THE BILLIONAIRES AND BABIES COLLECTION

The men in this special 2-in-1 collection rule their worlds with authority and determination. They're comfortable commanding those around them and aren't afraid to be ruthless if necessary. Independent and self-reliant, they are content with their money and lack of commitment.

Then the babies enter their lives and, before they know it, these powerful men are wrapped around their babies' little fingers!

With the babies comes the awareness of what else might be missing. Seems the perfect time for these billionaires to find the women who will love them forever.

Join us for two passionate, provocative stories where billionaires encounter the women—and babies—who will make them complete!

If you love these two classic stories, be sure to look for more Billionaires and Babies books from Harlequin Desire.

Andrea Laurence is an award-winning author of contemporary romance for Harlequin Desire and paranormal romance for Harlequin Nocturne. She has been a lover of reading and writing stories since she learned to read at a young age. She always dreamed of seeing her work in print and is thrilled to share her special blend of sensuality and humor with the world.

A dedicated West Coast girl transplanted into the Deep South, Andrea is working on her own happily-ever-after with her boyfriend and their collection of animals. Visit her website at andrealaurence.com; like her fan page on Facebook at facebook.com/authorandrealaurence; or follow her on Twitter, twitter.com/andrea_laurence.

Books by Andrea Laurence

Harlequin Desire

Dynasties: The Montoros

Seduced by the Spare Heir

Brides and Belles

Snowed In with Her Ex

Thirty Days to Win His Wife

Millionaires of Manhattan

What Lies Beneath

More Than He Expected

His Lover's Little Secret

Secrets of Eden

Undeniable Demands

A Beauty Uncovered

Heir to Scandal

Her Secret Husband

Visit the Author Profile page at Harlequin.com, or andrealaurence.com, for more titles!

Andrea Laurence

and

USA TODAY Bestselling Author

Michelle Celmer

HIS LOVER'S LITTLE SECRET

&

PRINCESS IN THE MAKING

HARLEQUIN® BILLIONAIRES AND BABIES

ISBN-13: 978-0-373-60150-9

His Lover's Little Secret & Princess in the Making

This edition published by arrangement with Harlequin Books S.A.

For questions and comments about the quality of this book, please contact us at CustomerService@Harlequin.com.

Printed in U.S.A.

CONTENTS

HIS LOVER'S LITTLE SECRET

Andrea Laurence

This book is dedicated to single mothers everywhere, including my own hardworking mother, Meg. You fight the good fight every day, often at the expense of your own well-being. Thank you for everything you do. (Treat yourself to some chocolate or shoes every now and then!)

One

"You'd better get on out of here, or you'll be late to stand on your head."

Sabine Hayes looked up from the cash drawer to see her boss, fashion designer Adrienne Lockhart Taylor, standing at the counter. She had worked for Adrienne the past thirteen months as manager of her boutique. "I'm almost done."

"Give me the nightly deposit and go. I'll stay until Jill shows up for her shift and then I'll stop by the bank on my way home. You have to pick up Jared by six, don't you?"

"Yes." The day care center would price gouge her for every minute she was late. Then she had to get Jared home and fed before the babysitter got there. Sabine loved teaching yoga, but it made those evenings even more hectic than usual. Single motherhood wasn't for wimps. "You don't mind making the deposit?"

Adrienne leaned across the counter. "Go," she said.

Sabine glanced quickly at her watch. "Okay." She put the deposit into the bank pouch and handed it over. Thank goodness Adrienne had come by this afternoon to put together the new window display. The trendy boutique was known for its exciting and edgy displays that perfectly showcased Adrienne's flair for modern pinup girl fashions. Sabine couldn't have found a better place to work.

Most places wouldn't look twice at an applicant with a nose piercing and a stripe of blue in her hair. It didn't matter that it was a small, tasteful diamond stud or that her hair was dyed at a nice salon in Brooklyn. Even after she'd bitten the bullet and had the bright color removed and left the piercing at home, she'd been turned down by every store on Fifth Avenue. The businesses that paid enough for her to support her son in New York were flooded with applicants more experienced than she was.

She thanked her lucky stars for the day she spied Adrienne walking down the street and complimented her dress. She never expected her to say she'd designed it herself. Adrienne invited her to come by her new boutique one afternoon, and Sabine was enamored with the whole place. It was fun and funky, chic and stylish. High-class fashion with an edge. When Adrienne mentioned she was looking for someone to run the store so she could focus on her designs, Sabine couldn't apply fast enough. Not only was it a great job with above-average pay and benefits, Adrienne was a great boss. She didn't care what color hair Sabine had—now she had purple highlights—and she was understanding when child illness or drama kept her away from the store.

Sabine grabbed her purse and gave a quick wave to Adrienne as she disappeared into the stockroom and out the back door. It was only a couple blocks to her son's day care, but she still had to hurry along the sidewalk, brushing past others who were leisurely making their way around town.

Finally rounding the last corner, Sabine swung open the gate to the small courtyard and leaped up the few steps to the door. She rang the buzzer at exactly three minutes to six. Not long after that, she had her toddler in her arms and was on her way to the subway.

"Hey, buddy," she said as they went down the street. "Did you have a good day?"

Jared grinned and nodded enthusiastically. He was starting to lose his chubby baby cheeks. He'd grown so much the past few months. Every day, he looked more and more like his father. The first time she'd held Jared in her arms, she looked into his dark brown eyes and saw Gavin's face staring back at her. He would grow up to be as devastatingly handsome as his father, but hopefully with Sabine's big heart. She should be able to contribute *something* to the genetic makeup of her child, and if she had her pick, that was what it would be.

"What do you want for dinner tonight?"

"A-sketti."

"Spaghetti, again? You had that last night. You're going to turn into a noodle before too long."

Jared giggled and clung to her neck. Sabine breathed in the scent of his baby shampoo and pressed a kiss against his forehead. He had changed her whole life and she wouldn't trade him for anything.

"Sabine?"

The subway entrance was nearly in sight when someone called her name from the restaurant she'd just passed. She stopped and turned to find a man in a navy suit drinking wine at one of the tables on the sidewalk. He looked familiar, but she couldn't come up with his name. Where did she know him from?

"It is you," he said, standing up and stepping toward

her. He took one look at her puzzled expression and smiled. "You don't remember me, do you? I'm Clay Oliver, a friend of Gavin's. I met you at a gallery opening a couple years back."

An icy surge rushed through Sabine's veins. She smiled and nodded, trying not to show any outward signs of distress. "Oh, yes," she said. She shifted Jared in her arms so he was facing away from his father's best friend. "I think I spilled champagne on you, right?"

"Yes!" he said, pleased she remembered. "How have you been?" Clay's gaze ran curiously over the child in her arms. "Busy, I see."

"Yes, very busy." Sabine's heart began pounding loudly in her chest. She glanced over her shoulder at the subway stop, desperate for an escape. "Listen, I'm sorry I can't stay to chat longer, but I've got to meet the babysitter. It was good to see you again, Clay. Take care."

Sabine gave him a quick wave and spun on her heel. She felt as if she was fleeing the scene of a crime as she dashed down the stairs. She nervously watched the people joining her on the platform. Clay wouldn't follow her. At least she didn't think so. But she wouldn't feel better until she was deep into Brooklyn and far out of Gavin's sphere of influence.

Had Clay seen Jared closely enough? Had he noticed the resemblance? Jared was wearing his favorite monkey T-shirt with a hood and ears, so perhaps Clay hadn't been able to make out his features or how old he was. She hoped.

She leaped onto the train the moment it arrived and managed to find a seat. Clutching Jared tightly as he sat in her lap, she tried to breathe deeply, but she just couldn't do it.

Nearly three years. Jared was fewer than two months from his second birthday, and she had managed to keep their son a secret from Gavin. In all this time she'd never run into him or anyone he knew. They didn't exactly move in the same social circles. That was part of why she'd broken it off with Gavin. They were a world apart. Unsuitable in every way. After she split with him, he'd never called or texted her again. He obviously wasn't missing her too badly.

But Sabine had never allowed herself to relax. She knew that sooner or later, Gavin would find out that he had a son. If Clay didn't tell him tonight, it would be the next time she bumped into someone Gavin knew. Sitting in the park, walking down the street…somebody would see Jared and know instantly that he was Gavin's son. The bigger he got, the more of a carbon copy of his father he became.

Then it was only a matter of time before Gavin showed up, angry and demanding. That was how he worked. He always got his way. At least until now. The only thing Sabine knew for certain was that he wouldn't win this time. Jared was her son. *Hers.* Gavin was a workaholic and wouldn't have a clue what to do with a child. She wasn't about to turn him over to the stuffy nannies and boarding schools that had raised Gavin instead of his parents.

As the train approached their stop, Sabine got up and they hurried to catch the bus that would take them the last few blocks to her apartment near Marine Park in Brooklyn, where she'd lived the past four years. It wasn't the fanciest place in the world, but it was relatively safe, clean and close to the grocery store and the park. The one-bedroom apartment was growing smaller as Jared grew older, but they were managing.

Originally, a large portion of the bedroom was used as her art studio. When her son came along, she packed up her canvases and put her artistic skills toward painting a cheerful mural over his crib. Jared had plenty of room to play, and there was a park down the street where he could run around and dig in the sandbox. Her next-door neighbor, Tina, would watch Jared when she had her evening yoga classes.

She had put together a pretty good life for her and Jared. Considering that when she moved to New York she was broke and homeless, she'd come quite a long way. Back then, she could live on meager waitressing tips and work on her paintings when she had the extra money for supplies. Now, she had to squeeze out every penny she could manage, but they had gotten by.

"A-sketti!" Jared cheered triumphantly as they came through the door.

"Okay. I'll make a-sketti." Sabine sat him down before switching the television on to his favorite show. It would mesmerize him with songs and funny dances while she cooked.

By the time Jared was done eating and Sabine was changed into her workout clothes, she had only minutes to spare before Tina arrived. If she was lucky, Tina would give Jared a bath and scrub the tomato sauce off his cheeks. Usually, she had him in his pajamas and in bed by the time Sabine got home. Sabine hated that he would be asleep when she returned, but going through his nightly routine after class would have Jared up way past his bedtime. He'd wake up at dawn no matter what, but he'd be cranky.

There was a sharp knock at the door. Tina was a little early. That was fine by her. If she could catch the earlier bus, it would give her enough time to get some good stretches in before class.

"Hey, Tina—" she said, whipping open the door and momentarily freezing when her petite, middle-aged neighbor was not standing in the hallway.

No. No, no, no. She wasn't ready to deal with this. Not yet. Not tonight.

It was Gavin.

Sabine clutched desperately at the door frame, needing its support to keep her upright as the world started tilting sharply on its axis. Her chest tightened; her stomach churned and threatened to return her dinner. At the same time, other long-ignored parts of her body immediately sparked back to life. Gavin had always been a master of her body, and the years hadn't dulled the memory of his touch.

Fear. Desire. Panic. Need. It all swirled inside her like a building maelstrom that would leave nothing but destruction in its path. She took a deep breath to clamp it all down. She couldn't let Gavin know she was freaking out. She certainly couldn't let him know she still responded to him, either. That would give him the upper hand. She plastered a wide smile across her face and choked down her emotions.

"Hello, Sabine," he said with the deep, familiar voice she remembered.

It was hard to believe the handsome and rich blast from her past was standing in front of her after all this time. His flawlessly tailored gray suit and shiny, sky-blue tie made him look every inch the powerful CEO of the BXS shipping empire. His dark eyes were trained on her, his gaze traveling down the line of his nose. He looked a little older than she remembered, with concern lining his eyes and furrowing his brow. Or maybe it was the tense, angry expression that aged him.

"Gavin!" she said with feigned surprise. "I certainly didn't expect to see you here. I thought you were my neighbor Tina. How have you—"

"Where is my son?" he demanded, interrupting her nervous twitter. His square jaw was rock hard, his sensual lips pressed into a hard line of disapproval. There had been a flash of that same expression when she'd left him all those years ago, but he'd quickly grown indifferent to it. Now he cared. But not about her. Only about their child.

Apparently news traveled fast. It had been fewer than two hours since she'd run into Clay.

"Your son?" she repeated, hoping to stall long enough to think of a plan. She'd had years to prepare for this moment and yet, when it arrived, she was thrown completely off guard. Moving quickly, Sabine rushed into the hallway and pulled the apartment door nearly closed behind her. She left just the slightest crack open so she could peek through and make sure Jared was okay. She pressed her back against the door frame and found it calmed her nerves just a little to have that barrier between Gavin and Jared. He'd have to go through her to get inside.

"Yes, Sabine," Gavin said, taking a step closer to her. "Where is the baby you've hidden from me for the last three years?"

Damn, she was still as beautiful as he remembered. A little older, a little curvier, but still the fresh, funky artist that had turned his head in that art gallery. And tonight, she was wearing some skimpy workout clothes that clung to every newly rounded curve and reminded him of what he'd been missing since she'd walked out on him.

People tended not to stay in Gavin's life very long. There had been a parade of nannies, tutors, friends and lovers his whole life as his parents hired and fired and then moved him from one private school to the next. The dark-haired beauty with the nose piercing had been no exception. She had walked out of his life without a second thought.

She'd said they weren't compatible in the long term because they had different priorities and different lives. Admittedly, they fell on opposite ends of the spectrum in most every category, but that was one of the things he'd been drawn to in Sabine. One of the reasons he thought she, of all people, might stay. She wasn't just another rich girl looking to marry well and shop often. What they had really seemed to matter. To mean something.

He'd been wrong.

He'd let her go—he'd learned early that there was no sense in chasing after someone who didn't want to be there—but she'd stayed on his mind. She'd starred in his dreams, both erotic and otherwise. She'd crept into his thoughts during the quiet moments when he had time to regret the past. More than once, Gavin had wondered what Sabine was up to and what she had done with her life.

Never in his wildest dreams did he expect the answer to be "raising his child."

Sabine straightened her spine, her sharp chin tipping

up in defiance. She projected an air of confidence in any situation and had the steel backbone to stand behind it. She certainly had spunk; he'd loved that about her once. Now, he could tell it would be an annoyance.

She looked him straight in the eye and said, "He's inside. And right now, that's where he's staying."

The bold honesty of her words was like a fist to his gut. The air rushed from his lungs. It was true. He had a son. *A son!* He hadn't entirely believed Clay's story until that precise moment. He'd known his best friend since they were roommates in college, one of the few constants in his life, but he couldn't always trust Clay's version of reality. Tonight, he'd insisted that Gavin locate Sabine as soon as possible to find out about her young son.

And he'd been right. For once.

Sabine didn't deny it. He'd expected her to tell him it wasn't his child or insist she was babysitting for a friend, but she had always been honest to a fault. Instead, she'd flat-out admitted she'd hidden his child from him and made no apologies about it. She even had the audacity to start making demands about how this was going to go down. She'd been in control of this situation for far too long. He was about to be included and in a big way.

"He's really my son?" He needed to hear the words from her, although he would demand a DNA test to confirm it no matter what she said.

Sabine swallowed and nodded. "He looks just like you."

The blood started pumping furiously in Gavin's ears. He might be able to understand why she kept it a secret if she was uncertain he was the father, but there was no doubt in her mind. She simply hadn't wanted him involved. She didn't want the inconvenience of having to share him with someone else. If not for Clay seeing her, he still wouldn't know he had a child.

His jaw tightened and his teeth clenched together. "Were you ever going to tell me I had a son, Sabine?"

Her pale green gaze burrowed into him as she crossed her arms over her chest. "No."

She didn't even bother to lie about it and make herself look less like the deceitful, selfish person she was. She just stood there, looking unapologetic, while unconsciously pressing her breasts up out of the top of her sports bra. His brain flashed between thoughts like a broken television as his eyes ran over the soft curves of her body and his ears tried to process her response. Anger, desire, betrayal and a fierce need to possess her rushed through his veins, exploding out of him in words.

"What do you mean, no?" Gavin roared.

"Keep it down!" Sabine demanded between gritted teeth, glancing nervously over her shoulder into the apartment. "I don't want him to hear us, and I certainly don't want all my neighbors to hear us, either."

"Well I'm sorry to embarrass you in front of your neighbors. I just found out I have a two-year-old son that I've never met. I think that gives me the right to be angry."

Sabine took a deep breath, amazing him with her ability to appear so calm. "You have every right to be angry. But yelling won't change anything. And I won't have you raising your voice around my son."

"*Our* son," Gavin corrected.

"No," she said with a sharp point of her finger. "He's

my son. According to his birth certificate, he's an immaculate conception. Right now, you have no legal claim to him and no right to tell me how to do *anything* where he's concerned. You got that?"

That situation would be remedied and soon. "For now. But don't think your selfish monopoly on our son will last for much longer."

A crimson flush rushed to her cheeks, bringing color to her flawless, porcelain skin. She had gotten far too comfortable calling the shots. He could tell she didn't like him making demands. Too bad for her. He had a vote now and it was long overdue.

She swallowed and brushed her purple-highlighted ponytail over her shoulder but didn't back down. "It's after seven-thirty on a Wednesday night, so you can safely bet that's how it's going to stay for the immediate future."

Gavin laughed at her bold naïveté. "Do you honestly think my lawyers don't answer the phone at 2:00 a.m. when I call? For what I pay them, they do what I want, when I want." He slipped his hand into his suit coat and pulled his phone out of his inner breast pocket. "Shall we call Edmund and see if he's available?"

Her eyes widened slightly at his challenge. "Go ahead, Gavin. Any lawyer worth his salt is going to insist on a DNA test. It takes no less than three days to get the results of a paternity test back from a lab. If you push me, I'll see to it that you don't set eyes on him until the results come back. If we test first thing in the morning, that would mean Monday by my estimation."

Gavin's hands curled into tight fists at his sides. She'd had years to prepare for this moment and she'd done her homework. He knew she was right. The labs probably wouldn't process the results over the weekend, so it would be Monday at the earliest before he could get his lawyer involved and start making parental demands. But once he could lay claim to his son, she had better watch out.

"I want to see my son," he said. This time his tone was less heated and demanding.

"Then calm down and take your thumb off your lawyer's speed dial."

Gavin slipped his cell phone back into his pocket. "Happy?"

Sabine didn't seem happy, but she nodded anyway. "Now, before I let you in, we need to discuss some ground rules."

He took a deep breath to choke back his rude retort. Few people had the audacity to tell him what to do, but if anyone would, it was Sabine. He would stick to her requirements for now, but before long, Gavin would be making the rules. "Yes?"

"Number one, you are not to yell when you are in my apartment or anywhere Jared might be. I don't want you upsetting him."

Jared. His son's name was Jared. This outrageous scenario was getting more and more real. "What's his middle name?" Gavin couldn't stop himself from asking. He suddenly wanted to know everything he could about his son. There was no way to gain back the time he'd lost, but he would do everything in his power to catch up on what he missed.

"Thomas. Jared Thomas Hayes."

Thomas was *his* middle name. Was that a coincidence? He couldn't remember if Sabine knew it or not. "Why Thomas?"

"For my art teacher in high school, Mr. Thomas. He's the only one that ever encouraged my painting. Since that was also your middle name, it seemed fitting. Number two," she continued. "Do not tell him you're his father. Not until it is legally confirmed and we are both comfortable with the timing. I don't want him confused and worried about what's going on."

"Who does he think his father is?"

Sabine shook her head dismissively. "He's not even two. He hasn't started asking questions about things like that yet."

"Fine," he agreed, relieved that if nothing else, his son hadn't noticed the absence of a father in his life. He knew how painful that could be. "Enough rules. I want to see Jared." His son's name felt alien on his tongue. He wanted a face to put with the name and know his son at last.

"Okay." Sabine shifted her weight against the door, slowly slinking into the apartment.

Gavin moved forward, stepping over the threshold. He'd been to her apartment before, a long time ago. He remembered a fairly sparse but eclectic space with mismatched thrift store furniture. Her paintings had dotted the walls, her portfolio and bag of supplies usually sitting near the door.

When he barely missed stepping on a chubby blue crayon instead of a paintbrush, he knew things were truly different. Looking around, he noticed a lot had changed. The furniture was newer but still a mishmash of pieces. Interspersed with it were brightly colored plastic toys like a tiny basketball hoop and a tricycle with superheroes on it. A television in the corner loudly played a children's show.

And when Sabine stepped aside, he saw the small, dark-haired boy sitting on the floor in front of it. The child didn't turn to look at him. He was immersed in bobbing his head and singing along to the song playing on the show, a toy truck clutched in his hand.

Gavin swallowed hard and took another step into the apartment so Sabine could close the door behind him. He watched her walk over to the child and crouch down.

"Jared, we have a visitor. Let's say hello."

The little boy set down his truck and crawled to his feet. When he turned to look at Gavin, he felt his heart skip a beat in his chest. The tiny boy looked exactly like he had as a child. It was as though a picture had been snatched from his baby album and brought to life. From his pink cheeks smeared with tomato sauce, to the wide, dark eyes that looked at him with curiosity, he was very much Gavin's son.

The little boy smiled, revealing tiny baby teeth. "Hi."

Gavin struggled to respond at first. His chest was tight with emotions he never expected in this moment. This morning, he woke up worried about his latest business acquisition and now he was meeting his child for the first time. "Hi, Jared," he choked out.

"Jared, this is Mommy's friend Gavin."

Gavin took a hesitant step forward and knelt down to bring himself to the child's level. "How are you doing, big guy?"

Jared responded with a flow of gibberish he couldn't understand. Gavin hadn't been around many small children, and he wasn't equipped to translate. He could pick out a few words—*school, train* and something close to *spaghetti.* The rest was lost on him, but Jared didn't seem to mind. Pausing in his tale, he picked up his favorite truck and held it out to Gavin. "My truck!" he declared.

He took the small toy from his son. "It's very nice. Thank you."

A soft knock sounded at the front door. Sabine frowned and stood up. "That's the babysitter. I've got to go."

Gavin swallowed his irritation. He'd had a whole two minutes with his son and she was trying to push him out the door. They hadn't even gotten around to discussing her actions and what they were going to do about this situation. He watched her walk to the door and let in a middle-aged woman in a sweater with cats on it.

"Hey, Tina. Come on in. He's had his dinner and he's just watching television."

"I'll get him in the bath and in bed by eight-thirty."

"Thanks, Tina. I should be home around the usual time."

Gavin handed the truck back to Jared and reluctantly stood. He wasn't going to hang around while the neighbor lady was here. He turned in time to see Sabine slip into a hoodie and tug a sling with a rolled-up exercise mat over her shoulder.

"Gavin, I've got to go. I'm teaching a class tonight."

He nodded and gave a quick look back at Jared. He'd returned to watching his show, doing a little monkey dance along with the other children and totally unaware of what was really going on around him. Gavin wanted to reach out to him again, to say goodbye or hug him, but he refrained. There would be time for all that later. For the first time in his life, he had someone who would be legally bound to him for the next sixteen years and wouldn't breeze in and out of his life like so many others. They would have more time together.

Right now, he needed to deal with the mother of his child.

Two

"I don't need you to drive me to class."

Gavin stood holding open the passenger door of his Aston Martin with a frown lining his face. Sabine knew she didn't want to get in the car with him. Getting in would mean a private tongue-lashing she wasn't ready for yet. She'd happily take the bus to avoid this.

"Just get in the car, Sabine. The longer we argue, the later you'll be."

Sabine watched the bus blow by the stop up the street and swore under her breath. She'd never make it to class in time unless she gave in and let him drive her there. Sighing in defeat, she climbed inside. Gavin closed the door and got in on his side. "Go up the block and turn right at the light," she instructed. If she could focus on directions, perhaps they'd have less time to talk about what she'd done.

She already had a miserably guilty conscience. It wasn't like she could look at Jared without thinking of Gavin. Lying to him was never something she intended to do, but the moment she found out she was pregnant, she was overcome with a fierce territorial and protective urge. She and Gavin were from different planets. He never really cared for her the way she did for him.

The same would hold true for their son. Jared would be *acquired* just like any other asset of the Brooks Empire. He deserved better than that. Better than what Gavin had been given.

She did what she thought she had to do to protect her child, and she wouldn't apologize for it. "At the second light, turn left."

Gavin remained silent as they drove, unnerving her more with every minute that ticked by. She was keenly aware of the way his hands tightly gripped the leather steering wheel. The tension was evident in every muscle of his body, straining the threads of his designer suit. His smooth, square jaw was flexed as though it took everything he had to keep his emotions in check and his eyes on the road.

It was a practiced skill of Gavin's. When they were together, he always kept his feelings tamped down. The night she told him they were over, there had barely been a flicker of emotion in his eyes. Not anger. Not sadness. Not even a "don't let the door hit you on the way out." Just a solemnly resigned nod and she was dismissed from his life. He obviously never really cared for Sabine. But this might be the situation that caused him to finally blow.

When his car pulled to a stop outside the community center where she taught, he shifted into Neutral, pulled the parking brake and killed the engine. He glanced down at his Rolex. "You're early."

She was. She didn't have to be inside for another fifteen minutes. He'd driven a great deal faster than the bus and hadn't stopped every block to pick up people. It was pointless to get out of the car and stand in front of the building to wait for the previous class to end. That meant time in the car alone with Gavin. Just perfect.

After an extended silence, he spoke. "So, was I horrible to you? Did I treat you badly?" His low voice was quiet, his eyes focused not on her but on something through the windshield ahead of them.

Sabine silently groaned. Somehow she preferred the yelling to this. "Of course not."

He turned to look at her then, pinning her with his dark eyes. "Did I say or do anything while we were together to make you think I would be a bad father?"

A bad father? No. Perhaps a distracted one. A distant one. An absent one. Or worse, a reluctant one. But not a *bad* father. "No. Gavin, I—"

"Then why, Sabine? Why would you keep something so important from me? Why would you keep me from being in Jared's life? He's young now, but eventually he'd notice he didn't have a daddy like other kids. What if he thought I didn't want him? Christ, Sabine. He may not have been planned, but he's still my son."

When he said it like that, every excuse in her mind sounded ridiculous. How could she explain that she didn't want Jared to grow up spoiled, rich but unloved? That she wanted him with her, not at some expensive boarding school? That she didn't want him to become a successful, miserable shell of a man like his father? All those excuses resulted from her primary fear that she couldn't shake. "I was afraid I would lose him."

Gavin's jaw still flexed with pent-up emotions. "You thought I would take him from you?"

"Wouldn't you?" Her gaze fixed on him, a challenge in her eyes. "Wouldn't you have swooped in the minute he was born and claimed him as your own? I'm sure your fancy friends and family would be horrified that a person like me was raising the future Brooks Express Shipping heir. It wouldn't be hard to deem me an unfit mother and have some judge from your father's social club grant you full custody."

"I wouldn't have done that."

"I'm sure you only would've done what you thought was best for your son, but how was I to know what that would entail? What would happen if you decided he would be better off with you and I was just a complication? I wouldn't have enough money or connections to fight you. I couldn't risk it." Sabine felt the tears prickling her eyes, but she refused to cry in front of Gavin.

"I couldn't bear the thought of you handing him off to nannies and tutors. Buying his affection with expensive gifts because you were too busy building the family company to spend time with him. Shipping him off to some boarding school as soon as he was old enough, under the guise of getting him the best education when you really just want him out of your hair. Jared wasn't planned. He wasn't the golden child of your socially acceptable marriage. You might want him on principle, but I couldn't be certain you would love him."

Gavin sat silent for a moment, listening to her tirade. The anger seemed to have run its course. Now he just looked emotionally spent, his dark eyes tired. He looked just like Jared after a long day without a nap.

Sabine wanted to brush the dark strands of hair from his weary eyes and press her palm against the rough stubble of his cheek. She knew exactly how it would feel. Exactly how his skin would smell…an intoxicating mixture of soap, leather and male. But she wouldn't. Her attraction to Gavin was a hurdle she had to overcome to leave him the first time. The years hadn't dulled her reaction to him. Now, it would be an even larger complication she didn't need.

"I don't understand why you would think that," he said at last, his words quieter now.

"Because that's what happened to you, Gavin." She lowered her voice to a soft, conversational tone. "And it's the only way you know how to raise a child. Nannies and boarding schools are normal to you. You told me yourself how your parents were always too busy for you and your siblings. How your house cycled through nannies like some people went through tissue paper. Do you remember telling me about how miserable and lonely you were when they sent you away to school? Why would I want that for Jared? Even if it came with all the money and luxury in the world? I wasn't about to hand him over to you so he could live the same hollow life you had. I didn't want him to be groomed to be the next CEO of Brooks Express Shipping."

"What's wrong with that?" Gavin challenged with a light of anger returning to the chocolate depths of his eyes. "There are worse things than growing up wealthy and becoming the head of a Fortune 500 company founded by your great-great-grandfather. Like growing up poor. Living in a small apartment with secondhand clothes."

"His clothes aren't secondhand!" she declared, her blood rushing furiously through her veins. "They're not from Bloomingdale's, but they aren't rags, either. I know that to you we look like we live in squalor, but we don't. It's a small apartment, but it's in a quiet neighborhood near the park where he can play. He has food and toys and most importantly, all the love, stability and attention I can possibly give him. He's a happy, healthy child."

Sabine didn't want to get defensive, but she couldn't help it. She recognized the tone from back when they were dating. The people in his social circles were always quick to note her shabby-chic fashion sense and lack of experience with an overabundance of flatware. They declared it charming, but Sabine could see the mockery in their eyes. They never thought she was good enough for one of the Brooks men. She wasn't about to let Gavin tell her that the way she raised her child wasn't good enough, either.

"I have no doubt that you're doing a great job with Jared. But why would you make it so hard on yourself? You could have a nice place in Manhattan. You could send him to one of the best private preschools in the city. I could get you a nice car and someone to help you cook and clean and take care of all the little things. I would've made sure you both had everything you needed—and *without* taking him from you. There was no reason to sacrifice those comforts."

"I didn't sacrifice anything," Sabine insisted. She knew those creature comforts came with strings. She'd rather do without. "I never had those things to begin with."

"No sacrifices?" Gavin shifted in the car to face her directly. "What about your painting? I've kept an eye out over the years and haven't noticed any showings of your work. I didn't see any supplies or canvases lying around the apartment, either. I assume your studio space gave way to Jared's things, so where did all that go?"

Sabine swallowed hard. He had her there. She'd moved to New York to follow her dream of becoming a painter. She had lived and breathed her art every moment of the day she could. Her work had even met with some moderate success. She'd had a gallery showing and sold a few pieces, but it wasn't enough to live on. And it certainly wasn't enough to raise a child on. So her priorities shifted. Children took time. And energy. And money. At the end of the day, the painting had fallen to the bottom of her list. Some days she missed the creative release of her work, but she didn't regret setting it aside.

"It's in the closet," she admitted with a frown.

"And when was the last time you painted?"

"Saturday," she replied a touch too quickly.

Gavin narrowed his gaze at her.

"Okay, it was finger paints," Sabine confessed. She turned away from Gavin's heavy stare and focused on the yoga mat in her lap. He saw more than she wanted him to. He always had. "But," she continued, "Jared and I had a great time doing it, even if it wasn't gallery-quality work. He's the most important thing in the world to me, now. More important than painting."

"You shouldn't have to give up one thing you love for another."

"Life is about compromises, Gavin. Certainly you know what it's like to set aside what you love to do for what you're obligated to do."

He stiffened in the seat beside her. It seemed they were both guilty of putting their dreams on the back burner, although for very different reasons. Sabine had a child to raise. Gavin had family expectations to uphold and a shipping empire to run. The tight collar of his obligations had chafed back when they were dating. It had certainly rubbed him bloody and raw by now.

When he didn't respond, Sabine looked up. He was looking out the window, his thoughts as distant as his eyes.

It was surreal to be in the same car with Gavin after all this time. She could feel his gravitational pull on her when they were this close. Walking away from him the first time had been hard. They dated for about a month and a half, but every moment they spent together had been fiercely passionate. Not just sexual, either. They enjoyed everything to the fullest, from spicy ethnic foods to political debates, museum strolls to making love under the stars. They could talk for hours.

Their connection was almost enough to make her forget they wanted different things from life. And as much as he seemed enticed by the exoticness of their differences, she knew it wouldn't last long. The novelty would wear off and they would either break up, or he would expect her to change for him. That was one thing she simply wouldn't do. She wouldn't conform for her parents and the small-minded Nebraska town she grew up in, and she wouldn't do it for him. She came to New York so she could be herself, not to lose her identity and become one of the Brooks Wives. They were like Stepfords with penthouse apartments.

She had briefly met some of Gavin's family, and it had scared the hell out of her. They hadn't been dating very long when they ran into his parents at a restaurant. It was an awkward encounter that came too early in the relationship, but the impact on Sabine had been huge. His mother was a flawless, polished accessory of his father's arm. Sabine was fairly certain that even if she wanted to be, she would be neither flawless nor polished. She didn't want to fade into the background of her own life.

It didn't matter how much she loved Gavin. And she did. But she loved herself more. And she loved Jared more.

But breathing the same air as Gavin again made her resolve weaken. She had neglected her physical needs for too long and made herself vulnerable. "So what do we do now?" Sabine asked at last.

As if he'd read her thoughts, Gavin reached over to her and took her hand in his. The warmth of him enveloped her, a tingle of awareness prickling at the nape of her neck. It traveled like a gentle waterfall down her back, lighting every nerve. Her whole body seemed to be awakening from a long sleep like a princess in a fairy tale. And all it had taken was his touch. She couldn't imagine what would happen if the dashing prince actually kissed her.

Kissed her? Was she insane? He was no dashing prince, and she had run from this relationship for a good reason. He may have tracked her down and she might be obligated to allow him to have a place in Jared's life, but that didn't mean they had to pick up where they left off. Quite the contrary. She needed to keep her distance from Gavin if she knew what was good for her. He'd let her go once, proving just how much she didn't matter to him. Anything he said or did now to the contrary was because of Jared. Not her.

His thumb gently stroked the back of her hand. Her body remembered that touch and everything it could lead to. Everything she'd denied herself since she became a mother…

He looked up at her, an expression of grave seriousness on his face. "We get married."

Gavin had never proposed to a woman before. Well, it wasn't really even a proposal since he hadn't technically asked. And even though it wasn't candlelight and diamonds, he certainly never imagined a response like this.

Sabine laughed at him. Loudly. Heartily. For an unnecessarily long period of time. She obviously had no idea how hard it had been for him to do this. How many doubts he had to set aside to ask *anyone* to be a permanent part of his life, much less someone with a track record of walking away from him.

He'd thought they were having a moment. Her glossy lips had parted softly and her pale eyes darkened when he'd touched her. It should've been the right time, the perfect moment. But he'd miscalculated. Her response to his proposal had proved as much.

"I'm serious!" he shouted over her peals of laughter, but it only made her giggle harder. Gavin sat back in his seat and waited for her to stop. It took a few minutes longer than his pride would've liked. Eventually, she quieted and wiped her damp eyes with her fingertips.

"Marry me, Sabine," he said.

"No."

He almost wished Sabine had gone back to laughing. The firm, sober rejection was worse. It reminded him of her pained, resolved expression as she broke off their relationship and walked out of his life.

"Why not?" He couldn't keep the insulted tone from his voice. He was a great catch. She should be thrilled to get this proposal, even as spur of the moment and half-assed as it was.

Sabine smiled and patted his hand reassuringly. "Because you don't want to marry me, Gavin. You want to do the right thing and provide a stable home for your son. And that's noble. Really. I appreciate the sentiment. But I'm not going to marry someone that doesn't love me."

"We have a child together."

"That's not good enough for me."

Gavin scoffed. "Making our son legitimate isn't a good enough reason for you?"

"We're not talking about the succession to the throne of England, Gavin. It's not exactly the horrid stigma it used to be. Having you in his life is more than enough for me. That's all I want from you—quality time."

"Quality time?" Gavin frowned. Somehow legally binding themselves in marriage seemed an easier feat.

"Yes. If you're committed enough to your son to marry his mother when you don't love her, you should be committed enough to put in the time. I'm not going to introduce a 'dad' into his life just so you can work late and ignore him. He's better off without a dad than having one that doesn't make an effort. You can't miss T-ball games and birthday parties. You have to be there when you say you will. If you can't be there for him one hundred percent, don't bother."

Her words hit him hard. He didn't have bad parents, but he did have busy ones. Gavin knew how it felt to be the lowest item on someone's priority list. How many times had he sat alone on the marble staircase of his childhood home and waited for parents who never showed up? How many times had he scanned the crowd at school pageants and ball games looking for family that wasn't there?

He'd always sworn he wouldn't do that to his own children, but even after having seen his son, the idea of him wasn't quite a firm reality in Gavin's mind. He had only this primitive need to claim the child and its mother. To finally have someone in his life that couldn't walk away.

That's why he'd rushed out to Brooklyn without any sort of plan. But she was right. He didn't know what to do with a child. His reflex would be to hand him off to someone who did and focus on what he was good at—running his family business. He couldn't afford the distraction, especially so close to closing his latest business deal.

And that was exactly what she was afraid of.

She had good reason, too. He'd spent most of their relationship vacillating between ignoring her for work and ignoring work for her. He never found the balance. A child would compound the problem. Part of the reason Gavin hadn't seriously focused on settling down was because he knew his work priorities would interfere with family life. He kept waiting for the day when things at BXS would slow down enough for him to step back. But it never happened. His father hadn't stepped back until the day he handed the reins over to Gavin, and he'd missed his children growing up to do it.

Gavin didn't have a choice any longer. He had a child. He would have to find a way—a better way than his father chose—to keep the company on top and keep his promises to his son and Sabine. He wasn't sure how the hell he would do it, but he would make it happen.

"If I put in the quality time, will you let me help you?"

"Help me with what?"

"With life, Sabine. If you won't marry me, let me get you a nice apartment in the city. Wherever you want to live. Let me help pay for Jared's education. We can enroll him in the best preschool. I can get someone to help around the house. Someone that can cook and clean, even pick up Jared from school if you want to keep working."

"And why would you want to do that? What you're suggesting is incredibly expensive."

"Maybe, but it's worth it to me. It's an investment in my child. Making your life easier will make you a happier, more relaxed mother to our son. He can spend more time playing and learning than sitting on the subway. And admittedly, having you in Manhattan will make it easier for me to see Jared more often."

He could see the conflict in Sabine's pale green eyes. She was struggling. She was proud and wouldn't admit it, but raising Jared on her own had to be difficult. Kids weren't cheap. They took time and money and effort. She'd already sacrificed her art. But convincing her to accept his offering would take time.

He knew Sabine better than she wanted to admit. She didn't want to be seen as one of those women who moved up in social status by calculated breeding. Jared had been an accident, of that he was certain. Judging by the expression on Sabine's face when she opened the door to her apartment, she would've rather had any man's son but his.

"Let's take this one step at a time, please," Sabine said, echoing his thoughts. There was a pained expression on her face that made him think there was more than just pride holding her back.

"What do you mean?"

"You've gone from having no kids to having a toddler and very nearly a fiancée in two hours' time. That's a big change for you, and for both Jared and me. Let's not uproot our lives so quickly." She sighed and gripped his hand. "Let's get the DNA results in, so there are no questions or doubts. Then we can introduce the idea of you to Jared and tell our families. From there, maybe we move into the city to be closer to you. But let's make these decisions over weeks and months, not minutes."

She glanced down at the screen on her cell phone. "I've got to get inside and set up."

"Okay." Gavin got out of the car and came around to open her door and help her out.

"I have tomorrow off. If you can make an appointment for DNA testing, call or text me and we'll meet you there. My number is the same. Do you still have it?"

He did. He'd very nearly dialed it about a hundred times in the weeks after she'd left. He'd been too proud to go through with the call. A hundred people had drifted in and out of his life, but Sabine leaving had caught him by surprise and it stung. He'd wanted to fight, wanted to call her and convince her she was wrong about them. But she wanted to go and he let her.

Now he could kick himself for not manning up and telling her he wanted her and didn't care what others thought about it. That he would make the time for her. Maybe then he would've been there to hear his son's heartbeat in the doctor's office, his first cries and his first words. Maybe then the mother of his child wouldn't look at him with wary eyes and laugh off his proposal of marriage like a joke.

He made a point of pulling out his phone and confirming it so she wouldn't think he knew for certain. "I do."

Sabine nodded and slowly started walking backward across the grass. Even after all this time apart, it felt awkward to part like strangers without a hug or a kiss goodbye. They were bonded for a lifetime now, and yet he had never felt as distant from her as he did when she backed away.

"I'll see you tomorrow, then," she said.

"Tomorrow," he repeated.

He watched as she regarded him for a moment at a distance. There was a sadness in her expression that he didn't like. The Sabine he remembered was a vibrant artist with a lust for life and experience. She had jerked him out of his blah corporate existence, demanded he live his life, not just go through the motions. Sabine was nothing like what he was supposed to have but absolutely everything he needed. He'd regretted every day since she'd walked out of his life.

Now, he regretted it more than ever, and not just because of his son. The sad, weary woman walking away from him was just a shadow of the person he once knew. And he hated that.

The outdoor lights kicked on, lighting the shimmer of tears in her eyes. "I'm sorry, Gavin," she said before spinning on her heels and disappearing through the doors of the community center.

She was sorry. And so was he.

Three

Gavin arrived at the office the next morning before seven. The halls were dark and quiet as he traveled to the executive floor of the BXS offices. The large corner office had once belonged to his father and his grandfather before him. Gavin's original office was down the hallway. He'd gotten the space when he was sixteen and started learning the business and then passed it along to his younger brother, Alan, when Gavin took over as CEO.

Opening the door, he walked across the antique rug and set his laptop bag and breakfast on the large wooden desk. The heavy mahogany furniture was originally from his great-grandfather's office and was moved here when BXS upgraded their location from the small building near the shipping yards.

His great-grandfather had started the company in 1930, Depression be damned. What began as a local delivery service expanded to trains and trucks and eventually to planes that could deliver packages all over the world. The eldest Brooks son had run the company since the day it opened. Everything about Brooks Express Shipping had an air of tradition and history that made it one of the most trusted businesses in America.

Frankly, it was a bit stifling.

Despite how he'd argued to the contrary with Sabine last night, they both knew this wasn't what he wanted to do with his life. The Brooks name came with responsibilities. Gavin had been groomed from birth to one day run BXS. He'd had the best education, interned with the company, received his MBA from Harvard… Each milestone putting him one step closer to filling his father's shoes. Even if they were too tight.

Sabine had been right about some things. He had no doubt his family would assume Jared would one day be the corporate successor to his father. The difference would be that Gavin would make certain *his* son had a choice.

He settled in at his desk, firing up his computer. He immediately sent an email to his assistant, Marie, about setting up a lab appointment for their DNA testing. With it, he included a note that this was a confidential matter. No one, literally no one, was to know what was going on. He trusted Marie, but she was friendly and chatty with everyone, including his father, who she used to work for. Gavin had barely come to terms with this himself. He certainly wasn't ready for the world, and especially his family, to know what was going on.

Marie wouldn't be in until eight, but she had a corporate smartphone and a long train ride in to work. He was certain she'd have everything handled before she arrived.

That done, he turned to the steaming-hot cup of coffee and the bagel he picked up on his way in. The coffee shop on the ground floor of the building was open well before most people stumbled into BXS for the day. Gavin spread cream cheese on his toasted bagel as he watched his in-box fill with new messages. Most were unimportant, although one caught his eye.

It was from Roger Simpson, the owner of Exclusivity Jetliners.

The small, luxury jet company specialized in private transportation. Whether you were taking a few friends for a weekend in Paris, transporting your beloved poodle to your summer home or simply refused to fly coach, Exclusivity Jetliners was ready and waiting to help. At least for now.

Roger Simpson wanted to retire. The business had been his life, and he was ready to finally relax and enjoy the fruits of his labor. Unlike BXS, he didn't have a well-groomed heir to take his place at the head of the company. He had a son, Paul, but from the discussions Roger and Gavin had shared, Roger would rather sell the company than let his irresponsible son drive it into the ground.

Gavin quickly made it known that he was interested. He'd been eight years old when his father let him ride in the cockpit of one of their Airbus A310 freighters. He'd immediately been enamored with planes and flying. For his sixteenth birthday, his parents had acquiesced and got him flying lessons.

He'd even entertained the idea of joining the Air Force and becoming a fighter pilot. There, sadly, was where that dream had died a horrible death. His father had tolerated Gavin's "hobby," but he wouldn't allow his son to derail his career path for a silly dream.

Gavin swallowed the old taste of bitterness on the back of his tongue and tried to chase it with his coffee. His father had won that battle, but he wasn't in charge anymore. He clicked on the email from Roger and scanned over the message.

BXS was about to offer a new service that would push them ahead of their shipping competitors—concierge shipping. It would appeal to the elite BXS clientele. Ones who wanted their things handled carefully and expeditiously and were willing to pay for the privilege.

The fleet of small planes from Exclusivity Jetliners would be transformed into direct freight jets that would allow the rich art lover to see to it that their new Picasso bought at auction over the phone would arrive safely at their home the same day. It would allow the fashion designer to quickly transport a dozen priceless gowns to an Academy Award nominee while she filmed on set two thousand miles from Hollywood.

It was a risk, but if it worked, it would give Gavin something he'd been wanting his whole life—the chance to fly.

Sabine had encouraged him years ago to find a way to marry his obligations and his passions. It had seemed impossible at the time, but long after she was out of his life, her words had haunted him.

Just as her words had haunted him last night. He'd lain in bed for hours, his brain swirling with everything that had happened after he'd answered Clay's phone call. Sabine had always had the innate ability to cut through his crap. She called it like she saw it, as opposed to all the polite society types who danced around delicate subjects and gossiped behind your back.

She didn't see Gavin as a powerful CEO. The money and the privilege didn't register on her radar at all, and really it never had. After years of women chasing after him, Sabine was the first woman he was compelled to pursue. He'd spied her across an art gallery and instantly felt the urge to possess her. She had no idea who he was or how much he was worth at first, and when she did, she didn't care. He insisted on taking her out to nice dinners, but Sabine was more interested in making love and talking for hours in bed.

But she couldn't ignore their differences. They'd lasted as long as they had by staying inside the protective bubble of the bedroom, but he could tell it was getting harder for Sabine to overlook the huge, platinum gorilla in the room. She didn't see his power and riches as an asset. It was just one thing on a list of many that made her believe they didn't have a future together. She would rather keep her son a secret and struggle to make ends meet than to have Jared live the life Gavin had.

What had she said? *...You know what it's like to set aside what you love to do for what you're obligated to do.*

He did. Gavin had done it his whole life because of some misguided sense of duty. He could've walked away at any time. Joined the Air Force. Sacrificed his inheritance and what little relationship he had with his parents. But then what would happen to the company? His brother couldn't run it. Alan hadn't so much as sat down in his token office in months. Gavin wasn't even sure if he was in the country. His baby sister, Diana, had a freshly inked degree from Vassar and absolutely no experience. His father wouldn't come out of retirement. That meant Gavin ran BXS or a stranger did.

And no matter what, he couldn't let that happen. It was a family legacy. One of his earliest memories was of coming into this very office and visiting his grandfather. Papa Brooks would sit Gavin on his knee and tell him stories about how his great-grandfather had started the company. Tears of pride would gather in the old man's dark eyes. Gavin and his father might have their differences, but he wouldn't let his grandfather down. He'd been dead for four years now, but it didn't matter. BXS and its legacy was everything to Papa Brooks. Gavin wouldn't risk it to chase a pipe dream.

A chime sounded at his hip. Gavin reached down to his phone to find a text from Marie. She'd arranged for an appointment at 4:15 with his concierge physician on Park Avenue. Excellent.

He could've just copied the information into another window and included the location to send it to Sabine, but he found himself pressing the button to call her instead. It was a dangerous impulse that he wished he could ignore, but he wanted to hear her voice. He'd gone so long without it that he'd gladly take any excuse to hear it again. It wasn't until after the phone began to ring that he realized it was 7:30 in the morning. Sabine had always been a night owl and slept late.

"Hello?" she answered. Her voice was cheerful and not at all groggy.

"Sabine? It's Gavin. I'm sorry to call so early. Did I wake you?"

"Wake me?" Sabine laughed. "Oh, no. Jared is up with the chickens, no later than 6:00 a.m. every morning. I tease him that he's going to grow up to be a farmer like his granddaddy."

Gavin frowned for a moment before he realized she was talking about her own father. Sabine spoke very rarely of her parents. Last he'd heard they were both alive and well in Nebraska, but Sabine wasn't in contact with them. It made Gavin wonder if he wasn't the only one who didn't know about Jared.

"My assistant got us an appointment." Gavin read her the information so she could write it down, including the address of the doctor's office.

"Okay," she said. "We'll meet you there at a little before 4:15."

"I'll pick you up," he offered.

"No, we'll take the subway. Jared likes the train. There's a stop about a block from there, so it's not a problem at all."

Sabine was fiercely independent. Always had been. It had made him crazy when they were dating. She wouldn't let him do anything for her. He wanted to argue with her now, but he wouldn't. His afternoon schedule was pretty hectic, and he'd have to shuffle a few things around to drive out to Brooklyn and get them in time unless he sent a car. And yet, he wasn't ready to end the conversation, either.

"After the appointment," he said, "may I take you and Jared to an early dinner?"

"Um…" Sabine delayed her response. She was probably trying to come up with a reason why she couldn't, but was failing.

"A little quality time," he added with a smile, happily using her own words to get his way.

"Sure," she said, caving. "That would be nice."

"I'll see you this afternoon."

"Goodbye," Sabine said, disconnecting the call.

Gavin smiled as he glanced down at his phone. He was looking forward to his afternoon with Jared. And even though the rational side of his brain knew that he shouldn't, he was looking forward to seeing Sabine again, as well.

Sabine was surprised that it didn't take long at the doctor's office. The paperwork took more time than anything else. Gavin and Jared got their cheeks swabbed, and they were told the office would call with the lab results on Monday.

By four forty-five, they were standing on the sidewalk watching the traffic stack up on Park Avenue. Sabine secured Jared in the collapsible umbrella stroller she sometimes took into the city. It was too busy to let him walk, even though he was getting more independent and wanted to.

"What would you like to eat?" Gavin asked.

Sabine was pretty sure that the majority of places he was used to eating at were not equipped to feed a picky toddler. She glanced around, getting her bearings for where she was in the city. "I think there's a good burger place about two blocks from here."

Gavin's gaze narrowed at her. "A burger?"

She swallowed her laugh. "Let's wait until Jared is at least five before we take him to Le Cirque. They don't exactly have a kid's menu."

"I know."

Sabine shook her head and started walking toward the restaurant. Gavin moved quickly to fall into step beside her.

"You're used to taking people out to nice places and spending a lot of money for dinner. I suppose that's what people expect of you, but that's not how Jared and I roll. We'll probably all eat for less than what you normally pay for a bottle of wine. And that's fine by us. Right, Jared?"

The little boy smiled and gave a thumbs-up. He'd learned the gesture in day care a few weeks ago and since then, a lot of things had called for it. "Cheeburger!"

"See?" Sabine said, looking over to Gavin. "He's easy to impress."

The restaurant was already a little busy, but they were able to order and get their food before their toddler started to revolt. Sabine tried to keep her focus on Jared, making sure he was eating small bites and not getting ketchup everywhere. It was easier than looking at Gavin and trying to guess what he was thinking.

Things were still very up in the air between them. He was being nice to her. More polite than she expected, under the circumstances. But once the test results came back, Sabine was certain that things would start to change. Gavin had sworn he wasn't about to snatch her baby from her arms, but she was more concerned about it happening slowly. A new apartment in the city. A new school for Jared. New clothes. New toys. Even if he gave up the idea of marrying for their child's sake, things would change for her, too. He'd insist she stop working. He'd give her spending money. Suggest they just move in with him.

And when the time came that she decided to move out, she was certain he'd see to it that Jared stayed behind in the stable home they'd created for him there. She'd be unemployed and homeless with no money of her own to fight him for custody.

These were the thoughts that had kept her quiet throughout her pregnancy. The same fears that made her hide Jared from his father. And yet, she found herself smiling as she watched Jared and Gavin color on the kid's menu together. There was a hamburger with legs dancing on one side. Jared was scribbling green across the bun. Gavin was more cautious, making the meat brown and the cheese orange as he stayed between the lines.

That was Gavin for you. No matter what he did, he always stayed between the lines. He never got dirty. Or screwed up anything.

Opposites attracted, but they were polar to the point of near incompatibility. A lot of Sabine's clothes had paint splattered on them from her art. She embraced that life was messy. You had to eat a little dirt before you died. Gavin was polished. Tailored. You couldn't find a speck of dirt beneath his fingernails.

How had she ever thought that dating Gavin was a good idea?

Her eyes drifted over his sharp features and thick, dark hair. His broad shoulders and strong jaw. In truth, that was why she'd let herself indulge. Gavin was a handsome, commanding specimen of a man. Every inch of him, from his large hands attempting to clutch a tiny crayon, to his muscular but trim frame, radiated health and power. He was interesting and thoughtful. Honorable and loyal to a fault.

If she'd *had* to get pregnant, her instincts had sought out a superior male to help her propagate the species.

Somehow, even that most scientific of thoughts spoke straight to her core. Her appraisal of Gavin had shot up her pulse. She felt a flush rise to her cheeks and chest. The heat spread throughout her body, focusing low in her belly. She closed her eyes, hoping to take a private moment to wish away her desire and regain control.

"Do you need to do anything else in the city before I take you back to your place?"

No such luck. Sabine's eyes flew open to see Gavin looking at her with a curious gaze. "You don't have to take us back," she snapped. She wasn't certain she could take being so close to him in the car. At least not at the moment. "We'll take the subway."

"No, I insist." Gavin paid the check and handed his crayon over to Jared.

"Gavin, you have a two-passenger roadster with no car seat. You can't drive us home."

He smiled and fished into his pocket, pulling out the ticket for the garage attendant. "Not today. Today I have a four-door Mercedes sedan…"

Sabine opened her mouth to reiterate the lack of car seat when Gavin continued, "…with a newly installed combination car seat that Jared can use until he's eighty-five pounds."

Her mouth snapped shut. He was determined to undermine any arguments she might make. Sure, it was harmless when it came to rides home from dinner, but what about when the decisions were important? Would Gavin find a way to make sure he got his way then, too? He'd always seemed to win when they were dating, so she wouldn't be surprised.

Tonight, Sabine didn't feel like arguing. She waited with Jared while Gavin had the attendant retrieve his car. Admittedly, it was nice to just sit in the soft leather seats and let Gavin worry about the stressful exodus of traffic into Brooklyn. No running down stairs to the train platforms…no crowded, B.O.-smelling subway cars…

And when he pulled up right in front of her building and parked, trimming several blocks from her walk, she said, "Thank you."

"For what?"

"Driving us home."

Gavin frowned slightly at her. "Of course I would drive you home. There's no need to thank me for that."

Sabine glanced over her shoulder and found Jared out cold in his new car seat. "I think he likes it," she said. She glanced at her watch. It was a little after seven. It was earlier than Jared usually went to bed, and he'd probably beat the sun to rise, but that was okay. If she could get him upstairs, change his Pull-Up and take off his shoes without waking him up, she'd consider it a victory.

They got out of the car. Sabine walked around to the other side, but Gavin had already scooped up the sleepy toddler in his arms. Without waking, Jared put his head on Gavin's shoulder and clung to his neck. Gavin gently ran his palm over the child's head, brushing back the baby-soft strands of his dark hair and resting his hand on Jared's back to keep him steady.

Sabine watched with a touch of tears distorting her vision. It was sweet watching the two of them, like carbon copies of one another. It was only their second day together and already she could see Jared warming up to Gavin.

Gavin carried Jared through the building and into her apartment after she unlocked the door. Sabine led the way down the hall to the bedroom. Flipping on the lights, they were greeted with calming mint-green walls, cream wainscoting and a mural of Winnie the Pooh characters she'd painted above the crib. Her double bed was an afterthought on the opposite wall.

She slipped off Jared's shoes. His soft cotton pants and T-shirt would be fine to sleep in. She gestured for Gavin to lay him on the crib mattress and made quick work of changing him.

Jared immediately curled into a ball, reaching out for his stuffed dinosaur and pulling it to his chest. Sabine covered him with his blanket. They slipped out quietly, the night-light kicking on as the overhead light went out.

Sabine pulled the door closed gently and made her way back into the living room. She expected Gavin to make noises about leaving, but instead he loitered, his eyes focused on a painting on the wall over the dining room table.

"I remember this one," Gavin said, his fists in his pants pockets.

Sabine looked up at the canvas and smiled. "You should. I was painting that one while we were dating."

The background of the painting was intricately layered with a muted palette of white, cream, ivory, off-white and ecru. The design was extremely structured and orderly. The variations of the pattern were really quite remarkable if you could differentiate the subtle color differences.

It was Gavin on canvas. And across it, splatters of purple, black and green paint. Disorder. Chaos. Color. That was Sabine. It was a striking juxtaposition. One that when it was complete, was the perfect illustration of why as a couple they made good art, but not good sense.

"You weren't finished with it when I saw it last.

Some of this is new, like the blue crosses. What did you end up calling it?"

The pale blue crosses were actually plus signs. The final addition to the work after seeing her own unexpected plus sign on a pregnancy test. "Conception," she said.

Gavin looked back at the painting and turned his head to look at it from a new angle. "It's very nice. I like the colors. It's a much-needed pop against the beige."

Sabine smiled. He didn't see the symbolism of their relationship in it at all and that was okay. Art was only half about what she created. The other half was how others perceived and experienced her work.

He turned back to her, his face serious. "You are a really talented artist, Sabine."

The compliment made her squirm a little. She was always uncomfortable with praise. Frankly, she wasn't used to it after growing up with parents who didn't understand why their daughter danced to a different drummer. "It's okay," she said with a dismissive wave of her hand. "Not my best work."

Gavin frowned and closed the gap between them. He clasped her hand in his and pulled it to the red silk of his tie. "No," he insisted. "It's not just okay. You're not just okay."

Sabine tried to pull away, but he wasn't having it. He bent his knees until he was at her eye level and she couldn't avoid his gaze.

"You are a gifted painter," he insisted. "You were then and you certainly are now. I was always amazed at how you could create such wonderful and imaginative things from just a blank canvas. You have a great deal of skill, Sabine, whether you think so or not. I hope our son has the same eye for the beautiful things in life."

The words were hard enough to hear when they were about her, but knowing he wished the same for their son was too much for her to take. Her parents hadn't wanted her to be a painter. It was frivolous. They'd wanted her to stay home and work on the farm, grow up and marry a farmer, and then raise a brood of tiny farmers. She was absolutely nothing like they wanted. And the day she left for New York, they said as much.

Before she could change her mind, Sabine threw herself against the wall of Gavin's chest and hugged him tight. He seemed surprised at first, but then he wrapped his strong arms around her and pulled her close. "Thank you," she whispered into his lapel.

It felt good to be in his arms, surrounded in his warmth and spicy cologne. Good to be appreciated for her work even when she hadn't lifted a brush in two years. Good to have someone believe in her, even if it was the same man who let her walk away from him. She would be happy with his professional admiration if nothing else.

And yet, with her head pressed to his chest, she could hear his heart racing. His muscles were tense as he held her. He was either extremely uncomfortable hugging her or there was more than just admiration there.

Sabine lifted her head and looked up at him. Her breath caught in her throat as her eyes met his. They glittered with what could only be desire. His jaw was tight, but unlike last night, he wasn't angry. He swallowed hard, the muscles in his throat working hard down the column of his neck. She recognized the signs in Gavin. She knew them well but thought she'd never see him look at her like that again.

The intensity of his gaze flipped a switch in her own body. As it had in the restaurant, heat pooled in her cheeks and then rushed through her veins to warm every inch of her. She couldn't help it. There had been few things as exquisite in her life as being made love to by Gavin. It had come as a huge surprise considering how tightly buttoned-up he was, but there was no denying he knew just how to touch her. It was probably the worst thing she could do considering what was going on between them, but she wanted Gavin to touch her again.

He must have read it in her eyes because a moment later he dipped his head and brought his lips to hers. They were soft at first, molding to her mouth and drinking her in. Sabine gently pressed her hands against his chest, pushing up onto her toes to get closer to him.

His hands glided across her back, the heat of him penetrating through the fabric of her blouse and searing her skin. She wanted to feel those hands all over her body. It had been so long since someone had touched her that way. She didn't want it to stop. Not ever.

Sabine was about to lean in. She wanted to wrap her arms around his neck and press her body tight against his. As if he sensed the move, Gavin started to retreat. She could feel him pulling away, the cool air rushing between them and bringing with it reality. She pulled away, too, wrapping her arms across her chest to ward off the chill and its evidence on her aching body.

Gavin looked down at her and cleared his throat. "I'd better go."

Sabine nodded and moved slowly with him toward the door.

"Good night, Sabine," he said in a hoarse whisper. He took a step back, straightening his suit coat, and then gripped the brass knob in his hand.

"Good night," she whispered, bringing her fingers up to gently touch her lips. They were still tingling with his kiss as he vanished through her doorway. "Good night."

Four

"We have a date this afternoon. I mean a playdate. I mean, aw hell, I have no idea what's going on," Sabine lamented. She was folding a stack of shirts and paused with one clutched to her chest. "You know, a few days ago I was living my life like a criminal on the run, but I felt like I had a better grip on things."

Adrienne smiled at her and turned to change the outfit on the mannequin by the wall. "It's a big change," she said. "But so far, it's not a bad change, right?"

"That's true. I guess that's what worries me. I keep waiting for the other shoe to drop."

The boutique was open, but the foot traffic usually didn't pick up until closer to lunchtime on a Saturday. At the moment, Sabine and Adrienne were alone in the store and able to speak freely about the dramatic turn of events in her life. Normally, Sabine ran the shop alone until another employee, Jill, came in later in the day. Today, Adrienne came in as well to relieve Sabine so she could meet Gavin.

"I don't think he's going to steal Jared away from you, Sabine. It sounds like he's been pretty reasonable so far."

"I know," she said, folding the last shirt and adding it

to the neat display. "But he doesn't have the DNA results back yet and won't until Monday. If he was going to make a move, it wouldn't be until he had the advantage. The Gavin I knew three years ago was...calculating and ruthless. He had absolutely no qualms about sitting back and waiting for the perfect moment to strike."

"This isn't a business deal and he's not a cobra. You two have a child together. It's different." Adrienne pulled out a pin and fitted the top of the dress to the form.

Sabine stopped and admired the outfit Adrienne had designed. The sexy sheath dress was fitted with a square neckline, but it had fun details like pockets and a bright print to make it pop. It was perfect for the summer with some strappy heels or colorful ballet flats. She'd been tempted to use her employee discount to buy it for herself, but there wasn't much point. That was the kind of dress a woman wanted to wear on a date or a night out with the girls. She hadn't had either in a very long time. And despite Gavin proposing one night and kissing her the next, she didn't think her Facebook relationship status would be changing anytime soon.

"Work and life are the same to Gavin. I mean, he didn't propose to me. Not really. It was more like an offer to buy out my company. A business merger. Just what a girl wants to hear, right?"

Adrienne turned and looked at Sabine with her hands planted on her hips. "And the kiss?"

The kiss. The one thing that didn't make sense. She knew he was her Achilles' heel so it didn't surprise her that she fell into his arms, but his motives were sketchy. "Strategy. He knows my weakness where he's concerned. He's just buttering up the competition to get his way."

"You really think that's all it was?" Her boss looked unconvinced.

Sabine flopped down onto an upholstered bench outside the changing rooms. "I don't know. It didn't feel like strategy. It felt..." Her mind drifted back to the way her body had responded to his touch. The way her lips tingled long after he'd left. She sighed and shook her head. "It doesn't matter what it felt like. The fact of the matter is that Gavin doesn't love me. He never has. His only interest in me back then was as a source of rebellion against his uptight family. Now, I'm nothing more than a vehicle to his son. And when he gets tired of the games, he'll remove the obstacle—*me*."

"You don't think he's interested in a relationship with you?" Adrienne sat down beside her.

"Why would he be? He wasn't interested the last time. At least not enough to so much as blink when it ended. I mean, I thought there was more between us than just sex, but he was always so closed off. I had no idea how he really felt, but when he let me walk out the door like I was nothing more than an amusement to occupy his time...I knew I was replaceable. Gavin never would've sought me out if it wasn't for Jared."

"You broke up with him," Adrienne reminded her. "Maybe his pride kept him from chasing after you. Listen, I'm married to one of those guys. They're all about running their little empires. They're the king of their own kingdoms. In the business world, showing weakness is like throwing chum in the ocean—the sharks start circling. They keep it all inside for so long that after a while, they lose touch with their own sense of vulnerability."

Her boss knew what she was talking about. Adrienne's husband was Will Taylor, owner of one of the oldest and most successful newspapers in New York. He came from a long line of CEOs, just as Gavin had. Even then, she'd seen Adrienne and Will together multiple times, and he was putty in her hands. And happily so. Will at work and Will at home were completely different people.

But somehow Sabine had a hard time picturing Gavin with a marshmallow center beneath his hard candy shell. They'd shared some intimate moments together while they'd dated, but there was always an element of control on his part. They were together only a short time, but it was an intense relationship. She gave so much and yet he held back from her. She had no way of knowing the parts he kept hidden, but more than likely, it was his apathy. "You're saying he let me walk away and cried himself to sleep that night?"

Adrienne chuckled. "Well, maybe that's taking it a little far. But he might have had regrets and didn't know what to do about it. Jared gives him a good reason to see you again without having to address any of those icky, uncomfortable feelings."

A pair of ladies came into the shop, so they put their conversation on hold for now. While the women looked around, Sabine moved over to the checkout counter and crouched down to inventory the stock of pink boutique bags with Adrienne's signature across the side. The passive activity helped her think.

Feelings were definitely not Gavin's forte. Or at least sharing them. She was certain he had them, he just bottled them up on the inside. But feelings for her? She doubted that.

Gavin might be attracted to her. The kiss they shared might've been him testing the waters of resuming a physical relationship. They'd always had an undeniable chemistry. She knew the minute she saw him the first time that she was in trouble. It was at a gallery showing for a local contemporary artist. Sabine had gotten lost in the lines and colors of one of the pieces and the rest of the world disappeared.

At least until she heard the low rumble of a man's voice in her ear. "It looks like an expensive mistake to me."

She'd turned in surprise and nearly choked on a sip of champagne when she saw him. He wasn't at all the kind of man she was used to. He wore an expensive suit and a watch that cost more money than she'd made in the past year. Men like Gavin typically turned their nose up at Sabine. But he'd looked at her with dark eyes that twinkled with amusement and desire.

Her pulse had shot up, her knees melted to butter beneath her, and she'd found herself without a witty response. Just that quickly, she was lost.

The weeks that followed were some of the greatest of her life. But not once in that time had he ever looked at her with anything more than lust. So as much as she'd like to think Adrienne was right, she knew better. He'd either been using their attraction to his advantage or using their situation to get laid.

One of the ladies tried on a blouse and then bought it, along with a scarf. Sabine rang her up and they left the store. The chime of the door signaled that her conversation with Adrienne could resume.

"So where are you guys going on your playdate today?" Adrienne called from the stockroom.

"We're going to the Central Park Zoo."

"That should be fun," Adrienne said, returning to the front with her arms full of one of her newest dress designs. "Was that his idea?"

"No," Sabine chuckled. She reached out to take several of the outfits from her. "He didn't have a clue of what to do with a two-year-old. I suggested the zoo because I wanted us to do something that didn't involve a lot of money."

Adrienne wrinkled her delicate nose. "What do you mean?"

They carried the dresses over to the empty rack and organized them by size. "I don't want Gavin buying Jared anything yet. At least not big, expensive things. He used to tell me that his father only ever took him shopping. I can't keep him from buying things forever, but that's not how I want to start off."

"Money isn't a bad thing, Sabine. I never had it until I married Will, and trust me, it takes some adjusting to get used to having a lot of it. But it can be used for good, too, not just for evil."

"It's also not a substitute for love or attention. I want Gavin to really try. Right now, Jared is still young, but before too long, he's going to be in the 'gimme' stage. I don't want Gavin buying affection with expensive gifts."

"Try to keep an open mind," Adrienne suggested. "Just because he buys Jared something doesn't mean he isn't trying. If getting him a balloon makes Jared smile, don't read too much into it. Just enjoy your afternoon." Adrienne stopped and crinkled her nose, making a funny face at Sabine.

"What's the matter?"

"I don't know. My stomach is a little upset all of a sudden. I think my smoothie is turning on me. Either that, or I'm nauseated by all your drama."

Sabine laughed. "I'm sorry my crazy life is making you ill. I've got some antacids in my purse if you need them."

"I'll be fine," Adrienne insisted. She looked down at her watch. "You'd better get going if you're going to meet him on time. Worry about having fun instead."

Sabine nodded. "Okay," she said. "We will have a good time, I promise."

She hoped she was right.

As Gavin stepped out of his apartment building onto Central Park South and crossed the street, he realized just how long it had been since he'd actually set foot in Central Park. He looked out at it every day but never paid any attention to the looming green hulk that sprawled out in front of him.

His first clue was that he was a little overdressed for a summer afternoon at the zoo. He'd left the tie at home, but he probably could've forgone the suit coat, too. A pair of jeans or khakis and a polo shirt would've suited just fine. He considered running his jacket back upstairs, but he didn't want to be late.

When he was younger, he'd enjoyed jogging along the paths or hanging out and playing Frisbee with friends in the Sheep Meadow. The more involved he got in the management of BXS, the less important trees and sunshine seemed in his agenda. He and Sabine had taken a horse-drawn carriage through the park one evening when they were dating, but the closest he had gotten to it since then was a gala at the Met last year.

By the time he reached the front entrance to the zoo, he could feel the sweat forming along his spine. He slipped out of the jacket and threw it over his arm after rolling up his sleeves. It helped, but not much. He was supposed to meet Sabine and Gavin just outside the brick archways that marked the entrance, but he didn't see them anywhere.

He unclipped his phone from his belt to look at the time. He was a few minutes early. He opted to flip through some emails. He'd hit a little bit of a snag with the Exclusivity Jetliners merger. The owner's son, Paul, had found out about his father's plans and was throwing a fit. Apparently he wasn't pleased about watching his inheritance getting sold off. Gavin was paying a pretty penny for the company, but Roger's son seemed to fancy playing CEO. Roger was starting to second-guess the sale.

He fired off a couple quick emails, but his attention was piqued by the sound of a child's laughter in the distance. It was one of those contagious giggles that made you smile just to hear it. He looked up in the direction of the sound and saw Sabine and Jared playing in the shade of a large tree.

Slipping his cell phone back in the holster, he made his way over to where they were. Sabine was crouched down beside Jared, dressed in capris and a tank top. Her dark hair was pulled back into a ponytail and a bright red backpack was slung over her shoulders.

Jared was playing with another one of his trucks. In the mud. Apparently, the kid had managed to find the only mud bog in the park. He was crouched barefoot in the brown muck, ramming his trucks through the sludge. He made loud truck noises with his mouth and then giggled hysterically when the mud splashed up onto his shirt. He was head-to-toe filthy and happy as a little piglet.

Gavin's instinct was to grab Jared and get him out of the dirt immediately. There had to be a restroom somewhere nearby where they could rinse him off. But then he saw the smile on Sabine's face. She wasn't even remotely concerned about what Jared was doing.

His mother would've had a fit if she had found him playing in the mud. His nanny would've had to hose him off outside and then thoroughly scrub him in the tub. When he was dry, he would've been given a lengthy lecture about how getting dirty was inappropriate and his nanny would've been fired for not keeping a better eye on him.

Jared dropped one of the trucks in the puddle and the water splashed up, splattering both him and Sabine. Gavin expected her to get upset since she'd gotten dirty now, but she just laughed and wiped the smear of muddy water off her arm. It was amazing. It made Gavin want to get dirty, too.

"Oh, hey," Sabine said, looking up to see him standing nearby. She glanced at her watch. "I'm sorry to keep you waiting. We got here a little early and Jared can't pass up some good mud." She stood up and whipped the backpack off her shoulders.

"Not a problem," he said as he watched her pull out an assortment of things including wet wipes, a large, plastic zip bag and a clean shirt.

"All right, buddy," she said. "Time to go to the zoo with Gavin. Are you ready?"

"Yeah!" Jared said, immediately perking up at the suggestion of a new adventure.

"Give me your trucks first." She put all the muddy toys in the bag and then used his dirty shirt to wipe up a good bit of the muck off his hands and feet before shoving it in there, as well. The baby wipes made quick work of the rest, then the clean shirt and the little socks and sneakers she'd taken off went back on. "Good job!" she praised, giving him a tiny high five and zipping up the backpack.

Gavin was amazed by the process. Not only did she let Jared get dirty, she was fully prepared for the eventuality. He'd always just thought of Sabine as the artistic type. She was laid-back and went with the flow as he expected, but she also had a meticulous bit of planning underneath it all that he appreciated. She had the motherhood thing down. It was very impressive.

"We're ready," she said, bending down to pick Jared up.

Gavin had to smile when he noticed the speck of mud on Sabine's cheek. "Not quite yet," he said. Without thinking, he reached out to her, running the pad of his thumb across her cheekbone and wiping it away. The moment he touched her, he sensed a change in the energy between them. Her pale green eyes widened, the irises darkening in the center to the deep hunter green he remembered from their lovemaking. A soft gasp of surprise escaped her glossy pink lips.

His body reacted, as well. The touch brought on the familiar tingle that settled between his shoulder blades and sent a shot of pure need down his spine. He wanted Sabine. There was no use in denying it. There was something about her that spoke to his most base instincts. Their time apart hadn't changed or dulled the attraction. In fact, it seemed to have amplified it.

That night at her apartment, he had to kiss her. There was no way he could walk out of there without tasting her again. Once he did, he could feel the floodgates giving way. He had to leave. And right then. If he had lingered a moment longer, he wouldn't have been able to stop himself.

Their relationship was complicated. There were a lot of proverbial balls still in the air. He wasn't dumb enough to get emotionally involved with Sabine again, but leaping back into a physical relationship with her, at least this soon, was a bad idea, too. For now, he needed to try and keep his distance on both fronts.

Why, then, was he standing in the middle of Central Park cradling Sabine's face with a throbbing erection? Because he was a masochist.

"A…uh…stray bit of Jared's handiwork," he said. He let his hand drop back to his side before he did something stupid in public. Instead, he turned to look at Jared. "Are you ready to see the monkeys?"

"Yeah!" he cheered, clapping his chubby hands together.

They bought their tickets and headed inside. Starting at the sea lion pool, they made their way around to visit the penguins and the snow leopards. He enjoyed watching his son's eyes light up when he saw the animals.

"Do you guys come here a lot?" he asked, leaning on the railing outside the snow monkey exhibit. "He really seems to like it."

"We actually haven't been here before. I was waiting until he was a little older. This seemed like the perfect opportunity."

Gavin was surprised. Somehow he'd thought he had missed all his son's firsts, but there were more to be had than he expected. "I've never been here, either."

Sabine looked at him with disbelief lining her brow. "You've lived in New York your whole life and you've never been to the zoo?"

"Saying I lived here my whole life isn't entirely accurate. My family lived here, but I was gone off to school a lot of the time."

"So not even as a child? Your nannies never brought you here?"

"Nope. Sometimes we came to the park to play or walk, but never to the zoo. I'm not sure why. My boarding school took a field trip to Washington, D.C., once. We went to the Smithsonian and the National Zoo on that trip. I think I was fourteen or so. But I've never had the chance to come here."

"Have you ever been to a petting zoo?"

At that, Gavin had to laugh. "A petting zoo? Absolutely not. My mother would have a fit at the thought of me touching dirty animals. I never even had pets as a kid."

Sabine wrinkled her nose at him. "Well, then, today is your day. We'll head over to the children's zoo after this and you and Jared can both pet your first goat."

A goat? He wasn't so sure that he was interested in that. Sabine seemed to sense his hesitation. "Maybe we can start you off slow. You can hold a rabbit. They have places to wash your hands. I also have hand sanitizer in my bag. You'll be okay, I promise."

Gavin chuckled at Sabine. She was mothering him

just the same as she did to coax Jared into trying something new. He wasn't used to that.

They were on their way to the children's zoo when he felt his cell phone buzzing at his hip. He looked down at the screen. It was Roger. He had to take this call.

"Excuse me one minute," he said.

Sabine frowned but nodded. "I'll take Jared to the restroom while we're waiting."

Gavin answered the phone and spent the next ten minutes soothing Roger's concerns. He didn't want this opportunity to slip through his fingers. Acquiring those private jets was as close to fulfilling his childhood dream as he might ever get. He had a plane of his own, but it was small and didn't have anywhere near the range of Roger's jets. He longed for the day when he could pilot one of those planes to some far-off destination. He was a falcon on a tether now. He wanted to fly free, and he wasn't going to let Paul Simpson's desire to play at CEO ruin it.

It was going well so far. He was able to address all of Roger's concerns. Things might be back on track if he could keep the owner focused on what was best for his family and his company. But it was taking some time. The conversation was still going when Sabine returned. She didn't seem pleased.

He covered the receiver with his hand. "I'm almost done. I can walk and talk," he said.

She turned and started walking away with Jared. He followed close behind them, but he was admittedly distracted. By the time he finally hung up, Gavin had already missed out on feeding the ducks. Jared was quacking and clumsily chasing one at the moment.

Sabine was watching him play with a twinkle in

her eye. She loved their son so much. He could tell that Jared was everything to her. He appreciated that about her. His parents had never been abusive or cruel, but they had been distant. Busy. They weren't hands-on at all. Jared hadn't had all the privileges that Gavin grew up with, but he did have a loving, doting mother.

Who was frowning intently at Gavin.

"I'm sorry," he said. "It was important."

She shook her head and turned back to look at Jared. One of the zoo employees was holding a rabbit so he could pet it. "That's the most important thing, right there, Gavin."

Jared turned around and grinned at his mother with such joy it made Gavin's chest hurt. "A bunny," he exclaimed, hopping around on his little legs like a rabbit.

She was right. He needed to be in this 100 percent. Jared deserved it. And so did Sabine.

Five

There was a knock on the door early Sunday morning. Sabine was making pancakes while Jared played with blocks on the floor. Sunday was their easy day. There was no work or preschool. They were both still in their pajamas and not expecting company.

She was surprised to find Gavin on her doorstep. She was even more surprised to find he was wearing jeans and a T-shirt. It was a Gucci T-shirt, but at least it wasn't a suit. And it looked good on him. The black shirt fit his muscular frame like a second skin, reminding her of the body he hid beneath blazers and ties. And the jeans…they were snug in all the right places, making her mouth go dry in an instant.

He caught her so off guard, she didn't notice at first that he had a large canvas and a bag of painting supplies in his hands.

"Gavin," she said. "I wasn't expecting you this morning." After yesterday, she didn't figure she would see him until the test results came back. She could tell that he was trying yesterday, but his thoughts were being pulled in ten different directions. Even after he got off the phone, he was checking it constantly and replying to emails. He had a business to run.

And yet, here he was.

"I know. I wanted it to be a surprise."

Sabine wasn't big on surprises. With Gavin, it was more that he wanted to do something his way and to keep her from arguing, he wouldn't tell her until the last second. Surprise! But still, she was curious. "Come on in," she said.

Gavin stepped in, leaning the canvas against the bookcase. "Hey, big guy," he said to Jared. He got up from his blocks and came over to hug Gavin's leg. Gavin scooped the toddler up and held him over his head, and then they "soared" around the living room making airplane noises. Jared the Plane crash-landed onto the couch in a fit of giggles and tickling fingers poking at his tummy.

It had only been a few days, but she could tell that Jared was getting attached to Gavin. It was a good thing. She knew that. But still, she worried. He'd put in a decent effort so far, but could he keep it up for the next sixteen years? She wasn't sure. But she did know that he'd better not screw this up.

"I was making pancakes," she said, turning and heading back into the kitchen. "Have you had breakfast?"

"That depends," he said, pausing in the tickle fight. "What kind of pancakes are they?"

"Silver-dollar pancakes with blueberries."

"Nope." Gavin smiled. "I haven't had breakfast." He let Jared return to his blocks. "I'll be right back, big guy."

He followed her into the kitchen, leaning against the entryway. The kitchen was too small for both of them to be in there and get anything done. She tried to ignore his physical presence and how much of the room he took up without even entering, but she failed. The sight of him in those tight jeans was more than she could take. Her body instantly reacted to his nearness, her mouth going dry and her nipples pebbling against the thin fabric of her T-shirt.

She spun to face the stove before he could notice and decided to focus on pancakes, not the sexy man lurking nearby. Eyeing the batter, she decided she needed a larger batch to feed a man of his size. "So what brings you here this morning?"

Gavin watched her fold in another handful of dried blueberries. "I wanted to make up for yesterday."

Sabine tried not to react. She was happy that he was making the effort, but failing Jared and then making a grand gesture to appease his conscience was a dangerous cycle. She'd rather he just be present the first time. "How's that?"

"I saw in the paper that the Big Apple Circus is here. I got tickets for this afternoon."

Just as she'd thought. She had no problems with going to the circus, but he didn't ask her. He didn't call to see if that was something they might want to do. What if Jared was petrified of clowns? Or if they had other plans today? Gavin just bought the tickets and assumed that everything would go the way he'd planned.

But—he was trying, she reminded herself. "Jared would probably enjoy that. What time do we need to leave for the show?"

"Well," Gavin said, "that's only part of the surprise. *We* aren't leaving. You're staying."

Sabine looked up from the griddle. "What do you mean?"

"I just got tickets for Jared and me. I thought you might enjoy an afternoon to yourself. I even brought you some painting supplies."

That explained the stuff he brought in with him. She'd been so thrown off by his unannounced arrival that she hadn't questioned it yet. She supposed that she should be excited and grateful, but instead, her stomach ached with worry. Gavin was taking her son someplace without her. She didn't really like the sound of that. He didn't know anything about children. What if Jared got sick? Or scared? Did Gavin even know that Jared wasn't fully potty trained yet? Just the idea of him changing dirty Pull-Ups started a rumble of nervous laughter in her chest that she fought down.

"I don't think that's a good idea," she managed to say.

Gavin's dark brow drew together in consternation. "Why not? You said you wanted me to be there. To be involved."

"It's been less than a week, Gavin. You've spent a couple hours with him, sure, but are you ready to take care of him on your own for a day?" Sabine turned back to the stove and flipped over the pancakes. She grabbed one of Jared's superhero plates and slid a couple tiny pancakes onto it beside the slices of banana she'd already cut up.

"You don't think I can handle it?"

She sighed heavily. Ignoring him, she poured some blueberry syrup into the small bowl built into the dish and grabbed a sippy cup with milk from the refrigerator. She brushed past him to go into the living room. Jared had a tiny plastic table and chair where he could eat. She set down his breakfast and called him over. Once he was settled, she turned back to look at Gavin. He was still standing in the doorway to the kitchen looking handsome and irritated all at once.

"I don't know," she admitted. "I don't know if you can handle it or not. That's the problem. We don't really know one another that well."

Gavin crossed his arms over his chest and leaned against the door frame. His biceps bulged against the constraints of the shirt, drawing her eyes down to his strong forearms and rock-hard chest. It was easier to focus on that than the strangely cocky expression on his face.

"We know each other *very* well," he said with a wicked grin curling his lips.

Sabine approached him, stopping just short of touching him. "Your ability to give me an orgasm has no bearing on whether or not you can care for a toddler."

At the mention of the word *orgasm* his gaze narrowed at her. He swallowed hard but didn't reach for her. "I disagree. Both require an attention to detail. Anticipating what another person wants or needs. I don't think it matters if what they need is a drink, a toy or a mind-blowing physical release."

Mind-blowing. Sabine couldn't stop her tongue from gliding out over her lips. They'd gotten painfully dry. His gaze dropped to her mouth, then back to her eyes. There was a touch of amusement in his gaze. He knew he was getting to her.

"What if what they need is their poopy diaper changed? Or you gave them too much cotton candy and they spew blue muck all over the backseat of your Mercedes? Not quite as sexy."

The light of attraction in his eyes faded. It was hard to keep up the arousal with that kind of imagery. That's why she hadn't bothered dating in all this time. Maybe she should reconsider. She might not feel as vulnerable to Gavin's charms if she had an outlet that didn't involve him.

His expression hardened for a moment. He seemed irritated with her. "Stop trying to scare me away. I know taking care of a child isn't easy. It can be messy. But it's just a few hours to start. I can handle it. Will you let me do this for you? Please?"

"Do this for *me?* Shouldn't you be doing this for your son?"

"I am. Of course, I am. I want a relationship with Jared more than anything. But to do that, you have got to trust me. I will return him to you tonight, well fed, well cared for and, for the most part, clean. But you have to do your part. You have to let me try. Let me mess up. Enjoy your free afternoon. Paint something beautiful because you can. Go get a pedicure."

Sabine had to admit that sounded wonderful. She hadn't had an afternoon to herself since she went into labor. She didn't have any family here to watch Jared. She tried to only use Tina's services when she had to for classes. She hadn't had a day just to relax. And to paint…

She pushed past him into the kitchen to finish making pancakes. Gavin stayed in the doorway, allowing her the space to think, while also keeping an eye on Jared. She appreciated having someone to do that. She hadn't had another set of eyes to help before. Since Jared became mobile, she hadn't been able to shower, cook or do anything without constantly peeking out to check on him. Life was a little easier when he sat in his swing or bouncy chair while she did what needed to be done.

A whole afternoon?

She wanted to say yes, but she couldn't shake the worry. It was probably going to be fine. There was only so much trouble that could befall them in an afternoon at the circus. If Jared came home covered in blue vomit, the world wouldn't end. And it was a family-oriented event. She had no doubt that if another mother saw Gavin and Jared in a meltdown moment, she would step in to help.

Sabine finished the pancakes and turned off the burner. She slid a stack onto her plate and the other onto a plate for Gavin. Turning around, she offered one to him. When he reached for it, she pulled it back slightly.

"Okay," she said. "You can go. But I want you to text and check in with me. And if anything remotely worrisome happens—"

Gavin took the plate from her. "I will call you immediately. Okay?"

Sharing Jared with someone else was going to be hard, she could tell already. But it could be good, too. Two parents were double the hands, double the eyes, double the love. Right? "Okay, all right. You win. Just don't feed him too much sugar. You'll regret it."

Gavin couldn't remember being this tired, ever. Not when he was on the college rowing team. Not when he stayed up late studying for an exam. Not even after spending all night making love to a beautiful woman. How on earth did parents do this every day? How did Sabine manage to care for Jared alone, work full-time, teach yoga…it was no wonder she'd stopped painting. He was bone-tired. Mentally exhausted.

And it was one of the best days of his life.

Seeing Jared's smile made everything worth it. That was what kept parents going. That moment his son's face lit up when he saw an elephant for the first time. Or the sound of his laughter when the clowns were up to their wacky antics.

The day hadn't been without its mishaps. Jared had dropped his ice cream and went into a full, five-alarm meltdown. Gavin knew Sabine didn't want him buying a bunch of things, but he gladly threw down the cash for the overpriced light-up sword to quiet him down. There was also a potty emergency that was timed just as they neared the front of the mile-long food line. Sabine had begun potty training recently and had told him that if Jared asked, they were to go, right then. So they did. And ended up at the end of the line, waiting another twenty minutes for hot dogs and popcorn.

But the world hadn't ended. There had been no tragedies, and he texted as much to Sabine every hour or so. The day had been filled with lights and sound and excitement. So much so that by the time they made it back to the apartment, Jared was out cold. Gavin knew exactly how he felt.

He carried the exhausted toddler inside, quietly tapping at the apartment door so as to not wake him up. When Sabine didn't answer, he tried the knob and found it unlocked. He expected to find Sabine frantically painting. This was her chance, after all, to indulge her suppressed creativity. Instead, she was curled up on the couch, asleep.

Gavin smiled. He had told her to spend the afternoon doing whatever she wanted. He should've guessed that a nap would be pretty high on the list. He tiptoed quietly through the living room and into the bedroom. Following the routine from Thursday night, he laid Jared in the crib and stripped him down into just his T-shirt and shorts. He covered him with the blanket and turned out the lights.

Sabine was still asleep when he came out. He knew he couldn't leave without waking her up, but he couldn't bear to disturb her. He eased down at the end of the couch and decided to just wait until she woke up.

He enjoyed watching Sabine sleep. She had always been one to work hard and play hard, so when she slept, it was a deep sleep and it came on quickly. There were many nights where he had lain in bed and just studied her face. Gavin had memorized every line and curve. He'd counted her eyelashes. There was just something about her that had fascinated him from the first moment he saw her.

The weeks they'd spent together were intense. He couldn't get enough of her. Sabine was a breath of fresh air to a man hanging from the gallows. She'd brought him back to life with her rebellious streak and quest for excitement. He'd loved everything about her, from her dazzling smile to her ever-changing rainbow-streaked hair. He'd loved how there was always a speck of paint somewhere on her body, even if he had to do a detailed search to find it. She was so different from every other woman he'd ever known.

For the first time, he'd allowed himself to start opening up to someone. He'd begun making plans for Sabine to be a permanent fixture in his life. He hadn't anticipated her bolting, and when she did, he shut down. Gavin hadn't allowed himself to realize just how much he'd missed her until this moment.

She didn't trust him. Not with her son and not with

her heart. Gavin hadn't appreciated it when he had it—at least not outwardly. He never told her how he felt or shared his plans for their future. That was his own fault, and they missed their chance at love. But even with that lost, he wanted her back in his bed. He ached to run his fingers through her hair. Tonight, it was pulled up on top of her head, the silky black and bright purple strands jumbled together. He wanted to touch it and see it sprawled across the pillowcase.

His eyes traveled down her body to the thin shirt and shorts she was wearing. He didn't think it was possible, but she was more beautiful now than she had been back then. She wouldn't believe him if he told her that, but it was true. Motherhood had filled out some of the curves she'd lacked as a struggling artist. He remembered her getting so engrossed in her work that sometimes she would simply forget to eat. Gavin would come to the apartment with takeout and force her to take a break.

Now she had nicely rounded hips that called to him to reach out and glide his palms over them. He wanted to curl up behind her and press her soft body into his. He wanted to feel her lean, yoga-toned muscles flexing against him. The sight of her in that skimpy workout outfit had haunted him since that first night.

Her newly developed muscles didn't make up for the mental strain, however. Even in her sleep, a fine line ran between her eyebrows. She made a certain face when she was frustrated or confused, and that line was the result. There were faint circles under her eyes. She was worn out. He was determined to make things easier for her. No matter how their relationship ended or his feelings where she was concerned, she deserved the help he could provide.

She just had to let him.

"Gavin," Sabine whispered.

He looked up, expecting to see her eyes open, but she was talking in her sleep. Calling his name in her sleep. He held his breath, waiting to see if she spoke again.

"Please," she groaned, squirming slightly on the sofa. "Yes. I need you."

Gavin nearly choked on his own saliva. She wasn't just dreaming about him. She was having an erotic dream about him. The mere thought made his jeans uncomfortably tight.

"Touch me."

Gavin couldn't resist. He reached out and placed his hand on the firm curve of her calf. He loved the feel of her soft skin against him. It made his palm tingle and his blood hum in his veins. Just a simple touch. No other woman had had this effect on him. Whatever it was that drew them together was still here, and as strong as ever.

"Gavin?"

He looked up to see Sabine squinting at him in confusion. She was awake now. And probably wondering why the hell he was fondling her leg. He expected her to shy away from his touch, but she didn't. Instead, she sat up. She looked deep into his eyes for a moment, the fire of her passionate dream still lighting her gaze.

She reached up, cradling his face in her hands and tugging his mouth down to hers. He wasn't about to deny her. The moment their lips met, he felt the familiar surge of need wash over him. Before when they'd kissed, he had resisted the pull, but he couldn't do it any longer. He wanted her and she wanted him. They could deal with the consequences of it later.

Her mouth was hungry, demanding more of him,

and he gave it. His tongue thrust inside her, matching her intensity and eliciting a groan deep in her throat. Her fingers drifted into his hair, desperately tugging him closer.

Gavin wrapped his arms around her waist and drew her up onto her knees. He explored every new curve of her body just as he'd fantasized, dipping low to cup the roundness of her backside. The firm press of her flesh against his fingertips was better than he ever could have imagined. He didn't think it was possible, but he grew even harder as he touched her.

Sabine's hands roamed as well, sliding down his chest, studying the ridges of his abs and then reaching around his back. She grasped the hem of his shirt and tugged until their lips parted and it came up and over his head. She did the same with her own shirt, throwing it to the floor and revealing full breasts with no bra to obscure them.

Before he could reach out to touch them, Sabine leaned back, cupping his neck with one hand and pulling him with her until she was lying on the couch and he was covering her body with his. Every soft inch of her molded to him. Her breasts crushed against his bare chest, the hard peaks of her nipples pressing insistently into his skin.

Gavin kissed her again and then let his lips roam along her jaw and down her throat. He teased at her sensitive skin, nipping gently with his teeth and soothing it with his tongue. He brought one palm to her breast, teasing the aching tip with slow circles and then massaging it with firm fingers. Sabine gasped aloud, her hips rising to meet his.

"I want you so badly," Gavin whispered against her collarbone.

Sabine didn't reply, but her hand eased between their bodies to unzip his jeans. She brought one finger up to her lips to gesture for him to be quiet, then her hand slipped under the waistband of his briefs. He fought for silence as her fingers wrapped around the length of him and stroked gently. He buried a moan against her breast, trying not to lose his grip of control. She knew just how to push him, just how to touch him to make him unravel.

He brushed her hand away and eased between her legs. He thrust his hips forward, creating a delicious friction as he rubbed against her through the thin cotton of her shorts.

"Ohh..." she whispered, her eyes closing.

She was so beautiful. He couldn't wait to watch her come undone. To bury himself deep inside her again after all this time.

"Please," he groaned, "tell me that you have something we can use." Gavin got up this morning thinking he was taking his son to the circus. He wasn't a teenager walking around with a condom in his pocket all the time. He hadn't come prepared for this.

Her eyes fluttered open, their green depths dark with desire. "I had an IUD put in after Jared was born," she said.

"Is that enough?" he asked.

At that, Sabine laughed. "It's supposed to be 99.8 percent effective, but with your super sperm, who knows? The condom didn't work so well for us the last time."

"Super sperm," Gavin snorted before dipping down and kissing her again. "Do you want me to stop?" he asked. He would if she wanted him to, as much as that would kill him. But she needed to decide now.

"Don't you dare," she said, piercing him with her gaze.

With a growl, he buried his face in her neck. His hand grasped at the waist of her shorts, tugging them and her panties down over her hips. She arched up to help him and then kicked them off to the floor.

Sabine pushed at his jeans without success until Gavin finally eased back to take them off. She watched him with careful study as he kicked off his shoes and slipped out of the last of his clothes.

He looked down at her, nude and wanting, and his chest swelled with pride. She was sexy and free and waiting for him. As he watched, she reached up and untied her hair. The long strands fell down over her shoulders, the ends teasing at the tips of her breasts.

He couldn't wait any longer. Gavin returned to the couch, easing between her thighs. He sought her out first with his hand. Stroking gently, his fingertips slid easily over her sensitive flesh, causing her to whimper with need.

"Gavin," she pleaded, her voice little more than a breath.

His hand continued to move over her until she was panting and squirming beneath him. Then he slipped one finger inside. Sabine threw her head back, a cry strangling to silence in her throat. She was ready for him.

Gavin propped onto one elbow and gripped her hip with his other hand. Surging forward, he pressed into the slick heat of her welcoming body. He lost himself in the pleasure for a moment, absorbing every delicious sensation before flexing his hips and driving into her again.

Sabine clung to him, burying her face in his shoulder to muffle her gasps and cries. She met his every advance, whispering words of encouragement into his ear. The intensity built, moment by moment, until he knew she was close.

Her eyes squeezed shut, her mouth falling open in silent gasps. He put every ounce of energy he had left into pushing her over the edge. He was rewarded with the soft shudder of her body against him, the muscles deep inside clenching around him. The string of tension in his belly drew tighter and tighter until it snapped. He thrust hard, exploding into her with a low growl of satisfaction.

They both collapsed against the couch cushions in a panting, gasping heap. No sooner had they recovered than Gavin heard Jared crying in the other room.

Sabine pressed against his chest until he backed off. She quickly tugged on her clothes and disappeared into the bedroom.

Things were officially more complicated.

Six

Jared went back down fairly quickly. Sabine changed his Pull-Ups, put him in his pajamas and he fell asleep in minutes. Even then, she stayed in her bedroom longer than necessary. Going back into the living room meant facing what she'd just done. She wasn't quite ready for that yet.

Damn that stupid, erotic dream. When she fell asleep on the couch, she never expected to sleep that long. Or that she would have a sexual fantasy about Gavin while he was sitting there watching her. When she opened her eyes and he was touching her with the spark of passion in his eyes, she had to have him. She needed him.

And now it was done. She'd refused his proposal of marriage because he didn't love her, yet she'd just slept with him. She was throwing mixed signals left, right and center.

But she had to go back out there eventually. Steeling her resolve, she exited the bedroom and pulled the door shut behind her. She made a quick stop in the restroom first, cleaning up and smoothing her hair back into a ponytail. When she returned to the living room, Gavin was fully dressed and sitting on the couch.

"Everything okay?" he asked.

"Yeah," she said. "He's back to sleep now. He probably won't wake up again until the morning." She nervously ran her hands over her shorts, not sure what to do with herself. "Did you guys have fun today?"

"We did. He's a very well-behaved kid. Gave me almost no trouble. Almost," he said with a smile.

Sabine was glad. She'd worried so much about them that she couldn't paint. At least at first. She'd tried, but it had been so long since she'd painted that she didn't know where to start. Instead, she'd taken a long, leisurely shower and indulged in extended grooming rituals she usually had to rush, like plucking her eyebrows and painting her toenails. One of her favorite chick flicks was on TV, so she sat down to watch it, and the next thing she knew, she was nodding off. She'd only expected to sleep for a half hour or so.

"I'm glad it went well." She eyed the spot on the couch where she'd just been and decided she wasn't quite ready to sit there yet. "Would you like some wine? I'm going to pour myself a glass."

"Sure," he said with a soft smile.

Sabine could tell this was awkward for him, too. And yet, he could've turned her down and left. But he didn't. She disappeared into the kitchen and returned a few minutes later with two glasses of merlot. "It came out of a box, but I like it," she said.

Gavin smiled in earnest, taking a large sip, then another. "It's pretty good," he admitted with surprise.

She sat down beside him and took her own sip. The wine seemed to flow directly into her veins, relaxing her immediately.

He pointed over at the blank canvas. "I'm surprised you didn't paint at all today."

Sabine looked at the white expanse that had been her nemesis for a good part of the afternoon. She couldn't count how many times she'd put her pencil to the canvas to sketch the bones of a scene and then stopped. "I think I've forgotten how to paint."

"That's not possible," Gavin argued. "You just need the right inspiration. I put you on the spot today. I bet if you relax and let the creative juices flow without the pressure of time, the ideas will come again."

"I hope so."

"You're too gifted to set your dream aside. Even for Jared. We can work together to get you back to what you love. I mean, after we get the results and I have visitation rights, you'll have more free time to yourself."

That was the wrong thing to say. She had been nervous enough about tomorrow and the lab results that were coming in. Knowing he was already planning to "exercise his rights" and take Jared for long stretches of time just made her chest tight with anxiety. It was a sharp reminder that even after they'd had sex, he was really here for Jared, not her. He hadn't mentioned anything about *all* of them spending time together. Or just the two of them. Any fantasies she had about there being any sort of family unit cobbled out of this mess were just that.

"And what about you?" she said, her tone a bit sharper than she'd planned. "You seem as wrapped up in the business as ever. We couldn't get you off your phone yesterday. I'm thinking you don't have much time to get in the cockpit anymore."

"It's been a while," he admitted. "But I'm working on it. All those calls I was taking at the zoo," he said, "were about a big deal I'm trying to pull together. Things were unraveling and I couldn't let it happen."

Sabine listened as he described his plans for BXS and Exclusivity Jetliners. It really did seem like a brilliant plan. There were plenty of wealthy and important people who would pay a premium for that kind of service. That didn't mean she appreciated it interloping on their day out together, but she could see it was important to him and not just day-to-day management crap.

"I'm hoping to fly one, too."

Her brows went up in surprise. "Did you get demoted from CEO to pilot?"

"I wish," he groaned. "But I've always wanted a Gulfstream model jet. The ones we're acquiring could go over four thousand miles on one tank of gas. That could get me to Paris. I've always dreamed of flying across the Atlantic. But even if I can't manage that, I can take one out from time to time. Even if it's just to do a delivery. I don't care. I just want to get out from behind the desk and get up there. It's the only place I can ever find any peace."

She understood that. Yoga did a lot to help center her mind and spirit, but nothing came close to losing herself in her art.

"I want more time out of the office, and Jared finally gives me a real reason to do it. There's no point in work-life balance when you've got no life. But spending time with Jared needs to be a priority for me. I've already missed so much."

Sabine was impressed by his heartfelt words. Gavin had quickly become enamored with Jared, and she was glad. Part of her had always worried that he might reject his son. The other part worried that he'd claim him with such force that he'd rip her child from her arms. This seemed a healthy medium. Maybe this wouldn't be so bad. He was trying.

"I found a great apartment in Greenwich Village overlooking Washington Square Park," he said. "It has three bedrooms and it's close to the subway."

Sabine took a large sip of her wine. Here we go, she thought. "I thought you liked your apartment," she said, playing dumb. "Getting tired of living at the Ritz-Carlton?"

Gavin frowned. "What? No. Not for me. For you. I'd prefer you to be closer to me, but I know you'd rather live downtown. You work in SoHo, right? You could easily walk to work from this apartment."

Walking to work. She wouldn't even allow herself to fantasize about a life without a long train commute each day. Or three bedrooms where she didn't have to share with Jared. "I'm pretty sure it's out of my budget."

Gavin set his wine down on the coffee table. "I told you I wanted to help. Let me buy you an apartment."

"And I told you I wanted to take this slowly. I probably couldn't even afford the maintenance fee, much less the taxes or the mortgage itself. Homeowner's insurance. The utilities on a place that large would be through the roof."

He turned in his seat to face her, his serious businessman expression studying her. "How much is your rent here?"

"Gavin, I—"

He interrupted her with a number that was fewer than fifty dollars off the mark.

"Yes, pretty much," she admitted, reluctantly.

"Tack on a couple hundred for utilities and such. So

what if I bought an apartment and rented it to you for the same amount you're paying now? That would be fair, right? You wouldn't have to worry about all the fees associated with owning the place."

She did have to admit that she preferred this idea. If she had to pay rent, she would continue working. She liked her job and wanted to keep doing it. But a three-bedroom apartment in the Village for the price of what she paid for a tiny place beyond the reach of the subway lines? That was insanity.

"That's a ridiculous suggestion. My rent is less than a tenth of what the mortgage on that kind of apartment would be."

Gavin shrugged. "I'm not concerned. You could live there rent-free for all I care. I just thought you would feel more comfortable if you contributed."

"There's a difference between helping us out and buying us a multimillion-dollar apartment."

"I want you close," he said. His dark eyes penetrated hers with an intensity that made her squirm slightly with a flush rising to her pale cheeks. Did he really mean *her?*

Sabine opened her mouth to argue, but he held up his hand to silence her protest. "I mean," he corrected, "living in Manhattan will make it easier to handle the custody arrangements and trade-offs. When he starts at his new school, he would be closer. It would be safer. More convenient for everyone."

Just as she thought. He wanted Jared close, not her. At least not for any reason more than the occasional booty call. "Especially for you," she snapped, irritably.

"And you!" he added. "If I got things my way, the two of you would just move in with me. That's certainly the cheapest option, since you seem so concerned about how much I spend, but I thought you would like having your own space better."

She must seem like the most ungrateful person on the planet, but she knew what this was. A slippery slope. He would push, push, push until he had things just the way he wanted them. If he wanted them—or Jared, she should say—living with him, eventually he would. This apartment in the Village would just be a pit stop to make it look as if he was being reasonable.

"I know it's a pain for you to drive all the way out here every time you want to see Jared. And I know that you and I just..." Her voice trailed off.

"Had sex?" he offered.

"Yes," she said with a heavy sigh. "But that doesn't change anything between us or about the things we've already discussed. We're not moving at all. Not in with you and not into that apartment. It sounds nice, but it's too soon. When we're ready, perhaps we could look together. I'd like some say in the decision, even if you're writing the checks. I'm pretty sure the place I pick will be significantly cheaper."

"I'm not concerned with the cost of keeping my child happy and safe."

A painful twinge nagged at Sabine right beneath her sternum. She should be happy the father of her child was willing to lay out millions for the health and welfare of their child. But a part of her was jealous. He was always so quick to point out that this was about their son. Each time he mentioned it, it was like he was poking the gaping wound of her heart with a sharp stick. She would benefit from the arrangement, but none of this was about her. The sex didn't change anything, just like it didn't change anything three years ago. He was attracted to her, but she was not his priority and never was.

"Thank you," she choked out. "I appreciate that you're so willing to create a stable, safe home for our son. Let's give it a week to sink in, all right? We've got a lot of hurdles to jump before we add real estate to the mix."

Gavin eyed her for a moment before silently nodding. Sabine knew this was anything but a victory. She was only pushing off the inevitable. He would get his way eventually.

He always did.

When Gavin arrived at Dr. Peterson's office at 10:00 a.m. Monday morning, Sabine was already there. She was lost in a fashion magazine and didn't notice him come in. "Morning," he said.

Sabine looked up and gave him a watery smile. "Hey." She looked a little out of sorts. Maybe she was nervous. Things would change after this and she probably knew it.

"Where's Jared?" he asked.

The smile faded. She slung the magazine she'd been reading onto the seat beside her. "At school, where he belongs. I'm sorry to disappoint, but you're stuck with me today."

He'd screwed up last night, he could tell. Not in seducing her—that would never be a bad idea—but in forcing the idea of the apartment on her. Anyone else would jump at the offer, but to her, it was him imposing on her. Demanding they be closer so he could see his son more easily. Not once mentioning that he'd like *her* closer as well because that opened the door to dangerous territory.

Sabine was skittish. She scared off easily last time. He wasn't about to tell her that he wanted to see her more because he was still fighting himself over the idea of it. He was usually pretty good at keeping his distance from people, but he'd already let Sabine in once. Keeping her out the second time was harder than he expected. Especially when he didn't want to. He wanted her in his bed. Across from him at a nice restaurant. Certainly he could have that and not completely lose himself to her.

"That's scarcely a hardship," he said, seating himself in the empty chair beside her. "I find your company to be incredibly…*stimulating*."

Sabine crossed her arms over her chest and smothered a snort of disbelief. "Well, you'll be stimulating yourself from now on. Last night was—"

"Awesome?" he interjected. Their physical connection could never be anything less.

"A mistake."

"Sometimes a mistake can be a happy accident. Like Jared, a happy accident."

Her moss-green eyes narrowed at him. "And sometimes it's just a mistake. Like sleeping with your ex when you're in the middle of a custody negotiation."

Gavin nodded and leaned into her, crossing his own arms. She really thought last night was a mistake? He hadn't picked up on it at the time. She was probably just worried it would give him the upper hand somehow. Knowing just how to touch a woman was always an advantage, but he didn't intend to use that knowledge against her. At least outside the bedroom.

"So I suppose you've got no business going to dinner with me tonight, either."

Her gaze ran over his face, trying to read into his motives. "Listen, Gavin," she started with a shake of her head. "I know I told you that I wanted you to put in quality time with Jared, but that doesn't mean you have to come see him *every* day. I know you've got a company to run and a life in progress before all this came out. I only meant that you had to keep your promises and make an effort."

She thought this was about Jared. Apparently he had not made it abundantly clear how badly he wanted her last night. Their tryst on the couch was nice, but it was just an appetizer to take the edge off three years apart. He wouldn't allow himself to fall for Sabine, but he wasn't going to deny himself the pleasure of making love to her. "Who said anything about Jared? I was thinking about you and me. Someplace dark and quiet with no kid's menu."

"That sounds lovely," she said, "but Jared isn't a puppy. We can't just crate him while we go out."

"I can arrange for someone to watch him."

A flicker of conflict danced across her face. She wanted to go. He could tell. She was just very protective and worried about leaving their son with a stranger. Hell, she hadn't even wanted to leave Jared with *him.*

"Someone? You don't even know who?"

"Of course I do. I was actually considering my secretary, Marie. She's got a new grandson of her own that she fawns over, but he lives in Vermont, so she doesn't see him nearly as much as she wants to. I asked her this morning if she was willing to watch Jared tonight. She'll even come out to your apartment so you don't have to pack up any of his things and he can sleep in his own bed when the time comes."

Sabine pursed her lips in thought and flipped her ponytail over her shoulder. "So you were so confident that I would go to dinner with you that you arranged a babysitter before you even bothered to ask if I wanted to go."

Her dream last night had tipped her hand. "Your subconscious doesn't lie."

Her cheeks flushed red against her pale complexion. She turned away from him and focused her attention on the television mounted on the opposite wall of the waiting room. "What if I have plans?"

"Do you have plans?" he asked.

"No," she admitted without facing him. "But that's not the point. You assume too much. You assume that just because we have a child together and we went too far last night that I want—"

"Brooks!" The nurse opened the side door and called out their name to come back.

Sabine's concerned expression faded, the lines disappearing between her brows. She seemed relieved to avoid this conversation. He wasn't going to let her off that easily.

"To be continued," Gavin said, looking her square in the eye. She met his gaze and nodded softly.

He climbed to his feet and offered his hand to help Sabine up. They made their way back to Dr. Peterson's personal office and sat in the two guest chairs across from his desk. It didn't take long before his physician strolled in with a file in his hands.

Dr. Peterson eased into his seat and flipped open the paperwork. His gaze ran over it for a moment before he nodded. In that brief flash of time, Gavin had his first flicker of doubt. Jared looked just like him. There was no real reason to believe he wasn't his son, but Sabine had seemed nervous in the lobby. He didn't know anything for certain until the doctor told him the results. He hadn't even wanted a son a week ago, and now he would be devastated to know Jared wasn't his.

"Well," the doctor began, "I've got good news for you, Mr. Brooks. It appears as though you're a father. Congratulations," he said, reaching across the desk to shake his hand.

"Thank you," Gavin replied with relief washing over him.

Dr. Peterson pulled out two manila envelopes and handed one to each of them. "Here's a copy of the DNA report for each of you to give your lawyers."

This apparently was not the doctor's first paternity test rodeo. "Thank you," he said, slipping the envelope into his lapel pocket.

"Let me know if you have any questions. Good luck to you both." Dr. Peterson stood, ushering them out the door.

They were back in the lobby of the building before they spoke again. Gavin turned to her as she was putting the envelope into her purse. "Now about that dinner. You never answered me."

Sabine looked up at him. She didn't have the relieved expression he was expecting. She seemed even more concerned than she had going in. "Not tonight, Gavin. I'm not much in the mood for that."

"What's the matter?" he asked. Some women would be leaping with joy to have scientific evidence that their child was the heir to a multibillion-dollar empire. Sabine was a notable exception. "This was your idea," he reminded her.

She sighed. "I know. And I knew what the results would be, but I wasn't prepared for the finality of it. It's done. Now the wheels start turning and the child that has been one hundred percent mine for the past two years will start slipping from my arms. It's selfish of me, I know, and I apologize, but that doesn't make me leap for joy."

Gavin turned to face her, placing his hands reassuringly on her shoulders. It gave her no real choice but to look at him. "Sabine, what can I possibly say to convince you that this isn't a bad thing?"

Her pale green eyes grew glassy with tears she was too stubborn to shed in front of him. "There's nothing you can say, Gavin. Actions speak louder than words."

Fair enough. "How about this," he offered. "I'll get Edmund to start the paperwork and put together a custody proposal for you to look over. When you're happy with it, we'll share a nice dinner, just the two of us, to celebrate that the sky didn't fall and things will be fine."

Her gaze dropped to his collar and she nodded so slightly, he could barely tell she'd agreed. "Okay," she whispered.

"Clear your schedule for Friday night," he said with confidence. "I have a feeling we're going to be sharing a lovely candlelit dinner together before the weekend arrives."

Sabine curled up on the couch and watched Gavin and Jared play on the living room floor. They were stacking Duplo blocks. Gavin was trying to build a plane, but Jared was determined to make a truck and kept stealing pieces off the clunky blue-and-red jet. It was amazing to see them together, the father and his tiny toddler clone.

It made her smile, even when she wasn't sure she should be smiling.

Gavin had done his best to reassure her that things would be fine. His lawyer had presented a very reasonable custody agreement. Her relief at reading the briefing was palpable. They were both giving a little and taking a little, which surprised her. Gavin got Jared on alternate weekends, rotating holidays and two weeks in the summer, but he would continue to reside primarily with Sabine. Her concession was to agree to move to Manhattan to make the arrangement easier on everyone.

They'd built in flexibility in the agreement to accommodate special requests, like birthdays. Unless Gavin pushed her, she intended to let him see Jared as often as he liked. How could she turn away a scene like the one playing out on her floor?

Tonight, they were telling Jared that Gavin was his father. It was a big moment for them. The DNA test had made it certain, but telling Jared made it real.

"Hey, big guy?" Gavin said.

Jared dropped a block and looked up. "Yep?"

"Do you know what a daddy is?"

Sabine leaned forward in her seat, resting her elbows on her knees. She agreed to let Gavin be the one to tell him, but she wasn't certain how much Jared would understand. He was still so young.

"Yeah," he said cheerfully, before launching into another of his long-winded and unintelligible speeches. Jared was a quiet child, slow to speak, although it seemed more that he didn't have a lot he wanted to say.

Only in the past few months had he started rattling on in his own toddler-speak. From what pieces she could pick out, he was talking about his friend at school whose daddy picked him up every day. Then he pointed at Sabine. “Mommy.”

“Right.” Gavin smiled. “And I am *your* daddy.”

Jared cocked his head to the side and wrinkled his nose. He turned to Sabine for confirmation. “Daddy?”

She let out the breath she’d been holding to nod. “Yeah, buddy. He’s your daddy.”

A peculiar grin crossed Jared’s face. It was the same expression he made when she “stole” his nose and he wasn’t quite sure he believed her. “Daddy?” He pointed at Gavin.

Gavin nodded, having only a moment to brace himself before his son launched into his arms.

“Daddy!” he proclaimed.

Sabine watched Gavin hold his son as fiercely as if someone were going to snatch him away. She understood how he felt. And then she saw the glassy tears in the eyes of her powerful CEO, and her chest tightened with the rush of confusing emotions. It hadn’t taken long, but Gavin was completely in love with his son.

She couldn’t help but feel a pang of jealousy.

Seven

"Damn you for always being right."

Gavin stood on Sabine's doorstep holding a bouquet of purple dahlias. She had opened the door and greeted him that way, stealing his "hello" from his lips. Fortunately she was smiling, so he did the same.

He held out the bundle of flowers with the nearly black centers that faded to bright purple tips. "These are for you. They reminded me of your hair."

Sabine brought the flowers up to her nose and delicately inhaled their scent. "They're beautiful, thank you."

"So are you," he added. And he meant it. She looked lovely tonight. She was wearing a fitted white dress with brightly colored flowers that looked like one of her watercolor paintings. It was sleeveless and clung to every curve of her body.

She smiled, wrinkling her nose with a touch of embarrassment. The movement caught the light on the tiny pink rhinestone in her nose. It was the same bright color as her lipstick and the chunky bracelet on her wrist. "Let me put these in some water and we can go."

Gavin nodded and stepped across the threshold into the apartment. It was Friday night and as predicted, they were having dinner. Everything had gone smoothly. The paperwork had been filed in family court to add Gavin's name to the birth certificate. Along with the addition, Jared's last name would be updated to Brooks. He'd suggested making Jared's middle name Hayes, but she said the name Thomas was more important to her. He'd thought Sabine would pitch a fit on the subject of Jared's name, but it hadn't concerned her.

The custody proposal Edmund put together was approved by both of them on the first draft. He hoped that he would see Jared more than required, but this established a minimum they were both comfortable with.

He noticed Marie's coat hanging by the door when he came in, so he knew she was already there to watch Jared. Gavin looked around the apartment, but he didn't see Marie or Jared anywhere. "Where is everyone?"

Then he heard giggles and splashing from the bathroom. He smiled, knowing Marie was probably soaked. After they'd told Jared that Gavin was his daddy, he'd insisted *Daddy* give him his bath that night. Gavin had gotten more water on him than the toddler in the tub, he was pretty certain.

Aside from that, the night had gone pretty smoothly. Apparently toddlers didn't angst about things the way grown-ups did. Gavin was his daddy—*great.* Let's go play.

"Marie is giving Jared a bath, although I think they're probably having more fun with the bathtub paints than actually washing."

Gavin wanted to peek in and say hello before they left, but he resisted. He'd gotten Sabine to agree to this dinner and the babysitter he provided. Right now, Jared was happy. If they went in to say goodbye, the giggles might disintegrate into tears. "Are you ready?"

She nodded, the luxurious black waves of her hair gracefully swaying along her jawline. "I already told Marie goodbye a few minutes ago so we could slip out. She seems to have everything under control."

Since it was just the two of them tonight, he'd opted for the Aston Martin. He held the door for her, noting the elegant curve of her ankles in tall pink pumps as she slipped inside. Gavin had no clue how women walked in shoes like that, but he was extremely thankful they did.

They had seven-thirty reservations at one of the most sought-out, high-end restaurants in Manhattan. He'd made the reservation on Monday, feeling confident they would come to an agreement in time, but even then, it had taken some persuading to get a table. Most people booked a table several months in advance, but they knew better than to tell a Brooks no. He tended to get in wherever he wanted to, and he made it worth the maître d's efforts.

They checked in and were immediately taken to an intimate booth for two. The restaurant was the brainchild of a young, up-and-coming chef who snagged a James Beard award at the unheard-of age of twenty-two. The decor was decidedly modern with lots of glass, concrete and colored lights that glowed behind geometric wall panels.

Their table was like a cocoon wrapping around them and shielding them from the world. A green glass container on the table had a flickering candle inside, giving a moody light to their space. It was just enough to read their menus, but not enough to draw attention to who was inside the booth. It made the restaurant popular with the young celebrity set who wanted to go out but maintain their privacy.

"Have you ever been here?" Gavin asked.

Sabine took in all the sights with wide eyes. "No, but I've heard of it. My boss said her husband took her here for her birthday."

"Did she like it?"

"She said the food was good. The decor was a little modern for her taste, which is funny considering her clothing design has a contemporary edge to it that would fit right in."

"I've been here once," Gavin said. "It's fine cuisine, but it's not stuffy. I thought you'd like that."

Sabine smiled and looked down. "Yes, there aren't fifteen pieces of silverware, so that's a relief."

Gavin smiled and looked over the menu. He'd learned his lesson the first time they dated. His attempts to impress her with nice restaurants had only intimidated her and pointed out the wide gap of their social standings. She wasn't like other women he'd dated. A lot of women in Manhattan expected to be wined and dined in the finest restaurants in town. Sabine was just as happy with Thai takeout eaten on the terrace of his apartment, if not more so.

This place was his attempt at a compromise and so far, it seemed to be a good choice. There wasn't a fixed tasting menu like so many other restaurants. Foie gras and caviar wasn't her style, and she wouldn't let him pay two hundred dollars a head for a meal she wouldn't eat. Here, diners got to mix and match their choice of Asian fusion dishes for the six courses.

The waiter brought their drinks, presenting him with a premium sake and Sabine with a light green pear martini that was nearly the color of her eyes. They ordered and the server disappeared to bring their first course selection.

"I'm glad we got everything worked out with Edmund. I've been looking forward to this night all week." He met her eyes across the table and let a knowing smile curl his lips. Gavin expected tonight to go well and for Sabine to end up back in his bed. He'd fantasized about her naked body lying across his sheets as he lay in bed each night.

Holding up his drink for a toast, he waited for Sabine to do the same. "To surviving the terrible twos," he said with a grin, "and everything else the future may hold."

Sabine tipped her glass against his and took a healthy sip. "Thank you for handling all of this so gingerly. You don't know how much I've worried."

"What are we drinking to?" A nasal voice cut into their conversation.

They both turned to find a blonde woman standing beside their table. *Ugh.* It was Viola Collins. The Manhattan society busybody was one of the last people he wanted to see tonight. She had a big mouth, an overabundance of opinions and a blatant desire for Gavin that he'd dodged for years.

"Viola," he said, ignoring her question and wishing he could ignore her, as well. "How are you?"

She smiled and showed off her perfect set of straightened, whitened teeth that looked a touch odd against her too-tan skin. "I'm just great." Her laser focus shifted toward Sabine, taking in and categorizing every detail with visible distaste. "And who do we have here?"

Gavin watched his date with concern. He wasn't certain how Sabine would react to someone like Viola.

Some people might shrink away under Viola's obvious appraisal, but she didn't. Sabine sat up straighter in her seat and met Viola's gaze with her own confident one.

"Viola Collins, this is my date, Sabine Hayes."

The women briefly shook hands, but he could tell there was no friendliness behind it. Women were funny that way, sizing one another up under the cool guise of politeness.

"Would I have met you before?" Viola asked.

"I sincerely doubt it," Sabine replied.

Gavin couldn't remember if they had or not. "You may have. Sabine and I dated a few years back."

"Hmm..." Viola said. Her nose turned up slightly, although Gavin thought that might be more the result of her latest round of plastic surgery. "I think I would've remembered *this.* That's interesting that you two are dating again. I would've thought the novelty would've worn off the first time."

"Oh, no," Sabine said, a sharp edge to her voice. "I'm very bendy."

Viola's eyes widened, her tight mouth twisting at Sabine's bold words. "Are you?" She turned to Gavin. "Well, I'll have to tell Rosemary Goodwin that you're off the market. *For now,*" she added. "I think she's still waiting for you to call her again after your last hot date. I'll just tell her to be patient."

"You'll have to excuse me." Sabine reached for her purse and slipped out of the booth, deliberately sweeping the green martini off the table. The concoction splattered across Viola's cream silk dress. "How clumsy of me!" she said. Ignoring the sputtering woman, Sabine bent down to pick up the glass and set it back on the table. "That's better." At that, she turned and bolted from the restaurant.

Viola gawked at Sabine as she disappeared, sputtering in outrage. The silk dress was ruined. No question of it.

Gavin didn't care. Viola could use a fist to the face, but no one wanted to pick up her plastic surgery tab to repair the damage. He got up, throwing cash onto the table for the bill and pressing more into Viola's hand for a new dress. "That wasn't your color anyway."

He jogged through the restaurant, pushing through the crowd waiting to be seated, and bursting out onto the street. He spied Sabine about a block away, charging furiously down the pavement despite the handicap of her heels.

"Sabine!" he yelled. "Wait."

She didn't even turn around. He had to run to catch up with her, pulling alongside and matching her stride.

"I should've known," she said, without acknowledging him. "You know there was a reason I ended this the last time. One of the reasons was that everyone in your world is a snob."

"Not everyone," he insisted. He wrapped his fingers around her delicate wrist to keep her from running off again and pulled her to a stop. "Just ignore Viola. She doesn't matter to anyone but herself."

She shook her head, the waves of her hair falling into her face as she looked down at the sidewalk. "It's the same as last time, Gavin. People in your world are never going to see me as anything other than an interloper. Like you're slumming for your own amusement. I don't fit in and I never will."

"I know," he said. "That's one of the many things that make you great."

Her light green eyes met his for a moment, a glimmer of something—hope, maybe—quickly fading away. "Stop fooling yourself, Gavin. You belong with someone like Viola or this Rosemary woman that's waiting on you to call again. We're all wrong for each other. You're only here with me now because of Jared."

"Let me assure you that if I wanted a woman like Viola I could have one. I could have *her,* if I wanted to. She's made that very clear over the years, but I'm not interested. I don't want her." He took a step closer, pulling Sabine against him. "I want you. Just as you are."

"You say that now, but you wouldn't answer her question," she said, resisting his pull on her.

"Answer what question?"

"She asked what we were drinking to. You don't want anyone to know about Jared, do you? Are you ashamed of him? Or of both of us?"

"Absolutely not!" he said as emphatically as he could. "I will gladly shout the news about my son from the rooftops. But I haven't told my family yet. If Viola found out, it would be all over town. I don't want them to hear it from her."

Gavin slipped his arms around her waist, enjoying the feel of her against him, even under these circumstances. "I'd like to tell them tomorrow afternoon. Would you be able to bring Jared to meet them? Maybe around dinnertime? That would give them some time to adjust to the idea before you show up."

"Why don't you just come get him?" she said. Her bravado from her interaction with Viola had crumbled. Now she just looked worn down.

"Because I want them to spend time with you, too," Gavin added. "I know you've met them before, but that was years ago. This is different."

"And say what, Gavin? 'Hey, everyone, you remember Sabine? Since you saw her last, she's had my son and lied to all of us for over two years. We've got that worked out now. Don't mind the nose ring.'"

"Pretty much," he said with a smile. "How did you guess?"

Sabine's gaze shot up to his. Red flushed her cheeks and she punched him in the shoulder. She hit him as furiously as she could and he barely felt it. He laughed at her assault, which only made it worse. She was like an angry kitten, hissing and clawing, but not dangerous enough to even break the skin. "I'm serious, Gavin!"

"I'm serious, too." He meant every word of it. Gavin had gone into this thinking that he could indulge in Sabine's body and keep his heart thoroughly out of the equation. She had no idea how badly she'd hurt him when she left, and he didn't want her to know. But he'd opened the door to her once. No matter how hard he fought, it was too easy to open up to her again. It wasn't love, but it was something more than his usual indifference.

Perhaps this time would be different. Even if they weren't together, they would always be connected through Jared. They would be constants in an ever-changing life and he welcomed it, even if he didn't know what they would do with it.

He slipped his finger under her chin and tipped her face up to him. "Serious about this."

Gavin's lips met hers before she could start arguing with him again. The moment he kissed her, she was lost. She melted into him, channeling her emotions into the kiss. Sabine let all of her anger, her frustration, her fear flow through her mouth and her fingertips. She buried her fingers through his dark hair, tugging his neck closer.

He responded in kind, his mouth punishing her with his kiss. His hands molded to her body, his fingers pressed hard into her flesh. The rough touch was a pleasure with a razor's edge. She craved his intensity. The physical connection made everything else fade away. At least for tonight. Tomorrow was…tomorrow.

"Take me to your place," she said.

Gavin reluctantly pulled away. "I'll have the valet bring the car."

Within a few minutes, they were strolling into the Ritz-Carlton Tower. They took the elevator up to Gavin's apartment. It had been a long time since she'd been here. She'd walked alone down this very hallway after she broke up with him. Pregnant and unaware of that fact. It felt strange to traverse the same carpeting after all these years.

Inside the apartment, little had changed. The same elegant, expensive and uncomfortable furniture that was better suited for a decorating magazine than to actually being used. The same stunning view of Central Park sprawled out of the arched floor-to-ceiling windows. There was a newer, larger, flatter television mounted to one wall, but that was about it.

"You've done a lot with the place since I saw it last," she said drily.

"There's new additions," he insisted. He pointed to a corner in the dining room where there was a stack of children's toys, new in the packages, and the car seat from the Mercedes. "I'm also doing some renovations to one of the bedrooms."

Gavin led her down the hallway to the rooms that had once functioned as a guest room and his office. Inside the old guest room, a tarp was draped over the hardwood floors. Several cans of paint were sitting in the middle of the floor, unopened. Construction was under way for some wainscoting and a window seat that would cover and vent the radiators. Jared was too young to enjoy it now, but she could just imagine him curling up there, looking out over Central Park and reading a book.

"You said his favorite color was red, so I was going to paint the walls red." He gestured over to the side. "I'm having them build a loft with a ladder into this niche here, so he'll have his own tree house–like space to play when he's older. They're delivering a toddler bed in a few days with a Spider-Man bedding set and curtains."

"It's wonderful," Sabine said. And it was. A million times better than anything she could afford to get him. "He will love it, especially when he gets a little older. What little boy wouldn't?"

Sabine took a last look and moved back out into the hallway and past the closed door to his home office. She didn't begrudge her son anything his father gave him, but it was hard for her to face that Gavin could provide Jared with things she couldn't. "What's this?" she asked, pointing toward a touch panel on the table near the phone.

Gavin caught up with her in the living room. "It's the new Ritz-Carlton concierge system. We didn't have dinner. Would you like me to order something?"

"Maybe later. It's still early." Sabine kicked off her

heels and continued through the apartment to the master suite. She reached behind her and began unzipping her dress as she disappeared around the corner.

She'd barely made it three feet inside before she felt Gavin's heat against her back. He brushed her hands away, tugging her zipper down the curve of her spine. His fingertips brushed at the soft skin there, just briefly, before he moved to her shoulders and pushed her dress off.

Sabine stepped out of her clothing, continuing across the room in nothing but the white satin bra and panties she'd worn with it. There were no lights on in that room, so she was free to walk to the window and look outside without being seen.

She heard Gavin close the door behind them, ensuring they were blanketed in darkness. The moonlight from outside was enough to illuminate the pieces of furniture she remembered from before.

She felt Gavin's breath on her neck before he touched her. His bare chest pushed into her back, his skin hot and firm. He swept her hair over her left shoulder, leaning down to press searing kisses along the line of her neck. One bra strap was pushed aside, then the other, before he unhooked the clasp and let the satin fall to the floor.

Sabine relaxed against him, letting her head roll back to rest on his shoulder and expose her throat. She closed her eyes to block out the distraction of the view and focus on the feeling of his lips, teeth and tongue moving over her sensitive flesh. His palms covered her exposed breasts, molding them with his hands and gently pinching the tips until she whimpered aloud with pleasure.

"Sabine," he whispered, biting at her earlobe. "You

don't know how long I've waited to have you back in my bed." He slid his hands down to her hips, holding her steady as he pressed his arousal into her backside with a growl.

The vibration of the sound rumbled through her whole body like a shock wave. Her nipples tightened and her core pulsed with need. Knowing she could turn him on like this was such a high. She never felt as sexy as she did when she was with Gavin. Somehow, knowing she could bring such a powerful man to his knees with desire and pleasure was the greatest turn-on.

Sabine turned in his arms, looking up at the dark shadows across his face before she smiled and slipped out of his grasp. Her eyes had adjusted to the light. It made it easy for her to find her way to the massive bed in the center of his room. She crawled up onto it, throwing a glance over her shoulder to make sure he was watching the swell of her backside peeking out from the satin panties. Of course he was.

"This bed?" she asked sweetly, although she felt anything but sweet.

Gavin had his hands balled into fists at his side. "What are you trying to do to me?"

He was fighting for control, but she didn't want him to win. She wanted him to break, to lose himself in her. It would only require her to push a little bit harder. She climbed up to her knees and hooked her thumbs beneath her panties. Looking him in the eye, she bit her lips and glided the slick fabric over her hips.

His breath was ragged in his chest, but he held his place. Gavin's burning gaze danced between the bite of her teeth into her plump pink lips to her full, pert breasts, to the ever-lowering panties. When the cropped dark curls of her sex peeked out from the top, he swallowed hard. His hands went to his belt. His eyes never left her body as he removed the last of his clothes.

Now they were both naked with no more barriers between them. She was ready for him to unleash his passion on her.

With a wicked smile, Sabine flicked her dark hair over her shoulder and curled her finger to beckon Gavin to come to her. He didn't hesitate, surging forward onto the bed until she fell backward onto the soft comforter.

Every inch of her was suddenly covered by the massive expanse of his body. The weight of him pressed her into the mattress, molding her against him. He entered her quickly as well, causing Sabine to cry out before she could stop herself.

"Yes," Gavin hissed in encouragement. "Be loud. You can scream the walls down tonight." He thrust hard into her again. "I want hotel security knocking on the door."

Sabine laughed and drew her knees up to cradle him. When he surged forward again, he drove deeper. She groaned loud, the sound echoing off the walls of the room. He wanted her loud and she would be happy to oblige.

Eight

Sabine rang the doorbell with her elbow, fighting to keep ahold of her son. Jared squirmed furiously in her arms, and she didn't blame him. For their trip to see Gavin's parents she'd dressed him in his best outfit—a pair of khakis, a short-sleeved plaid shirt and a little bow tie. Adrienne had bought the outfit for him and he looked adorable in it. When he stopped squirming. His two-year-old heart much preferred hoodies and T-shirts with cartoon characters on them.

Putting him on the ground, she crouched down to his level and straightened his clothes. "Hey, buddy," she said. "I know you don't like this, but I need you to be a good boy today. You're going to see Daddy and meet some nice people who are very excited to see you."

"Don't wanna." He pouted, with one lip sticking out so far, she was tempted to kiss it away. "Want truck."

"I've got your truck in my bag, and you can have it later. If you're a good boy today, we'll get ice cream on the way home, okay?"

The dark, mischievous eyes of her son looked up at her, considering the offer. Before he could answer, the door opened and Sabine looked up into the same eyes. Gavin was in the doorway.

"Hi, Jared," Gavin said, his whole face lighting up at the sight of his son. He knelt down and put out his arms, and Jared immediately stopped pouting and ran to him. Gavin scooped him up and swung him in the air while Jared giggled hysterically.

Sabine stood and smiled, nervously readjusting her purse on her shoulder and smoothing a hand over her hair. She'd pulled the black-and-purple strands back into a bun at the nape of her neck. The violet highlights were still visible, but not so "in their face." Adrienne had insisted she wear one of her newly designed tops today, a silky, scoop-neck red top that gathered at the waist. She'd paired it with some black pants and a patent leather belt. It looked good on her, but it was hardly the armor she'd wanted going into this.

She sucked a deep breath into her lungs, trying to even out her frantic heartbeat, but it did little good. She was about to see Gavin's parents again, and this time, as the mother of their grandchild. They had been polite but distant the last time. Obviously, they hadn't felt the need to get invested in Gavin's latest dating novelty.

She didn't anticipate this going well. They might hate her for keeping Jared a secret. They might turn their noses up at her like Viola had. Only today, she couldn't dump a drink on the bitch and run out.

"How'd it go?" she asked.

Gavin settled Jared in his arms and turned to her. "Well, I think. They were surprised. Okay, *more* than surprised. But we talked a lot, and they've had some time to process it. Now I think they're excited at the prospect of their first grandchild."

It was too early for Sabine to feel optimistic. She was about to reply when she heard a woman's voice from inside the apartment. "Are they here? Ohmigosh, look at him!"

Sabine was expecting his mother, but instead, the face of a younger woman appeared over Gavin's shoulder. She had long, dark brown hair like his, but her eyes were a steely gray color. It had to be his sister, Diana.

Gavin turned toward her, showcasing his son. "This is Jared. Jared, this is your auntie Diana."

Jared played shy, turning his face into Gavin's shirt when Diana tried to coax him to say hello. More voices sounded inside with footsteps pounding across the floor. How many people were in there? A crowd of four or five people gathered, all fussing at Jared and Gavin at once.

"He looks just like you did at that age!"

"What a handsome boy!"

Sabine was happy to stay safely in the hallway and play spectator for the moment. It was easier. She always knew they would accept Jared. He was their blessed heir. The vessel that brought him into existence was another matter.

She could feel the moment the first set of eyes fell on her. It was Diana. She slipped around Gavin into the hallway, rushing Sabine with a hug she wasn't anticipating.

"It's so nice to finally meet you," Diana said.

Sabine patted weakly at the young woman's back and pulled away as soon as she could. "Finally?"

Diana smiled and threw a conspiratorial look over her shoulder. "Gavin had mentioned you to me when you were first dating. He just went on and on about you. I'd never heard him do that about another woman before. And then it ended and I was so disappointed. When he called and asked me to come over today to meet his son, I was so happy to hear that you were the mother." She grinned wide and nudged Sabine with her elbow. "I think it's fate."

Sabine tried not to laugh at the young woman's enthusiasm. She couldn't be more than twenty-two or twenty-three. She still believed in all that. And since Diana was the beautiful only daughter of a billion-dollar empire, Sabine was pretty certain no man had the nerve to break her heart. At least, not yet.

Diana snatched up Sabine's hand in hers and tugged her over the threshold of the entryway. The polished parquet floors were too slick for her to resist the movement and before she knew it, the door was closed and she was standing in the apartment of Byron and Celia Brooks.

Okay, apartment was a misnomer. This was a mansion slapped on the top of an apartment building. In front of her was a grand marble staircase with a gold-and-crystal chandelier twinkling overhead from the twenty-foot ceilings. On each side of the doorway were large urns filled with bouquets of fresh flowers that were nicer than the arrangements at some people's weddings.

That was all she could see with the press of people, but it was enough to let her know she wasn't in Nebraska anymore.

"Everyone, you remember Sabine Hayes. She's Jared's mother."

Sabine's chest tightened instantly, her breath going still in her lungs of stone. Every eye in the room flew from Jared to her. His father's. His mother's. His brother Alan's. She tried to smile wide and pretend she wasn't having a panic attack, but she wasn't certain how convincing she was.

His mother stepped forward first. She looked just as she had the last time. Sabine and Gavin had run into them at a restaurant as they were going in and his parents were leaving. It had been an accidental meeting really, given their relationship hadn't called for the meeting of the parents yet. Sabine had been struck by how refined and effortlessly elegant his mother was. Today was no exception.

Celia's light brown hair was pulled back in a bun like Sabine's. She was wearing a gray silk dress with a strand of dark gray pearls around her neck and teardrops with diamonds from her ears. The dress perfectly matched her eyes, so much like Diana's. Her gaze swept quickly over Sabine from head to toe but stopped at her eyes with a smile of her own. "It's lovely to see you again, Sabine."

"Likewise," she said, politely shaking the woman's hand. Every description Gavin ever gave her of his mother had built an image of a cold, disinterested woman in Sabine's mind. Their meeting before hadn't been very revealing, but today, she instantly knew that was not the case. There was a light in her eyes that was very warm and friendly. Celia Brooks had just been raised well and taught early the rules of etiquette and civility that a woman of her class needed. Yes, she could've been a more hands-on mother and let her children get dirty every now and then, but that wasn't how she was brought up.

"Please, come in and meet everyone. You remember my husband, Byron, and this is my other son, Alan."

Sabine shook each of their hands and was amazed at

how much alike the Brooks men looked. Thick brown hair, eyes like melted dark chocolate, strong builds. Just one glance and Sabine could tell exactly how Jared would look when he was twenty-five and when he was fifty-five.

"Nora has refreshments set up for us in the parlor," Celia said, ushering everyone out of the hallway.

The farther they went into the apartment, the more nervous Sabine became. Not because of his family, but because of their stuff. Every item her eyes lit upon looked fragile and priceless. "Do not put him down," Sabine whispered to Gavin.

At that, Gavin chuckled. "Do you have any idea how many things my siblings and I have broken over the years? I assure you, if it's important, it's not sitting out."

"Oh, yes," Celia insisted. "Don't worry about a thing. It has been quite a while since we had a youngster here, but we'd better get used to it, right?" She got a wistful look in her eye and glanced over at Jared. "A grandchild. What an unexpected and wonderful surprise."

Sabine wasn't quite sure what to say. She expected the other shoe to drop at any moment. But time went on, and it didn't. They chatted and nibbled on treats their housekeeper, Nora, made. His family asked questions about her with genuine interest. Jared was turned loose and managed not to break anything. To her shock, Byron, the former CEO of BXS, got on the floor and played with him and his dump truck.

She had made herself sick worrying about today. Thinking they would hate her. That they'd never accept her or her son. But as time went by, she found herself to be incredibly at ease with his family. They were polished and polite, but not cold and certainly not blatantly rude like Viola. It was nothing like she'd expected.

It seemed Sabine was as guilty of prejudice as she worried they would be. Just as she feared they would look at her and make snap judgments, so had she. She had this idea of what rich people were like. Gavin's stories of his distant, workaholic family had only reinforced the image in her mind.

But she was wrong. And it made her angry. People like Viola had made her believe that she could never have Gavin. That she would never fit in. She was angry at herself, really. She was the one who was too afraid to find out if their wicked whispers were true. She pushed away the only man she'd ever loved, deprived him of his son for two years, because she was certain they could never last.

She was wrong. At least in part. They might never truly be together as a couple again, but they could be a family and make it work.

Sabine had wasted so much time being afraid. She wasn't about to make the same mistake twice.

"You don't have to keep trying to take me out to dinner, Gavin."

"If at first you don't succeed, try, try again." Gavin smiled and helped her out of the car and onto the curb outside a restaurant.

"You didn't fail the last time." Sabine slowly approached him, pressed herself against the length of his body and wrapped her arms around his neck. "I seem to recall that evening ending in quite a…spectacular fashion."

"Spectacular, eh?" Gavin growled near her ear. "I'm

glad you seemed to think so. But—" he planted a kiss on her neck and whispered to her "—we never actually ate."

"That was okay with me." She looked up at him with her wide green eyes and a wicked smile curling her lips. "We could have the same thing tonight, if you'd like."

He smiled and let his hands roam across the silky fabric of her dress. She was trying to lure him back to bed, but he wouldn't let her. Couldn't let her. At least not tonight. "Well, as tempting as that is, I'll have to pass. You see, I brought in reinforcements to make sure this meal was a success. We can't stand up our guests."

Sabine frowned at him, her nose wrinkling. "Guests?"

"Sabine!"

She pulled away from Gavin and turned to find Adrienne and Will behind her. "Adrienne? Will? What are you two doing here?"

Adrienne leaned in to give her a hug with an amused smirk on her face. "Gavin invited us to have dinner with you tonight. Did he not tell you?"

"Uh, no, he didn't." Sabine looked over her shoulder at Gavin, who appeared appropriately admonished, at least for the moment. "How did you even know how to get in touch with either of them?"

"Gavin and I have been acquaintances for several years," Will said. "We play the occasional game of racquetball together."

Sabine just shook her head. "So…what? Do all young, rich guys know each other? Is there some kind of club or something where you all hang out and be rich together?"

"Yes, we have a support group—Rich and Sexy

Anonymous," Gavin offered with a smile. "Let's get inside or we'll be late for our reservation."

They were seated at a table for four near the window. He'd known Will for several years but hadn't connected that the Adrienne that Sabine worked for was the same Adrienne that married Will the year before. When the pieces finally clicked, he thought having dinner together would be nice. Not even Viola would have the nerve to come up to a table like this and make a fuss. They were guaranteed a fun night out with people that he already knew would make Sabine comfortable.

He had also been curious to meet Adrienne in person. He'd read about her in the newspaper a few years ago after her plane crash and the scandal that followed. She had lost her memory for weeks, and everyone thought she was Will's fiancée, who actually died in the wreck. It was the stuff of dramatic movies, but she had made herself into quite the success story. Her clothing line had soared in the past year, and her boutique was one of the most popular destinations for the young and hip in Manhattan. He just never thought to look for his runaway girlfriend behind the counter of the store.

The waiter came to take their drink orders. "Is anyone interested in some wine?"

"None for me," Adrienne said.

"We can order something sweeter," Sabine offered. "I know you like a Riesling or a Moscato, right?"

"I do normally—" she smiled "—but I'm not drinking at all for the next eight months or so."

The sharp squealing noise that followed was nearly enough to pierce Gavin's eardrums. Sabine leaped up from her chair and ran around to embrace Adrienne. That kicked off a rapid-fire female discussion about things that Gavin would rather not be privy to. Instead, he ordered sparkling water for Adrienne and wine for everyone else.

"Congrats, Daddy," he said to Will.

Will chuckled. "Congrats to you, as well. It seems to be going around."

"It has. I can assure you that mine was more of a surprise, since my child was walking and talking by the time I found out about it."

"Yeah, but you lucked out. You missed the morning sickness, the wild hormonal swings, the Lamaze classes, the birthing room where she threatens to castrate you. After the child is born there's the midnight feedings, the colic…"

Gavin listened to Will talk for a moment and shook his head to interrupt. "I'd gladly take all that and more in exchange for the rest of what I missed. I also didn't get to be there when she heard his heartbeat or saw his image on the sonogram for the first time. I missed his birth, his first steps, his first words…. Enjoy every moment of this experience with Adrienne. Things that don't seem very important now will be the very stuff that will keep you up at night when you're older. One day, you'll look up from your BlackBerry and your kid will be in high school."

Gavin couldn't stop the words from flying out of his mouth. Every single one of them was true, although he'd barely allowed himself the time to think about what he'd missed. He tried to focus on what was ahead. Jared wasn't going to drift in and out of his life like so many others, so he had no excuse. If he missed moments going forward, it was his own fault. He didn't want any more regrets.

The waiter brought their wine, and Gavin took a large sip. "Sorry about that," he said.

"No, don't be," Will answered. "You're right. Time goes by so quickly, especially to guys like us. The priorities start to change when you fall in love and even more so when kids come into the picture. I'll try to keep it in perspective when she's sending me out in the night on strange cravings runs."

"Gavin is taking us to look at apartments on my day off," he heard Sabine say.

"There's an apartment down the street from us that's for sale," Adrienne said. "A really nice brownstone. It's on the second floor, so there's some stairs, but not many."

"I think I'd prefer her to be in a building with a doorman and some security. It would make me feel better."

"It's not like my current apartment has surveillance cameras and security," Sabine said.

"It doesn't matter. If you continue to refuse living with me, I want you in someplace secure. I don't want just anyone strolling up to your door. This can be a dangerous town sometimes, and I want you and Jared protected when I can't be there."

"Yes, that viciously dangerous Upper West Side," Sabine said with a smile. "I actually read that the Village has one of the higher crime rates, but you seemed okay with that."

"Hence the doorman."

"Okay, fine, no brownstones." The two women exchanged knowing looks and shrugged.

They placed their orders and continued chatting easily during the meal. Given they actually got as far as having food on the table, this was their most successful dinner yet. At this point, Gavin was thinking of opening a door to a line of conversation he was extremely interested in. He hadn't brought it up to Sabine—she would likely shoot him down—but with Will and Adrienne as backup, he might be successful.

"So, are you guys planning to take any romantic prebaby vacations sometime soon?"

The couple looked at each other. "That's not a bad idea," Will said. "We honestly haven't given it much thought. It really will be a challenge to travel with little ones. Honey," he said, turning to Adrienne, "we should definitely do something. Let's go somewhere glamorous and decidedly un-kid-friendly to celebrate. We're going to be making pilgrimages to the Mouse from now on, so we need to enjoy an adult vacation while we can."

"You really should," Sabine echoed. "That escape to your place in the Hamptons this summer was the only vacation I've taken since Jared was born. You should take the time to pamper yourself now. The spring lines are almost finished for Fashion Week. You should definitely go somewhere after the show."

Gavin perked up at her words. That was exactly what he was hoping to hear. "You've only had one vacation in two years?"

"More than that, really," she admitted. "Since I had Jared, I haven't had the time. Before I had Jared, I didn't have the money. Adrienne twisted my arm into going this summer. Prior to that, the last real vacation I took was my senior trip to Disney World in high school."

"That hardly counts," Will pointed out.

"Yes," Adrienne agreed. "You need a vacation as badly as I do. Maybe more. Thank goodness I got you to come to the beach house. I had no idea you were so vacation-deprived."

"I save all my hours in case Jared gets sick. And I don't have anyone to watch him while I'm gone. Tina had him over the Fourth of July trip, but I think that was too much for her. I couldn't ask her to do it again."

"You wouldn't have to," Gavin said.

"Are you offering to watch him while I go on vacation?" she challenged with a smile.

"Not exactly."

Nine

"This one is nice."

Sabine was gripping the handles of Jared's stroller as she shot him a glance that told him he was incorrect. She wasn't impolite enough to say that in front of the Realtor, though.

They were in the seventh apartment of the day. They had crisscrossed Manhattan, looking at places uptown, downtown, east and west. This last apartment, in midtown, had three spacious bedrooms, a large kitchen, a balcony and a spa tub in the master bath. And of course, it did not impress her nearly as much as some of the others. Unfortunately, it was the closest of all the apartments to his own place.

She favored the West Village, and there was no convincing her otherwise.

"This is probably a no," he said. "And I think we're done for the day. The kid is getting tired." That was an understatement. He'd been conked out in his stroller since they arrived at this building.

"I really do like the one in the Village. I just want to know what all my options are before we spend that much. It's more than we need, really."

The woman sighed and closed her leather portfolio.

"I'll keep looking and contact you next week with a list of other options. I worry you might lose out on that place if you don't put an offer in soon."

The Realtor was eyeing him from the other room. She was far too eager to push him into an expensive sale, and he wouldn't be rushed. Sabine would have what she wanted, and for the price he was willing to pay, this lady needed to find it for them.

"There are two million apartments in Manhattan," Gavin said. "We'll find another one if we have to."

They were escorted out of the apartment and downstairs. After they parted ways with the Realtor, they started strolling down the block. The street sounds roused Jared from his nap just as they neared Bryant Park.

"Could we take Jared over to the carousel? He loves that."

"Absolutely."

They took Jared for a spin on the carousel and then settled onto a bench to enjoy the nice afternoon. Gavin went to buy them both a drink, and when he returned, Jared was playing with another child who'd brought bubbles to the park.

"I've got a surprise for you."

Gavin had to smile at the mix of concern and intrigue on Sabine's face. He was excited about the prospect of what he had planned, but he also enjoyed watching her twist herself into knots trying to figure out what he was doing. She hated not knowing what was going on, which made him all the more determined to surprise her.

"Really?" Sabine turned away, feigning disinterest and watching Jared play with the bubbles.

It had been a couple days since she'd met his family.

Things seemed to be going well on all fronts. Edmund said the custody and other legal paperwork should be finalized any day now. Gavin and his legal team were signing off on the merger agreement with Exclusivity Jetliners next week. Roger Simpson's son had finally stopped his loud protests about the acquisition, and things were moving forward.

Everything was going to plan, and Gavin wanted to celebrate the best way he knew how—an exhilarating flight and a luxurious weekend on the beach. For the first time in his life, he wanted to share that experience with someone else. He wanted Sabine beside him as he soared through the clouds and buried his toes in the sand. He just had to talk her into going along with it, which would be harder than securing an Exclusivity Jetliners jet and reserving a private beachfront bungalow in Bermuda on short notice.

"When you go home tonight, I want you to pack for a long weekend away."

Her head snapped back to look at him, a frown pulling down the corners of her pink lips. "I have to work this weekend, Gavin. I've already taken off too much time from the store. I can't go anywhere."

"Yes, you can," he said with a wide smile. Did she really think he would make a suggestion like this without having every detail handled? He ran an international shipping empire; he could manage taking her away for the weekend. "The lovely Adrienne and I spoke about my plans at dinner while you were in the ladies' room. She seemed very enthusiastic about it. You have the next three days off. She told me to tell you to have a good time and not to worry about anything."

Red rushed to Sabine's pale cheeks as her brow furrowed and she started to sputter. "What? You—y-you just went to my boss and made arrangements without asking me? Seriously? Gavin, you can't just make decisions like this and leave me out of them."

"Relax," he said, running a soothing hand over her bare shoulder. She was wearing a sleeveless blouse in a bright kelly green that made her eyes darken to the color of the oak leaves overhead. It was almost the same shade as when she looked at him with desire blazing in her eyes. "I'm not trying to take over your life. I'm just trying to take you on a little surprise getaway. You wouldn't do it if I didn't twist your arm."

His fingertips tingled as they grazed over her skin, rousing a need inside him that was inappropriate for the park. He hadn't made love to Sabine since they went to his apartment. She might have her concerns, but he was determined to take her to a tropical location where he could make love to her for hours, uninterrupted.

He wasn't sure whether it was his words or his touch, but the lines between her brows eased up. With a heavy sigh, she turned her attention back to the playground. "What will we do about Jared? You haven't mentioned him coming with us."

It was all handled. "My parents have volunteered to keep him for the weekend. They're quite excited about the prospect, actually."

Sabine's lips twisted as she tried, and failed, to hold in her concerns. "Your parents? The ones who left you with nannies, refused to let you get dirty or be loud or do anything remotely childlike? I don't see that going very well, to be perfectly honest."

Gavin shrugged. What was the worst that could happen? His parents had all the resources in the world at their fingertips. They could manage any contingency, even if it meant breaking down and hiring in someone to help them for the weekend. "I think it will be fine. This is completely different. From what I hear, being a grandparent has a different set of rules. They were distracted by work and responsibilities when I was a kid. Now, they've got nothing but time, cash and two years of indulging to catch up on. Worst-case scenario, we come home to a spoiled-rotten brat."

A soft chuckle escaped Sabine's lips as she turned back to the playground again. He followed her line of sight to the patch of grass where Jared and another little boy were chasing bubbles and giggling hysterically.

She was a great mother. She worried about their son and his welfare every second of the day and had done so for two straight years all on her own. A mother's protective nature never really went away, but Sabine needed a break. A weekend trip wouldn't hurt anything. In fact, she might come home refreshed and be a better parent for it.

"If it helps," Gavin added, "Nora, the housekeeper, used to work as a nanny. She's great with kids. If my parents need reinforcements, she'll be there to help. Nothing will go wrong. You deserve some time to relax."

"I don't know, Gavin. When you took him to the circus, I was nearly panicked the whole time. That was the first time he'd gone somewhere without me aside from day care. And now you want to take me on a trip? How far are we going?"

"Only a short plane ride away."

"Plane?" she cried, turning on the bench to face him

full-on. "I really don't want to be that far from him, Gavin."

"It's only about a two-hour flight. If we drove to the Hamptons it would take just as long to get back home with summer traffic." He reached out and took her hand, relishing the cool glide of her skin against his. She had such delicate, feminine hands, more so than he remembered. He was used to them being rough with calluses from her wooden brushes, with paint embedded under her nails and along her cuticles. He hadn't managed to get her back to painting yet, but this trip was a sure start.

"Please let me do this for you. Not only will you have a great time, but it's my chance to share my passion with you the way you once shared your painting with me."

Her green eyes met his, and he felt some of her resistance fading away. She knew how important this was to him. "You're flying us there?"

Gavin smiled and nodded. It hadn't been an original part of his plan, but when he asked Roger about chartering one of his jets, he'd laughed and told him they were practically his already. If he wanted to take one, he was welcome to it, and he could fly it himself.

"Roger is loaning me one of his jets for the trip. I've been dying to fly one, and I really want you to be up there with me when I do. That would make the experience that much more special."

He loved to fly. Soaring through the air was the greatest high he'd ever experienced. It wasn't the same when you weren't sitting at the controls. The only thing that could make it better would be sharing it with her. Somehow, the idea of having Sabine beside him in the cockpit made his chest tight. He wanted to share this with her. He wanted to spoil her. She just had to let him.

She finally let the slightest smile curl her lips. He'd won, he could tell. The tiny smirk made him want to lean in and kiss her until she was blushing again, but this time with passion instead of irritation. But he'd have time soon enough. He wanted her in a swimsuit, her skin glistening with suntan oil. He couldn't wait to feel the press of her bikini bottom against him as he held her in the ocean. They both needed this trip away for a million different reasons.

"I suppose you're not going to tell me where we're flying to."

"Nope." He grinned.

"Then how do I know what to pack?"

"Dress for sizzling-hot days lounging on the beach and cool nights overlooking the ocean. Throw a couple things in a bag and leave the rest up to me."

Sabine wasn't a big fan of flying, but she wasn't about to tell Gavin that. It was his big love, like painting was for her, so she took her Dramamine, packed her bag and hoped for the best.

"You look nervous," Gavin said after locking the door and sliding into the cockpit beside her.

"Me?" she asked with a nervous twitter of laughter. "Never." She was thankful she'd worn large sunglasses today. Maybe he wouldn't notice her eyes were closed the whole time.

The taxi down the runway wasn't so bad. Gavin seemed very at ease with his headset on and vast display of controls in front of him. He had given her a headset of her own to wear so she could hear the air traffic controllers talking. She heard the tower give them clearance to take off.

"Here we go," Gavin said with an impish smile that reminded her of Jared when he thought he was getting away with something naughty.

Gavin eased the accelerator forward and the jet started down the runway. At that point, Sabine closed her eyes and took a deep breath. She felt the lift as the plane surged into the sky, but she didn't open her eyes.

"Isn't it beautiful?" Gavin asked after a few minutes.

"Oh, yeah," she said, seeing nothing but the dark inside of her eyelids.

"Sabine, open your eyes. Are you afraid to fly?"

She turned to him with a sheepish smile. "No, I'm afraid to crash. You know my boss survived a plane crash a few years ago, right? When you know someone it happened to, it makes it more real in your mind." It was then that she looked through the glass and noticed nothing but ocean around them. He hadn't mentioned flying over the ocean. She swallowed hard. She could do this. She didn't really have a choice.

"We're not going to crash."

"No one plans to."

"Just breathe and enjoy the freedom of zooming through the sky like a bird. Soaring above everyone and everything."

She pried her gaze away from the vast stretch of ocean that surrounded them and decided to focus on Gavin instead. His eyes were alight with excitement. Her serious businessman was grinning from ear to ear like a child with his first bicycle. He adjusted the controls like a pro, setting the cruising altitude and putting them on a course to...*somewhere*.

It was an amazing transformation. Sabine had seen Gavin happy. Angry. Sad. She'd watched his face contort in the pinnacle of passion and go blank with deep thought. But not once had she ever seen him truly joyful. It suited him. He should've joined the Air Force. He might not have a thirty-million-dollar apartment on Central Park South, but he would've been happier. Sometimes you have to make the hard choices to chase your dream. She'd left her entire family behind to follow hers and had rarely regretted the decision.

Two hours later, Gavin started talking into the headset again, and they were granted permission to land although she didn't see anything but miles of blue sea. The plane slowly dropped in altitude. The ocean lightened to a bright turquoise blue, and mossy-green islands appeared through the clouds. She closed her eyes when they landed, but Gavin did a great job at that.

They taxied around the small island airport, finally passing a sign to help her figure out where she was. Welcome to Bermuda.

Bermuda!

At the hangar, they were directed to a location to leave the jet. Gavin shut all the equipment down and they opened the door, extending steps to the ground. Sabine was excited about the trip but grateful to finally have her sandals touching the earth again.

Gavin directed a couple men to unload luggage from the cargo hold and move it to a black town car waiting outside. The driver then whisked them through the narrow, winding streets. After a while, they turned off the main road to a sand-and-gravel drive that disappeared through the thick cover of trees. The world seemed to slip farther away with every turn until at last they came upon a secluded two-story home right on the beach. The house was bright yellow with a white roof and white shutters around each window.

The driver carried their bags inside, leaving them on the tile floor of the master bedroom suite. Sabine followed behind him, taking in every detail of their home away from home. It was decorated in a casual beach style with bright colors and lots of light. There were large French doors off the living room that opened onto a deck. She walked outside, stepping onto it and realizing that it actually extended out over the water.

Sabine leaned against the railing and looked all around her. She didn't see another house or boat anywhere. There was nothing but palm trees, black volcanic rock, clear blue water and pink sand. It was unexpected, but peachy-pink sand stretched out on either side of them.

"The sand is pink," she said, when she heard Gavin step out onto the patio behind her.

"I thought you'd like that." He pressed against her back and wrapped his arms around her waist.

Sabine sighed and eased against him. She could feel the tension start to drift away just being here in his arms. He was right. As much as she'd protested, she needed this vacation.

"I didn't even know such a thing existed. It's beautiful." Her gaze fell on some multicolored glittering stones in the sand. "What is that?" She pointed to the beach. "Shells?"

"Sea glass. They have some beaches here that are just covered in it."

Sabine had the urge to walk along the beach and collect some glass to take home. Maybe she could work it into her art. She hadn't done any painting yet, but she had begun allowing herself to think about it again. The ideas were forming, waiting for her to execute when she was ready. Sea glass might very well feature prominently in the first piece.

"This place is amazing. I want to paint it."

Gavin nuzzled his nose along the shell of her ear. "Good. I want you to paint. I even brought supplies with me."

Sabine turned in his arms with a small frown. "I didn't notice any canvases."

He grinned and planted his hands on the railing to trap her there. "That's because they're body paints. I'm your canvas."

"Oohhh..." Sabine cooed, the possibilities flowing into her mind. This could certainly be fun. "When can we start my next masterpiece?"

Gavin captured her lips with his own, coaxing her blood to move faster and her skin to flush with the heat of desire. One hand moved to her waist and slid beneath her shirt to caress her bare skin. "Right now," he whispered against her lips.

He took her hand and led her back inside. In the bedroom, his luggage was open, and sitting on the dresser was a box of body paints. Gavin must've unpacked it after their driver left. She picked up the pink box and eyed it with curiosity. "You didn't mention it was edible."

"I thought it might bother you to destroy your own creation."

Sabine pulled a jar of strawberry-flavored red paint from the box with a wicked grin. "Given I'd be destroying it with my tongue, I don't mind so much."

She advanced toward the bed, Gavin stepping backward until his calves met with the mattress. Sabine set down the paints long enough to help him slip out of his clothes and lie out on the king-size bed.

There wasn't anything quite as inspirational as seeing his powerful, naked body sprawled in front of her. His arms were crossed behind his head, his rock-hard chest and chiseled abs just waiting for her artistic improvements. This was an exciting new canvas, and unlike the one he brought to her apartment, there was no blank, white surface to mock her.

Easing onto the bed beside him, she arranged her jars and pulled out the brush that came with it. It wasn't exactly the highest-quality equipment, but this wasn't going to hang in the Louvre one day.

Thinking for a moment, she dipped the brush into the blueberry paint and started swirling it around his navel. He hissed for a moment at the cold paint and then smiled. Next, she added some strawberry paint. Then green watermelon and purple grape. She lost herself in the art, mixing the colors around his skin until he looked like her own twisted, edible version of an abstract Kandinsky painting.

After nearly an hour, she sat back on her heels and admired her canvas. She liked it. It really was a shame it wouldn't last through his next shower.

"I like watching you work."

Sabine turned to look at him, his face one of the only parts of his body that didn't look like a unicorn had thrown up a rainbow on him. "Thanks."

"You get this intensity in your eyes that's amazingly sexy." He sat up to admire his body. "I can say with certainty that this is probably the greatest abstract art piece ever created with edible body paints. And," he added with a grin, "the only one that smells like a bowl of Froot Loops."

She reached out with her brush and dabbed a dot of purple paint on his lips, then leaned in to lick it away. Her tongue glided slowly along his bottom lip, her gaze never leaving his. "Tasty."

He buried his fingers in her hair and tugged her mouth back to his. His tongue dipped inside and glided along her own. "Indeed. The grape is very tasty."

Sabine smiled and pushed him back against the bed. "That was fun, but now it's time to clean up."

She started with his chest, licking a path across his pecs and flicking her tongue across his nipples. She made her way down the flavorful canvas, teasing at his rib cage and the sensitive plane of his stomach. When she glanced up, she noticed Gavin watching just as eagerly as when she was painting.

"I told you I liked watching you work," he said with a grin.

Sabine dipped lower to the firm heat of his erection and wiped away his smile with her tongue. Taking it deep into her mouth, she worked hard to remove every drop of paint, leaving Gavin groaning and clutching at the blankets with his fists.

"Sabine," he whispered, reaching for her wrist. He found her and tugged until her body was sprawled across his. "You're wearing too much clothing," he complained.

Sitting astride him, Sabine slipped out of her top and bra and then stood to push down her capris and panties. She tossed everything onto the floor and crouched back down. With little effort, she was able to take him into her body and thrust him deep inside.

His hands moved quickly to her hips, guiding her movements. Sabine closed her eyes and tried to absorb the sensations, but found that without the distraction of painting, her emotions were starting to creep in.

From the moment he first kissed her, Sabine had worried that she was fighting a losing battle. Not for custody of Jared, but for custody of her heart. No matter how many times she told herself that none of this was about them, that it was about his son, she couldn't help but think it was more.

Sure, everything he offered would make her a happier mother for their child. But he didn't need to bring her here, to make love to her like this. He didn't have to be so supportive of her art when no one else was. It made it seem like more. And she wanted it to be more. She was just afraid.

Sabine loved him. She always had. There were plenty of reasons why they wouldn't make a good couple, but in the end, only one reason mattered. She left because she loved him enough to change for him—the one thing she swore she'd never do. She'd been disowned by her family for her unwillingness to bend, and yet she would be whatever Gavin wanted her to be. And it scared the hell out of her. So she made her excuses and ran before she did something she might hate herself for.

There was no running from Gavin now. He would forever be a part of her life. And she didn't have the strength to keep fighting this. He might never love her the way she loved him. But she couldn't pretend that this meant nothing to her.

Gavin groaned loudly, pulling her from her thoughts. He moved his hand up to cup her breast, the intensity of their movements increasing with each moment that went by. She wouldn't be able to hold out much longer.

Opening her eyes, she looked down at Gavin. His eyes were closed, his teeth biting down on his lip. He was completely wrapped up in his desire for her. For *her.* Just the way she was. He'd told her that the night she fought with Viola, but she wasn't ready to listen. Perhaps he really meant it. Perhaps he wouldn't ask her to change and she wouldn't betray how weak she was by giving in to his demands.

Perhaps one day he might love her for being herself.

That thought made her heart soar with hope and her body followed. The pleasure surged through her, her cries echoing in the large, tile-floored room. Gavin quickly followed, digging his fingers into the flesh of her hips and growling with satisfaction.

When their heartbeats slowed and they snuggled comfortably into each other's arms, Sabine spoke. Not the words she wanted to say, but the ones she needed to say. "Thank you."

"For what?"

"For the paint. And all of this, really. But mostly the paint."

"I assure you, the pleasure was all mine."

Sabine laughed and nestled tighter against his still somewhat rainbow-colored chest. "That's not what I meant. You've always been such a big supporter of my work. I haven't…" Her voice trailed off as tears crept into her words. She cleared her throat. "I haven't always had that in my life.

"After I had Jared and stopped painting, I began to worry that I might lose my touch. When you brought that canvas the other day and the ideas didn't come,

I was really worried my art career was done. Today showed me that I still have the creativity inside me. I just need to not put so much pressure on myself and have fun with it again. It doesn't seem like much, but those body paints were a big deal. For me."

"I'm glad," Gavin said, holding her tight. "I have to say it's the best fifteen bucks I've ever spent at the adult novelty store."

Ten

"We should really call and check in on Jared."

Gavin tugged her tight against him and shook his head. They had made love, showered off her artwork, eaten—as body paints are not a replacement for real food—made love again and taken a nap. He wasn't anywhere near ready to let go of her. Not even just so she could grab her phone from the other room.

"I told my parents to call if there was a problem. I want you one hundred percent focused on enjoying yourself and relaxing. They've got it under control. We've only been gone for eight hours."

He could feel her start to squirm, but he wasn't budging. "How about we call in the morning?"

"Okay. I'm sure everything's fine, but I'm just a nervous mama. I worry."

"I know. But remember, our parents raised us, at least yours did. Mine hired very qualified people to do it. They know what they're doing."

"I'd rather you not use my parents as an example of good parenting."

Gavin had never heard Sabine speak at length about her family or where she grew up. He knew it was somewhere in the Midwest, but she always seemed hesitant to talk about it. Since she opened the door, he'd take the opportunity. "Do your parents know about Jared?"

He felt Sabine stiffen in his arms. "No," she finally said.

"Why not?"

She wiggled until he allowed her to roll onto her back and look at him. "They are very religious, very hard-working Midwestern farmers. They worship God, the Cornhuskers and John Deere, in that order. I grew up in a small town that was nothing but cornfields and the occasional church for miles. From the time I was a teenager, I started to divert from the path they all followed. My parents tried their hardest to guide me back, but it didn't work. They decided they didn't want anything to do with me and this crazy life I wanted to lead. I refuse to expose Jared to grandparents that would just look at him as my shameful illegitimate son that my wild city life earned me."

"What happened between you and your family?" Gavin asked.

Sabine sighed, her kiss-swollen lips pursing in thought. She didn't really want to talk about it, but she needed to and they both knew it.

"Like I said, I wasn't the child they wanted. I wasn't willing to change who I was or what I dreamed of for them. They wanted me to be a quiet, mousy girl that would get up at dawn to cook for my husband and the other farmhands, take care of a brood of children and be content to sit on the porch and snap green beans. My two sisters didn't see anything wrong with that, but it wasn't what I wanted for my life. They couldn't understand why I wanted a nose ring instead of a wedding ring. The first time I dyed my bangs pink, my mother nearly had a heart attack. My art, my dreams of New York and being a famous painter…that was all childish nonsense to them. They wanted me to 'grow up' and do something respectable."

Gavin knew what it was like not to have his family support his choices. But he hadn't been brave like Sabine. He'd caved to the pressure. He envied her strength, especially knowing the high price she'd paid for her dreams. She had no contact with her family at all?

"You don't even speak to your sisters, then?"

"Very rarely. They're both older than I am, but the younger of the two talks to me on Facebook now and then. When we do talk, it's like chatting superficially with an old friend from junior high you barely remember. We don't share much. I don't post anything about Jared online, so none of them know about him. It seems that when I refused the life they chose I was insulting them, too. In trying to make myself happy, I made everyone else mad."

"So how did you end up in New York?"

"After graduation, I was toying with the idea of leaving Nebraska. I was working as a checkout girl at the grocery store and hoarding every penny I made. My parents had started this ridiculous parade of eligible farmers through the house each week at Sunday dinner just like they had with my older sisters. I could feel my opportunity to leave slipping away. If I wasn't careful, eventually one of the men would catch my eye. Then I'd end up pregnant or married, and I'd never get to New York.

"One night, after I walked the latest guy out, I returned to the living room and announced to my parents that I was moving out. I'd finally saved up enough to get there and a little money to live on. I told them I had a bus ticket to Manhattan and I would be leaving in the morning. It scared the daylights out of me, but I had to do it."

Gavin noticed the faint shimmer of tears in her eyes. The room was dark, but there was enough moonlight to catch it. Her parents hurt her and he hated them for it. "What did they say when you told them?"

She didn't reply right away. When she finally spoke, the tears had reached her voice, her words wavering with emotions. "They said to go on and go, then. Why wait for the morning? My dad grabbed the bag I had packed and threw it in the back of his truck."

Sabine sniffed delicately and wiped her eyes. "They were done with me. If I wasn't going to be the daughter they wanted me to be, then I just wouldn't be their daughter. My mama didn't say a word. She just shook her head and went to do the dishes. That's all she ever did was clean that damned kitchen. So I climbed into the truck and left. I wasn't even finished packing, but I couldn't make myself go upstairs to get the last of my things. I ended up sleeping in the bus station that night because I couldn't change my ticket."

"Just like that?"

"Just like that." She sighed, pulling her emotions back into check. "They disowned me. I don't know if they secretly thought I would fail and come running home, or if they were just tired of dealing with my eccentricities. I wasn't the town tramp. I wasn't pregnant or on drugs. I was smart, I graduated high school with good grades. I worked and did my share around the farm. But I didn't fit this mold they tried to force me into.

"That was the last time I saw or spoke to my parents. The saddest part is that despite the fact that I wanted to go, I wanted them to ask me to stay. But they didn't. They just let me walk out like I meant nothing to them."

Gavin felt a sick knot start to form in his stomach. He'd done the exact same thing to her. All this time, he'd only focused on the fact that Sabine had left like everyone else in his life. He'd never considered that she might stay if he'd asked. And he'd wanted to. Every nerve in his body was screaming for him to say something—do *something*—to keep Sabine from leaving him, but he'd sat quietly and let her walk away.

"You know, people make mistakes. I'm willing to bet that they love you and miss you. Maybe they thought they were giving you one of those hard life lessons thinking you would come back and be more grateful for what you had. And when you didn't…they didn't know what to do. Or how to find you."

"I'm not that hard to find. Like I said, I'm on Facebook. For a while, I even had a website for my art."

Gavin shook his head. "It's not always as easy as that, especially when you know you're in the wrong. I mean, I did the same thing, didn't I? I was stupid and stubborn and let you walk away. I had a million idiotic reasons for it at the time, but none of them held up the moment that door slammed. Whenever I think back on that day, I wonder what would've happened if I'd run after you. If I'd pulled you into my arms and told you that I needed you to stay."

"You wanted me to stay?"

There was such astonishment in her voice that made him feel even worse. She thought he didn't care. All this time. A part of her probably still did. He hadn't asked for more than her body. Perhaps that's all she thought he wanted. It was all he thought he wanted, until this moment.

"Of course I wanted you to stay. I was just so caught off guard. I had let myself believe that you were different, that you wouldn't leave because you cared about me. When you broke it off, my world started to crumble. I just didn't know how to ask you to stay. You know that I'm not good with that kind of thing. Feelings..." His voice drifted off as he shook his head. He sucked at the emotional stuff.

"It's easier than you think."

Gavin planted a kiss against the crown of her head. "It is?"

"Yes." She propped up onto one elbow and looked him in the eyes. "All you had to say is 'stay.' Just that one word is enough."

"If I had said it the day you left..." He hated to ask, but he had to know.

"I would have stayed."

Gavin swallowed hard and nodded. So many people had come and gone from his life. How many of them might still be around if he'd had the nerve to ask them to stay? Some things were out of his control, but at least he could've salvaged the past few years with Sabine.

It was hard to face the fact that one little word could've changed their entire lives. But sometimes that was all it took. He looked down at the beautiful woman in his arms, the mother of his child, and he vowed he would never let something that insignificant get in the way again.

Sabine stretched out on the lounge chair and sighed. Gavin was snoozing in the chair beside her as they both soaked in the warm sunshine and light breeze. She was really enjoying this little vacation. They had eaten too much, drank too much, slept late and made love more times than she could count. Gavin had even taken her to the Bermuda Botanical Gardens and the art museum there. She'd lost herself in room after room of paintings and sculptures, lighting the fires of her long-cold creative flames.

It was all too perfect.

She couldn't believe how wrong she'd been. About everything. From the day she took that first pregnancy test, she worried that Gavin would take over her life, steal her son and leave her powerless to stop him. So far, he'd wanted to help, wanted to have his time with his son, but had respected her boundaries. Things would change, but they would compromise on the decisions. There would be no boarding schools, no nannies taking the place of loving parents…

She'd thought Gavin didn't want her, only to find out he'd been devastated when she left. He hadn't told her that he loved her, but she could tell he had feelings for her. They might not be as strong as what she felt for him, but it was more than she ever expected to have.

She thought that she would never fit into Gavin's world or be the woman he wanted her to be. Now, she realized he didn't want her to fit in. He wanted her to be herself. There would always be people with something rude to say, but if his family welcomed her with open arms, she didn't really care what anyone else thought.

Things were going amazingly well.

A soft chirp distracted Sabine from her thoughts. It was Gavin's cell phone. It had been remarkably quiet since they'd arrived. He'd done well in focusing on their vacation, too. She watched him reach for it and frown at the screen before answering.

"Hi, Dad," he said. "Is everything okay?"

Immediately, Sabine's stomach sank. They had called yesterday to check in and everything was fine. He'd told her that his parents would only call if there was a problem. She tried to will herself to relax as she listened to half of the conversation.

"What?" Gavin's tone was sharp and alarmed. He shot up on the lounge chair, his worried gaze searching the ocean for answers he wouldn't find there. "Are you sure? Did you look in all the closets and under the beds? He likes to play hide-and-seek."

Sabine sat up in her chair, swinging her legs over the side to turn toward him. "What is it? Is Jared okay?"

Gavin wouldn't look at her. He was totally focused on the call. "How did they get in the apartment?"

They? Her heart was racing.

"Did you call the police?"

"Gavin!" Sabine cried, unable to stand not knowing what was going on any longer. If Jared fell and skinned his knee, the police wouldn't be involved. This was something far worse than she could imagine.

"No, that was the right thing to do. We'll be home in three hours." Gavin turned off his phone and finally looked at her. He had the shimmer of glassy tears in his eyes as he spoke. "Jared is gone."

A strangled cry escaped her throat. "Gone? He's missing? How?"

Gavin shook his head softly. "Not missing. Kidnapped. A ransom note was left."

Sabine's brain started to swim in panic. She could barely follow his words. She couldn't possibly have heard him right. No one would take Jared. Why would anyone take Jared? "What?" she said, but she couldn't understand his answer. Nothing made sense.

Gavin stood up and offered his hand to her, but she didn't know why. "Sabine, please," he said at last. "We have to get back to New York."

She took his hand, standing slowly until she was looking into his eyes. His eyes. Just like her son's. That's when the fog in her brain cleared, and all that was left behind was red fury.

Her baby had been taken. Her sweet little boy, who had been nothing but safe under her care. Until now. Until he became the son of one of the wealthiest men in Manhattan. Then he was just a pawn in the games of the rich.

"Sabine?"

Her gaze locked on his, her lips tightening with anger. Gavin reached out to touch her face, but she swatted his hand away. "Don't you touch me," she warned through gritted teeth. "This is all your fault."

It was as though she'd slapped him across the face. He flinched and stepped back. "What?"

"I never should've listened to you. You said he would be safe with your parents."

"Of course. Why would I think someone would kidnap our son?"

"Because that's the world you live in, Gavin. You might be appalled by the way we lived with our tiny apartment and our old, worn furniture, but you know what? Jared was safe! He was a safe, happy little boy who didn't know what he was missing. And now he's a rich little boy, scared and alone because being *your son* made him a target."

"You think I'm the reason he was kidnapped?"

There was hurt in Gavin's eyes, but she ignored it. She was too deep in her rage to care. "You are *absolutely* the reason he was kidnapped. What did the ransom note say? Did they want millions of dollars? They wouldn't have gotten that from me, no matter what. I have nothing to offer, nothing anyone could possibly want, unlike you."

"I don't know what the ransom note said aside from the fact that they would call with instructions at 5:00 p.m. If we leave now, we can get back in plenty of time. Can you stop yelling long enough to pack and get on the plane?"

"You bet I can. I don't want to be on the island with you for another minute anyway." Sabine spun on her heel and ran from him, kicking pink sand as she headed for the stairs. She leaped up them two at a time until she reached the deck and raced for the master bedroom.

"What is that supposed to mean?" he said, charging in behind her.

"It means I wish I'd never run into Clay on the street. That the last two weeks had never happened. I should've gone home to Nebraska so you could never find me. If you weren't a part of Jared's life, I would have my son with me right now. This is exactly why I didn't tell you that you were a father."

The hurt expression on Gavin's face quickly morphed into anger. His dark eyes narrowed dangerously at her. "That is a load of crap and you know it. You didn't tell me about Jared because you're a control freak who couldn't stand someone else being involved in decisions for *your* son. You didn't tell me because you're selfish and you wanted him all to yourself, no matter what the cost to him."

"You bastard! I was protecting him from the life you hated."

"Yes, because it was so much better to suffer for your child and get sympathy than to give up your child dictatorship. Martyrdom doesn't look good on you, Sabine."

Her cheeks flushed red with anger. She didn't know what to say to him. There wasn't anything else to say. She turned her back on him and focused on packing and getting home to her son. She threw open her bag and chucked everything within reach into it. Whatever was too far away wasn't important enough to worry about. By the time she had her things together, so did he. He was standing at the front door, a car waiting for them in the driveway.

She couldn't speak. If she opened her mouth, she would say more horrible things. Some she meant, some she didn't. It was probably the same for him. Yelling made her feel better when she felt so helpless. Instead, she brushed past him to the car, giving her bags over to the driver and climbing inside.

The ride to the airport was just as silent. Her anger had begun to dissipate; this wasn't the time to start blaming and arguing. That time would come later, when Jared was home safely and she could think of something, anything, but her son's welfare.

The plane was well on its way back to New York before she so much as looked in Gavin's direction. There was only a foot between them, but it could've been miles. "Listen, fighting isn't going to get us anywhere, so let's call a truce until this whole mess is over."

Gavin's fingers flexed around the controls with anger

and anxiety, but the plane didn't so much as waver under his steady command. "Agreed."

"What else did your parents say when they called?"

"They had taken him to the park and then brought him home to take a nap before lunch. My mother said she fell asleep herself on the chaise in the living room. When she got up to check on him, he was gone and the ransom note was left on the bed."

"No one else was home?"

"My father was in his office. Nora had gone out to pick up groceries."

Sabine shook her head and focused her gaze on the miles of ocean between her and her baby. "How can someone just walk into a multimillion-dollar apartment building and walk out with our son? Did no one see him? Not even the doorman? Surely there are cameras everywhere."

"Whoever it was didn't go through the front door. They probably went in through the parking garage. There are cameras all over, but it requires a police request for them to pull the surveillance tapes."

"And?"

"And," Gavin said with a heavy sigh, "we haven't called the cops yet. The note threatened Jared's safety if we involved the police. I want to wait and take the kidnapper's call tonight. Then we might have a better idea of who we're working with here. At that point, we might get the NYPD to come in."

Sabine wasn't sure if she liked this plan or not. This was her first involvement with a kidnapping outside episodes of *Law & Order,* but calling the cops always seemed to be step number one in those situations. But perhaps Gavin had more insight into this than he was sharing. "You said 'a better idea of who we're working with.' Do you know who might be involved in this?"

Gavin shrugged, the dismissive gesture making her angrier than she already was. "It might not be anyone I know. With this kind of thing, it could just be some random creep out to make a quick buck in ransom money. You were right to say that claiming my son made him a target. It did. I hadn't really considered that until now.

"But I can't help but think this is someone I know. Jared isn't common knowledge yet. I can't be certain, but I've got a pretty short suspect list. Despite what you might think, I don't go around ruining my competitors and giving them reason to hate me."

"Who, out of those people, would despise you enough to kidnap your son?"

"Three, tops. And that's a stretch."

"And how many," Sabine asked with a tremble in her voice, "would be willing to *kill* your son for revenge?"

Gavin turned and looked at her, the blood draining from behind his newly tanned skin. "No one," he said, although not with enough confidence to make her feel better. "No one."

Eleven

Truthfully, Gavin only had one suspect on his list. As the time drew close for the call from the kidnappers, he was fairly certain who would be on the other end.

They had arrived safely at the airport and made their way to his parents' apartment as quickly as they could. His parents looked nearly ill when they walked in. His father's larger-than-life confidence had crumbled. His mother looked paper-thin and fragile. This had shaken them and it was no wonder. Their home, the one they'd shared for over thirty years, had been tainted by someone bold enough to stroll inside and walk out with the most precious treasure in their possession.

Sabine and his mother hugged fiercely and then went to sit together on the couch. His father paced in the corner, staring out the window at the city that had somehow betrayed him. Nora brought a tray with hot tea and nibbles that no one could stomach touching. Gavin just sat and waited for the call.

When the phone finally rang, Gavin's heart leaped into his throat. He answered on the second ring, gesturing for silence in the room. They had not called the police, but if the four nervous adults swarming him weren't quiet, the kidnapper might think the mansion was overrun with investigators and hostage negotiation teams.

"Hello?" he choked out.

"Gavin Brooks," the man said with an air of confidence that bordered on arrogance. Gavin didn't recognize the voice, but he hadn't spoken to his primary suspect. "So glad you could come home from your luxury vacation for our little chat."

"I want to talk to Jared," Gavin demanded as forcefully as he could.

Sabine leaped up and sat beside him on the couch. They hadn't really spoken much since their fight, and things might be irrevocably broken between them, but in this moment, they were united in finding their son and making sure Jared returned home safe and sound. He reached out and took her trembling hand in his. He was just as nervous, just as scared as she was, but he was better at not showing it. Holding her hand and keeping her calm was like an anchor on his own nerves. It kept the butterflies in his stomach from carrying him off into the sky.

"I bet you do. But you're not in charge here. I am. And you've got a couple hoops to jump through before that's even on the table."

"How do I know that you really have him?"

"If I don't…who does? You haven't misplaced your son, have you?"

"Is he okay?"

"For now. I haven't harmed a hair on his handsome little head. If you want to keep it that way, you'll do exactly as I ask and not involve the police. If you call the cops, we're done negotiating and you'll never see your little boy again."

Gavin nervously squeezed Sabine's hand. She smiled weakly at him, confusing his gesture as one of reassurance. He felt anything but sure. "I'm not calling the police. I want to keep this between you and me. But I have to know. What, exactly, do you want, Paul?"

The man on the other end of the line chuckled bitterly. "Aww, shoot. I was hoping it would take longer for you to figure out who was behind this. How did you guess it was me? I thought you'd be ruining the lives of half a dozen people right now, but you narrowed the field pretty quickly."

Paul Simpson. He had been right on the money with his original guess. Roger's irresponsible only son was the heir to Exclusivity Jetliners. At least until his father signed over the company to Gavin on Tuesday. The looming deadline must have pushed Paul too far. He had no choice but to act. That left little question of what his ransom demand would be.

"Only a handful of people knew I was going out of town. Even fewer knew that I had a son. That's not common knowledge yet."

Gavin had mentioned the trip to Roger when they spoke on the phone Thursday. He'd mentioned taking Sabine to Bermuda and that his parents would be watching Jared. That's when Roger had graciously offered the jet. If Paul was listening in on their conversation, all he had to do was wait for the right moment to slip in and steal away their son. He had handed his enemy the ammunition to attack him and didn't even realize it.

The only plus to this scenario was that Paul was spineless. Or so he seemed. Roger didn't have much faith in his son. When he snapped, Paul jumped to attention. That said, Gavin wouldn't have given him the credit to plan a scheme like this, so maybe he was wrong. He wouldn't push Paul to find out.

"Ahh. Well, mistakes are bound to be made in a scenario like this. Fortunately, we don't have to worry about any of that because this is going to go smoothly and without issue."

Somehow, Gavin doubted it. "What do you *want,* Paul? You still haven't told me what you're after with all this, although I have a pretty good guess."

"It's simple, really. First, you're going to call my father. You tell him that you have to back out of the merger deal. Give him whatever excuse you want to. Aside from blackmail, of course. But end it, and now."

The sinking feeling in his gut ached even more miserably than it had before. His dream of having his own jet fleet was slipping through his fingers. Everything he'd worked for, everything he'd built toward in the past few years would be traded away for his son. Gavin hadn't been a father for long, but he would do anything to keep Jared safe. If that meant losing Exclusivity Jetliners, that was the price he would pay. But that didn't mean it wouldn't hurt.

He should've seen this coming. Paul had silenced his complaints about the sale recently. Roger had thought that he had finally convinced his son to see reason, but the truth was that Paul was quietly looking into alternatives to get his way. Going around his father was the best plan. But it wouldn't solve all of his problems.

"If I don't buy the company, your father will just sell it to someone else."

"No!" Paul shouted into the line. "He won't. If this falls through, he'll give me the chance to try running the company on my own. Then I can prove to him that I can do it and he won't sell."

Gavin wanted to tell Paul he was delusional, but he couldn't. The moment Jared was safely in his arms, he'd have the NYPD swarming this guy and hauling his ass to Rikers Island for the foreseeable future. He wouldn't be running a company anytime soon.

"After I call Roger and cancel the deal, we get our son back?"

"Not exactly," Paul chuckled. "First, I have to confirm with my father that the merger is out for good. After that, I need a little financial insurance. I expect to see you at the bank bright and early in the morning—and yes, I am watching you. You'll withdraw a million in small bills and put it into a backpack. I'll call again in the morning with the rendezvous point."

"And then we get Jared back."

"And then," Paul sighed in dismay, "yes, you get your precious little boy back. But first, phone my father and call off the deal. I'll be calling him in half an hour, and I expect him to share the disappointing news when I speak to him. You'll hear from me at 10:00 a.m. tomorrow."

The line went dead.

Gavin dropped the phone onto the table and flopped back into the cushions of his couch. He was fighting to keep it together, but inside, it felt as if his world was crumbling. His son was in danger. The one person he believed was in his life for good could be permanently snatched away on the whim of a ruthless man. His dreams of owning private jets were about to be crushed. The woman he cared for blamed him for all of it and might never forgive him if something went wrong. She was already one foot out of his life, he could tell.

But nothing he could say or do would guarantee that Jared would be handed over, unharmed. Or that Sabine would ever look at him with love in her eyes again.

She was watching him silently from the seat beside him. He was still clutching her hand, worried if he let go, he'd lose her forever. "Well," she said at last. "What did you find out?"

"Is Jared okay?" his mother asked.

"Yes, I think so. I know who has orchestrated this and why. I don't have any reason to believe that he won't return Jared to us safe and sound as long as I meet his demands."

She breathed a visible sigh of relief. "Who has him?"

"Paul Simpson. No one you know."

"What did he ask for?" His father finally entered the conversation.

"A million-dollar ransom, delivered tomorrow in exchange for Jared."

"Our accountant can make that happen," Byron confirmed.

"And today," Gavin continued, "the cancellation of my latest business deal."

Sabine gasped and squeezed his hand even tighter. "The one you were working with the private jet company?"

Gavin nodded, his gaze dropping down to his lap. "Yes. I hope you enjoyed riding in that plane to Bermuda. That will probably be the last time."

"Oh, Gavin, I'm so sorry." Her pale eyes, lined with worry, were at once glassy with tears. For a moment he was jealous that she could cry for what he was losing and he couldn't. "I know how important that was to you. Maybe you can still—"

Gavin pulled his hand away and held it up to silence her. He wasn't in the mood to deal with the maybes and other consolations she could offer. It wouldn't matter. "Even if this all works out, I think my dealings with the Simpson family are over."

"We can acquire more planes, son."

He shook his head at his father. "Finding another company with a quality fleet I can afford is nearly impossible. The shareholders won't back a more expensive merger. The whole concierge plan is dead."

He turned away from his family and picked up his phone. He needed to call Roger, but that would wait a few more minutes. More important was calling his accountant. He didn't exactly leave thousands of dollars just lying around, much less a million. Some things would need to be shifted around so he had liquid assets for the ransom. His accountant would get everything together for him with little fuss.

The awkward call to his accountant took only a few minutes. The man seemed confused by the sudden and out-of-ordinary request, but he didn't question it. The money would be ready for pickup in the morning. That done, he couldn't put off the inevitable any longer.

Gavin slowly dialed the familiar number of Roger Simpson. With every fiber of his being, he didn't want to back out of this deal. It was everything he'd desired, and it was mere days from being his at last. He wasn't even sure how he would say the words out loud. His tongue might not cooperate. He'd rather shout at Roger about how his son was volatile, if not plain disturbed.

But he wouldn't. Not while Jared's life was in another person's hands.

"Gavin?" Roger answered. "I didn't expect to hear from you today. You're back early from Bermuda. Did something happen? Was something wrong with the jet I loaned you?"

"The jet was fine. Don't worry about any of that. Something came up and we had to come back ahead of schedule." He just couldn't tell him that the something involved blackmail and kidnapping. "I—I'm sorry to have to make this call, Roger. I'm afraid I have to withdraw my offer to buy Exclusivity Jetliners."

"What?" Roger's voice cracked over the line. "You were thrilled about the offer when we last spoke just a few days ago. What's wrong? What happened to change your mind so suddenly? Did you find a better company to meet your needs? Our arrangement is completely negotiable."

"No, please, Roger. I'm sorry, but I can't really elaborate on the subject. I hate that I have to do this, but I must. I'm sorry for the trouble I'm causing you, but I have to go."

Gavin hung up the phone before Roger could grill him for more information. He did what he had to do for Jared's sake, but he didn't have to like it. Dropping his phone onto the coffee table, he got up, brushing off the questions and sympathetic looks of Sabine and his family, and walked out of the room. He needed some space to mourn his dreams, privately.

It was 10:00 a.m. and Gavin had returned from the bank with the million-dollar ransom a few minutes ago. The whole family was gathered around the phone waiting for Paul's call and the instructions for today's trade-off.

Sabine hadn't slept. They had all stayed at the Brooks mansion, but even an expensive mattress with luxury linens couldn't lure her to sleep. And from the looks of it, Gavin hadn't slept, either. Never in her life had she seen him look like he did right now. His eyes were lined with exhaustion and sadness. Gray smudges circled beneath them. He wasn't frowning, but he wasn't smiling, either. He had shut everything off. She recognized that in him. There was too much to deal with, too much that could go wrong, so he had chosen to numb himself to the possibilities.

She knew it was hard on him. Not only because of his concern for Jared but what it cost him to ensure his son's safety. That jet acquisition had meant everything to him. Seeing him in the cockpit of that plane had been an eye-opening experience. She had experienced what she thought was the pinnacle of passion when she made love to Gavin. But for him, there was a higher joy, a greater pleasure.

He'd been so close to merging his work and his dreams. And he'd been forced to throw it away.

Sabine placed a reassuring hand on his knee, and he covered it with his own. The warmth of his skin against hers chased away the fears that threatened from the corners of her mind. She wouldn't allow herself to indulge those thoughts. She'd be no good to her son if she was a hysterical mess.

As much as she'd yelled at Gavin, and blamed him for this whole mess, she was glad to have him here with her during this. No one should have to deal with this sort of thing alone. He had handled everything, and well.

There were benefits to having a take-charge man in her life, even when it was sometimes frustrating.

Gavin would do whatever it took to see that their son came home safely. Jared was their number one priority.

The phone rang. The loud sound was amplified in the silent room, sending Sabine straight up out of her seat. Gavin calmly reached out and hit the button for the speakerphone. Sabine hated listening to only half the conversation and had asked him to let her listen this time, as well.

"Yes?"

"I'm surprised, Gavin." Paul's voice boomed through the speaker. "You've done everything I've asked so far without a whisper to the police. My father was quite disappointed that your deal fell through. It was hard not to laugh in his face. You've been so cooperative you must really care about this brat. Funny, considering you've only known about him for two weeks."

Sabine fought back her urge to scream profanities into the phone. They were too close to getting Jared home safely. She could say or do whatever she wanted after that.

"I've got the money," Gavin said, ignoring his taunts. "What now?"

"Meet me in an hour in Washington Square Park. I'll be waiting by the arch with junior. You hand over the backpack, I hand over the kid."

"I'll be there."

"If I so much as smell a cop, we're done. And so is the kid."

Paul hung up, leaving them all in a stunned silence. After a moment, Celia started crying. Byron put his arm around her.

"Don't worry, dear. He doesn't have the nerve to actually hurt Jared, no matter what he says."

Gavin stood up and nodded. "He's right. Roger told me once that Paul didn't have enough ambition to get out of bed before noon most days. This is just the quickest, easiest way to make some money and get his father to do what he wants." He slung the backpack with the money onto his shoulder. "I'd better go."

Sabine leaped up, as well. "I'm going with you."

Gavin's jaw tightened. He looked as though he wanted to argue with her, but he didn't. Gavin might be able to get his way when it came to unimportant things, but that was because most times, Sabine didn't care. She cared about this, and she wouldn't take no for an answer.

"Okay. Let's go."

Sabine grabbed her own red backpack. It had a change of clothes, Pull-Ups, dry cereal, Jared's favorite stuffed dinosaur and one of his trucks. She wanted to have everything she needed to clean him up and comfort him the minute she could finally get herself to let go.

Gavin had a car drive them downtown. It let them off about a block from the park and would circle until he called to be picked up. If all went well, this shouldn't take long.

Sabine's heart was pounding wildly in her chest as they walked through the park and headed toward the arch. She could barely hear the sounds of the traffic and people surrounding them. Gavin clutched her hand in his, steadying and guiding her to the rendezvous point.

They were about five minutes early. She didn't know what Paul Simpson looked like, but Jared was nowhere in sight.

The minutes ticked by. Anxiously waiting. Then she heard it.

"Mommy!"

Like an arrow through her brain, Sabine immediately recognized the voice of her child amid the chaos of downtown. Her head turned sharply to the left. There, an older man was walking toward them carrying Jared in his arms.

She broke into a sprint, closing the gap between them. It wasn't part of the plan, but Sabine didn't care. She could hear Gavin running behind her. She stopped herself short of the man, who looked nothing like she expected him to. He was in his late fifties easily, in a nice suit. He also immediately lifted Jared from his hip and handed him into her arms.

Something about this didn't seem right, but it didn't matter. All that mattered was the warm, snuggling body of her baby back in her arms. Jared clung to her neck, his breathing a little labored as she nearly squeezed the life out of him. When she could finally ease up, she inspected her son for signs of his abduction. He was clean. Rosy-cheeked. Smiling. He actually didn't appear to think anything was awry.

What the hell was really going on?

"Roger?"

Sabine pried her attention away to listen to Gavin's conversation. Roger? That was Paul's father. Was he involved in this, too?

"Gavin, I am so sorry. You have no idea how disturbed I was to find out what was really going on. My son..." His voice trailed off. "It's inexcusable. There are no words to express how horrified I am. This must have been a day of pure hell for you both."

"What happened, Roger? We were supposed to be meeting Paul here." Gavin's dark eyes flickered over Sabine and Jared, but he didn't dare try to hold his son. He'd have to pry him from Sabine's dead arms.

"After your call last night, I got concerned. When I went into the office this morning, I heard Paul talking to someone in the day care center of our offices. He doesn't have children, so there was no reason for him to be there. Later, I overheard him talking on the phone to you. After he hung up, I confronted him and he confessed everything to me. My wife and I have been concerned about him for a while, but you never believe your children could ever do something as horrible as this."

"Where is he now?"

"He's in one of my jets on his way to a very expensive long-term rehab facility in Vermont. It was that or I disinherited him. If you want to press charges, I completely understand. I can give you the facility address for the police to pick him up. I just wanted to start getting him help right away. It seems he had more problems than even I knew, including an expensive drug habit. He owed his dealer quite a bit and had worked out a deal where he would let them use our planes to import and export drugs. That was the only reason he wanted the company. Can you imagine?"

"I'm sorry to hear that, Roger."

The old man shook his head sadly and looked over at Jared. It must be hard to know your child did something terrible when all you can see is them when they were little.

"I want you to know your little boy was in the best possible care the entire time he was gone. Paul put him in the Exclusivity Jetliners day care center. We run a twenty-four-hour facility for our employees who might have to go on long flights or overnight trips. Jared spent the last day playing with the other children. I personally guarantee there's not a scratch on him."

Sabine felt a wave of relief wash over her. No wonder Jared seemed perfectly contented. He thought he had spent the day at school with new friends and had no clue he was a kidnapping victim. Thank goodness for that. She ran her palm over his head, messing up the soft, dark hairs and standing them on end.

Jared rubbed his hair back down with both hands. "Dinosaur?" he asked.

Sabine crouched down, settling him on his feet and pulling her bag off her shoulder. "He's right here." She pulled out the plush triceratops from their trip to the American Museum of Natural History.

Jared happily hugged the dinosaur and leaned against her leg. He wasn't traumatized by the whole ordeal, but Mommy was gone a little too long for his taste. She wasn't going to be out of his sight for a while, and she knew exactly how he felt.

"I want to make this up to you," Roger said. He was shuffling awkwardly in his loafers. "At least I want to try. I doubt anything can make it better."

"Don't beat yourself up over this, Roger. You can't control what your kids do when they're adults."

"No, Gavin. I'm taking responsibility for this whole mess. I kept waiting for him to grow up, and I let things go too far. Now I want to change what I can. If you're still interested, I want to make sure you get these planes you're after. There's no way in hell I want my son to ever have his hands in the company—rehab or no. Because of everything that happened, I'd like to sell it to you for twenty percent less than we previously negotiated. How's that sound?"

Sabine watched Gavin's eyes widen in surprise. Twenty percent of the money they were talking about was apparently a huge amount. She couldn't even imagine it.

"Roger, I—"

"And I'll throw in *Beth.*"

"No." Gavin shook his head. "Absolutely not. That's your private jet. You named it after your wife!"

Roger smiled and patted Gavin on the shoulder. "My first wife," he clarified. "She's not a part of the Exclusivity Jetliners fleet, I know. But I want to give her to you. Not to BXS, but to *you.* Even if the merger is off the table. I know you've always wanted your own jet, and it doesn't get much better than my *Beth,* I assure you."

"What about you?" Gavin asked.

"I'll take some of the money I make off the sale and maybe I'll buy a smaller plane. I don't need such a big one anymore. Anyway, I don't want to give Paul too many options. Maybe I'll just get a nice yacht instead and take the missus to Monaco."

"Are you sure?"

"Absolutely. I'll have my lawyers redraft the agreement and we'll be back on for Tuesday." Roger smiled and looked down at Jared with a touch of sadness in his eyes. "Again, I'm sorry about all of this. Please, take your son home and enjoy your afternoon with him."

Then he leaned in closer to Gavin. "And for the love of God, stop by the bank and get that cash put back someplace safe. You can't just walk around with a million dollars in a backpack."

Twelve

"Well," Gavin said, breaking the long silence. "Tomorrow I'm going to call the Realtor and let her know that the apartment overlooking Washington Square Park is out."

"Out? Why?" Sabine asked from the seat beside him. The town car had picked them up after Roger left and was taking them back uptown to his apartment.

"I'm not paying five million dollars for a place that will do nothing but remind you of all of this every time you look out the window. This location is tainted."

Sabine sighed. "We looked at over half a dozen apartments last week, and that was the only one I really liked. I understand your concerns, but I hate to start over."

Thankfully, Gavin had no intention of putting her through all that again. There was only one apartment she needed to tour. It had taken him a long time to come to this conclusion, but now his mind was made up. "We're not. A place has come available that no one knows about yet. I think you're really going to love it."

Her brows arched in question, but she didn't press him. At least not now. She was too busy holding a squirming Jared in her lap. After the past twenty-four hours of hell, she probably didn't think apartment hunting was high on their agenda. She would question him later.

Besides, they hadn't spoken—really spoken—since their fight on the beach. They were angry with one another and then they set that aside while they focused on getting Jared back. Now, with all of that behind them, they had nothing to do but deal with each other and the fallout of their heated and regretful words.

Gavin wasn't ready to start that awkward conversation yet. He was much happier to watch Sabine and Jared interact as they drove home. Occasionally she leaned down and inhaled the scent of his baby shampoo and smiled, very nearly on the verge of tears. How could she ever have thought he could split the two of them up? It was an impossible task.

And as time went by, splitting Gavin from Sabine and Jared was an even more impossible task.

He'd signed off on the custody agreements because they were fair and reasonable, but he didn't like them. He wouldn't see Jared nearly enough. And aside from the occasional custody trade-off, nowhere in the pile of paperwork did it say how often he would get to see Sabine. There was no such thing as visitation with the mother.

At this point, she might not want anything else to do with him. They had both said terrible things to each other. He hadn't meant a word of it. He'd been hurt by her blame and flung the most convenient insults he could find. He could tell her that. But he knew Sabine. She wouldn't pay any attention to his apologies. They were just words, and she had told him more than once that actions spoke louder.

Now was the time for action.

The car finally pulled up outside of the Ritz-Carlton. He ushered them both inside through the crowd of tourists and over to the residential elevator. He swiped the card that had special access to his floor of the hotel. In his apartment with the door locked, Gavin finally felt secure again. His family was safe and intact and he was never going to let them out of his sight again.

Once they settled in, he called his parents to let them know Jared was okay. He should've called from the car, but he needed time to mentally unwind and process everything that happened.

Jared was playing with his dinosaur on the floor when he got off the phone. Sabine was staring out the window at Central Park, her arms crossed protectively over her chest.

"Sabine?" She turned to look at him, an expression of sadness on her face. "Are you okay?"

She nodded softly. "Yes. I wanted to tell you that I'm sorry about everything I said to you. I was upset and scared when I found out something had happened to Jared. Blaming you was the easiest thing to do. It was wrong of me. Your son was in danger, too."

"I said things I didn't mean, too."

"Yes, but you were right. I was being selfish. I was so afraid of not having Jared all to myself that I kept him from you. I shouldn't have done that. I'm glad that Clay saw me and told you about him. It was a step I couldn't make on my own. I'm really glad you're going to be a part of his life."

"What about your life?"

Sabine's eyes narrowed. "Of course Jared is already a huge part of my life. Any more, he is my life."

Gavin took a few steps closer to her. "I wasn't talking about Jared. I was talking about me. Will I get to be a part of your life, too?"

She sighed and let her gaze drop to the floor. "I don't know, Gavin. The last few weeks have been nice, but it has been a lot, and fast. We have a lifetime of sharing our son. I don't want anything to mess that up. I know how important he is to you."

"*You're* important to me," he emphasized. "Both of you. Not just Jared. All this time, all that we've shared together these weeks… It wasn't just about our son or wooing you into giving me what I wanted. You know that, right?"

Sabine looked up at him, her pale green eyes still sad and now, a touch wearier than before. "I want to believe that, Gavin. Truly, I do. But how can I know anything about our relationship when you won't tell me how you feel? You'd rather let me walk away than tell me you want me to stay. I can't spend all our time together guessing. I need you to talk to me."

"You know that's hard for me. I've never been good at voicing my feelings. I've spent my whole life watching people walk away and never come back. My parents were always busy, foisting me and my siblings off on one nanny after the next until I was old enough for boarding school. They were so worried about keeping up appearances that I changed schools every few years to move on to a more prestigious program. It didn't take long for me to learn to keep my distance from everyone."

"Not everyone is going to leave you, Gavin."

"You did. You said that you would've stayed if I had asked, but how do I know that for certain? What if I told them how I felt and they left anyway? I'm not good with words. Can't I just show you how I feel?"

"More kisses? More gifts and fancy dinners? That doesn't mean anything to me. I need more, Gavin. I need to hear the words coming from your lips."

He reached out for her hand. "I'm offering more. But first, please, I want to show you something." He tugged gently until she followed him down the hallway toward Jared's newly renovated bedroom.

"You already showed me Jared's room."

"I know. This time I want to show you the other room."

Gavin turned the knob and pushed open the door to what used to be his office. When he flipped on the light switch, he heard Sabine gasp beside him.

"Remember in the car when I said that I knew of an available property that you would love? This is it. I had the old office done up for you. An art studio just for you to work. You don't have to share it with a toddler or storage boxes or cleaning supplies. It's all yours for you to do whatever you like."

Sabine stepped ahead of him into the large, open room. He'd had the hardwood floors refinished. The walls were painted a soft, matte green very close to the color of her eyes. "The consultant I worked with told me that this shade of green was a good choice for an art studio because it wouldn't influence the color of your work and would provide enough light with the off-white ceilings."

There was one large window that let in plenty of natural light and several nonfluorescent fixtures that he was told were good for art. A leather love seat sat along one wall. Several cabinets lined the other, each filled with every painting supply he could order. Several easels were already set up with blank canvases perched on them, and a few framed paintings were hanging on the walls.

"That shade of green also looked wonderful with the paintings I had of yours."

"It's beautiful. Perfect." Sabine approached one of the three canvases hanging on the wall and let her finger run along the large wooden frame. "I didn't know you had bought any of my work. Why didn't you tell me?"

"Because I bought the pieces after you left me. It was my way of keeping you in my life, I guess."

She spun on her heel to face him, her brow knit together with excitement tampered by confusion. "When did you decide to do all this?"

"Three years ago."

"What?" she gasped.

"The room was nearly finished when you broke it off. I was planning on asking you to move in with me and giving you the room as a housewarming gift. I decided to go ahead and complete it, and then I didn't have the heart to do anything else with it. I've just kept the door shut."

"You wanted me to move in with you?" Sabine's hands dropped helplessly at her sides. "I wish to God you would've said something. I didn't think I mattered to you. I loved you, but I thought I was a fool."

"I was the fool for letting you walk away. I wanted you here with me then, and I was too afraid to admit to myself that I still wanted you here with me now. I would've bought you any apartment you chose, but I knew you were meant to be here with me."

"Why didn't you tell me about it when you showed me Jared's new room?"

Gavin took a deep breath. "I thought it was too soon to show it to you. We were slowly rebuilding our relationship. I didn't know where we would end up. I thought that I might scare you away if you saw it. Too much, too soon."

"Why would you think that?"

"You'd already laughed off my proposal and shot down any suggestion of moving in with me."

"To be fair, it wasn't much of a proposal."

"True. Which is why I worried you would think the studio was my way of trying to bribe you into moving in with me after you told me no already. It's not a bribe. It's a homecoming gift. I started working on this place years ago because I wanted it to be a home for us. Now, a home for *all* of us. Not a part-time, alternate weekends and holidays home. For every day. All three of us together."

He watched tears start welling in her eyes and didn't know if it was a good or bad sign. He decided to go with it. The moment felt right even though he wasn't as prepared as he would like to be.

"Sabine, I know I'm no good at talking about my feelings. I built this space for you because I…I love you. I loved you then and I love you now. This was the only way I could think of to show you how I felt."

"You love me?" Sabine asked with a sly smile curling her lips.

"I do. Very much."

"Then say it again," she challenged.

"I love you," he repeated, this time without hesitation. A grin of his own spread wide across his face.

It was getting easier every time he said it. "Now it's your turn."

Sabine leaned into him, her green gaze focused intently on him. "I love you, Gavin," she said without a moment's indecision. Then she placed her hands on his face and leaned in to kiss him.

Gavin wrapped his arms around her, thankful to have this again after two days without her touch or her kisses to help him get through it. He'd worried that he'd ruined it again.

"I'm glad you do," he said. Gavin pulled her hands from his face and held them in his. "That will make this next part less embarrassing. I want to ask again if you'll marry me, but this time, even if the answer is no, please don't laugh. A man's ego can't take that twice."

"Okay," Sabine said, her face now perfectly solemn in preparation for his query.

Gavin dropped down to one knee, her hands still grasped in his own. "Sabine Hayes, I love you. And I love our son. I want us to be a family. There is nothing on this earth—not a jet, not money—that I want more than for you to be my wife. Will you marry me?"

Sabine could barely withstand the rush of emotions surging through her. She really was on an emotional roller coaster. She'd experienced the highest of highs and the lowest of lows all in a few hours' time. If Gavin wasn't looking up at her with dark, love-filled eyes, she might start nervously twittering with laughter again simply from the stress of it all.

But she couldn't laugh. Not this time. Gavin wanted to marry her and there was nothing funny about that.

"Yes. I will marry you."

Gavin stood back up and swept her into his arms. His mouth eagerly captured hers, sealing their agreement with a kiss that made her blood sizzle through her veins. She wanted to make love to him on the leather couch of her new studio. The sooner she could start creating memories in her new home, the better.

Of course, that would have to wait for nap time.

Instead, she looked up into the dark eyes of her fiancé. The man she loved. The father of her child. There, in his arms, everything felt right. This is what she'd missed, the thing that made all those other apartments seem cold and unappealing.

"Gavin, do you know why I didn't like any of the apartments we looked at?"

He gave her a lopsided smile in response to her unexpected question. "You wanted crown molding and granite countertops?"

"No. Guess again."

He shrugged. "I'm out of guesses. Why didn't you like them?"

"Because they were all missing something—*you*."

Gavin laughed. "Of course. There's only one apartment in Manhattan that comes equipped with Gavin Brooks. It's a very exclusive address. The only way to get into the place is through marriage."

"Well, wouldn't you know that THE Gavin Brooks just asked me to be his wife?"

He picked up her left hand and eyed the bare ring finger. "This won't do. The first thing everyone will do when you tell them we're engaged is look at your hand. We need to get you an engagement ring."

"Right now?"

"We're two blocks away from Tiffany's. Why not right now?"

Sabine sighed. It had been an exciting couple of days. Too exciting if you asked her. She was happy to spread out some of the big moments to later in the week. "There's no rush. I know you're good for it. There's a million dollars in cash lying around on the living room floor in a JanSport."

"Okay, you win. What about tomorrow?"

"I have to work tomorrow morning."

Gavin eyed her with dismay. "No, you don't."

"Yes, I do. I'm not going to abandon my wonderful, pregnant boss when she needs me. You're the one that suggested a vacation. I at least have to stay at the store long enough for her to take one."

"What about if we go early, before the boutique opens?"

"Okay," Sabine relented. If he wanted so badly to put a dangerously expensive rock on her hand, she would let him. "But make sure you don—"

"Spider-Man!"

Sabine and Gavin turned to find Jared standing in the doorway of his new bedroom. He flung the door the rest of the way open and charged in the space that was custom-made for a little boy with dreams of being a superhero.

The workers had done an excellent job on the room. It was just as Gavin had described. Red walls, a loft with a rope swing for an adventurous young boy, and a comic-book motif sure to please. All it needed was his favorite toys from their place in Brooklyn and it would be perfect.

Jared crawled up on the new bed, bouncing ever so slightly on the new Spider-Man comforter. “Big bed!”

“Yep, it’s a big boy bed.”

“Mine?”

“It is,” Gavin replied. “Do you like it?”

Jared flipped two thumbs up. “Love Spider-Man!”

Sabine was nearly overwhelmed by the joy and excitement on their small son’s face. Gavin turned to look at her and frowned when he noted the tears pooling in her eyes.

“And I love you,” she said.

“More than Spider-Man?” Gavin asked.

“Oh, yeah,” she replied, leaning in to kiss him and prove her point.

Epilogue

Sabine was exhausted. There wasn't really another word to describe the state a woman was in immediately following childbirth. The messy business was over. The doctors and nurses had cleared out and the family went home. Now it was just Sabine and Gavin in a quiet hospital suite.

Well, make that just Sabine, Gavin *and* the brand-new Miss Elizabeth Anne Brooks in a quiet hospital suite.

Beth made her arrival at 4:53 p.m., weighing seven pounds, two ounces and shrieking with the finest set of lungs to ever debut at St. Luke's Hospital. They named her after Gavin's private plane—*Beth*—and Sabine's mother, with whom she'd recently reconciled.

Gavin's parents, siblings and the housekeeper had left a few hours ago with Jared in tow. Their son had been very excited to see his new sister, but the novelty wore off pretty quickly when she didn't do anything but sleep. He insisted that Grandpa and Grandma take him for ice cream and when visiting hours ended, they relented.

It had been a long day filled with excitement, nerves,

joy and pain. And now, she was enjoying a private moment she would remember for her whole life.

Gavin was beside her in the reclining chair. Beth was bundled up in a white blanket with pastel stripes. She was perfect, tiny and pink with Sabine's nose. The nurses had put a hat on to keep her head warm. It hid away the wild mohawk of dark hair she'd been born with. Gavin said her crazy hair was from Sabine, too. Beth had fallen asleep with her small hand clutching his pinky finger, content, warm and safe in her daddy's arms.

But the best part was watching Gavin.

The past nine months had been an adventure for her husband. Since he'd missed out on her first pregnancy, Gavin wanted to be a part of every moment from sonograms to Lamaze classes. Sometimes she wondered if he regretted getting so immersed in the details of the process.

He could handle running shipping empires and flying jets, but preparing for the arrival of a new baby—and a girl at that—nearly did him in. During labor, he was wide-eyed and panicked. Occasionally even a little green around the gills. It was pretty adorable.

Then she was born, shouting her displeasure to everyone in the maternity ward. Of course, Sabine looked at her baby first, cataloging fingers and toes and noting how beautiful and perfect she was. But the moment Beth was laid on her chest, Sabine's eyes went to Gavin. The expression on his face was priceless. It was quite literally love at first sight.

And now, while he held her, a marching band could parade through the room and Gavin probably wouldn't notice. He couldn't tear his gaze away from his daughter. It was as though the answers to all the questions in the universe were wrapped up in that blanket. It was the most precious thing Sabine had ever seen.

"You're my hero."

Sabine didn't realize Gavin was looking at her until he spoke. "Your hero?"

"Absolutely. You were amazing today." Gavin stood slowly so he didn't wake their daughter and carried Beth over to her.

Sabine accepted the bundle and smiled up at him. "Eh, piece of cake. I think I only threatened your life once."

"Twice, but who's counting?" Gavin eased down to sit on the edge of the bed and put his arm around her shoulders. "Seriously, though, I don't know how you did it. *Before.* With Jared. I mean, I knew that *I* had missed a lot, but one thing I never really considered was how it was for you. To do this all alone…"

It certainly was different this time. Before, one of her gallery friends came by the next day. That was it. This time, she had an entire cheering squad waiting in the next room, a crew in Nebraska staying up to date on Facebook and a husband holding her hand. What a difference a few years could make.

"That was the choice I made." She shrugged. "The wrong one, obviously. It was definitely better with you here."

Gavin leaned in to place a kiss on her lips and another on Beth's forehead. "I have to say I agree."

They both spent a moment looking down at their daughter. "She looks like you," Gavin said.

"That's fair since Jared looks like you. Besides, it would be unfortunate for a girl to have your chin."

"I can tell she's going to give me trouble. If she's half as beautiful and smart and talented as her mother, the boys will be lined up the block."

"She's four hours old. I don't think you need to start polishing the shotgun just yet. You've got years of ballet recitals and princess parties before we need to start worrying about that."

Gavin smiled and leaned his head against hers. "I'm looking forward to every pink, glittery second."

* * * * *

Michelle Celmer is a *USA TODAY* bestselling author of more than thirty books for Harlequin. When she's not writing, she likes to spend time with her husband, kids, grandchildren and a menagerie of animals. Michelle loves to hear from readers. Visit her website, michellecelmer.com, like her on Facebook or write her at PO Box 300, Clawson, MI 48017.

Books by Michelle Celmer

Harlequin Desire

The Nanny Bombshell
Princess in the Making

Black Gold Billionaires

The Tycoon's Paternity Agenda
One Month with the Magnate
A Clandestine Corporate Affair
Much More Than a Mistress

The Caroselli Inheritance

Caroselli's Christmas Baby
Caroselli's Baby Chase
Caroselli's Accidental Heirt

The Texas Cattleman's Club: After the Storm

More Than a Convenient Bride

Visit the Author Profile page at Harlequin.com for more titles!

PRINCESS IN THE MAKING

Michelle Celmer

To Patti, who has been an invaluable source of support through some rough times.

One

From a mile in the air, the coast of Varieo, with its crystal blue ocean and pristine sandy beaches, looked like paradise.

At twenty-four, Vanessa Reynolds had lived on more continents and in more cities than most people visited in a lifetime—typical story for an army brat—but she was hoping that this small principality on the Mediterranean coast would become her forever home.

"This is it, Mia," she whispered to her six-month-old daughter, who after spending the majority of the thirteen-hour flight alternating between fits of restless sleep and bouts of screaming bloody murder, had finally succumbed to sheer exhaustion and now slept peacefully in her car seat. The plane made its final descent to the private airstrip where they would be greeted by Gabriel, Vanessa's…it seemed silly and a little juvenile to call him her boyfriend, considering he was fifty-six. But he wasn't exactly her fiancé either. At least, not yet. When he asked her to marry him she hadn't said yes, but she hadn't said no either. That's what this visit would determine, if she wanted to marry a man who was not only thirty-two years her senior and lived halfway around the world, but a *king.*

She gazed out the window, and as the buildings below grew larger, nervous kinks knotted her insides.

Vanessa, what have you gotten yourself into this time?

That's what her father would probably say if she'd had the guts to tell him the truth about this visit. He would tell her that she was making another huge mistake. And, okay, so maybe she hadn't exactly had the best luck with men since…well, *puberty.* But this time it was different.

Her best friend Jessy had questioned her decision as well. "He seems nice now," she'd said as she sat on Vanessa's bed, watching her pack, "but what if you get there and he turns out to be an overbearing tyrant?"

"So I'll come home."

"What if he holds you hostage? What if he forces you to marry him against your will? I've heard horror stories. They treat women like second-class citizens."

"That's the other side of the Mediterranean. Varieo is on the European side."

Jessy frowned. "I don't care, I still don't like it."

It's not as if Vanessa didn't realize she was taking a chance. In the past this sort of thing had backfired miserably, but Gabriel was a real gentleman. He genuinely cared about her. He would never steal her car and leave her stranded at a diner in the middle of the Arizona desert. He wouldn't open a credit card in her name, max it out and decimate her good credit. He wouldn't pretend to like her just so he could talk her into writing his American history term paper then dump her for a cheerleader. And he certainly would never knock her up then disappear and leave her and his unborn child to fend for themselves.

The private jet hit a pocket of turbulence and gave a violent lurch, jolting Mia awake. She blinked, her pink bottom lip began to tremble, then she let out an ear-piercing wail that only intensified the relentless throb in Vanessa's temples.

"Shh, baby, it's okay," Vanessa cooed, squeezing her chubby fist. "We're almost there."

The wheels of the plane touched down and Vanessa's heart climbed up into her throat. She was nervous and excited and relieved, and about a dozen other emotions too jumbled to sort out. Though they had chatted via Skype almost daily since Gabriel left Los Angeles, she hadn't been face-to-face with him in nearly a month. What if he took one look at her rumpled suit, smudged eyeliner and stringy, lifeless hair and sent her right back to the U.S.?

That's ridiculous, she assured herself as the plane bumped along the runway to the small, private terminal owned by the royal family. She had no illusions about how the first thing that had attracted Gabriel to her in the posh Los Angeles hotel where she worked as an international hospitality agent was her looks. Her beauty—as well as her experience living abroad—was what landed her the prestigious position at such a young age. It had been an asset and, at times, her Achilles' heel. But Gabriel didn't see her as arm dressing. They had become close friends. Confidants. He loved her, or so he claimed, and she had never known him to be anything but a man of his word.

There was just one slight problem. Though she respected him immensely and loved him as a friend, she couldn't say for certain if she was *in love* with him—a fact Gabriel was well aware of. Hence the purpose of this extended visit. He felt confident that with time—six weeks to be exact, since that was the longest leave she could take from work—Vanessa would grow to love him. He was sure that they would share a long and happy life together. And the sanctity of marriage was not something that Gabriel took lightly.

His first marriage had spanned three decades, and he claimed it would have lasted at least three more if cancer hadn't snatched his wife from him eight months ago.

Mia wailed again, fat tears spilling down her chubby, flushed cheeks. The second the plane rolled to a stop Vanessa turned on her cell phone and sent Jessy a brief text, so when she woke up she would know they had arrived safely. She then unhooked the straps of the plush, designer car seat Gabriel had provided and lifted her daughter out. She hugged Mia close to her chest, inhaling that sweet baby scent.

"We're here, Mia. Our new life starts right now."

According to her father, Vanessa had turned exercising poor judgment and making bad decisions into an art form, but things were different now. *She* was different, and she had her daughter to thank for that. Enduring eight months of pregnancy alone had been tough, and the idea of an infant counting on her for its every need had scared the crap out of her. There had been times when she wasn't sure she could do it, if she was prepared for the responsibility, but the instant she laid eyes on Mia, when the doctor placed her in Vanessa's arms after a grueling twenty-six hours of labor, she fell head over heels in love. For the first time in her life, Vanessa felt she finally had a purpose. Taking care of her daughter, giving her a good life, was now her number one priority.

What she wanted more than anything was for Mia to have a stable home with two parents, and marrying Gabriel would assure her daughter privileges and opportunities beyond Vanessa's wildest dreams. Wouldn't that be worth marrying a man who didn't exactly...well, *rev her engine?* Wasn't respect and friendship more important anyway?

Vanessa peered out the window just in time to see a limo pull around the building and park a few hundred feet from the plane.

Gabriel, she thought, with equal parts relief and excitement. He'd come to greet her, just as he'd promised.

The flight attendant appeared beside her seat, gesturing to the carry-on, overstuffed diaper bag and purse in a pile at Vanessa's feet. "Ms. Reynolds, can I help you with your things?"

"That would be fantastic," Vanessa told her, raising her voice above her daughter's wailing. She grabbed her purse and hiked it over her shoulder while the attendant grabbed the rest, and as Vanessa rose from her seat for the first time in several hours, her cramped legs screamed in protest. She wasn't one to lead an idle lifestyle. Her work at the hotel kept her on her feet eight to ten hours a day, and Mia kept her running during what little time they had to spend together. There were diaper changes and fixing bottles, shopping and laundry. On a good night she might manage a solid five hours of sleep. On a bad night, hardly any sleep at all.

When she met Gabriel she hadn't been out socially since Mia was born. Not that she hadn't been asked by countless men at the hotel—clients mostly—but she didn't believe in mixing business with pleasure, or giving the false impression that her *hospitality* extended to the bedroom. But when a king asked a girl out for drinks, especially one as handsome and charming as Gabriel, it was tough to say no. And here she was, a few months later, starting her life over. Again.

Maybe.

The pilot opened the plane door, letting in a rush of hot July air that carried with it the lingering scent of the ocean. He nodded sympathetically as Mia howled.

Vanessa stopped at the door and looked back to her seat. "Oh, shoot, I'm going to need the car seat for my daughter."

"I'll take care of it, ma'am," the pilot assured her, with a thick accent.

She thanked him and descended the steps to the tarmac, so relieved to be on steady ground she could have dropped to her knees and kissed it.

The late morning sun burned her scalp and stifling heat drifted up from the blacktop as the attendant led her toward the limo. As they approached, the driver stepped out and walked around to the back door. He reached for the handle, and the door swung open, and Vanessa's pulse picked up double time. Excitement buzzed through her as one expensive looking shoe—Italian, she was guessing—hit the pavement, and as its owner unfolded himself from the car she held her breath…then let it out in a whoosh of disappointment. This man had the same long, lean physique and chiseled features, the deep-set, expressive eyes, but he was *not* Gabriel.

Even if she hadn't done hours of research into the country's history, she would have known instinctively that the sinfully attractive man walking toward her was Prince Marcus Salvatora, Gabriel's son. He looked exactly like the photos she'd seen of him—darkly intense, and far too serious for a man of only twenty-eight. Dressed in gray slacks and a white silk shirt that showcased his olive complexion and crisp, wavy black hair, he looked more like a *GQ* cover model than a future leader.

She peered around him to the interior of the limo, hoping to see someone else inside, but it was empty. Gabriel had promised to meet her, but he hadn't come.

Tears of exhaustion and frustration burned her eyes. She *needed* Gabriel. He had a unique way of making her feel as though everything would be okay. She could only imagine what his son would think of her if she dissolved into tears right there on the tarmac.

Never show weakness. That's what her father had drilled into her for as long as Vanessa could remember. So she took a deep breath, squared her shoulders and greeted the prince with a confident smile, head bowed, as was the custom in his country.

"Miss Reynolds," he said, reaching out to shake her hand. She switched Mia, whose wails had dulled to a soft whimper, to her left hip to free up her right hand, which in the blazing heat was already warm and clammy.

"Your highness, it's a pleasure to finally meet you," she said. "I've heard so much about you."

Too many men had a mushy grip when it came to shaking a woman's hand, but Marcus clasped her hand firmly, confidently, his palm cool and dry despite the temperature, his dark eyes pinned on hers. It lasted so long, and he studied her so intensely, she began to wonder if he intended to challenge her to an arm wrestling match or a duel or something. She had to resist the urge to tug her hand free as perspiration rolled from under her hair and beneath the collar of her blouse, and when he finally did relinquish his grip, she experienced a strange buzzing sensation where his skin had touched hers.

It's the heat, she rationalized. And how did the prince appear so cool and collected when she was quickly becoming a soggy disaster?

"My father sends his apologies," he said in perfect English, with only a hint of an accent, his voice deep and velvety smooth and much like his father's. "He was called out of the country unexpectedly. A family matter."

Out of the *country?* Her heart sank. "Did he say when he would be back?"

"No, but he said he would be in touch."

How could he leave her to fend for herself in a palace full of strangers? Her throat squeezed tight and her eyes burned.

You are not going to cry, she scolded herself, biting the inside of her cheek to stem the flow of tears threatening to leak out. If she had enough diapers and formula to make the trip back to the U.S., she might have been tempted to hop back on the plane and fly home.

Mia wailed pitifully and Marcus's brow rose slightly.

"This is Mia, my daughter," she said.

Hearing her name, Mia lifted her head from Vanessa's shoulder and turned to look at Marcus, her blue eyes wide with curiosity, her wispy blond hair clinging to her tearstained cheeks. She didn't typically take well to strangers, so Vanessa braced herself for the wailing to start again, but instead, she flashed Marcus a wide, two-toothed grin that could melt the hardest of hearts.

Maybe he looked enough like his father, whom Mia adored, that she instinctively trusted him.

As if it were infectious, Marcus couldn't seem to resist smiling back at her, and the subtle lift of his left brow, the softening of his features—and, oh gosh, he even had dimples—made Vanessa feel the kind of giddy pleasure a woman experienced when she was attracted to a man. Which, of course, both horrified and filled her with guilt. What kind of depraved woman felt physically attracted to her future son-in-law?

She must have been more tired and overwrought than she realized, because she clearly wasn't thinking straight.

Marcus returned his attention to her and the smile disappeared. He gestured to the limo, where the driver was securing Mia's car seat in the back. "Shall we go?"

She nodded, telling herself that everything would be okay. But as she slid into the cool interior of the car, she couldn't help wondering if this time she was in way over her head.

She was even worse than Marcus had imagined.

Sitting across from her in the limo, he watched his new rival, the woman who, in a few short weeks, had managed to bewitch his grieving father barely eight months after the queen's death.

At first, when his father gave him the news, Gabriel thought he had lost his mind. Not only because he had fallen for an American, but one so young, that he barely knew. But now, seeing her face-to-face, there was little question as to why the king was so taken with her. Her silky, honey-blond hair was a natural shade no stylist, no matter how skilled, could ever reproduce. She had the figure of a gentlemen's magazine pinup model and a face that would inspire the likes of da Vinci or Titian.

When she first stepped off the plane, doe-eyed and dazed, with a screaming infant clutched to her chest, his hope was that she was as empty-headed as the blonde beauties on some of those American reality shows, but then their eyes met, and he saw intelligence in their smoky gray depths. And a bit of desperation.

Though he hated himself for it, she looked so disheveled and exhausted, he couldn't help but feel a little sorry for her. But that didn't change the fact that she was the enemy.

The child whimpered in her car seat, then let out a wail so high-pitched his ears rang.

"It's okay, sweetheart," Miss Reynolds cooed, holding her baby's tiny clenched fist. Then she looked across the car to Marcus. "I'm so sorry. She's usually very sweet natured."

He had always been fond of children, though he much preferred them when they smiled. He would have children one day. As sole heir, it was his responsibility to carry on the Salvatora legacy.

But that could change, he reminded himself. With a pretty young wife his father could have more sons.

The idea of his father having children with a woman like her sat like a stone in his belly.

Miss Reynolds reached into one of the bags at her feet, pulled out a bottle with what looked to be juice in it and handed it to her daughter. The child popped it into her mouth and suckled for several seconds, then made a face and lobbed the bottle at the floor, where it hit Marcus's shoe.

"I'm so sorry," Miss Reynolds said again, as her

daughter began to wail. The woman looked as if she wanted to cry, too.

He picked the bottle up and handed it to her.

She reached into the bag for a toy and tried distracting the baby with that, but after several seconds it too went airborne, this time hitting his leg. She tried a different toy with the same result.

"Sorry," she said.

He retrieved both toys and handed them back to her.

They sat for several minutes in awkward silence, then she said, "So, are you always this talkative?"

He had nothing to say to her, and besides, he would have to shout to be heard over the infant's screaming.

When he didn't reply, she went on nervously, "I can't tell you how much I've looked forward to coming here. And meeting you. Gabriel has told me so much about you. And so much about Varieo."

He did not share her enthusiasm, and he wouldn't pretend to be happy about this. Nor did he believe even for a second that she meant a word of what she said. It didn't take a genius to figure out why she was here, that she was after his father's vast wealth and social standing.

She tried the bottle again, and this time the baby took it. She suckled for a minute or two then her eyelids began to droop.

"She didn't sleep well on the flight," Miss Reynolds said, as though it mattered one way or another to him. "Plus, everything is unfamiliar. I imagine it will take some time for her to adjust to living in a new place."

"Her father had no objection to you moving his child to a different country?" he couldn't help asking.

"Her father left us when he found out I was pregnant. I haven't seen or heard from him since."

"You're divorced?"

She shook her head. "We were never married."

Marvelous. And just one more strike against her. Divorce was bad enough, but a child out of wedlock? What in heaven's name had his father been thinking? And did he honestly believe that Marcus would ever approve of someone like that, or welcome her into the family?

His distaste must have shown in his face, because Miss Reynolds looked him square in the eyes and said, "I'm not ashamed of my past, your highness. Though the circumstances may not have been ideal, Mia is the best thing that has ever happened to me. I have no regrets."

Not afraid to speak her mind, was she? Not necessarily an appropriate attribute for a future queen. Though he couldn't deny that his mother had been known to voice her own very potent opinions, and in doing so had been a role model for young women. But there was a fine line between being principled and being irresponsible. And the idea that this woman would even think that she could hold herself to the standards the queen had set, that she could replace her, made him sick to his stomach.

Marcus could only hope that his father would come to his senses before it was too late, before he did something ridiculous, like *marry* her. And as much as he would like to wash his hands of the situation that very instant, he had promised his father that he would see that she was settled in, and he was a man of his word. To Marcus, honor was not only a virtue, but an obligation. His mother had taught him that. Although even he had limits.

"Your past," he told Miss Reynolds, "is between you and my father."

"But you obviously have some strong opinions about it. Maybe you should try getting to know me before you pass judgment."

He leaned forward and locked eyes with her, so there was no question as to his sincerity. "I wouldn't waste my time."

She didn't even flinch. She held his gaze steadily, her smoky eyes filled with a fire that said she would not be intimidated, and he felt a twinge of…something. An emotion that seemed to settle somewhere between hatred and lust.

It was the lust part that drew him back, hit him like a humiliating slap in the face.

And Miss Reynolds had the audacity to *smile*. Which both infuriated and fascinated him.

"Okay," she said with a shrug of her slim shoulders. Did she not believe him, or was it that she just didn't care?

Either way, it didn't make a difference to him. He would tolerate her presence for his father's sake, but he would never accept her.

Feeling an unease to which he was not accustomed, he pulled out his cell phone, dismissing her. For the first time since losing the queen to cancer, his father seemed truly happy, and Marcus would never deny him that. And only because he believed it would never last.

With any luck his father would come to his senses and send her back from where she came before it was too late.

Two

This visit was going from bad to worse.

Vanessa sat beside her sleeping daughter, dread twisting her stomach into knots. Marcus, it would seem, had already made up his mind about her. He wasn't even going to give her a chance, and the idea of being alone with him until Gabriel returned made the knots tighten.

In hindsight, confronting him so directly probably hadn't been her best idea ever. She'd always had strong convictions, but she'd managed, for the most part, to keep them in check. But that smug look he'd flashed her, the arrogance that seemed to ooze from every pore, had raked across her frayed nerves like barbed wire. Before she could think better of it, her mouth was moving and words were spilling out.

She stole a glance at him, but he was still focused on his phone. On a scale of one to ten he was a solid fifteen in the looks department. Too bad he didn't have the personality to match.

Listen to yourself.

She gave her head a mental shake. She had known the man a total of ten minutes. Was she unfairly jumping to conclusions, judging him without all the facts? And in doing so, was she no better than him?

Yes, he was acting like a jerk, but maybe he had a good reason. If her own father announced his intention to marry a much younger woman whom Vanessa had never even met, she would be wary too. But if he were a filthy rich king to boot, she would definitely question the woman's motives. Marcus was probably just concerned for his father, as any responsible son should be. And she couldn't let herself forget that he'd lost his mother less than a year ago. Gabriel had intimated that Marcus had taken her death very hard. He was probably still hurting, and maybe thought she was trying to replace the queen, which could not be further from the truth.

Looking at it that way made her feel a little better.

But what if he disliked her so much that he tried to come between her and Gabriel? Did she want to go through life feeling like an intruder in her own home? Or would it never feel like home to her?

Was this just another huge mistake?

Her heart began to pound and she forced herself to take a deep breath and relax. She was getting way ahead of herself. She didn't even know for certain that she wanted to marry Gabriel. Wasn't that the whole point of this trip? She could still go home if things didn't work out. Six weeks was a long time, and a lot could happen between now and then. For now she wouldn't let herself worry about it, or let it dash her excitement. She was determined to make the best of this, and if it didn't work out, she could chalk it up to another interesting experience and valuable life lesson.

She smiled to herself, a feeling of peace settling over her, and gazed out the window as the limo wound its way through the charming coastal village of Bocas, where shops, boutiques and restaurants lined cobblestone streets crowded with tourists. As they pulled up the deep slope to the front gates of the palace, in the distance she could see the packed public beach and harbor where everything from sailboats and yachts to a full-size cruise ship were docked.

She'd read that the coastal tourist season stretched from April through November, and in the colder months the tourist trade moved inland, into the mountains, where snowboarding and skiing were the popular activities. According to Gabriel, much of the nation's economy relied on tourism, which had taken a financial hit the last couple of years.

The gates swung open as they approached and when the palace came into view, Vanessa's breath caught. It looked like an oasis with its Roman architecture, sprawling fountains, green rolling lawns and lush gardens.

Things were definitely starting to look up.

She turned to Marcus, who sat across from her looking impatient, as though he couldn't wait to be out of the car and rid of her.

"Your home is beautiful," she told him.

He glanced over at her. "Had you expected otherwise?"

Way to be on the defensive, dude. "What I meant was, the photos I've seen don't do it justice. Being here in person is really a thrill."

"I can only imagine," he said, with barely masked sarcasm.

Hell, who was she kidding, he didn't even *try* to mask it. He really wasn't going to cut her a break, was he?

She sighed inwardly as they pulled up to the expansive marble front steps bracketed by towering white columns. At eighty thousand square feet the palace was larger than the White House, yet only a fraction of the size of Buckingham Palace.

The instant the door opened, Marcus was out of the car, leaving it to the driver to help Vanessa with her things. She gathered Mia, who was still out cold, into her arms and followed after Marcus, who stood waiting for her just inside the massive, two-story high double doors.

The interior was just as magnificent as the exterior, with a massive, circular foyer decorated in creamy beiges with marble floors polished to a gleaming shine. A ginormous crystal chandelier hung in the center, sparkling like diamonds in the sunshine streaming through windows so tall they met the domed ceiling. Hugging both sides of the curved walls, grand staircases with wrought iron railings branched off to the right and the left and wound up to the second floor. In the center of it all sat a large, intricately carved marble table with an enormous arrangement of fresh cut exotic flowers, whose sweet fragrance scented the air. The impression was a mix of tradition and modern sophistication. Class and a bit of excess.

Only then, as Vanessa gazed around in wonder, did the reality of her situation truly sink in. Her head spun and her heart pounded. This amazing place could be her home. Mia could grow up here, have the best of everything, and even more important than that, a man who would accept her as his own daughter. That alone was like a dream come true.

She wanted to tell Marcus how beautiful his home was, and how honored she felt to be there, but knew it would probably earn her another snotty response, so she kept her mouth shut.

From the hallway that extended past the stairs, a line of nearly a dozen palace employees filed into the foyer and Marcus introduced her. Celia, the head housekeeper, was a tall, stern-looking woman dressed in a starched gray uniform, her silver hair pulled back into a tight bun. Her three charges were similarly dressed, but younger and very plain looking. No makeup, no jewelry, identical bland expressions.

Vanessa smiled and nodded to each one in turn.

"This is Camille," Celia told her in English, in a flat tone that perfectly matched her dour expression, signaling for the youngest of the three to step forward. "She will be your personal maid for the duration of your stay."

Duration of her stay? Were they anticipating that she wouldn't be sticking around? Or more to the point, hoping she wouldn't?

"It's nice to meet you, Camille," she said with a smile, offering her hand.

Looking a little nervous, the young woman took it, her eyes turned downward, and with a thick accent said, "Ma'am."

The butler, George, wore tails and a starched, high collar. He was skin and bones with a slight slouch, and looked as though he was fast approaching the century mark…if he hadn't hit it already. His staff consisted of two similarly dressed assistants, both young and capable looking, plus a chef and baker, a man and a woman, dressed in white, and each looking as though they frequently tested the cuisine.

Marcus turned to George and gestured to the luggage the driver had set inside the door. Without a word the two younger men jumped into action.

A smartly dressed middle-aged woman stepped forward and introduced herself as Tabitha, the king's personal secretary.

"If there is anything you need, don't hesitate to ask," she said in perfect English, her expression blank. Then she gestured to the young woman standing beside her, who wore a uniform similar to those of the maids. "This is Karin, the nanny. She will take care of your daughter."

Vanessa was a little uncomfortable with the idea of a total stranger watching her baby, but she knew Gabriel would never expose Mia to someone he didn't trust implicitly.

"It's very nice to meet you," Vanessa said, resisting the urge to ask the young woman to list her credentials.

"Ma'am," she said, nodding politely.

"Please, call me Vanessa. In fact, I've never been one to stand on formality. Everyone should feel free to use my first name."

The request received no reaction whatsoever from the staff. No one even cracked a smile. Were they always so deadpan, or did they simply not like her? Had they decided, as Marcus had, that she wasn't to be trusted?

That would truly suck. And she would have to work extra hard to prove them wrong.

Marcus turned to her. "I'll show you to your quarters."

Without waiting for a reply, he swiveled and headed up the stairs to the left, at a pace so brisk she nearly had to jog to keep up with him.

Unlike the beige theme of the foyer, the second floor incorporated rich hues of red, orange and purple, which personally she never would have chosen, but it managed to look elegant without being too gaudy.

Marcus led her down a long, carpeted hall.

"So, is the staff always so cheerful?" she asked him.

"It's not enough that they'll cater to your every whim," Marcus said over his shoulder. "They have to be happy about it?"

With a boss who clearly didn't like her, why would they?

At the end of the hallway they turned right and he opened the first door on his left. Gabriel told her that she would be staying in the largest of the guest suites, but she hadn't anticipated just how large it would be. The presidential suite at the hotel where she worked paled in comparison. The main room was big and spacious with high ceilings and tall windows that bracketed a pair of paned French doors. The color scheme ran to muted shades of green and yellow.

There was a cozy sitting area with overstuffed, comfortable-looking furniture situated around a massive fireplace. There was also a dining alcove, and a functional desk flanked by built-in bookcases whose shelves were packed with hardback books and knickknacks.

"It's lovely," she told Marcus. "Yellow is my favorite color."

"The bedroom is that way." Marcus gestured toward the door at the far end of the suite.

She crossed the plush carpet to the bedroom and peeked inside, her breath catching. It was pure luxury with its white four-poster king-size bed, another fireplace and a huge, wall-mounted flat screen television. But she didn't see the crib Gabriel had promised.

The weight of her sleeping daughter was starting to make her arms ache, so she very gently laid Mia down in the center of the bed and stacked fluffy pillows all around her, in case she woke up and rolled over. She didn't even stir.

On her way back to the living area Vanessa peered inside the walk-in closet where her bags were waiting for her, and found that it was large enough to hold a dozen of her wardrobes. The bathroom, with its soaking tub and glass-enclosed shower, had every modern amenity known to man.

She stepped back into the living space to find Marcus standing by the door, arms crossed, checking his watch impatiently.

"There's no place for Mia to sleep," she told him, and at his blank expression added, "Gabriel said there would be a crib for her. She moves around a lot in her sleep, so putting her in a normal bed, especially one so high off the ground, is out of the question."

"There's a nursery down the hall."

There was an unspoken "duh" at the end of that sentence.

"Then I hope there's a baby monitor I can use. Otherwise, how will I hear her if she wakes in the middle of the night?" Though Mia slept through most nights, Vanessa was still accustomed to the random midnight diaper changes and feedings, and an occasional bad dream.

He looked puzzled. "That would be the responsibility of the *nanny*."

Right, the nanny. Vanessa had just assumed the nanny was there for the times when Mia needed a babysitter, not as a full-time caregiver. She wasn't sure how she felt about that. Vanessa worked such long hours, and was away from home often. Part of this trip was about spending more time with her daughter.

"And where does the nanny sleep?" she asked Marcus.

"Her bedroom is attached to the nursery," he said, in a tone that suggested she was asking stupid questions. In his world it was probably perfectly natural for the staff to take full responsibility for the children's care, but she didn't live in his world. Not even close. Surely he knew that, didn't he?

She would have to carefully consider whether or not she wanted the nanny to take over the nightly duties. She didn't want to be difficult, or insult Karin, who was probably more than capable, but when it came to Mia, Vanessa didn't fool around. If necessary, she would ask Marcus to move the crib into her bedroom, and if he had a problem with that, she would just sleep in the nursery until Gabriel returned. Hopefully it wouldn't be more than a few days.

"If there's nothing else you need," Marcus said, edging toward the door. He really couldn't wait to get away, could he? Well, she wasn't about to let him off the hook just yet.

"What if I do need something?" she asked. "How do I find someone?"

"There's a phone on the desk, and a list of extensions."

"How will I know who to call?"

He didn't roll his eyes, but she could see that he wanted to. "For a beverage or food, you call the kitchen.

If you need clean towels or fresh linens, you would call the laundry…you get the point."

She did, although she didn't appreciate the sarcasm. "Suppose I need you. Is your number on there?"

"No, it isn't, and even if it were, I wouldn't be available."

"Never?"

A nerve in his jaw ticked. "In my father's absence, I have a duty to my country."

Why did he have to be so defensive? "Marcus," she said, in a voice that she hoped conveyed sincerity, "I understand how you must be feeling, but—"

"You have no *idea* how I'm feeling," he ground out, and the level of animosity in his tone drew her back a step. "My father asked me to get you settled in, and I've done that. Now, if there's nothing else."

Someone cleared their throat and they both looked over to see the nanny standing in the doorway.

"I'll leave you two to discuss the child's care," Marcus said, making a hasty escape, and any hope she'd had that they might be friends went out the door with him.

"Come in," she told Karin.

Looking a little nervous, the girl stepped inside. "Shall I take Mia so you can rest?"

She still wasn't sure about leaving Mia in a stranger's care, but she was exhausted, and she would have a hard time relaxing with Mia in bed with her. If Vanessa fell too deeply asleep, Mia could roll off and hurt herself. And the last thing she needed was Marcus thinking that not only was she a money-grubbing con artist, but a terrible mother as well.

"I really could use a nap," she told Karin, "but if she wakes up crying, I'd like you to bring her right to me.

She's bound to be disoriented waking up in a strange place with someone she doesn't know."

"Of course, ma'am."

"Please, call me Vanessa."

Karin nodded, but looked uncomfortable with the idea.

"Mia is asleep on the bed. Why don't I carry her, so I can see where the nursery is, and you can bring her bag?"

Karin nodded again.

Not very talkative, was she?

Vanessa scooped up Mia, who was still sleeping deeply, and rolled her suitcase out to Karin, who led her two doors down and across the hall to the nursery. It was smaller than her own suite, with a play area and a sleeping area, and it was decorated gender-neutral. The walls were pale green, the furniture white and expensive-looking, and in the play area rows of shelves were packed with toys for children of every age. It was clearly a nursery designed for guests, and she supposed that if she did decide to stay, Mia would get her own nursery closer to Gabriel's bedroom.

The idea of sharing a bedroom with Gabriel, and a bed, made her stomach do a nervous little flip-flop.

Everything will work out.

She laid Mia in the crib and covered her with a light blanket, and the baby didn't even stir. The poor little thing was exhausted.

"Maybe I should unpack her things," she told Karin.

"I'll do it, ma'am."

Vanessa sighed. So it was still "ma'am"? That was something they would just have to work on. "Thank you."

She kissed the tips of her fingers, then gently pressed them to Mia's forehead. "Sleep well, sweet baby."

After reiterating that Karin was to come get her when Mia woke, she walked back to her suite. She pulled her cell phone out of her bag and checked for calls, but there were none. She dialed Gabriel's cell number, but it went straight to voice mail.

She glanced over at the sofa, thinking she would sleep there for an hour or so, but the bed, with its creamy silk comforter and big, fluffy pillows, called to her. Setting her phone on the bedside table, she lay back against the pillows, sinking into the softness of the comforter. She let her eyes drift closed, and when she opened them again, the room was dark.

Three

After leaving Miss Reynolds's suite, Marcus stopped by his office, where his assistant Cleo, short for Cleopatra—her parents were Egyptian and very eccentric—sat at her computer playing her afternoon game of solitaire.

"Any word from my father?" he asked.

Attention on the screen, she shook her head.

"I'm glad to see that you're using your time productively," he teased, as he often did when he caught her playing games.

And obviously she didn't take him seriously, because she didn't even blink, or look away from the cards on the screen. "Keeps the brain sharp."

She may have been pushing seventy, but no one could argue that she wasn't still sharp as a pin. She'd been with the royal family since the 1970s, and used to be his mother's secretary. Everyone expected she would retire after the queen's death, and enjoy what would be a very generous pension, but she hadn't been ready to stop working. She claimed it kept her young. And since her husband passed away two years ago, Marcus suspected she was lonely.

She finished the game and quit out of the software, a group photo of her eight grandchildren flashing on to her computer screen. She turned to Marcus and caught him in the middle of a yawn and frowned. "Tired?"

After a month-long battle with insomnia, he was always tired. And he wasn't in the mood for another lecture. "I'm sure I'll sleep like a baby when *she* is gone."

"She's that bad?"

He sat on the edge of her desk. "She's awful."

"And you know this after what, thirty minutes with her?"

"I knew after five. I knew the second she stepped off the plane."

She leaned forward in her chair, elbows on her desk, her white hair draped around a face that was young for her years, and with no help at all from a surgeon's knife. "Based on what?"

"She only wants his money."

Her brows rose. "She told you that?"

"She didn't have to. She's young, and beautiful, and a single mother. What else would she want from a man my father's age?"

"For the record, your highness, fifty-six is not that old."

"For her it is."

"Your father is an attractive and charming man. Who's to say that she didn't fall head over heels in love with him."

"In a few *weeks?*"

"I fell in love with my husband after our first date. Never underestimate the powers of physical attraction."

He cringed. The idea of his father and that woman… he didn't even want to think about it. Though he didn't doubt she had seduced him. That was the way her kind operated. He knew from experience, having been burned before. And his father, despite his staunch moral integrity, was vulnerable enough to fall under her spell.

"So, she's really that attractive?" Cleo asked.

Much as he wished he could say otherwise, there was no denying her beauty. "She is. But she had a child out of wedlock."

She gasped and slapped a hand to her chest. "Off with her head!"

He glared at her.

"You do remember what century this is? Women's rights and equality and all that."

"Yes, but *my* father? A man who lives by tradition. It's beneath him. He's lonely, missing my mother and not thinking straight."

"You don't give him much credit, do you? The king is a very intelligent man."

Yes, he was, and clearly not thinking with his brain. No one could convince Marcus that this situation was anything but temporary. And until she left, he would simply stay out of her way.

Vanessa bolted up in bed, heart racing, disoriented by the unfamiliar surroundings. Then, as her eyes adjusted to the dark and the room came into focus, she remembered where she was.

At first she thought that she'd slept late into the night, then realized that someone had shut the curtains. She grabbed her cell phone and checked the time, relieved to see that she had only slept for an hour and a half, and there were no missed calls from Gabriel.

She dialed his cell number, but like before it went straight to voice mail. She hung up and grabbed her laptop from her bag, hoping that maybe he'd sent her an email, but the network was password protected and she couldn't log on. She would have to ask someone for the password.

She closed the laptop and sighed. Since she hadn't heard a word from Karin, she could only assume Mia was still asleep, and without her daughter to take care of, Vanessa felt at a loss for what to do. Then she remembered all the bags in the closet waiting to be unpacked—basically her entire summer wardrobe—and figured she could kill time doing that.

She pushed herself up out of bed, her body still heavy with fatigue, and walked to the closet. But instead of finding packed suitcases, she discovered that her clothes had all been unpacked and put away. The maid must have been in while she was asleep, which was probably a regular thing around here, but she couldn't deny that it creeped her out a little. She didn't like the idea of someone else handling her things, but it was something she would just have to get used to, as she probably wouldn't be doing her own laundry.

She stripped out of her rumpled slacks and blouse and changed into yoga pants and a soft cotton top, wondering, when her stomach rumbled, what time she would be called for dinner. She grabbed her phone off the bed and walked out to the living room, where late afternoon sunshine flooded the windows and cut paths across the creamy carpet. She crossed the room and pulled open the French doors. A wall of heat sucked the breath from her lungs as she stepped out onto a balcony with wrought iron railings and exotic plants. It overlooked acres of rolling green grass and colorful flower beds, and directly below was the Olympic-size pool and cabana Gabriel had told her about. He put the pool in, he'd bragged, because Marcus had been a champion swimmer in high school and college, and to this day still swam regularly. Which would account for the impressively toned upper body.

But she definitely shouldn't be thinking about Marcus's upper body, or any other part of him.

Her cell phone rang and Gabriel's number flashed on the screen. Oh, thank God. Her heart lifted so swiftly it left her feeling dizzy.

She answered, and the sound of his voice was like a salve on her raw nerves. She conjured up a mental image of his face. His dark, gentle eyes, the curve of his smile, and realized just then how much she missed him.

"I'm so sorry I couldn't be there to greet you," he told her, speaking in his native language of Variean, which was so similar to Italian they were practically interchangeable. And since she was fluent in the latter, learning the subtle differences had been simple for her.

"I miss you," she told him.

"I know, I'm sorry. How was your flight? How is Mia?"

"It was long, and Mia didn't sleep much, but she's napping now. I just slept for a while too."

"My plane left not twenty minutes before you were due to arrive."

"Your son said it was a family matter. I hope everything is okay."

"I wish I could say it was. It's my wife's half sister, Trina, in Italy. She was rushed to the hospital with an infection."

"Oh, Gabriel, I'm so sorry." He'd spoken often of his sister-in-law, and how she had stayed with him and his son for several weeks before and after the queen died. "I know you two are very close. I hope it's nothing too serious."

"She's being treated, but she's not out of danger. I hope you understand, but I just can't leave her. She's a widow, and childless. She has no one else. She was there for me and Marcus when we needed her. I feel obligated to stay."

"Of course you do. Family always comes first."

She heard him breathe a sigh of relief. "I knew you would understand. You're an extraordinary woman, Vanessa."

"Is there anything I can do? Any way I can help?"

"Just be patient with me. I wish I could invite you to stay with me, but…"

"She's your wife's sister. I'm guessing that would be awkward for everyone."

"I think it would."

"How long do you think you'll be?"

"Two weeks, maybe. I won't know for sure until we see how she's responding to the treatment."

Two weeks? Alone with Marcus? Was the universe playing some sort of cruel trick on her? Not that she imagined he would be chomping at the bit to spend quality time with her. With any luck he would keep to himself and she wouldn't have to actually see Marcus at all.

"I promise I'll be back as soon as I possibly can," Gabriel said. "Unless you prefer to fly home until I return."

Home to what? Her apartment was sublet for the next six weeks. She lived on a shoestring budget, and being on unpaid leave, she hadn't had the money for rent while she was gone. Gabriel had offered to pay, but she felt uncomfortable taking a handout from him. Despite what Marcus seemed to believe, the fact that Gabriel was very wealthy wasn't all that important to her. And until they were married—if that day ever came—she refused to let him spoil her. Not that he hadn't tried.

The wining and dining was one thing, but on their third date he bought her a pair of stunning diamond earrings to show his appreciation for her professional services at the hotel. She had refused to take them. She had drooled over a similar pair in the jewelry boutique at the hotel with a price tag that amounted to a year's salary.

Then there had been the lush flower arrangements that began arriving at her office every morning like clockwork after he'd flown back home, and the toys for Mia from local shops. She'd had to gently but firmly tell him, no more. There was no need to buy her affections.

"I'll wait for you," she told Gabriel. Even if she did have a place to go home to, the idea of making that miserably long flight two more times with Mia in tow was motivation enough to stay.

"I promise we'll chat daily. You brought your laptop?"

"Yes, but I can't get on the network. And I'll need plug adaptors since the outlets are different."

"Just ask Marcus. I've instructed him to get you anything that you need. He was there to greet you, wasn't he?"

"Yes, he was there."

"And he was respectful?"

She could tell Gabriel the truth, but what would that accomplish, other than to make Gabriel feel bad, and Marcus resent her even more. The last thing she wanted to do was cause a rift between father and son.

"He made me feel very welcome."

"I'm relieved. He took losing his mother very hard."

"And it's difficult for him to imagine you with someone new."

"Exactly. I'm proud of him for taking the change so well."

He wouldn't be proud if he knew how Marcus had really acted, but that would remain hers and Marcus's secret.

"Your room is satisfactory?"

"Beyond satisfactory, and the palace is amazing. I plan to take Mia for a walk on the grounds tomorrow, and I can hardly wait to visit the village."

"I'm sure Marcus would be happy to take you. You should ask him."

When hell froze over, maybe. Besides, she would much rather go exploring on her own, just her and Mia.

"Maybe I will," she said, knowing she would do no such thing.

"I know that when you get to know one another, you'll become friends."

Somehow she doubted that. Even if she wanted to, Marcus clearly wanted nothing to do with her.

"I left a surprise for you," Gabriel said. "It's in the top drawer of the desk."

"What sort of surprise?" she asked, already heading in that direction.

"Well, it won't be a surprise if I tell you," he teased. "Look and see."

She was already opening the drawer. Inside was a credit card with her name on it. She picked it up and sighed. "Gabriel, I appreciate the gesture, but—"

"I know, I know. You're too proud to take anything from me. But I *want* to do this for you."

"I just don't feel comfortable spending your money. You're doing enough already."

"Suppose you see something in the village that you like? I know you have limited funds. I want you to have nice things."

"I have you, that's all I need."

"And that, my dear, is why you are such an amazing woman. And why I love you. Promise me you'll keep it with you, just in case. I don't care if it's five euros or five thousand. If you see something you really want, please buy it."

"I'll keep it handy," she said, dropping it back in the drawer, knowing she would never spend a penny.

"I've missed you, Vanessa. I'm eager to start our life together."

"If I stay," she reminded him, so he knew that nothing was set in stone yet.

"You will," he said, as confident and certain as the day he'd asked her to marry him. Then there was the sound of voices in the background. "Vanessa, I have to go. The doctor is here and I need to speak with him."

"Of course."

"We'll chat tomorrow, yes?"

"Yes."

"I love you, my sweet Vanessa."

"I love you, too," she said, then the call disconnected.

She sighed and set her phone on the desk, hoping there would come a day when she could say those words, and mean them the way that Gabriel did. That there would be a time when the sort of love she felt for him extended past friendship.

It wasn't that she didn't find him attractive. There was no doubt that he was an exceptionally good-looking man. Maybe his jaw wasn't as tight as it used to be, and there was gray at his temples, and he wasn't as fit as he'd been in his younger years, but those things didn't bother her. It was what was on the inside that counted. And her affection for him felt warm and comfortable. What was missing was that…*zing.*

Like the one you felt when you took Marcus's hand?

She shook away the thought. Yes, Marcus was an attractive man, too, plus he didn't have the sagging skin, graying hair and expanding waist. He also didn't have his father's sweet disposition and generous heart.

When Gabriel held her, when he'd brushed his lips across her cheek, she felt respected and cherished and safe. And okay, maybe those things didn't make for steamy hot sex, but she knew from personal experience that sex could be highly overrated. What really mattered was respect, and friendship. That's what was left when the *zing* disappeared. And it always did.

Men like Marcus thrilled, then they bailed. Usually leaving a substantial mess in their wake. She could just imagine the string of broken hearts he'd caused. But Gabriel was dependable and trustworthy, and that's exactly what she was looking for in a man now. She'd had her thrills, now she wanted a mature, lasting relationship. Gabriel could give her that. That and so much more, if she was smart enough, and strong enough, to let him.

Four

Marcus was halfway through his second set of laps that evening, the burn in his muscles shaking off the stress that hung on his shoulders like an iron cloak, when he heard his cell phone start to ring. He swam to the side of the pool, hoisted himself up onto the deck and walked to the table where he'd left his phone, the hot tile scorching his feet. It was his father.

He almost didn't answer. He was sure his father would have spoken to Miss Reynolds by now, and she had probably regaled him with the story of Marcus's less than warm welcome. The first thing on her agenda would be to drive a wedge between him and his father, which the king would see through, of course. Maybe not right away, but eventually, and Marcus was happy to let her hang herself with her own rope. Even if that meant receiving an admonishment from his father now. So he took the call.

"Father, how is Aunt Trina?"

"Very sick, son," he said.

His heart sank. He just wasn't ready to say goodbye to yet another loved one. "What's the prognosis?"

"It will be touch and go for a while, but the doctors are hoping she'll make a full recovery."

He breathed a sigh of relief. No one should ever have to endure so much loss in the span of only eight months. "If there's anything you need, just say so."

"There is something, but first, son, I wanted to thank you, and tell you how proud I am of you. And ashamed of myself."

Proud of him? Maybe he hadn't spoken to Miss Reynolds after all. Or was it possible that he'd already seen though her scheme and had come to his senses? "What do you mean?"

"I know that accepting I've moved on, that I've fallen in love with someone new—especially someone so young—has been difficult for you. I was afraid that you might treat Vanessa…well, less than hospitably. But knowing that you've made her feel welcome…son, I'm sorry that I didn't trust you. I should have realized that you're a man of integrity."

What the hell had she told him exactly?

Marcus wasn't sure what to say, and his father's words, his misplaced faith, filled him with guilt. How would he feel if he knew the truth? And why had she lied to him? What sort of game was she playing? Or was it possible that she really did care about his father?

Of course she didn't. She was working some sort of angle, that was how her kind always operated.

"Isn't her daughter precious?" his father said, sounding absolutely smitten. Marcus couldn't recall him ever using the word *precious* in any context.

"She is," he agreed, though he'd seen her do nothing but scream and sleep. "Is there anything pressing I should know about, business that needs tending?"

"There's no need to worry about that. I've decided to fly my staff here and set up a temporary office."

"That's really not necessary. I can handle matters while you're away."

"You know I would go out of my mind if I had nothing to do. This way I can work and still be with Trina."

That seemed like an awful lot of trouble for a short visit, unless it wasn't going to be short. "How long do you expect you'll be gone?"

"Well, I told Vanessa two weeks," he said. "But the truth is, it could be longer."

He had a sudden, sinking feeling. "How much longer?"

"Hopefully no more than three or four weeks."

A *month.* There was no question that Trina—*family*—should come first, but that seemed excessive. Especially since he had a guest. "A month is a long time to be away."

"And how long did Trina give up her life to stay with us when your mother was ill?"

She had stayed with them for several months in the final stages of his mother's illness, then another few weeks after the funeral. So he certainly couldn't fault his father for wanting to stay with her. "I'm sorry, I'm being selfish. Of course you should be there with her. As long as she needs you. Maybe I should join you."

"I need you at the palace. Since Tabitha will be with me, it will be up to you to see that Vanessa and Mia have anything they need."

"Of course." He could hardly wait.

"And I know this is a lot to ask, but I want you to keep them entertained."

Marcus hoped he didn't mean that the way it sounded. *"Entertained?"*

"Make them feel welcome. Take them sightseeing, show them a good time."

The idea had been to stay away from her as much as humanly possible, not be her tour guide. "Father—"

"I realize I'm asking a lot of you under the circumstances, and I know it will probably be a bit awkward at first, but it will give you and Vanessa a chance to get to know one another. She's truly a remarkable woman, son. I'm sure that once you get to know her you'll love her as much as I do."

Nothing his father could say would make Marcus want to spend time with that woman. And no amount of time that he spent with her would make him "love" her. "Father, I don't think—"

"Imagine how she and her daughter must feel, in a foreign country where they don't know a soul. And I feel terrible for putting her in that position. It took me weeks to convince her to come here. If she leaves, she may never agree to come back."

And that would be a bad thing?

Besides, Marcus didn't doubt for an instant that she had just been playing hard to get, stringing his father along, and now that she was here, he seriously doubted she had any intention of leaving, for any reason. But maybe in this case absence wouldn't make the heart grow fonder. Maybe it would give his father time to think about his relationship with Miss Reynolds and realize the mistake he was making.

Or maybe, instead of waiting for this to play out, Marcus could take a more proactive approach. Maybe he could persuade her to leave.

The thought brought a smile to his face.

"I'll do it," he told his father.

"I have your word?"

"Yes," he said, feeling better about the situation already. "You have my word."

"Thank you, son. You have no idea how much this means to me. And I don't want you to worry about anything else. Consider yourself on vacation until I return."

"Is there anyplace in particular you would like me to take her?"

"I'll email a list of the things she might enjoy doing."

"I'll watch for it," he said, feeling cheerful for the first time in weeks, since his father had come home acting like a lovesick teenager.

"She did mention a desire to tour the village," the king said.

That was as good a place to start as any. "Well then, we'll go first thing tomorrow."

"I can't tell you what a relief this is. And if ever you should require anything from me, you need only ask."

Send her back to the U.S., he wanted to say, but he would be taking care of that. After he was through with her, she would be *sprinting* for the plane. But the key with a woman like her was patience and subtlety.

He and his father hung up, and Marcus dropped his phone back on the table. He looked over at the pool, then up to the balcony of Miss Reynolds's room. He should give her the good news right away, so she would have time to prepare for tomorrow's outing. He toweled off then slipped his shirt, shorts and sandals on, combing his fingers through his wet hair as he headed upstairs. He half expected to hear her daughter howling as he approached her room, but the hallway was silent.

He knocked, and she must have been near the door because it opened almost immediately. She had changed into snug black cotton pants, a plain pink T-shirt, and her hair was pulled up in a ponytail. She looked even younger this way, and much more relaxed than she had when she stepped off the plane. It struck him again how attractive she really was. Without makeup she looked a little less exotic and vampy, but her features, the shape of her face, were exquisite.

He looked past her into the suite and saw that she had spread a blanket across the carpet in the middle of the room. Mia was in the center, balanced on her hands and knees, rocking back and forth, shaking her head from side to side, a bit like a deranged pendulum. Then she stopped, toppled over to the left, and rolled onto her back, looking dazed.

Was she having some sort of fit or seizure?

“Is she okay?” Marcus asked, wondering if he should call the physician.

Miss Reynolds smiled at her daughter. “She’s fine.”

“What was she doing?” Marcus asked.

“Crawling.”

Crawling? “She doesn’t seem to be getting very far.”

“Not yet. The first step is learning to balance on her hands and knees.”

She apparently had a long way to go to master that.

Mia squealed and rolled over onto her tummy, then pushed herself back up and resumed rocking. She seemed to be doing all right, until her arms gave out and she pitched forward. Marcus cringed as she fell face-first into the blanket, landing on her button nose. She lifted her head, looking stunned for a second, then she screwed up her face and started to cry.

When Miss Reynolds just stood there, Marcus asked, “Is she okay?”

"She's probably more frustrated than injured."

After several more seconds of Mia wailing, when she did nothing to comfort the child, he said, "Aren't you going to pick her up?"

She shrugged. "If I picked her up every time she got discouraged, she'd never learn to try. She'll be fine in a second."

No sooner had she spoken the words than Mia's cries abruptly stopped, then she hoisted herself back up on her hands and knees, starting the process all over again. Rocking, falling over, wailing…

"Does she do this often?" he asked after watching her for several minutes.

She sighed, as if frustrated, but resigned. "Almost constantly for the past three days."

"Is that…normal?"

"For her it is. She's a very determined child. She'll keep doing something over and over until she gets it right. She gets that from my father, I think."

He could tell, from the deep affection in her eyes, the pride in her smile as she watched her daughter, that Miss Reynolds loved the little girl deeply. Which made her attempts to con his father all the more despicable.

"I'm sorry," she said, finally turning to him. "Was there something you wan…" She trailed off, blinking in surprise as she took in the sight of him, as if she just now noticed how he was dressed. Starting at his sandals, her eyes traveled up his bare legs and over his shorts, then they settled on the narrow strip of chest where the two sides of his shirt had pulled open. For several seconds she seemed transfixed, then she gave her head a little shake, and her eyes snapped up to his.

She blinked again, looking disoriented, and asked, "I'm sorry, what did you say?"

He began to wonder if maybe he'd been mistaken earlier, and she really was a brainless blonde. "I didn't say anything. But I believe you were about to ask me if there was something that I wanted."

Her cheeks blushed bright pink. "You're right, I was. Sorry. Was there? Something you wanted, I mean."

"If you have a moment, I'd like to have a word with you."

"Of course," she said, stepping back from the door and pulling it open, stumbling over her own foot. "Sorry. Would you like to come in?"

He stepped into the room, wondering if perhaps she'd been sampling the contents of the bar. "Are you all right?"

"I took a nap. I guess I'm not completely awake yet. Plus, I'm still on California time. It's barely seven a.m. in Los Angeles. Technically I was up most of the night."

That could explain it, he supposed, yet he couldn't help questioning her mental stability.

She closed the door and turned to him. "What did you want to talk about?"

"I want to know why you lied to my father."

She blinked in surprise, opened her mouth to speak, then shut it again. Then, as if gathering her patience, she took a deep breath, slowly blew it out, and asked, "Refresh my memory, what did I lie about?"

Did she honestly not know what he meant, or were there so many lies, she couldn't keep track? "You told my father that I made you feel welcome. We both know that isn't true."

She got an "oh *that*" look on her face. "What was

I supposed to tell him? His son, who he loves and respects dearly, acted like a big jer—" She slapped a hand over her mouth, but it was pretty obvious what she'd been about to say.

Marcus had to clench his jaw to keep it from falling open. "Did you just call me a *jerk?*"

She shook her head, eyes wide. "No."

"Yes, you did. You called me a *big jerk*."

She hesitated, looking uneasy. "Maybe I did."

"Maybe?"

"Okay, I did. I told you, I'm half asleep. It just sort of…slipped out. And let's be honest, Marcus, you were acting like a jerk."

He was sure people said unfavorable things about him all the time, but no one, outside of his family, had ever dared insult him to his face. Twice. He should feel angry, or annoyed, yet all he felt was an odd amusement. "Are you *trying* to make me dislike you?"

"You already don't like me. At this point I doubt anything I say, or don't say, will change that. Which I think is kind of sad but…" She shrugged. "And for the record, I didn't *lie* to Gabriel. I just…fudged the truth a little."

"Why?"

"He has enough on his mind. He doesn't need to be worrying about me. Besides, I can fight my own battles."

If he didn't know better, he might believe that she really did care about his father. But he knew her type. He'd dated a dozen women just like her. She was only after one thing—his legacy—and like the others, he would make sure that she never got her hands on it.

"I would hardly call this a battle," he told her.

She folded her arms, emphasizing the fullness of her breasts. "You would if you were me."

Marcus had to make an effort to keep his eyes on her face. But even that was no hardship. She was exceptionally attractive and undeniably sexy. A beautiful woman with a black heart.

Her eyes wandered downward, to his chest, lingering there for several seconds, then as if realizing she was staring, she quickly looked away.

She didn't strike him as the type to be shy about the male physique. Or maybe it was just his that bothered her.

"Look," she said. "You don't like me, and that's fine. I can even understand why. It's disappointing that you aren't going to give me a chance, but, whatever. And if I'm being totally honest, I'm not so crazy about you either. So why don't we just agree to stay out of each other's way?"

"Miss Reynolds—"

"It's *Vanessa*. You could at least have the decency to use my first name."

"Vanessa," he said. "How would you feel if we called a truce?"

Five

A truce?

Vanessa studied Marcus's face, trying to determine if his words were sincere. Instead, all she could seem to concentrate on was his damp, slicked-back hair and the single wavy lock that had fallen across his forehead. She felt the strongest urge to brush it back with her fingers. And why couldn't she stop looking at that tantalizing strip of tanned, muscular, bare chest?

"Why would you do that?" she asked, forcing her attention above his neck. He folded his arms over his chest and she had to wonder if he'd seen her staring. Was she creeping him out? If she were him, she would probably be creeped out.

"I thought you wanted me to give you a chance," he said.

But why the sudden change of heart? A couple of hours ago he could barely stand to be in the same room with her. She couldn't escape the feeling that he was up to something. "Of course I do, you just didn't seem too thrilled with the idea."

"That was before I learned that for the next few weeks, we're going to be seeing a lot of each other."

She blinked. "What do you mean?"

"My father thinks it would be a good idea for us to get to know one another, and in his absence has asked me to be your companion. I'm to show you and your daughter a good time, keep you entertained."

Oh no, what had Gabriel done? She wanted Marcus to give her a chance, but not by force. That would only make him resent her more. Not to mention that she hadn't anticipated him being so…

Something.

Something that made her trip over her own feet and stumble over her words, and do stupid things like stare at his bare chest and insult him to his face.

"I don't need a companion," she told him. "Mia and I will be fine on our own."

"For your safety, you wouldn't be able to leave the palace without an escort."

"My safety?"

"There are certain criminal elements to consider."

Her heart skipped a beat. "What kind of criminal elements?"

"The kind who would love nothing more than to get their hands on the future queen. You would fetch quite the ransom."

She couldn't decide if he was telling the truth, or just trying to scare her. Kidnappings certainly weren't unheard of, but Varieo was such a quiet, peaceful country. No handguns, very little crime. Gabriel hadn't mentioned any potential threat or danger.

And why would he when he was trying to convince her to marry him? There was a reason royalty had bodyguards, right?

Wait a minute. Who even knew that she was here? It wasn't as if Gabriel would broadcast to the country that eight months after his wife's death he was bringing his new American girlfriend in for a visit.

Would he?

"The point is," Marcus said, "my father wanted you to have an escort, and that person is me."

"What about Tabitha?"

"She's flying to Italy to be with my father. He takes her everywhere. Some people have even thought..." He paused and shook his head. "Never mind."

Okay, now he *was* trying to mess with her.

But how well do you really know Gabriel, that annoying voice of doubt interjected. He could have a dozen mistresses for all she knew. Just because he claimed to have been faithful to his wife didn't mean it was true. Maybe there was no sick sister-in-law. Maybe he was with another one of his girlfriends. Maybe there had been a scheduling conflict and he chose her over Vanessa. Maybe he—

Ugh! What are you doing?

She *trusted* Gabriel, and she hated that Marcus could shake her faith with one simple insinuation. And a ridiculous one at that. Maybe she hadn't known Gabriel long, but in that short time he had never been anything but honest and dependable. And until someone produced irrefutable evidence to the contrary, she was determined to trust him.

This wasn't another dumb mistake.

It wasn't Gabriel's fault that she'd had lousy luck with relationships, and it wasn't fair to judge him on her own bad experiences. If he wanted her to spend a couple of weeks getting to know his son, that's what she would do, even if she didn't exactly trust Marcus, and questioned his motives. She would just be herself, and hope that Marcus would put aside his doubts and accept her.

"I guess I'm stuck with you then," she told him.

Marcus frowned, looking as if she'd hurt his feelings. "If the idea of spending time with me is so offensive—"

"No! Of course not. That isn't what I meant." No matter what she said, it always seemed to be the wrong thing. "I really would like us to get acquainted, Marcus. I just don't want you to feel pressured, as if you have no choice. I can only imagine how awkward this is for you, and how heartbreaking it was to lose your mother. It sounds as if she was a remarkable woman, and I would never in a million years try to replace her, or even think that I could. I just want Gabriel to be happy. He deserves it. I think that would be much more likely to happen if you and I are friends. Or at the very least, not mortal enemies."

"I'm willing to concede that I may have rushed to judgment," he said. "And for the record, my father is not *forcing* me. I could have refused, but I know it's important to him."

It was no apology for his behavior earlier, but it was definitely a start. And she hoped he really meant it, that he didn't have ulterior motives for being nice to her. "In that case, I would be honored to have you as my escort."

"So, truce?" he said, stepping closer with an outstretched hand. And boy did he smell good. Some sort of spicy delicious scent that made her want to bury her face in his neck and take a big whiff.

No, she *definitely* didn't want to do that. And she didn't want to feel the zing of awareness when he clasped her hand, the tantalizing shiver as his thumb brushed across the top of her hand, or the residual buzz after he let go.

How could she zing for a man she didn't even like?

"My father will be sending me a list of activities he thinks you'll enjoy, and he's asked me to accompany you to the village tomorrow. If there's anything in particular you'd like to do, or someplace you would like to see, let me know and we'll work it into the schedule."

Honestly, she would be thrilled to just lie around by the pool and doze for a week, but she knew Gabriel wanted her to familiarize herself with the area, because how could she decide if she wanted to live somewhere if she didn't see it? "If there's anything I'll let you know."

"Be ready tomorrow at ten a.m."

"I will."

He nodded and walked out, closing the door behind him.

Vanessa sat on the floor beside her daughter, who had tired of rocking, and was now lying on her tummy gnawing contentedly on a teething ring.

The idea of spending so much time alone with Marcus made her uneasy, but she didn't seem to have much choice. To refuse would only hurt Gabriel's feelings, and make her look like the bad guy. At the very least, when the staff saw that Marcus was accepting her, they might warm up to her as well.

Vanessa's cell phone rang and she jumped up to grab it off the desk, hoping it was Gabriel.

It was her best friend Jessy.

"Hey! I just woke up and got your text," Jessy said, and Vanessa could picture her, sitting in bed in her pajamas, eyes puffy, her spiky red hair smashed flat from sleeping with the covers pulled over her head. "How was the flight?"

"A nightmare. Mia hardly slept." She smiled down at her daughter who was still gnawing and drooling all over the blanket. "But she seems to be adjusting pretty well now."

"Was Gabriel happy to see you?"

Vanessa hesitated. She didn't want to lie to Jessy, but she was afraid the truth would only add to her friend's doubts. But if she couldn't talk to her best friend, who could she talk to?

"There was a slight change of plans." She explained the situation with Gabriel's sister-in-law, and why he felt he had to be with her. "I know what you're probably thinking."

"Yes, I have reservations about you taking this trip, but I have to trust that you know what's best for you and Mia."

"Even if you don't agree?"

"I can't help but worry about you, and I absolutely hate the idea of you moving away. But ultimately, what I think doesn't matter."

To Vanessa it did. They had been inseparable since Vanessa moved to L.A. With her statuesque figure and exquisitely beautiful features—assets that, unlike Vanessa, she chose to cleverly downplay—Jessy understood what it was like to be labeled the "pretty" girl. She knew that, depending on the circumstances, it could be more of a liability than an asset. They also shared the same lousy taste in men, although Jessy was now in a relationship with Wayne, a pharmaceutical rep, who she thought might possibly be the *one*. He was attractive without being too handsome—since she'd found most of the really good-looking guys to be arrogant—he had a stable career, drove a nice car and lived in an oceanside condo. And aside from the fact that he had a slightly unstable and bitter ex-wife and a resentful teenaged daughter with self-cutting issues in Seattle, he was darn close to perfect.

Vanessa hoped that they had both found their forever man. God knows they had paid their dues.

"So, what will you do until Gabriel comes back?" Jessy asked, and Vanessa heard the whine of the coffee grinder in the background.

"His son has agreed to be my companion." Just the thought caused a funny little twinge in her stomach.

"Companion?"

"He'll take me sightseeing, keep me entertained."

"Is he as hot in person as he is in the photos you showed me?"

Unfortunately. "On a scale of one to ten, he's a solid fifteen."

"So, if things don't work out with Gabriel…" she teased.

"Did I mention that he's also a jerk? And he doesn't seem to like me very much. Not that I don't understand why." She picked a hunk of carpet fuzz from Mia's damp fingers before she could stuff it in her mouth. "Gabriel wants us to be friends. But I think I would settle for Marcus not hating my guts."

"Vanessa, you're one of the sweetest, kindest, most thoughtful people I've ever met. How could he not like you?"

The problem was, sometimes she was too nice and too sweet and too thoughtful. To the point that she let people walk all over her. And Marcus struck her as the sort of man who would take advantage of that.

Or maybe she was being paranoid.

"He's very…intense," she told Jessy. "When he steps into a room he's just so…*there.* It's a little intimidating."

"Well, he is a prince."

"And Gabriel is a king, but I've never felt anything but comfortable with him."

"Don't take this the wrong way, but maybe Gabriel, being older, is more like…a father figure."

"Jessy, my dad has been enough of a father figure to last a dozen lifetimes."

"And you've told me a million times how his criticism makes you feel like a failure."

She couldn't deny that, and Gabriel's lavish attention did make her feel special, but she wasn't looking for a substitute father. Quite the opposite in fact. In the past she always found herself attracted to men who wanted to control or dominate her. And the worst part was that she usually let them. This time she wanted a partner. An *equal.*

Maybe the main thing that bothered her about Marcus—besides the fact that he despised her—was that he seemed a bit too much like the sort of man she used to date.

"I don't trust Marcus," she told Jessy. "He made it clear the minute I stepped off the plane that he didn't like me, then a couple of hours later he was offering to take me sightseeing. He said he's doing it for his father, but I'm not sure I buy that. If he really wanted to please Gabriel, wouldn't he have been nice to me the second I stepped off the plane?"

"Do you think he's going to try to come between you and Gabriel?"

"At this point, I'm not sure what to think." The only thing she did know was that something about Marcus made her nervous, and she didn't like it, but she was more or less stuck with him until Gabriel returned.

"I have some good news of my own," Jessy said. "Wayne has invited me to Arkansas for a couple of days for his parents' fortieth anniversary party. He wants me to meet his family."

"You're going, right?"

"I'd love to. Do you realize how long it's been since I've met a man's family, since I've even wanted to? The thing is, they live in a remote area that doesn't have great cell coverage and I might be hard to get ahold of. I'm just a little worried that if you end up needing me—"

"Jessy, I'll be fine. Worst-case scenario, I can call my dad." Although things would have to be pretty awful for her to do that.

"Are you sure? I know you say everything is okay, but I still worry about you."

"Well, don't," she told Jessy. "I can handle Prince Marcus."

She just hoped that was true.

Six

Marcus was sure he had Vanessa pegged, but after spending a day with her in the village, he was beginning to wonder if his original assumptions about her were slightly, well…unreliable.

His first hint that something might be off was when he arrived at her door at 10 a.m. sharp, fully anticipating a fifteen-or twenty-minute wait while she finished getting ready. It was a game women liked to play. They seemed to believe it drew out the anticipation or gave them power, or some such nonsense, when in reality, it just annoyed him. But when Vanessa opened the door dressed in conservative cotton shorts, a sleeveless top, comfortable-looking sandals and a floppy straw hat, she was clearly ready to go, and with a camera hanging from a strap around her neck, a diaper bag slung over one shoulder and her daughter on her hip, she looked more like an American tourist than a gold digger angling for the position of queen.

His suspicions grew throughout the day while he witnessed her shopping habits—or lack thereof. Tabitha, with only the king's best interest at heart, had warned Marcus of the credit card his father had requested for Vanessa, and its outrageous credit limit. Therefore,

Marcus requested his driver be at the ready in anticipation of armfuls of packages. But by midafternoon they had visited at least a dozen shops showcasing everything from souvenirs to designer clothing to fine jewelry, and though he'd watched her admire the fashions, and seen her gaze longingly at a pair of modestly priced, hand-crafted earrings, all she'd purchased was a T-shirt for her daughter, a postcard that she said she intended to send to her best friend in L.A. and a paperback romance novel—her one guilty pleasure, she'd explained with a wry smile. And she'd paid with cash. He had an even bigger surprise when he heard her speaking to a merchant and realized she spoke his language fluently.

"You never mentioned that you could speak Variean," he said, when they left the shop.

She just shrugged and said, "You never asked."

She was right. And everything about her puzzled him. She was worldly and well traveled, but there was a childlike delight and curiosity in her eyes with each new place she visited. She didn't just see the sights, but absorbed her surroundings like a sponge, the most trivial and mundane details—things he would otherwise overlook—snagging her interest. And she asked a million questions. Her excitement and enthusiasm were so contagious he actually began to see the village with a fresh pair of eyes. Even though they were tired and achy from lack of sleep.

She was intelligent, yet whimsical, and at times even a little flighty. Poised and graceful, yet adorably awkward, occasionally bumping into a store display or another shopper, or tripping on a threshold—or even her own feet. Once, she was so rapt when admiring the architecture of a historical church, she actually walked right into a tourist who had paused abruptly in front of her to take a photo. But instead of looking annoyed, Vanessa simply laughed, apologized and complimented the woman on her shoes.

Vanessa also had an amusing habit of saying exactly what she was thinking, while she was thinking it, and oftentimes embarrassing herself or someone else in the process.

Though she was obviously many things—or at least wanted him to believe she was—if he had to choose a single word to describe her it would probably be… *quirky.*

Twenty-four hours ago he would have been content never to see her again. But now, as he sat across from her on a blanket in the shade of an olive tree near the dock, in the members-only park off the marina, watching her snack on sausage, cheese and crackers—which she didn't eat so much as inhale—with Mia on the blanket between them rocking back and forth, back and forth on her hands and knees, he was experiencing a disconcerting combination of perplexity, suspicion and fascination.

"I guess you were hungry," he said as she plucked the last cheese wedge from the plate and popped it in her mouth.

Most women would be embarrassed or even offended by such as observation, but she just shrugged.

"I'm borderline hypoglycemic, so I have to eat at least five or six times a day. But I was blessed with a fast metabolism, so I never gain weight. It's just one more reason for other women to hate me."

"Why would other women hate you?"

"Are you kidding? A woman who looks like I do,

who can eat anything and not gain an ounce? Some people consider that an unforgivable crime, as though I have some sort of control over how pretty I am, or how my body processes nutrients. You have no idea how often as a teenager I wished I were more ordinary."

Acknowledging her own beauty should have made her come off as arrogant, but she said it with such disdain, so much self-loathing, he actually felt a little sorry for her.

"I thought all women wanted to be beautiful," he said.

"Most do, they just don't want *other* women to be beautiful too. They don't like competition. I was popular, so I had no real friends."

That made no sense. "How could you be popular if you had no friends?"

She took a sip of her bottled water than recapped it. "I'm sure you know the saying, keep your friends close and your enemies closer."

"And you were the enemy?"

"Pretty much. Those stereotypes you see in movies about popular girls aren't as exaggerated as you might think. They can be vicious."

Mia toppled over and wound up lying on her back against his leg. She smiled up at him and gurgled happily, and he couldn't help but smile back. He had the feeling she was destined to be as beautiful as her mother.

"So, if the popular girls were so terrible, why didn't you make friends who weren't popular?"

"Girls were intimidated by me. It took them a long time to get past my face to see what was on the inside. And just when they would begin to realize that I wasn't a snob, and I started to form attachments, my dad would uproot us again and I'd have to start over in a new school."

"You moved often?"

"At least once a year, usually more. My dad's in the army."

He had a difficult time picturing that. He'd imagined her as being raised in an upscale suburban home, with a pampered, trophy wife mother and an executive father who spoiled her rotten. Apparently he'd been wrong about many things.

"How many different places have you lived?" he asked.

"Too many. The special weapons training he did meant moving a lot. Overseas we were based in Germany, Bulgaria, Israel, Japan and Italy, and domestically we lived in eight different states at eleven bases. All by the time I was seventeen. Deep down, I think all the moving was just his way of coping with my mom's death."

The fact that she, too, had lost her mother surprised him. "When did she die?"

"I was five. She had the flu of all things."

His mother's death, the unfairness of it, had left him under a cloud so dark and obliterating, he felt as if he would never be cheerful again. Yet Vanessa seemed to maintain a perpetually positive attitude and sunny disposition.

"She was only twenty-six," Vanessa said.

"That's very young."

"It was one of those fluke things. She just kept getting worse and worse, and by the time she went in for treatment, it had turned into pneumonia. My dad was away at the time, stationed in the Persian Gulf. I don't think he ever forgave himself for not being there."

At least Marcus had his mother for twenty-eight years. Not that it made losing her any easier. And though he knew it happened all the time, it still struck him as terribly unjust for a child to lose a parent so young, and from such a common and typically mild affliction.

"How about you?" she asked. "Where have you lived?"

"I've visited many places," Marcus said, "but I've never lived anywhere but the palace."

"Haven't you ever wanted to be independent? Out on your own?"

More times than he could possibly count. When people heard *royalty,* they assumed a life of grandeur and excess, but the responsibilities attached to the crown could be suffocating. When it came to everything he did, every decision he made, he had to first consider his title and how it would affect his standing with the people.

"My place is with my family," he told Vanessa. "It's what is expected of me."

Mia gurgled and swung her arms, vying for his attention, so he tickled her under the chin, which made her giggle.

"If I'd had to live with my dad all these years, I would be in a rubber room," Vanessa said, wearing a sour expression, which would seem to suggest animosity.

"You don't get along?"

"With my father, it's his way or the highway. Let's just say that he has a problem with decisions I've made."

"Which ones, if you don't mind my asking?"

She sighed. "Oh, pretty much all of them. It's kind of ironic if you think about it. There are people who dislike me because I'm too perfect, but in my dad's eyes I've never done a single thing right."

He couldn't help thinking that must have been an exaggeration. No parent could be that critical. "Surely he's pleased now that you're planning to marry a king."

"I could tell him I'm the new Mother Teresa and he'd find a way to write it off as a bad thing. Besides, I haven't told him. The only person who knows where I am is my best friend Jessy."

"Why keep it a secret?"

"I didn't want to say anything to anyone until I knew for sure that I really was going to marry Gabriel."

"What reason would you have not to marry him?" Marcus asked, and Vanessa hesitated. While she wanted to get to know Marcus better, she wasn't sure how she felt about discussing the private details of her relationship with his father. But at the same time, she hated to clam up now, as this outing was definitely going better than expected. And as she sat there on the rough wool blanket in the shade, the salty ocean air cooling her sunbaked skin, her daughter playing happily between them, she felt a deep sense of peace that she hadn't experienced in a very long time.

The first hour or so had been a bit like tiptoeing around in a minefield, her every move monitored, each word dissected for hidden meaning. But little by little she began to relax, and so did Marcus. The truth is, he was more like his father than she'd imagined. Sure, he was a bit intense at times, but he was very intelligent with a quick wit, and a wry sense of humor. And though it was obvious that he wasn't quite sure what to make of her—which wasn't unusual as she always seemed to fall somewhere outside of people's expectations—she had the feeling that maybe he was starting to like her. Or at the very least dislike her less. And he clearly adored Mia, who—the little flirt—hadn't taken her eyes off him for hours.

"Unless you'd rather not discuss it," Marcus said, his tone, and the glint of suspicion in his dark eyes, suggesting that she had something to hide.

She fidgeted with the corner of the blanket. Even though her relationship with Gabriel was none of his business, to not answer would look suspicious, but the truth might only validate his reservations about her. "My relationship with Gabriel is…complicated."

"How complicated could it be? You love him, don't you?"

There was a subtle accusation in his tone. Just when she thought things were going really well, when she believed he was having a change of heart, he was back to the business of trying to discredit her, to expose her as a fraud. Well, maybe she should just give him what he wanted. It didn't seem as though it would make a difference at this point.

"I love him," she said. "I'm just not sure I'm *in* love with him."

"What's the difference?"

Did he honestly not know, or did he think she didn't? Or was he possibly just screwing with her? "Your father is an amazing human being. He's smart and he's kind and I respect him immensely. I love him as a friend, and I want him to be happy. I know that marrying me would make him happy, or at least he's told me it will. And of course I would love for Mia to have someone to call Daddy."

"But?" Marcus asked, leaning back on his arms, stretching his long legs out in front of him, as if he were settling in for a good story.

"But I want *me* to be happy, too. I deserve it."

"My father doesn't make you happy?"

"He does but…" She sighed. There was really no getting around this. "What are your feelings about intimacy before marriage?"

He didn't even hesitate. "It's immoral."

His answer took her aback. "Well, this is a first."

"What?"

"I've never met a twenty-eight-year-old virgin."

His brows slammed together. "I never said that I'm…"

He paused, realizing that he'd painted himself into a corner, and the look on his face was priceless.

"Oh, so what you're saying is, it's only immoral for your father to be intimate before marriage. For you it's fine?"

"My father is from a different generation. He thinks differently."

"Well, that's one thing you're right about. And it's a big part of my problem."

"What do you mean?"

"I believe two people should know whether or not they're sexually compatible before they jump into a marriage, because let's face it, sex is a very important part of a lasting relationship. Don't you agree?"

"I suppose it is."

"You suppose? Be honest. Would you marry a woman you'd never slept with?"

He hesitated, then said, "Probably not."

"Well, Gabriel is so traditional he won't even kiss me until we're officially engaged. And he considers sex before the wedding completely out of the question."

"You seriously want me to believe that you and my father have never…" He couldn't seem to make himself say the words, which she found kind of amusing.

"Is that really so surprising? You said yourself he's from a different generation. He didn't have sex with your mom until their wedding night, and even then he said it took a while to get all the gears moving smoothly."

Marcus winced.

"Sorry. TMI?"

"TMI?"

"Too much information?"

He nodded. "A bit."

"Honestly, I don't know why I'm telling you *any* of this, seeing as how it's really none of your business. And nothing I say is going to change the way you feel about me."

"So why are you telling me?"

"Maybe it's that I've gone through most of my life being unfairly judged and I'm sick of it. I really shouldn't care if you like me or not, but for some stupid reason, I still do."

Marcus looked as if he wasn't sure what to believe. "I don't *dis*like you."

"But you don't trust me. Which is only fair, I guess, since I don't trust you either."

Seven

Instead of looking insulted, Marcus laughed, which completely confused Vanessa.

"You find that amusing?" she asked.

"What I find amusing is that you said it to my face. Do you ever have a thought that you *don't* express?"

"Sometimes." Like when she hadn't told him how his pale gray linen pants hugged his butt just right, and the white silk short sleeved shirt brought out the sun-bronzed tones of his skin. And she didn't mention how the dark shadow of stubble on his jaw made her want to reach up and touch his face. Or the curve of his mouth made her want to…well, never mind. "When I was a kid, every time I expressed an idea or a thought, my father shot it down. He had this way of making me feel inferior and stupid, and I'm *not* stupid. It just took a while to figure that out. And now I say what I feel, and I don't worry about what other people think, because most of them don't matter. When it comes to my self-worth, the only opinion that really matters is my own. And though it took a long time to get here, I'm actually pretty happy with who I am. Sure, my life isn't perfect, and I still worry about making mistakes, but

I know that I'm capable and smart, and if I do make a mistake, I'll learn from it."

"So what will you do?" he asked. "About my father, I mean. If he won't compromise his principles."

"I'm hoping that if we spend more time together, I'll just know that it's right."

"You said it yourself, you're a very beautiful woman, and my father seems to have very strong feelings for you. I'm quite certain that with little effort you could persuade him to compromise his principles."

Was he actually suggesting she *seduce* Gabriel? And why, when Marcus said she was beautiful, did it cause a little shiver of delight? She'd heard the same words so many times from so many men, they had lost their significance. Why was he so different? And why did she care *what* he thought of her?

And why on earth had she started this conversation in the first place?

"I would never do that," she told Marcus. "I respect him too much."

Mia began to fuss and Vanessa jumped on the opportunity to end this strange and frankly *inappropriate* chat. No matter what she did or said, or how she acted, the situation with Marcus just seemed to get weirder and weirder.

"I should get her back to the palace and down for a nap. And I could probably use one too." She was still on L.A. time, and despite being exhausted last night, she'd slept terribly.

He pushed himself to his feet. "Let's go."

Together they cleaned up the picnic, and to Vanessa's surprise, Marcus lifted Mia up and held her while she folded the blanket. Even more surprising was how natural he appeared holding her, and how, when she reached to take her back, Mia clung to him and laid her head on his shoulder.

Little traitor, she thought, but she couldn't resist smiling. "I guess she wants you," she told Marcus, who looked as if he didn't mind at all.

They gathered the rest of their things and walked back to the limo waiting in the marina parking lot. They piled into the air-conditioned backseat, and she buckled Mia into her car seat. She expected that they would go straight back to the palace but instead, Marcus had the driver stop outside one of the shops they had visited earlier and went inside briefly. He came out several minutes later carrying a small bag that he slipped into his pants pocket before climbing back in the car, and though she was curious as to what was in it, she didn't ask, for fear of opening up yet another can of worms. He'd probably picked out a gift for his girlfriend. Because men who looked the way he did, and were filthy rich princes, always had a lady friend—if not two or three. And according to Gabriel, his son was never short on female companionship.

Mia fell asleep on the ride back, and when they pulled up to the front doors to the palace, before Vanessa had a chance, Marcus unhooked her from the car seat and plucked her out.

"I can carry her," she told him.

"I've got her," he said, and not only did he carry her all the way up to the nursery, he laid her in her crib and covered her up, the way a father would if Mia had one. And somewhere deep down a part of Vanessa ached for all the experiences her daughter had missed in her short life. Because she knew what it was like to lose a parent, to miss that connection. She hoped with all her heart that Gabriel could fill the void, that these months without a father hadn't left a permanent scar on Mia.

"She was really good today," he said, grinning down at Mia while she slept soundly.

"She's a pretty easygoing baby. You saw her at her very worst yesterday."

Vanessa let Karin know to listen for Mia so she could take a quick nap herself—thinking this nanny business was sort of nice after all—then Marcus walked her down the hall to her room. She stopped at the door and turned to him. "Thank you for taking me to the village today. I actually had a really good time."

One brow lifted a fraction. "And that surprises you?"

"Yeah, it does. I figured it could go either way."

The corners of his mouth crept up into a smile and those dimples dented his cheeks. Which made her heart go pitter-patter. He was too attractive for his own good. And hers.

"Too honest for you?" she asked him.

He shrugged. "I think I'm getting used to it."

Well, that was a start.

"My father would like me to take you to the history museum tomorrow," he said.

"Oh."

One brow rose. "Oh?"

"Well, I'm still pretty exhausted from the trip and I thought a day to just lie around by the pool might be nice. Mia loves playing in the water and I desperately need a tan. Back home I just never seem to have time to catch any sun. And you don't need to feel obligated to hang out with us. I'm sure you have things you need to do."

"You're sure?"

"I am."

"Then we can see the museum another day?"

She nodded. "That would be perfect."

He started to turn, then paused and said, "Oh, I almost forgot."

He pulled the bag from the shop out of his pocket and handed it to her. "This is for you."

Perplexed, she took it from him. "What is it?"

"Look and see."

She opened the bag and peered inside, her breath catching when she recognized the contents. "But…how did you know?"

"I saw you admiring them."

He didn't miss a thing, did he?

She pulled the earrings from the bag. They were handcrafted with small emeralds set inside delicate silver swirls, and she'd fallen in love with them the instant she'd seen them in the shop, but at one hundred and fifty euros they had been way out of her budget.

"Marcus, they're lovely." She looked up at him. "I don't get it."

Hands hooked casually in his pants pockets, he shrugged. "If you had been there with my father, I don't doubt that he would have purchased them on the spot. It's what he would have wanted me to do."

She couldn't help but think that this meant something. Something significant. "I don't even know what to say. Thank you so much."

"What is it you Americans say? It's not a big deal?"

No, it was a *very* big deal.

It bothered her when Gabriel bought her things. It was as if he felt it necessary to buy her affections. But

Marcus had no reason to buy her anything, other than the fact that he *wanted* to. It came from the heart. More so than any gift Gabriel had gotten her—or at least, that was the way she saw it.

Swallowing back tears of pure happiness—unsure of why it even mattered so much to her—she smiled and said, "I should go. Gabriel will be Skyping me soon."

"Of course. I'll see you tomorrow."

She watched him walk down the hall until he disappeared around the corner, then slipped into her room and shut the door behind her. Knowing how much it meant to Gabriel, she had really been hoping that she and Marcus could be friends. And now it seemed that particular wish might actually come true.

Marcus pushed off the edge of the pool for his final lap, his arms slicing through the water, heavy with fatigue due to the extra thirty minutes he'd spent in the pool pondering his earlier conversation with Vanessa. If what she said was true, and she and his father hadn't been intimate, what else could have possibly hooked him in? Her youth, and the promise of a fresh beginning, maybe?

Marcus's mother had confided once, a long time ago, that she and his father had hoped to have a large family, but due to complications from Marcus's birth—details she'd mercifully left out—more children became an impossibility. Maybe he saw this as his chance to start the family he always wanted but could never have. Because surely someone as adept at parenting as Vanessa would want more children.

Or maybe he saw what Marcus had seen today. A

woman who was smart and funny and a little bizarre. And of course beautiful.

So much so that you had to buy her a present?

He reached the opposite end of the pool, debated stopping, then flipped over and pushed off one last time.

He really had no idea why he'd bought Vanessa the earrings. But as they were on their way back to the palace and he saw the shop, he heard himself asking the driver to stop, and before he knew what he was doing, he was inside, handing over his Visa card, and the clerk was bagging his purchase.

Maybe he and Vanessa had made some sort of...*connection*. But that wasn't even the point, because what he'd told her was true. If his father had seen her admiring the earrings he would have purchased them on the spot. Marcus did it to please his father and nothing more.

But the surprise on her face when she opened the bag and realized what was inside...

She looked so impressed and so grateful, he worried that she might burst into tears. That would have been really awful, because there was nothing worse than a woman in the throes of an emotional meltdown. And all for such a simple and inexpensive gift. If her only concern was wealth, wouldn't she have balked at anything but diamonds or precious gems? And if she were using his father, why would she admit that she wasn't in love with him? Why would she have discussed it at all?

Maybe, subconsciously, he'd seen it as some sort of test. One that she had passed with flying colors.

Marcus reached the opposite edge and hoisted himself up out of the water, slicking his hair back, annoyed that he was wasting any time debating this with himself.

He sighed and squinted at the sun, which hung close to the horizon, a reddish-orange globe against the darkening sky. The evening breeze cooled his wet skin. The fact of the matter was, though he didn't want to like Vanessa, he couldn't seem to help himself. He'd never met anyone quite like her.

From the table where he'd left it, his cell phone began to ring. Thinking it could be his father with an update about Aunt Trina, he pushed himself to his feet and grabbed the phone, but when he saw the number he cursed under his breath. He wasn't interested in anything his ex had to say, and after three weeks of avoiding her incessant phone calls and text messages, he would have expected that she'd gotten the point by now.

Apparently not. Leaving him to wonder what it was he'd seen in her in the first place. How could someone who had bewitched him so thoroughly now annoy him so completely?

Aggressive women had never really been Marcus's first choice in a potential mate. But sexy, sultry and with a body to die for, Carmela had pursued him with a determination that put other women to shame. She was everything he could have wanted in a wife, or so he believed, and because she came from a family of considerable wealth and power, he never once worried that she was after his money. Six months in he'd begun to think about engagement rings and wedding arrangements, only to discover that he'd been terribly wrong about her. And though the first week after the split had been difficult, he'd gradually begun to realize his feelings for her were based more on infatuation and lust than real love. His only explanation was that he'd been emotionally compromised by his mother's death. And the fact that she had taken advantage of that was, in his opinion, despicable. And unforgivable.

He shuddered to think what would have happened had he actually proposed, or God forbid *married* her. And he was disappointed in himself that he'd let it go as far as he had, that he'd been so blinded by her sexual prowess. And honestly, the actual sex wasn't that great. Physically, she gave him everything he could ask for and more, but emotionally their encounters had left him feeling…empty. Maybe it had been an unconscious need for a deeper connection that had kept him coming back for more, but now, looking back, he could hardly believe what a fool he'd been.

His text message alert chimed, and of course it was from her.

"Enough already," he ground out, turning on his heel and flinging his cell phone into the pool. Only when he looked up past the pool to the garden path did he realize that he had an audience.

Vanessa stood on the garden path watching Marcus's cell phone hit the surface of the water, then slowly sink down, until it was nothing but a murky shadow against the tile bottom.

"You know," she told Marcus, who clearly hadn't realized that she was standing there, "I have that same impulse nearly every day of my life. Although I usually imagine tossing it off the roof of the hotel, or under the wheels of a passing semi."

He sighed and raked a hand through his wet hair, the last remnants of evening sunshine casting a warm glow over his muscular arms and chest, his toned to perfection thighs. And though the Speedo covered the essentials, it was wet and clingy and awfully…well, revealing.

Ugh, what was she, *twelve?* It wasn't as if she hadn't seen a mostly naked man before. Or a completely naked one for that matter. Of course, none of them had been quite so…yummy.

Remember, this is your almost fiancé's son you're ogling. The thought filled her with guilt. Okay, maybe that was an exaggeration, but she did feel a mild twinge.

"That was childish of me," he said, looking as if he were disappointed in himself.

"But did it feel good?" she asked.

He hesitated, then a smile tilted the corners of his mouth. "Yeah, it did. And I needed a new one anyway."

"Then it's worth it."

"What are you doing out here?" He grabbed his towel from the table and began to dry himself. His arms, his pecs, the wall of his chest…

Oh boy. What she wouldn't give to be that towel right now.

Think son-in-law, Vanessa.

"Mia went down early, and I was feeling a little restless," she told him. "I thought I would take a walk."

"After all the walking we did today? You should be exhausted."

"I'm on my feet all day every day. Today was a cakewalk. Plus I'm trying to acclimate myself to the time change. If I go to bed too early I'll never adjust. And for the record, I am exhausted. I haven't slept well since I got here."

"Why not?" He draped the towel over the back of a chair, then took a seat, leaning casually back, with not a hint of shame. Not that he had anything to be ashamed of, and there was nothing more appealing than a man so comfortable in his own skin. Especially one who looked as good as he did.

"I keep waking up and listening for Mia, then I remember that she's down the hall. And of course I feel compelled to get up and go check on her. Then it's hard to get back to sleep. I thought a walk might relax me."

"Why don't you join me for a drink?" he said. "It might take the edge off."

She'd never been one to drink very often, and lately, with an infant in her care, she'd more or less stopped altogether. But now there was a nanny to take over if Vanessa needed her. Maybe it would be okay, just this once, to let her hair down a little.

And maybe Marcus would put some clothes on.

"Yeah, sure. I'd love one," she told him, and as if by magic, or probably ESP, the butler materialized from a set of French doors that led to…well, honestly, she wasn't sure where they led. She had gone out a side door to the garden, one patrolled by armed guards. She probably wouldn't have been able to find even that if Camille hadn't shown her the way. The palace had more twists and turns than a carnival fun house.

"What would you like?" Marcus asked.

"What do you have?"

"We have a fully stocked bar. George can make anything you desire."

She summoned a list of drinks that she used to enjoy, and told George, "How about…a vodka tonic with a twist of lime?"

George nodded, turned to Marcus, and in a voice as craggy and old as the man said, "Your highness?"

"The same for me. And could you please let Cleo

know that I'll be needing a new phone, and a new number."

George nodded and limped off, looking as if every step took a great deal of effort.

Vanessa took a seat across from Marcus and when George was out of earshot asked, "How old is he?"

"I'm really not sure. Eighties, nineties. All I know is that he's been with the family since my father was a child."

"He looks as if he has a hard time getting around."

"He has rheumatoid arthritis. And though his staff does most of the real work these days, I assure you he's still quite capable, and has no desire to retire anytime soon. Honestly, I don't think he has anywhere else to go. As far as I'm aware, he's never been married. He has no children. We're his only family."

"That's kind of sad," Vanessa said, feeling a sudden burst of sympathy for the cranky old butler. She couldn't imagine being so alone in the world. Or maybe he didn't see it that way. Maybe his career, his attachments with the royal family and the other staff, were all the fulfillment he needed.

"If you'll excuse me a moment," Marcus said, rising from his seat. "I should probably go change before I catch a chill."

She had wanted him to put clothes on, but she couldn't deny being slightly disappointed. But the blistering heat of the afternoon did seem to be evaporating with the setting sun, and a cool breeze had taken its place.

While he was gone, Vanessa slipped her sandals off and walked over to the pool. She sat on the edge, dipping her feet in water warm enough to bathe in. She'd never been much of a swimmer—or into any sort of exercise, despite how many times her father had pushed her to try different sports and activities. She had the athletic prowess of a brick, and about as much grace. And firearms being his passion, he'd tried relentlessly to get her on the firing range. He'd gone as far as to get her a hunting rifle for her fourteenth birthday, but guns scared her half to death and she'd refused to even touch it. She'd often entertained the idea that he would have been much happier with a son, and had someone offered a trade, he'd have jumped at the chance.

As the last vestiges of daylight dissolved into the horizon and the garden and pool lights switched on, Vanessa noticed the shadow of Marcus's cell phone, wondering what—or *who*—had driven him to chuck it into the water. From what Gabriel had told her, Marcus was even-tempered and composed, so whatever it was must have really upset him.

She sighed, wondering what Gabriel was doing just then. Probably sitting at the hospital, where he spent the majority of his day. Trina was still very sick, but responding to the treatment, and the doctors were cautiously optimistic that she would make a full recovery. Though Vanessa felt selfish for even thinking it, she hoped that meant Gabriel would be home soon. She wanted to get her life back on track and plan her future, because at the moment she'd never felt more unsettled or restless. And it wasn't fair to Mia to keep her living in limbo, although to be honest she seemed no worse for wear.

"Your drink," Marcus said, and the sound of his voice made her jump.

She turned to find him dressed in khaki shorts and a

pale silk, short sleeved shirt, that could have been gray or light blue. It was difficult to tell in the muted light.

"Sorry, didn't mean to startle you." He handed her one of the two glasses he was holding and sat next to her on the edge, slipping his bare feet into the water beside hers. He was so close, she could smell chlorine on his skin, and if she were to move her leg just an inch to the right, her thigh would touch his. For some reason the idea of actually doing it made her heart beat faster. Not that she ever would.

Eight

"I guess I was lost in thought," she said. "When I talked to Gabriel today he said that your aunt is responding to the treatment."

Marcus nodded, sipping his drink, then setting it on the tile beside him. "I spoke with him this afternoon. He said they're optimistic."

"I was kind of hoping that meant he would be home sooner. Which is pretty thoughtless, I know." She took a swallow of her drink and her eyes nearly crossed as it slid down her throat, instantly warming her insides. "Wow! That's strong."

"Would you care for something different?"

"No, I like it." She took another sip, but a smaller one this time. "It has kick, but the vodka is very…I don't know, smooth, I guess."

"George only stocks the best. And for the record, you're not thoughtless. I would say that you've been tremendously patient given the circumstances. Had it been me, considering my less than warm greeting, I probably would have turned around and gotten back on the plane."

"If it hadn't been for Mia, I might have. But another thirteen hours in the air would have done me in for sure."

Marcus was quiet for a minute, gazing at the water and the ripples their feet made on the surface. Then he mumbled something that sounded like a curse and shook his head.

"Is something wrong?" she asked him.

"Your proclivity toward brutal honesty must be rubbing off on me."

"What do you mean?"

"I probably shouldn't tell you this, and I would be breaking a confidence in doing so, but I feel as if you deserve the truth."

Vanessa's heart sank a little. "Why do I get the feeling I'm not going to like this?"

"My father told me that he would likely be three or four weeks. He didn't want you to know for fear that you wouldn't stay. It's why he wanted me to keep you entertained."

Her heart bottomed out. "But my visit will only be for six weeks. Which will leave us only two or three to get to know one another better."

What if that wasn't enough time?

Marcus shrugged. "So you'll stay longer."

Feeling hurt and betrayed, her nerves back on edge, Vanessa took another swallow of her drink. If Gabriel lied about this, what else was he lying about? "I can't stay longer. My leave from work is only six weeks. If I don't go back I'll get fired. Until I know for sure whether I'm staying here, I need that job. Otherwise I would have nothing to go back for. I have very little savings. Mia and I would essentially be on the streets."

"My father is a noble man," Marcus said. "Even if

you decided not to marry him, he would never allow that to happen. He would see that you were taken care of."

"If he's so noble why would he lie to me in the first place?"

"He only did it because he cares for you."

It was a moot point because she would never take his charity. And even if she would, there was no guarantee that Gabriel would be so generous.

Marcus must have read her mind, because he added, "If he didn't see that you were taken care of, *I* would."

His words stunned her. "Why? As of this afternoon, you still believed that I'm using him."

"I guess you could say that I've had a change of heart."

"But, *why?*"

His laugh was rich and warm and seemed to come from deep within him. "You perplex me, Vanessa. You tell me that I should give you a chance, but when I do, you question my motives. Perhaps it's you who needs to give *me* a chance."

She had indeed said that. "You're right. I guess I'm just feeling very out of sorts right now." She touched his arm lightly, found it to be warm and solid under her palm. "I'm sorry."

He looked at her hand resting on his forearm, then up into her eyes, and said, "Apology accepted."

There was something in their sooty depths, some emotion that made her heart flip in her chest, and suddenly she felt warm all over.

It's just the vodka, she assured herself, easing her hand away and taking a deep swallow from her glass.

"Would you care for another?" Marcus asked.

She looked down and realized that her glass was empty, while his was still more than half full.

"I probably shouldn't," she said, feeling her muscles slacken with the warm glow of inebriation. It was the most relaxed she had felt in weeks. Would one more drink be such a bad thing? In light of what she'd just learned, didn't she deserve it? With Mia in the care of her nanny, what reason did Vanessa have to stop? "But what the hell, why not? It's not as if I have to drive home, right?"

Marcus gestured randomly and George must have been watching for it—which to her was slightly creepy—because moments later he appeared with a fresh drink. And either this one wasn't as strong, or the first had numbed her to the intensity of the vodka. Whatever the reason, she drank liberally.

"So, would I be overstepping my bounds to ask why you drowned your phone?" Vanessa said.

"A persistent ex-lover."

"I take it you dumped her."

"Yes, but only after I caught her in the backseat of the limo with my best friend."

"Ouch. Were they…you know…"

"Yes. Quite enthusiastically."

She winced. So he'd lost his mother, his girlfriend and his best friend. How sucky was that? "I'm sorry."

He slowly kicked his feet back and forth through the water, the side of his left foot brushing against her right one. She had to force herself not to jump in surprise.

"Each tried to pin it on the other. She's still trying to convince me that he lured her there under false pretenses, and once he had her in the car he more or less attacked her."

She let her foot drift slightly to the left, to see if it would happen again. "She cried rape?"

"More or less."

"What did your friend say?"

"That she lured him into the car, and she made the first move."

"Who do you believe?"

"Neither of them. In the thirty seconds or so that I was standing there in shock, she never once told him no, and she wasn't making any attempt to stop him. I think all the moaning they were both doing spoke for itself."

His foot bumped hers again, and a tiny thrill shot up from her foot and through her leg, settling in places that were completely inappropriate considering their relationship.

"Were you in love with her?" Vanessa asked him.

"I thought I was, but I realize now it was just lust."

"Sometimes it's hard to tell the two apart."

"Is that how it is with you and my father?"

What she felt for Gabriel was definitely not lust. "Not at all. Gabriel is a good friend, and I love and respect him for that. It's the lust part we need to work on."

Her candor seemed to surprise him. "And he knows you feel that way?"

"I've been completely honest with him. He's convinced that my feelings for him will grow. And I'm hoping he's right."

His foot brushed hers again, and this time she could swear it was intentional. Was he honestly playing footsies with her? And why was her heart beating so fast, her skin tingling with awareness? And why was she mentally willing him to touch her in other places too, but with his hands?

Because there is something seriously wrong with you, honey. But knowing that didn't stop her from leaning back on her arms and casually shifting her leg so her thigh brushed his.

Now this, what she was feeling right now, *this* was lust. And it was so wrong.

"I learned last week that her father's company is in financial crisis and on the verge of collapse," Marcus said, and it took Vanessa a second to realize that he was talking about his ex. "I guess she thought that an alliance with the royal family would have pulled him from the inevitable depths of bankruptcy."

"So you think she was using you?"

"It seems a safe assumption."

Well, that at least explained why he was so distrustful of Vanessa. He obviously looked at her and saw his ex. She shook her head in disgust and said, "What a bitch."

Marcus's eyes widened, and Vanessa slapped a hand across her mouth. Why couldn't she learn to hold her tongue? "Sorry, that was totally inappropriate of me."

Instead of looking angry, or put out, Marcus just laughed.

"No, it was more appropriate than you would imagine. And unfortunately she wasn't the first. But usually I'm better at spotting it. I think my mother's death left such a gaping hole, and I was so desperate to fill it I had blinders on."

"You want to hear something ironic? In my junior year of high school, I caught my boyfriend in the back of his car with my so-called friend."

His brow lifted. "Was it a limo?"

She laughed. "Hardly. It was piece of crap SUV."

"What did you do when you caught them?"

"Threw a brick through the back window."

He laughed. "Maybe that's what I should have done."

"I was really mad. I had just written his history term paper for him, and he got an A. I found out later from one of my 'friends' that he'd only dated me because I was smart, and in most of the same classes and willing to help him with his homework. I was stupid enough to do it for him. And let him copy off my tests. He played football, and if his grades dropped he would be kicked off the team. Pretty much everyone knew he was using me."

"And no one told you?"

"Suffice it to say they weren't my friends after that. My dad was reassigned a month later. It was one of the few times I was really relieved to be starting over."

"I hope you at least reported him to the headmaster," Marcus said.

"You have no idea how badly I wanted to go to our teachers and the principal and tell them what I'd been doing, that his work was really my work. Not only could I have gotten him kicked off the team, he would have been expelled."

"Why didn't you?"

"Because I would have been expelled too. And my father would have *killed* me. Not to mention that it was completely embarrassing. I should have known, with his reputation, he would never seriously date a girl who didn't put out unless he was after something else. Not that he didn't try to get in my pants every chance he got."

"You shouldn't blame yourself. You have a trusting nature. That's a good thing."

Not always. "Unfortunately, I seem to attract untrustworthy men. It's as if I have the word *gullible* stamped in invisible ink on my forehead, and only jerks can see it."

"Not all men use women."

"All the men I've known do."

"Surely not everyone has been that bad."

"Trust me, if there was a record for the world's worst luck with men, I would hold it. When Mia's dad walked out on me, I swore I would never let a man use me again. That I would never trust so blindly. But then I met Gabriel and he's just so…wonderful. And he treated me as if I were something special."

"That's because he thinks you are. From the minute he returned home he couldn't stop talking about you." He laid a hand on her arm, gave it a gentle squeeze, his dark eyes soft with compassion. "He's not using you, Vanessa."

Weird, but yesterday he was convinced she was using his father. When had everything gotten so turned around?

And why, as they had a heart-to-heart talk about his father—one that should have drawn her closer to Gabriel—could she only think about Marcus? Why did she keep imagining what it would be like to lay her hand on his muscular thigh, feel the crisp dark hair against her palm? Why did she keep looking at his mouth, and wondering how it would feel pressed against hers?

Maybe they both would have been better off if he kept acting like a jerk, because it was becoming painfully clear that Vanessa had developed a major crush. On the wrong man.

* * *

"Do you think someone can fall in love, real love, in a matter of two weeks?" Vanessa asked Marcus.

He could tell her that he believed falling in love so fast was nothing but a fairy tale, and that he thought his father was rebounding. What he felt for Vanessa was infatuation and nothing more, and he would realize that when he returned from Italy. Marcus knew if he told Vanessa that, she was confused and vulnerable enough that she might actually believe him. Which would discourage her, and fill her with self-doubt, and might ultimately make her leave. And wasn't that what he'd wanted?

But now, he couldn't make himself say the words. Something had changed. He was instead telling her things that would make her want to stay, and for reasons that had nothing to do with his father's happiness, and everything to do with Marcus's fascination with her. She wasn't helping matters by encouraging him, by moving closer when he touched her, looking up at him with those expressive blue eyes. And did she have to smell so good? Most of the women he knew bathed themselves in cloying perfume, Carmela included, but Vanessa smelled of soap and shampoo. And he could smell that only because they were sitting so close to one another. *Too* close. If he had any hope of fighting these inappropriate feelings, he really needed to back off.

"I believe that when it comes to love, anything is possible," he told her, which wasn't a lie exactly. He just didn't believe it in this case. And the idea that she might be hurt again disturbed him more than he could have ever imagined possible. Maybe because he knew it was inevitable. He just hoped that when his father let her down, he did it gently. Or maybe after waiting for his father for so many weeks, she would grow frustrated and decide she didn't want to stay after all.

Now that Marcus had gotten to know her better, he wasn't any more sure of what to expect. He'd never met a woman more confusing or unpredictable. Yet in a strange way, he felt he could relate to her—understand her even—which made no sense at all.

But what baffled him most was how wrong he'd been about her, when he was so sure he'd had her pegged. He hadn't given his father nearly enough credit, had just assumed he was too vulnerable to make intelligent choices, and for that Marcus would always feel foolish.

George appeared at his side with two fresh drinks. Marcus took them and held one out to Vanessa. She looked in the glass she was still holding as if she were surprised to realize that it was empty.

"Oh, I really shouldn't," she said, but as he moved to give it back to George, added, "But it would be a shame to let the good stuff go to waste. No more after this though."

George shuffled off with their empty glasses, shaking his head in either amusement or exasperation, Marcus couldn't be sure which. None of the staff were sure what to think of her, and that was in large part Marcus's fault, as he'd made his feelings about her visit quite clear from the moment his father had broken the news. Now he knew that he'd unfairly judged her, and that was something he needed to rectify.

"Your dad said that when he met your mom it was love at first sight," she said. "And it was a big scandal because she wasn't a royal."

"Yes, my grandparents were very traditional. There

was already a marriage arranged for him but he loved my mother. They threatened to disown him. He said it was the only time in his life that he rebelled against their wishes."

"That must have been difficult for your mom. To know that they hated her so much they would disown their own child."

"It wasn't her so much as the idea of her that they resented, but things improved after I was born. My father was an only child, so they were happy that she'd given my father a male heir."

"So your father wouldn't mind if you married a non-royal?"

"My parents have been very insistent my entire life that as sole heir it's imperative I also produce an heir, but they want me to marry for love."

"Like they did."

He nodded.

"What was your mom like?" she asked.

Just thinking of her brought a smile to his face. "Beautiful, loyal, outspoken—more so than some people thought a queen should be. She grew up in a middle-class family in Italy, so she had a deep respect for the common man. You actually remind me of her in a way."

She blinked in surprise. "*I* do?"

"She was brave and smart, and she wasn't afraid to speak her mind. Even if it got her into trouble sometimes. And she was a positive role model to young women."

"Brave?" she said, looking at him as though he'd completely lost his mind. "I'm constantly terrified that I'm doing the wrong thing, or making the wrong choice."

"But that doesn't stop you from *making* the choice, and that takes courage."

"Maybe, but I fail to see how I'm a role model to women. My life has been one bad move after another."

How could she not see it, not be proud of her accomplishments? "You're well traveled, intelligent, successful. You're an excellent mother, raising a child with no help. What young woman wouldn't look up to you?"

She bit her lip, and for a second he thought she might start crying. "That's probably the nicest thing anyone has ever said to me. Though I'm pretty sure that I don't deserve it. I'm a gigantic walking disaster waiting to happen."

"That's your father talking," he said.

"In part. But I can't deny that I've made some really dumb decisions in my life."

"Everybody does. How will you learn if you don't make occasional mistakes?"

"The problem is, I don't seem to be learning from mine."

Why couldn't she see what he did? Was she really so beaten down by her father's overinflated ideals that she had no self-confidence left? And what could he do to make her believe otherwise? How could he make her see how gifted and special and unique she really was? "You don't give yourself enough credit. If you weren't an extraordinary person, do you really think my father would have fallen so hard for you so fast?"

Nine

Their eyes met and Vanessa's were so filled with hope and vulnerability, Marcus had to resist the urge to pull her into his arms and hold her. His gaze dropped to her mouth, and her lips looked so plump and soft, he couldn't help but wonder how they would feel, how they would taste.

The sudden pull of lust in his groin caught him completely off guard, but he couldn't seem to look away.

Carmela and most other women he'd dated favored fitted, low-cut blouses and skintight jeans. They dressed to draw attention. In shorts and a T-shirt and with no makeup on her face, her pale hair cascading down in loose waves across her shoulders, Vanessa didn't look particularly sexy. Other than being exceptionally beautiful, she looked quite ordinary, yet he couldn't seem to keep his eyes off her.

Vanessa was the one to turn her head, but not before he saw a flash of guilt in her eyes, and he knew, whatever these improper feeling were, she was having them too.

Vanessa rubbed her arms. "It's getting chilly, huh?"

"Would you like to go inside?" he asked.

She shook her head, gazing up at the night sky. "Not yet."

"I could have George bring us something warm to drink."

"No, thank you."

They were both quiet for several minutes, but there was a question that had been nagging him since their conversation this afternoon in the park. "You said that you were afraid two or three weeks wouldn't be long enough to get to know my father better. I'm wondering, what guarantee did you have that four weeks would be? Or six?"

She shrugged. "There was no guarantee. But I had to at least try. For him. And for Mia."

"What about you?"

"For me, too," she said, avoiding his gaze.

Why did he get the feeling her own needs were pretty low on the priority scale? The way he saw it, either you were physically attracted to someone or you weren't. There was no gray area. And it seemed a bit selfish of his father to push her into something she clearly was unsure about.

She took a swallow of her drink, then blinked rapidly, setting her glass on the tile beside her. "You know, I think I've had enough. I feel a little woozy. And it's getting late. I should check on Mia."

It was odd, but although he'd had no intention of spending the evening with her, now he wasn't ready for it to end. All the more reason that it should. "Shall I walk you back to your room?"

"You might have to. I'm honestly not sure I could find it by myself."

"Tomorrow I'll have Cleo print a map for you."

Two days ago it wouldn't have mattered to him, now he wanted her to feel comfortable in the palace. It was the least he could do.

He set his drink down and pulled himself to his feet, the night air cool against his wet skin, and extended a hand to help her. It felt so small and fragile, and it was a good thing he was holding on, because as he pulled her to her feet, she was so off balance she probably would have fallen into the pool.

"Are you okay?" he asked, pulling her away from the edge.

"Yeah." She blinked several times then gave her head a shake, as if to clear it, clutching his hand in a death grip. "Maybe I shouldn't have had that last drink."

"Would you like to sit back down?"

She took several seconds to get her bearings, then said, "I think I should probably just get to bed."

His first thought, depraved as it was, was "Why don't I join you." But, while he could think it, and perhaps even wish it a little, it was something he would never say out loud. And even more important, never do.

Could this be more embarrassing?

Feeling like an idiot, Vanessa clung to Marcus's arm as he led her across the patio. So much for letting her hair down a little.

"On top of everything else, now you probably think I have a drinking problem," she said.

Marcus grinned, his dimples forming dents in both cheeks, and she felt that delicious little zing. Did he have to be so…*adorable?*

"Maybe if you'd had ten drinks," he said, stopping by the table so she could grab her phone and they could both slip into their sandals. "But you only had three, and you didn't even finish the last one. I'm betting it has more to do with the jet lag."

"Jet lag can do that?"

"Sure. So can fatigue. Are you certain you can make it upstairs? I could carry you."

Yeah, because that wouldn't be completely humiliating. Besides, she liked holding on to his arm. And she couldn't help wondering what it would be like to touch him in other places. Not that she would ever try. She probably wouldn't be feeling this way at all if it weren't for the alcohol.

Well, okay, she probably would, but never in a million years would she act on it. Even though he thought she was smart and brave and successful. Plus, he'd left out beautiful. That was usually the first, and sometimes the only thing, that people noticed about her. Gabriel must have told her a million times. Remarkably, Marcus seemed to see past that.

"I think I can manage," she told him.

Clutching her cell phone in one hand and his forearm in the other, she wobbled slightly as he led her across the patio, but as they reached the French doors, she stopped. "Could we possibly walk around the side, through the garden?"

"What for?"

She chewed her lip, feeling like an irresponsible adolescent, which is probably how everyone else in the palace would see her as well. "I'm too embarrassed to have anyone see me this way. The entire staff already thinks I'm a horrible person. Now they're going to think I'm a lush, too."

"What does it matter what they think?"

"Please," she said, tugging him toward the garden path. "I feel so stupid."

"You shouldn't. But if it means that much to you, we'll go in the side entrance."

"Thank you."

Actually, now that she was on her feet, she felt steadier, but she kept holding on to his arm anyway. Just in case. Or just because it felt nice. He was tall and sturdy and reliable. And warm. He made her feel safe. She tried to recall if any man had made her feel that way before and drew a blank. Surely there must have been someone.

They headed down the path, around the back of the palace to the east side. At least, she was pretty sure it was east, or maybe it was west. Or north. Suddenly she felt all turned around. But whichever way it was, she remembered it from earlier, even though it was a lot darker now, despite the solar lights lining the path.

They were halfway around the building when Vanessa heard a sound on the flagstones behind them and wondered fleetingly if they were being followed. Being an L.A. resident, her first instinct was to immediately whip out her phone in case she needed to dial 911, which was how she realized her cell phone was no longer in her hand. The noise must have been her phone falling onto the path.

She let go of Marcus's arm and stopped, squinting to see in the dim light.

"What's wrong," he asked. "Are you going to be sick?"

She huffed indignantly. "I'm not *that* drunk. I dropped my phone."

"Where?"

"A few feet back, I think. I heard it hit the ground."

They backtracked, scouring the ground for several minutes, but it wasn't on or even near the path.

"Maybe it bounced into the flower bed," she said, crouching down to peer into the dense foliage, nearly falling on her butt in the process.

Marcus shook his head, looking grim. "If it did, we'll never find it at night."

"Call it!" Vanessa said, feeling rather impressed with herself for having such a brilliant idea in her compromised condition. "When we hear it ring, we'll know where it is."

"Right," he said hooking a thumb in the direction of the pool. "I'll go fish my phone out of the water and do that."

"Oh yeah, I forgot about that. Can't you borrow one?"

"Or we could look for your phone tomorrow."

"No!" Maybe he could blithely toss his electronic equipment away, but she worked for a living. Nor did she have a secretary to keep track of her life. "Besides the fact that it cost me a fortune, that phone is my life. It has my schedule and all my contacts and my music. What if it rains, or an animal gets it or something?"

He sighed loudly. "Wait here and I'll go get a phone."

She frowned. "By myself, in the dark?"

"I assure you the grounds are highly guarded and completely safe."

"What about that certain criminal element who would love to ransom the future queen?"

He smiled sheepishly. "Maybe that was a slight exaggeration. You'll be fine."

She'd expected as much. He'd been trying to drive her away, to make her *want* to leave. And as much as it annoyed her, she couldn't hold it against him. Not after all the nice things he'd said about her. Which she supposed was a big part of her problem. Someone said something nice about her and she went all gooey.

"You should stay in the general vicinity of where you lost it," Marcus warned her. "Or this could take all night."

"I'll stay right here," she said, flopping down on the path cross-legged to wait, the flagstone still warm from the afternoon sun.

Marcus grinned and shook his head. She watched as he backtracked from where they'd come, until he disappeared around a line of shrubs.

She sat there very still, listening to sounds of the night—crickets chirping and a mild breeze rustling the trees. And she swore, if she listened really hard, she could hear the faint hiss of the ocean, that if she breathed deep enough, she could smell the salty air. Or maybe it was just her imagination. Of all the different places her father had been stationed over the years, her favorite bases had been the ones near the water. And while she loved living close to the sea, the coast of California was exorbitantly expensive. Maybe someday. Maybe even here. The palace wasn't right on the water, but it was pretty darn close.

After a few minutes of waiting, her butt started to get sore, so she scooted off the flagstone path into the cool, prickly grass. Falling backward onto the spongy sod, she looked up at the sky. It was a crystal-clear night with a half moon, and even with the lights around the grounds, she could see about a million stars. In L.A. the only way to see the stars was to drive up to the mountains. She and Mia's dad used to do that. They would camp out in the bed of his truck, alternating between making love and watching the stars. She couldn't be sure, but she suspected that Mia may have actually been conceived in the bed of that truck. An unusual place to get pregnant, but nothing about her relationship with Paul had been typical. She used to think that was a good thing, and one of their strengths, because God knew those "normal" relationships she'd had were all a disaster. Until she came home to find a "Dear Vanessa" letter and realized she was wrong. Again. He hadn't even had the guts to tell her to her face that he wasn't ready for the responsibility of a child, and they were both better off without him.

So normal was bad, and eccentric was bad, which didn't leave much else. But royal, that was one she'd never tried, and never expected to have a chance to. Yet here she was. Lying on the palace lawn on a cool summer night under a sky cloaked with stars.

Which she had to admit wasn't very royal of her. She wondered if Gabriel's wife, or even Gabriel, had ever sprawled out on the grass and gazed up at the sky. Or skipped in the rain, catching drops on their tongues. Or snowflakes. Had Gabriel and Marcus ever bundled up and built a snowman together? Had they given it coal eyes and a carrot nose? Had they made snow angels or had snowball fights? And would she really be happy married to someone who didn't know how to relax and have fun, do something silly? Would Mia miss out on an important part of her childhood? Because *everyone* had to be silly every now and then.

Or was she worrying for nothing? Suffering from a typical case of insecurity? Was she creating problems where none really existed? Was she trying to sabotage a good thing because she was too afraid to take a chance?

So much for her being brave, huh?

She pondered that for a while, until she heard footsteps on the path, and glanced over to see Marcus walking toward her, looking puzzled. He stopped beside her, hands on his slim hips, and looked down. “You okay?”

She smiled and nodded. “It’s a beautiful night. I’m looking at the stars.”

He looked up at the sky, then back down at her. “Are you sure you didn’t fall down?”

She swatted at him, but he darted out of the way, grinning.

“Could you join me?” she said. “Unless you’re not allowed.”

“Why wouldn’t I be?”

“I thought maybe it wasn’t royal enough.”

“You know, you’re not making a whole lot of sense.”

“Do I ever?”

He laughed. “Good point.”

And that apparently didn’t matter, because he lay down beside her in the grass, so close their arms were touching. And she liked the way it felt. *A lot.* She liked being close to him, liked the warm fuzzy feeling coupled with that zing of awareness, and that urge to reach over and lace her fingers through his. It was exciting, and scary.

But of course she wouldn’t do it, because even she wasn’t that brave.

“You’re right,” he said, gazing up at the sky. “It is beautiful.”

She looked over at him. “You think I’m weird, don’t you.”

"Not weird, exactly, but I can safely say that I've never met anyone like you."

"I don't know if I'm royalty material. I don't think I could give this up."

"Lying in the grass?"

She nodded.

"Who said you have to?"

"I guess I just don't know what's acceptable, and what isn't. I mean, if I marry Gabriel can I still build snowmen?"

"I don't see why not."

"Can I catch rain and snowflakes on my tongue?"

"You could try, I suppose."

"Can I walk in the sand in my bare feet, and make mud pies with Mia?"

"You know, we royals aren't so stuffy and uptight that we don't know how to have fun. We're just people. We lead relatively normal lives outside of the public eye."

But normal for him, and normal for her, were two very different things. "This all happened so abruptly. I guess I just don't know what to expect."

Marcus looked over at her. "You know that if you marry my father, you'll still be the same person you are right now. There's no magic potion or incantation that suddenly makes you royal. And there are no set rules." He paused then added, "Okay, I guess there are some rules. Certain protocol we have to follow. But you'll learn."

And Gabriel should have been the one explaining that to her, not Marcus. It was Gabriel she should have been getting to know, Gabriel she needed to bond with. Instead she was bonding with Marcus, and in a big way.

She could feel it. She was comfortable with him, felt as if she could really be herself. Maybe because she wasn't worried about impressing him. Or maybe she was connecting in a small way. The truth was, everything had gotten so jumbled and confused, she wasn't sure how she felt about anything right now. And she was sure the drinks weren't helping.

Everything will be clearer tomorrow, she told herself. She would talk to Gabriel again, and remember how much she cared about him and missed him, and everything would go back to normal. She and Marcus would be friends, and she would stop having these irrational feelings.

"I've been thinking," Marcus said. "You should call your father and tell him where you are."

His suggestion—the fact that he'd even thought it—puzzled her. "So he can tell me that I'm making another stupid mistake? Why would I do that?"

"*Are* you making a mistake?"

If only she could answer that question, if she could hop a time machine and flash forward a year or so in the future, she would know how this would all play out. But that would be too easy. "I guess I won't know for sure until things go south."

He exhaled an exasperated sigh. "Okay, do you *think* you're making a mistake? Would you be here if you were sure this was going to end in disaster?"

She considered that, then said, "No, *I* don't think I'm making a mistake, because even if it doesn't work out, I got to visit a country I've never been to, and meet new people and experience new things. I got to stay in a palace and meet a prince. Even if he was kind of a doofus at first."

He smiled. "Then it doesn't matter what your father thinks. And I think that keeping this from him only makes it seem as though you have something to hide. If you really want him to respect you, and have confidence in your decisions, you've got to have faith in yourself first."

"Wow. That was incredibly insightful." And he was right. "You're speaking from experience, I assume."

"I'm the future leader of this country. It's vital I convey to the citizens that I'm confident in my abilities. It's the only way they'll trust me to lead them."

"Are you confident in your abilities?"

"Most of the time. There are days when the thought of that much responsibility scares the hell out of me. But part of being an effective leader means learning to delegate." He looked at her and grinned. "And always having someone else to pin the blame on when you screw up."

He was obviously joking, and his smile was such an adorable one, it made her want to reach out and touch his cheek. "You know, you have a really nice smile. You should do it more often."

He looked up at the stars. "I think this is probably the most I've smiled since we lost my mother."

"Really?"

"Life has been pretty dull since she died. She made everything fun and interesting. I guess that's another way that you remind me of her."

The warm fuzzy feeling his words gave her were swiftly replaced by an unsettling thought. If she was so much like Marcus's mom, could that be the reason Gabriel was so drawn to her? Did he see her as some sort of replacement for the original?

Second best?

That was silly. Of course he didn't.

And if it was so silly, why did she have a sudden sick, hollow feeling in the pit of her stomach?

Ten

Remember what you told Marcus, Vanessa reminded herself. *Even if this doesn't work out, it's not a mistake.* The thought actually made her feel a tiny bit better.

"Oh, by the way..." Marcus pulled a cell phone from his shorts pocket. "What's your number?"

She'd actually forgotten all about her phone. She told him the number and he dialed, and she felt it begin to rumble...in the front pocket of her shorts! "What the—"

She pulled it out, staring dumbfounded, and Marcus started to laugh. "But...I heard it fall."

"Whatever you heard, it obviously wasn't your phone."

"Oh, geez. I'm sorry."

"It's okay." He pushed himself to his feet and extended a hand to help her up. "Why don't we get you upstairs."

As stupid as she felt right now, she was having such a nice time talking to him that she hated to actually go to her room. But it was late, and he probably had more important things to do than to entertain her in the short amount of evening that remained. He'd already sacrificed most of his day for her.

She took his hand and he hiked her up, but as he

pulled her to her feet her phone slipped from her hand and this time she actually did drop it. It landed in the grass between them. She and Marcus bent to pick it up at the exact same time, their heads colliding in the process. Hard.

They muttered a simultaneous "Ow."

She straightened and reached up to touch the impact point just above her left eye, wincing when her fingers brushed a tender spot. Great, now she could look forward to a hangover *and* a concussion. Could she make an even bigger ass of herself?

"You're hurt," he said, looking worried, which made her feel even stupider.

"I'm fine. It's just a little tender."

"Let me see," he insisted, gently cradling her cheek in his palm, turning her toward the light for a better look. With his other hand he brushed her hair aside, his fingertips grazing her forehead.

Her heart fell to the pit of her stomach, then lunged upward into her throat. *Oh my god.* If her legs had been a little wobbly before, her senses slightly compromised, that was *nothing* compared to the head-to-toe, limb-weakening, mind-altering, knock-me-off-my-feet rush of sensation she was experiencing now. His face was so close she could feel his breath whisper across her cheek, and the urge to reach up and run her hand across his stubbled chin was almost irresistible.

Her breath caught and she got a funny feeling in the pit of her stomach. Then his eyes dropped to hers and what she saw in them made her knees go weak.

He wanted her. *Really* wanted her.

Don't do it, Vanessa. Don't even think *about it.*

"Does it hurt?" he asked, but it came out as a raspy whisper.

The only thing hurting right now—other than her bruised pride—was her heart, for what she knew was about to happen. For the betrayal she would feel when she talked to Gabriel tomorrow. But even that wasn't enough to jar her back to reality. She invited the kiss, begged for it even, lifted her chin as he dipped his head, and when his lips brushed hers…

Perfection.

It was the kind of first kiss every girl dreamed of. Indescribable really. Every silly cliché and romantic platitude all rolled in one. And even though it had probably been inevitable, they simply could not let it happen again. To let it happen at all had been…well, there was no justification for it. To say it was a mistake was putting it mildly. But the problem was, it didn't *feel* like a mistake. She felt a bit as though this was the first smart thing, the first *right* thing, she had done in years.

Which is probably why she was *still* kissing him. Why her arms were around his neck, her fingers curled into his hair. And why she would have kept on kissing him if Marcus hadn't backed away and said, "I can't believe I just did that."

Which made her feel even worse.

She pressed a hand to her tingling lips. They were still damp, still tasted like him. Her heart was still pounding, her knees weak. He'd *wrecked* her.

Marcus looked sick with guilt. Very much, she imagined, how she probably looked. She had betrayed Gabriel. With his own *son*. What kind of depraved person was she?

A slap to the face couldn't have sobered her faster.

"It's not your fault. I let you," she said.

"Why did you?" he asked, and she could see in his eyes that he wanted some sort of answer as to why this was happening, why they were feeling this way.

"Because..." she began, then paused. She could diffuse the situation. She could tell him that she was just lonely, or he reminded her so much of Gabriel that she was confused. But it felt wrong to lie, and there was only one honest answer to give him. "Because I wanted you to."

He took a second to process that, looking as though he couldn't decide if it was a good or a bad thing, if he should feel relieved that it wasn't all his fault, or even more guilty. "If it was something I did—"

"It wasn't!" she assured him. "I mean, it was, but it was me too. It was both of us. We're obviously just, confused, or...*something.* And it would probably be best if we don't analyze it to death. I mean, what would be the point? It doesn't matter why we did it. We know that we shouldn't have, and even more important, we know that it can't happen again. Right?"

"Right."

"So that's that?"

He was quiet for several long seconds and she waited for his confirmation, because they really needed to put an end to this now.

But instead of agreeing with her, Marcus shook his head and said, "Maybe not."

Though it seemed impossible that a heart could both sink and lift at the same time, hers managed it. "Why not?"

"Because maybe if we figure out why we did it, I'll stop feeling like I want to do it again."

* * *

Marcus watched Vanessa struggle for what to say next, feeling a bit as though he were caught up in some racy evening television drama. This sort of thing didn't happen in real life. Not in civilized society anyway. Men did not have affairs with their fathers' female companions, and that was exactly what he thinking of doing.

What was *wrong* with him?

She'd admitted that she was not *in* love with his father, nor was she physically attracted to him. And Marcus truly believed they would never marry. But until Vanessa's relationship with his father was completely over, he had no right to lay a finger on her. Even then a relationship with her could potentially come between him and his father.

Not that he even *wanted* a relationship. After Carmela, he had vowed to practice the single life for a while. Like his father he was probably just rebounding, and this strange fascination was probably fleeting. He would be wise to remember that.

Like father, like son, right?

"Marcus—"

"No, you're right," he interrupted. "This was a mistake. I promise it won't happen again."

"Okay," she said, but he couldn't tell if she was relieved, or disappointed. Or if she even believed him. He wasn't sure if he believed himself.

They walked in silence up to her room, and she must have sobered up, because she was steadier now. When they reached her door she turned to him.

"I had a really good time tonight. I enjoyed our talk."

"So did I."

"And...well, thank you."

He wasn't quite sure what she was thanking him for, but he nodded anyway.

Without a backward glance, she stepped into her room and closed the door, and for a full minute Marcus just stood there, plagued with the sensation that nothing had been resolved, feeling the overpowering urge to knock on her door. The only problem was, he had no idea what he wanted to say to her.

That should have been the end of it, but something wasn't right. He just couldn't put his finger on what.

You're losing your mind, he thought with a bitter laugh, then he turned and walked down the hall. He pulled out the cell phone from his pocket, with the private number that not even Cleo knew about, and tapped on the outgoing calls icon. Vanessa's number popped up. Though he wasn't sure why he did it, he programmed the number into his address book, then stuck the phone back in his pocket.

Tomorrow would be better, he assured himself. Considering how stressful the past few months had been, and the fact that he'd been sleeping—on a good night—four or five restless hours, it was no wonder he wasn't thinking clearly. His physician had offered a prescription for sleeping pills, but Marcus was against taking medication unless absolutely necessary. The meditation that Cleo had suggested hadn't helped much either. There were times, especially in the evening, when he felt a bit as if he were walking around in a fog.

Tonight I'll sleep, he told himself, then things would be clearer in the morning. Instead, he laid in bed, tossing and turning, unable to keep his mind off Vanessa and the kiss that never should have happened. He drifted in and out of sleep, his dreams filled with hazy images that made no sense, but left him feeling edgy and restless.

Marcus dragged himself out of bed at 6 a.m. with thoughts and feelings just as jumbled as the day before. He showered, dressed and had breakfast, then he tried to concentrate on work for a while, but his mind kept wandering back to Vanessa and Mia. George had informed him that they went down to use the pool around eleven, and though he found himself wanting to join them, he knew it was a bad idea. Thinking that it might help to get away for the afternoon, he called a few acquaintances to see if anyone was free for lunch, but everyone was either busy or didn't answer their phone. Instead he ate his lunch from a tray in his suite while he read the newspaper, but after he was finished he went right back to feeling restless.

"Laps," he said to himself. Swimming laps always relieved stress. He didn't even know for sure that Vanessa was still down there. It was past one-thirty, so wouldn't Mia be due for a nap? Besides, maybe it was best to confront these feelings head-on, prove to himself that he was strong enough to resist this.

He dressed in his swimsuit, pulled on a shirt and headed down to the pool. He stepped out into the blistering afternoon heat to find that Vanessa was still there, in the water, her hair pulled back in a ponytail, not a stitch of makeup on her face. In that instant the emptiness melted away, replaced by a longing, a desire to be close to her that made it difficult to breathe. And all he could think was, *Marcus, you are in big trouble.*

Vanessa carried Mia around the shallow end of the pool, swishing her back and forth while Mia plunged

her little fists into the water, giggling and squealing, delighting in the fact that she was splashing them both in the face. After what had turned out to be a long and restless night, all Vanessa really wanted to do was collapse in a lounge chair and doze the afternoon away. Thinking, of course, about anything but last night's kiss. Which she could do if she called Karin, but Mia was having so much fun, Vanessa hated to take her out of the water.

Deep down she knew it was a good thing that Marcus had decided not to join them today. Still, she couldn't deny the jerk of disappointment every time she looked over at the door and he didn't come through it. Maybe, like her, he just needed a day or two to cool down. Or maybe it had nothing to do with that, and he just had more important things to do. Either way, by lunchtime she had resigned herself to the fact that he wasn't going to show. Of course that still hadn't stopped her from looking over at the door every five minutes, just in case.

"I guess today we're on our own," she told Mia.

"You two look like you're having fun."

Vanessa nearly jumped out of her skin at the unexpected voice, and whipped around to see Marcus walking toward the pool, wearing nothing but a shirt and a little black Speedo.

Holy cow.

Her heart plunged to her knees, then shot back up into her throat, and she snapped her mouth shut before her jaw had a chance to drop open. Did the man not own a pair of swim trunks? The baggy variety that hung to the knee?

"Hi there!" she said, hoping she came across as friendly, without sounding too enthusiastic. Mia, on the other hand, heard his voice and practically dislocated her neck trying to turn and see him, and when she got a glimpse of him she let out a screech and batted at the water excitedly.

Marcus sat on the edge of the pool, dipping his feet in the water, putting his crotch exactly at eye level, and with his knees slightly spread, it was difficult not to stare.

"It's a hot one," he said, shading his eyes to look up at the clear blue sky.

It certainly was, and she wasn't referring to the weather. Maybe wishing he were in the pool with them had been a bad idea. Her gaze wandered to his mouth, which of course made her think about that kiss last night, and what they might have done if they kept kissing. If she invited him into her room.

Disaster, that's what would have happened. As it stood, the damage they had done wasn't irreparable. She could write it off as a serious lapse in judgment. Another kiss, and that may have been no longer the case.

Mia on the other hand had no shame. She practically jumped out of Vanessa's arms trying to reach him.

Vanessa laughed. "I think she wants you to come in."

He pushed off the edge and slid into the water, looking even better wet. But on the bright side, she didn't have to look at as much of him.

Mia reached for him and Marcus asked, "May I?"

"Of course," she said, handing Mia over.

He held her tightly to his bare chest, as if he were afraid he might drop her, and all Vanessa could think was, *you lucky kid.* But Mia wiggled in Marcus's arms, trying to get closer to the water.

"If you turn her around and hook your arm across

her belly she can play in the water," Vanessa told Marcus, and the second he turned her, she began to splash and squeal.

"It's okay if the water gets in her eyes?" he asked, looking concerned.

"Are you kidding, she loves it. She does the same thing in the bathtub. You wouldn't believe the mess she makes. When she's all soapy it's a lot like trying to bathe a squid."

"She's pretty slippery without the soap too," Marcus said, but he was grinning.

"If you want to put her in her floating ring she likes to be pulled around the pool. The faster the better." Vanessa grabbed the ring from the side and Mia shrieked.

Marcus laughed. "Let's give it a try."

Vanessa held the ring still while Marcus maneuvered her inside, which, with all of her squirming, was a bit like wrestling a baby octopus. When she was securely seated, he tugged her across the pool, swimming backward into the deeper water, then he spun her in circles and Mia giggled and swung her arms, beside herself with joy. It warmed her heart, but also broke it a little, to see Mia so attached to him.

She backed up against the edge of the pool and just watched them.

"She really does like this," Marcus said, looking as if he was having just as much fun.

"She loves being in the water. I wish I had more time to take her swimming, but our complex back home doesn't have a pool. I could take her to the hotel, but if I dare show my face on my day off, I inevitably get wrangled into working."

"Maybe she'll be a champion swimmer someday," Marcus said.

"Gabriel told me you used to compete."

"I was working toward a spot on the Olympic team, which meant intense training. I swam at least fifteen to twenty thousand meters a day, plus weight training and jogging."

"Wow, that is intense."

"Yeah, and it began to interfere with my royal duties, so I had to give it up. Now it's just a good way to stay in shape."

It certainly was, she thought, admiring all the lean muscle in his arms and shoulders. "It's sad that you weren't able to follow your dream."

"I was disappointed, but not devastated. My life was just meant for different things."

"It must have been really amazing growing up with all this," she said, looking up at the palace.

"Well, it didn't suck," Marcus said with a grin, all dimples and white teeth.

Vanessa laughed. Sometimes it was easy to forget that he was a future king. He just seemed so…ordinary. Gabriel, though just as approachable, had a more serious and formal manner. His confidence, his sense of self-worth, had been intoxicating, and a little thrilling. Even if he had doubts about his abilities as king he would never admit them. And though Marcus possessed that same air of conviction, he wasn't afraid or ashamed to show vulnerability, and there was something unbelievably sexy about that. Especially for a woman like her, who was constantly second-guessing herself.

"The truth is, I was away at boarding school for the

better part of my childhood," Marcus said. "But I did come home for school breaks and summer vacations."

"I'm not sure if I could do that," Vanessa said.

"Go to boarding school?"

"Send my child away to be raised by someone else. It would break my heart."

"In my family it's just what was expected, I guess. It was the same for my father, and his father before him."

"But not your mother, right? She didn't mind letting you go?"

"I know she missed me, but as I said, that's just the way things were. She had her duties as queen, and I had mine."

Vanessa had a sudden heart-wrenching thought. "If I marry your father, would I have to send Mia away to boarding school?"

For several seconds he looked as if he wasn't sure how to answer, or if she could handle the truth.

"I can only assume that's what he would want," he finally said.

"And if I refused?"

"She's your child, Vanessa. You should raise her the way you see fit."

But if Gabriel were to adopt her, then Mia would be both of theirs. Which he had already said would be an eventuality. Until just this moment, she had only imagined that as a good thing. Now she wasn't so sure. What if they had contrasting views about raising children? And suppose they had a baby together? Would she have even less control then?

"I guess that's just another thing we'll have to discuss when he gets back," she said, then for reasons she didn't fully understand, heard herself ask, "How would you feel about sending your children away to school?"

Why would she ask such a thing when his opinions about child-rearing had no bearing on her life in the least?

"I guess I've never really considered that," Marcus said. "I suppose it would be something I would have to discuss with my wife."

She couldn't help but wonder if he was just giving her the PC answer, or if he really meant it. And honestly, why did it matter?

Eleven

Vanessa heard her phone ringing from the chair where she'd set her things. Thinking that it might be Gabriel, she pushed herself up out of the pool and rushed to grab it, the intense afternoon heat drying her skin in the few seconds it took to reach it. Her heart sank when she saw her father's number on the display. She had played over in her mind about a million times what she would say to him when he finally called, yet she was still too chicken to answer. She let the call go to voice mail, waited until her alert chimed, then listened to the message.

"Hey Nessy, it's Daddy," he said and she cringed, in part because she was a grown woman and he still referred to himself as Daddy, and also because she absolutely hated being called Nessy. It made her sound as though she belonged in a Scottish loch. "I thought I might catch you before you left for work. I just called to tell you that my platoon reunion will be in Los Angeles next week so I'm flying in."

Oh, crap. She closed her eyes and sighed.

"The reunion is a week from Friday night and I want time to see my grandbaby, so I'll be taking a flight early Thursday morning."

He wasn't coming there to see Vanessa, just Mia.

Ironic considering he'd barely acknowledged her existence until she was almost three months old. Before then he referred to her as Vanessa's *latest mistake.* Knowing how disappointed he would be, she hadn't even told him she was pregnant until it was no longer possible to hide it. And when she had, he'd responded in that same tired, disappointed tone, "Vanessa, when will you learn?"

"I'll call with my flight information when I get it," his message said. "You can swing by and pick me up from the airport. See you soon!"

He never asked, he only demanded. Suppose she'd had other plans? Or was it that he just didn't care? It wasn't unlike him to visit on a whim and expect her to drop everything and entertain him. She had to endure that same old look of disappointment when she didn't cater to his every whim. It had always been that way, even when she was a kid. God forbid if she didn't get the laundry washed and ironed and the dishes done, not to mention the vacuuming and the dusting and the grocery shopping. And of course she was expected to maintain straight As in school. He ran a tight ship, and she had been expected to fall in line. And he wondered why she lit out of there the day she graduated high school. Which was, of course, another mistake.

This time she wouldn't be there to disappoint him… which in itself would be a disappointment, she supposed. The truth is, no matter what she did, in his opinion it would never be the right thing.

She sighed and dropped the phone back onto the chair, then looked up, surprised to find Marcus and Mia floating near the edge watching her.

"Everything okay?" he asked.

She forced a smile. "Sure. Fine."

"You're lying," he said.

She went for an innocent look, but was pretty sure it came out looking more like a grimace. "Why would you think that?"

"Because you're chewing on your thumbnail, and people generally do that when they're nervous."

She looked down to find she'd chewed off the tip of her left thumbnail. Damn. He didn't miss a thing, did he? And the way he was looking up at her, she began to wonder if choosing her bikini over the conservative one-piece had been a bad idea. She felt so…exposed, yet at the same time, she *liked* that he was looking at her. She *wanted* him to.

Vanessa, that is just so wrong.

"It's fine if you don't want to talk about it," he said.

She sat on the edge of the pool, dipping her feet in the water. "My father just left a message. He's coming to Los Angeles to visit next week."

"Does that mean you'll be leaving?"

The old Vanessa may have. She would have been worried about disappointing him yet again. But she was twenty-four years old, damn it. It was time to cut the umbilical cord and live her life the way she wanted. But she was the new Vanessa now, and that Vanessa was confident and strong and no longer cared what her father thought.

She hoped so at least.

"I'm not leaving," she told Marcus. "I'm going to call him back and tell him that I won't be there, and we'll have to reschedule for another time."

"And when he asks where you are?"

That was the tricky part.

"I'll tell him the truth." Maybe.

You're strong, she reminded herself. *You are responsible for your own destiny and what he thinks doesn't matter.*

And if she told herself enough times, she just might start to believe it.

Marcus stood behind Vanessa while she examined an exhibit at the museum, thinking that of all the visitors he had escorted there over the years—and there had been many—she showed by far the most intense interest. She didn't just politely browse while looking bored out of her skull. She absorbed information, reading every sign and description carefully, as if she were dedicating it to memory.

"You do realize that there's no quiz when we get back to the palace," he teased, as she read the fine print on a display of artifacts from the Varieo civil war of 1899.

She smiled sheepishly. "I'm taking forever, I know, but I just love history. It was my favorite subject in school."

"I don't mind," he told her, and he honestly didn't. Just like he hadn't minded spending the afternoon at the pool with her and Mia the day before. And not because of that hot pink bikini she'd worn. Okay, not completely because of the bikini. He just…liked her.

"I just wish Mia would sit in her stroller," Vanessa said, hiking her daughter, who had been unusually fidgety and fussy all day, higher on her hip. "She desperately needs a nap." But every time Vanessa tried to strap her into the stroller Mia would begin to howl.

"Why don't you let me hold her for a while," he said, extending his arms. Mia lunged for him.

"Jeez, kid!" Laughing, Vanessa handed her over, and

when Mia instantly settled against his shoulder, said, "She sure does like you."

The feeling was mutual. He even sort of liked having a baby around the palace. Although the idea that this little person could become his stepsister was a strange one. Not that he believed it would ever really happen. But did that possibly mean he was ready to start a family of his own? Eight months ago he would have said absolutely not. But so much had changed since then. He felt as if he'd changed, and he knew for a fact that it had everything to do with Vanessa's visit.

They walked to the next display, where Vanessa seemed intent on memorizing the name of every battle and its respective date. He stood behind her to the left, watching her, memorizing the curve of her face, the delicate shell of her ear, wishing he could reach out and touch her. He felt that way all the time lately, and the impulse was getting more difficult to ignore. And he knew, by the way she looked at him, the way her face flushed when they were close, the way her breath caught when he took her hand to help her out of the car, she felt it too.

When she was finished, she turned to Marcus, looked at him and laughed.

"What are you? The baby whisperer?"

He looked down at Mia to find that she was sleeping soundly on his shoulder. "Well, you said she needed a nap."

"You could try sitting her in the stroller now."

"I don't mind holding her."

"Are you sure?"

"Why risk waking her," he said, but the truth was, he just liked holding her. And he'd been doing it a lot more often. Yesterday he'd carried her on his shoulders as they strolled down the stretch of private beach at the marina—Vanessa wearing that ridiculous floppy hat—and Mia delighted in tugging on handfuls of his hair. Later they sat on a blanket close to the shore and let Mia play in the sand and splash in the salty water. Those simple activities had made him feel happier, feel more *human*, than he had in ages.

With Mia asleep in his arms, they turned and walked toward the next section of the museum.

"You're really good with her," Vanessa said. "Are you around kids much?"

"I have a few friends with young children, but I don't see them very often."

"The friends, or the children?"

"Either, really. Since we lost my mother I haven't felt much like socializing. The only time I see people now is at formal events where I'm bound by duty to attend, and children, especially small ones, are not typically included on the guest list."

She gazed up at him, looking sad. "It sounds lonely."

"What does?"

"Your life. Everyone needs friends. Would your mother be happy if she knew how you've isolated yourself?"

"No, she wouldn't. But the only true friend I had betrayed me. Sometimes I think I'm better off alone."

"I could be your friend," she said. "And having experienced firsthand what it feels like to be betrayed by a friend, you can trust that I would never do that to you."

Despite everything he'd learned of her the past three days, the blunt statement still surprised him. And he couldn't help but wonder if that might be a bad idea, that if being her friend would only strengthen the physical attraction he felt growing nearly every time he looked at her, every time she opened her mouth and all that honesty spilled out. Which is why he shouldn't have said what he said next.

"In that case, would you care to join me for dinner on the veranda tonight?"

The invitation seemed to surprise her. "Um, yeah, I'd love to. What time?"

"How about eight?"

"Mia goes to bed right around then, so that would be perfect. And I assume you mean the veranda in the west wing, off the dining room?"

"That's the one. I see you've been studying your map."

"Since I'm going to be here a while either way, I should probably learn my way around." She glanced at her watch, frowned and said, "Wow, I didn't realize how late it is. Maybe we should think about getting back."

"I'm in no hurry if you want to stay."

"I really do need to get back," she said, looking uncomfortable. "Gabriel promised to Skype me at four today, so..."

So she obviously was looking forward to speaking to him. And was that jealousy he was feeling? He forced a smile and kept his tone nonchalant. "Well then, by all means, let's go."

You have no reason to be nervous, Vanessa told herself for the tenth time since she'd left her room and made her way to the veranda. They'd spent all day together and though it had been a little awkward at times, Marcus had been a perfect gentleman, and she was sure tonight would be no exception. He probably only invited her to dinner because he felt obligated to entertain her. Or maybe he really did want to be friends.

And what a sophomoric thing that had been to say to him, she thought, offering to be his friend. As if he probably didn't already have tons of people lining up to be his friend. What made her so special?

Or was that just her way of subtly telling him that's all they could ever be. Friends. And she was sure that with time, she would stop fantasizing about him taking her in his arms, kissing her, then tearing off her clothes and making passionate love to her. Tearing, because he wasn't the kind of man to take things slow. He would be hot and sexy and demanding and she would of course have multiple orgasms. At least, in her fantasy she did. The fantasy she had been playing over and over in her head since he'd kissed her.

Get a grip, Vanessa. You're only making this harder on yourself.

She found the dining room and stepped through the open doors onto the veranda at exactly seven fifty-nine. Taper candles burned in fresh floral centerpieces on a round bistro table set for two, and champagne chilled in an ice bucket beside it. Beyond the veranda, past lush, sweetly scented flower gardens, the setting sun was a stunning palette of brilliant red and orange streaking an indigo canvas sky. A mild breeze swept away the afternoon heat.

It was the ideal setting for a romantic dinner. But this was supposed to be a meal shared between friends. Wasn't it?

"I see you found it."

She spun around to find Marcus standing behind her.

He stood leaning casually in the dining room doorway, hands tucked into the front pockets of his slacks, his white silk shirt a stark contrast to his deep olive skin and his jacket the exact same rich espresso shade as his eyes. His hair was combed back but one stubborn wavy lock caressed his forehead.

"Wow, you look really nice," she said, instantly wishing she could take the words back. This is a casual dinner between *friends,* she reminded herself. She shouldn't be chucking out personal compliments.

"You sound surprised," he said with a raised brow.

"No! Of course not. I just meant…" She realized Marcus was grinning. He was teasing her. She gestured to the sleeveless, coral-colored slip dress she was wearing. She had wanted to look nice, without appearing blatantly sexy, and this was the only dress she'd brought with her that seemed to fit the bill. It was simple, and shapeless without looking frumpy. "I wasn't really sure how formal to dress."

His eyes raked over her. Blatantly, and with no shame. "You look lovely."

He said it politely, but the hunger in his gaze, and the resulting tug of lust deep in her belly, was anything but polite. And as exposed as she felt just then, she might as well have been wearing a transparent negligee, or nothing at all. And the worst part was, she liked it. She liked the way she felt when he looked at her. Even though it was so very wrong.

He gestured to the table. "Shall we sit?"

She nodded, and he helped her into her chair, the backs of his fingers brushing her bare shoulders as he eased it to the table, and she actually shivered. Honest to goodness goose bumps broke out across her skin.

Oh my.

She'd read in stories about a man making a woman shiver just by touching her, but it had never actually happened to her. In fact, she thought the whole thing sounded sort of silly. Not so much anymore.

"Champagne?" Marcus asked.

Oh, that could be a really bad idea. The last thing she needed was something to compromise her senses. They were compromised enough already. But the bottle was open, and she hated to let good champagne—and noting the label, it was *good* champagne—go to waste.

"Just one glass," she heard herself say, knowing she would have to be careful not to let one glass become two and so on.

Marcus poured it himself, then took a seat across from her. He lifted his glass, pinned his eyes on her and said, "To my father."

There was some sort of message in his eyes, but for the life of her, she wasn't sure what it was. Was toasting his father his way of letting her know the boundaries they'd established were still firmly in place, or did it mean something else entirely?

She'd just as soon they didn't talk about Gabriel at all. And rather than analyze it to death, she lifted her own glass and said, "To Gabriel." Hoping that would be the end of it.

She took a tiny sip, then set her glass down, and before she could even begin to think of what to say next, one of the younger butlers appeared with a gleaming silver tray and served the soup. He even nodded cordially when she thanked him. Karin definitely seemed to be warming to her as well, and Vanessa's maid had actually smiled and said good morning when she came in to make the bed that morning. They weren't exactly rolling out the red carpet—more like flopping down the welcome mat—but it was progress.

The soup consisted of bite-sized dumplings swimming in some sort of rich beef broth. And it was delicious. But that didn't surprise her considering the food had been exemplary since she arrived.

"You spoke with my father today?" he asked.

Ugh, she really didn't want to do this, but she nodded. "This afternoon."

"He told you that my aunt is still in intensive care?"

"He said she had a bad night. That her fever spiked, and she may need surgery. It sounds as if he won't be home anytime soon." Despite what she had hoped.

"He told me she's still very ill," Marcus said, then his eyes lifted to hers. "He asked if I've been keeping you entertained."

Oh, he had definitely been doing that.

"He asked if I've been respectful."

Her heart skipped a beat. "You don't think he…"

"Suspects something?" Marcus said bluntly, then he shook his head. "No. I think he's still worried that I won't be nice to you."

Oh, he'd been "nice" all right. A little too nice, some might say.

"He said you seemed reluctant to talk about me."

The truth was, she hadn't known what to tell Gabriel. She worried that if she said too much, like mentioning the earrings, or their evening stroll, Gabriel might get suspicious. She didn't know what was considered proper, and what was pushing the boundaries, so she figured it was better not to say anything at all.

"I didn't mean to be elusive, or give him the impression I felt unwelcome."

"I just don't want him to think that I've neglected my duty," Marcus said.

"Of course. I'll be sure to let him know that you've been a good host."

They both quietly ate their soup for several minutes, then Marcus asked, "Have you spoken with your father yet?"

She lowered her eyes to her bowl. "Uh, nope, not yet."

She took a taste of her soup and when she looked up, he was pinning her with one of those brow-tipped stares.

"I *will*," she said.

"The longer you wait, the harder it will be."

She set her spoon down, her belly suddenly knotted with nerves. She lifted her glass and took another sip. "I know. I just have to work up the nerve. I'll do it, I just…I need to wait until the time is right."

"Which will happen when?"

When he was at the airport waiting for her to pick him up, maybe. "I'll do it. Probably tomorrow. The problem is, whenever I have the time, it's the middle of the night there."

The brow rose higher.

She sighed. "Okay, that's a lie. I'm a big fat chicken. There, I said it."

One of the butlers appeared to clear their soup plates. While another served the salad, Vanessa's phone started to ring. Would it be funny—not ha-ha funny, but ironic funny—if that were him right now.

She pulled it out of her pocketbook and saw that it wasn't her father, but Karin. As crabby as Mia had been today, maybe she was having trouble getting her to settle.

"Mia woke with a fever, ma'am."

It wasn't unusual for Mia to run a low-grade fever when she was teething, and that would explain her foul mood. "Did you take her temperature?"

"Yes, ma'am. It's forty point five."

The number confused her for a second, then she realized Karin meant Celsius. She racked her brain to recall the conversion and came up with a frighteningly high number. Over one hundred and *four* degrees!

She felt the color drain from her face. Could that be right? And if it was, this was no case of teething. "I'll be right up."

Marcus must have seen the fear in her eyes, because he frowned and asked, "What's wrong?"

Vanessa was already out of her chair. "It's Mia. She has a fever. A high one."

Marcus shoved himself to his feet, pulled out his phone and dialed. "George, please get Dr. Stark on the line and tell him we need him immediately."

Twelve

Other than a mild cold in the spring, Mia had never really been sick a day in her life. Imagining the worst, Vanessa's heart pounded a mile a minute as she rushed up the stairs to her suite, Marcus trailing close behind. When she reached the nursery she flung the door open.

Karin had stripped Mia down to her diaper and was rocking her gently, patting her back. Mia's cheeks were bright red and her eyelids droopy, and Vanessa's heart sank even lower as she crossed the room to her. How, in a couple of hours' time, could she have gotten so sick?

"Hey, baby," Vanessa said, touching Mia's forehead. It was burning hot. "Did you give her anything?"

Karin shook her head. "No, ma'am. I called you the minute she woke up."

Vanessa took Mia from her. She was limp and listless. "In the bathroom there's a bottle of acetaminophen drops. Could you get it for me, please?"

Karin scurried off and Marcus, who stood by the door looking worried, asked, "Is there anything I can do?"

"Just get the doctor up here as fast as possible." She cradled Mia to her chest, her hands trembling she was so frightened.

Karin hurried back with the drops and Vanessa measured out the correct dose. Mia swallowed it without a fuss.

"I don't know what this could be. She's barely ever had a cold."

"I'm sure it's nothing serious. Probably just a virus."

"I wonder if I should put her in a cool bath to bring her temperature down."

"How high is it?"

"Over one hundred and four."

His brows flew up.

"Fahrenheit," she added, and his face relaxed.

"Why don't you wait and see what the doctor says?"

She checked the clock across the room. "How soon do you think he'll be here?"

"Quickly. He's on call 24/7."

"Is he a pediatrician?"

"A family practitioner, but I assure you he is more than qualified."

She didn't imagine the royal family would keep an unqualified physician on call.

"Why don't you sit down," Marcus said, gesturing to the rocker. "Children can sense when parents are upset."

He was right, she needed to pull it together. The way the baby lay limp in Vanessa's arms, whimpering pathetically, it was as if she didn't have the energy to cry. She sat in the chair, cradling Mia in her arms and rocked her gently. "I'm sorry to have interrupted dinner. You can go back down and finish."

He folded his arms. "I'm not going anywhere."

Though she was used to handling things on her own when it came to her daughter, she was grateful for his company. Sometimes she got tired of being alone.

Dr. Stark, a kind-faced older gentleman, arrived just a few minutes later carrying a black medical bag.

He shook her hand and asked in English, "How old is the child?"

"Six months."

"Healthy?"

"Usually, yes. The worst she's ever had was a mild cold. I don't know why she would have such a high fever."

"She's current on her vaccinations?"

She nodded.

"You flew here recently?"

"Five days ago."

He nodded, touching Mia's forehead. "You have records?"

She was confused for a second, then realized he meant medical records. "Yes, in my bedroom."

"I'd like to see them."

Marcus held out his arms. "I'll hold her while you get them."

She handed her to him and Mia went without a fuss.

She darted across the hall to her room, grabbed the file with Mia's medical and immunization records, then hurried back to the bedroom. Marcus was sitting in the rocking chair, cradling Mia against his shoulder. Karin stood by the door looking concerned.

"Here they are," she said, and the doctor took the folder from her.

He skimmed the file then set it aside. "You'll need to lay her down."

Marcus rose from the chair and set Mia down on the changing table with all the care and affection of a father, watching with concern as the doctor gave her a thorough exam, asking random questions. When he looked in her ears she started to fuss.

When he was finished, Vanessa asked, "Is it serious?"

"She'll be fine," he assured her, patting her arm. "As I suspected, it's just an ear infection."

Vanessa was so relieved she could have cried. She picked Mia up and held her tight. "How could she have gotten that?"

"It could have started as a virus. A round of antibiotics should clear it right up. The acetaminophen you gave her should bring the fever down."

It looked as if it already had started to work. Mia's cheeks weren't as red and her eyes seemed less droopy. "Could that be why she was so crabby during the flight here?"

"I doubt it. Some children are just sensitive to the cabin pressure. It could have been hurting her ears."

It broke her heart to think that all the time they'd been in the air, Mia had been in pain and Vanessa hadn't even known it. "What can I do to keep it from happening in the future?"

"I would keep her out of the air until the infection clears, then, when you fly home, try earplugs. It will help regulate the pressure."

If she went home, that is. She glanced over at Marcus, who was looking at her. Was he thinking the same thing?

"Right now the best thing for her is a good night's rest. I'll have the antibiotics delivered right away. Just follow the directions. Call if she hasn't improved by morning. Otherwise I'll check her again in two days."

"Thank you, Dr. Stark," she said, shaking his hand.

"Shall I put her back in her crib?" Karin asked Vanessa after he left.

Vanessa shook her head. "I'm going to take her to my room, so you can have the night off. Thanks for calling me so quickly."

Karin nodded and started to walk to her room, then she stopped, turned back and said, "She's a strong girl, she'll be fine in no time." Then she actually smiled.

When she was gone, Vanessa turned to Marcus. He'd removed his jacket and was leaning against the wall, arms crossed. "Thank you," she said.

He cocked his head slightly. "For what?"

"Getting the doctor here so fast. For just being here with me. I don't suppose you have a portable crib anywhere around here. She rolls so much that I get nervous keeping her in bed with me."

Marcus pulled out his phone. "I'm sure we have one."

The medicine arrived fifteen minutes later and Vanessa gave her a dose, and within half an hour a portable crib had been set up in her bedroom. Vanessa laid Mia, who had fallen asleep on her shoulder, inside and covered her with a light blanket. She gently touched Mia's forehead, relieved to find that her temperature had returned almost to normal.

She walked back out into the sitting room where Marcus waited. It was dark but for a lamp on the desk. He stood by the French doors, the curtain pulled back, gazing into the night. Her first instinct was to walk up to him, slide her arms around his waist and lay her head against his back. She imagined that they would stay that way for a while, then he would turn and take her in his arms, kiss her the way he did the other night.

But as much as she wanted to—ached for it even—she couldn't do it.

"She's in bed," she said, and Marcus turned to her, letting the curtain drop. "I think she's better already."

"That's good."

The phone on her desk began to ring and she crossed the room to pick it up. It was Gabriel. Thank goodness he couldn't see her face or surely he would recognize the guilt there for the thoughts she had just been having.

"George called," he said, sounding worried. "He told me that Mia is ill."

"She woke with a fever."

"The doctor was there?"

"He came right away. It's an ear infection. He put her on antibiotics."

"What can I do? Do you need me to come home? I can catch a flight first thing in the morning."

This was it. She could say yes, and get Gabriel back here and be done with this whole crazy thing with Marcus. Instead she heard herself saying, "In the time it would take you to get here, she'll probably be fine. Her fever is already down."

"Are you sure?"

"Trina needs you more than I do. Besides, Marcus is helping," she said, glancing his way.

His expression was unreadable.

"Call me if you need anything, day or night," Gabriel said.

"I will, I promise."

"I'll let you go so you can tend to her needs. I'll call you tomorrow."

"Okay."

"Good night, sweet Vanessa. I love you."

"I love you, too," she said, and she did. She loved him as a friend, so why did she feel like a fraud? And why did she feel so uncomfortable saying the words in front of Marcus?

Well, duh, of course she knew why.

She set the phone down and turned to Marcus. He stood by the sofa, his arms folded across his chest. "Your father," she said, as if he needed an explanation.

"He offered to come home?" he asked.

She nodded.

"You told him no?"

She nodded again.

He started walking toward her. "Why? Isn't that what you wanted?"

"It was…I mean, it *is*. I just think…" The truth was, she was afraid. Afraid that Gabriel would come home, see her face and instantly know what she was feeling for Marcus. He trusted her, *loved* her, and she'd betrayed him. And she continued to betray him every time she had an inappropriate thought about his son, but she just couldn't seem to stop herself. Or maybe she didn't want to stop. "Maybe we need some time to sort this out before he comes back."

"Sort what out?"

"This. Us."

"I thought there was no us. That we were going to pretend like it never happened."

That had seemed like a good idea yesterday, but now she wasn't so sure she could do that. Not right away, anyhow. "We are. I just…need some time to think."

He stepped closer, his dark eyes serious and pinned to hers. Her stomach bottomed out and her heart started to beat faster.

"Please don't look at me like that."

"Like what?"

"Like you want to kiss me again."

"But I do."

Oh boy. Her knees felt squishy. "You know that would be a really bad idea."

"Yeah, it probably would."

"You really shouldn't."

"So tell me no."

He wanted *her* to be the responsible one? Seriously?

"Have you not heard a thing I've said this week?"

"Every word of it."

"Then you know that you really shouldn't trust me with a responsibility like that, considering my tendency to make bad decisions."

His grin warmed her from the inside out. "Right now, I'm sort of counting on it."

Thirteen

Vanessa reached up and cupped Marcus's cheek, running her thumb across that adorable dimple, something she'd wanted to do since the first time she'd seen him smile.

This was completely insane, what they were about to do, because she knew in her heart that this time it wouldn't just be a kiss. But with him standing right in front of her, gazing into her eyes with that hungry look, she just couldn't make herself stop him. And her last thought, as he lowered his head and leaned in, as she rose up to meet him halfway, was how wrong this was, and how absolutely wonderful.

Then he kissed her. But this time it was different, this kiss had a mutual urgency that said neither would be having a crisis of conscience. In a weird way it felt as if they had been working toward this moment since the minute she'd stepped off the plane. Like somewhere deep down she just knew it had been inevitable. It was difficult to imagine that at one time she hadn't even liked him. A big fat jerk, that's what she'd thought him to be. She'd been so wrong about him. About so many things.

"I want you Vanessa," he whispered against her lips. "I don't care if it's wrong."

She pulled back to look him in the eyes. How could she have known this beautiful man only five days when right now it felt like an eternity?

And right now their feelings were the only ones that mattered to her.

She shoved his jacket off his shoulders, down his arms, and it dropped to the floor. She ran her hands up the front of his shirt, over his muscular chest, the way she had wanted to since he stood in her doorway that day with his shirt unbuttoned. And he felt just as good as she knew he would.

Marcus groaned deep in his throat. Then, as if the last bit of his control snapped, he kissed her hard, lifting her off her feet and pinning her to the wall with the length of his body. She gasped against his lips, hooked her legs around his hips, curling her fingers into the meat of his arms. This was the Marcus she had fantasized about, the one who would sweep her off her feet and take her with reckless abandon, and everything inside her screamed, "Yes!"

Marcus set her on her feet and grabbed the hem of her dress, yanking it up over her head—as close to tearing as he could get without actually shredding the delicate silk fabric. When she stood there in nothing but a bra and panties, he stopped and just looked at her.

"You're amazing," he said.

Not beautiful, but amazing. Was it possible that he really did see more in her than just a pretty face? When she looked at Marcus she saw not royalty, not a prince, but a man who was charismatic and kind and funny. And maybe a little vulnerable too. A man who was looking back at her with the same deep affection. Could it be that her feelings for Gabriel were never meant to be more than friendship? That Marcus was the one she was destined to fall in love with? Because as much as she'd tried to fight it, she was definitely falling in love with him.

She took his hand and walked backward to the sofa, tugging him along with her. A part of her said that she should have been second-guessing herself, or feeling guilty—and a week ago, she probably would have—but as they undressed, kissing and touching each other, it just felt right.

When he was naked, she took a moment to just look at him. Physically he was just as perfect as he could possibly be, but she didn't really care about that. It was his mind that fascinated her most, who he was on the inside.

She lay back against the sofa, pulling him down with her, so he was cradled between her thighs. He grinned down at her, brushing her hair back from her face. "You know that this is completely crazy."

"I know. I take it you don't do crazy things?"

"Never."

"Me neither." She stroked the sides of his face, his neck, ran her hands across his shoulders. She just couldn't stop touching him. "Maybe that's why this feels so good. Maybe we both need a little crazy."

"That must be it." He leaned down to kiss her, but just as his lips brushed hers, he stopped, uttering a curse.

"If you're about to tell me we have to stop, I'm going to be very upset," she said.

"No, I just realized, I don't have protection with me."

"You *don't?* Aren't princes supposed to be prepared

at all times?" She paused, frowning. "Or is that the scouts?"

"I wasn't exactly planning for this, you know."

"Really?"

He laughed. "Yes, really. But then you walked into the room wearing that dress..."

"*That* dress? Are you kidding me? It's like the least sexy thing I own. I wore it so I *wouldn't* tempt you."

"The truth is, you could have been wearing a paper sack and I would have wanted to rip it off you. It's you that I want, not your clothes."

It was thrilling to know he wanted her that much, that he would be attracted to her even at her worst.

"I'm going to have to run back to my room," he said, not sounding at all thrilled with the idea.

"I'm on birth control, so you don't have to."

"Are you sure?"

"I'm sure. And now that we have that settled, could we stop talking and get to the good stuff?"

He grinned. "I thought women liked to talk."

"Yes, but even we have our limits."

She didn't have to ask twice, and lying there with him, kissing and touching, felt completely natural. There was none of the usual first time fumbling or awkwardness. And any vestige of reservations, or hint of mixed feelings that may have remained evaporated the instant he thrust inside her. Everything else in the world, any cares or worries or feelings of indecision that were always there somewhere in the back of her mind, melted away. She knew from the instant he began to move inside her—slow and gentle at first, then harder and faster, until it got so out of control they tumbled off the couch onto the rug—that this was meant to be.

He made her feel the way a woman was supposed to feel. Adored and desired and protected, and *strong*, as if no one or no thing could ever knock her back down.

And she felt heartbroken, all the way down to her soul, because as much as she wanted Marcus, she couldn't have him, and she was terrified that no man would ever make her feel this way again.

"We're totally screwed, aren't we?" Vanessa asked Marcus, lying next to him naked on the floor beside the sofa, her breath just as raspy and uneven as his own, glowing from what had been for him some of the best sex of his entire life. Actually no, it had been *the* best.

Maybe it was the anticipation that had made it so exciting, or the forbidden nature of the relationship. Maybe it was that she had no hang-ups about her looks or insecurities about her body, or that she gave herself heart and soul and held nothing back. It could have been that unlike most women, whatever she took, she gave back tenfold.

Or maybe he just really liked her.

At this point, what difference did it make? Because she was right. They were screwed. How could he possibly explain this to his father? "Sorry, but I just slept with the woman you love, and I think I might be falling in love with her myself, but don't worry, you'll find someone else."

There was a code among men when it came to girlfriends and wives, and that was even more true among family. It was a line a man simply did not cross. But he had crossed it, and the worst part was that he couldn't seem to make himself feel guilty about it.

"My father can't ever know," he said.

She nodded. “I know. And I can’t marry him now.”

“I know.” He felt bad about that, but maybe it was for the best. He believed that Vanessa came here with the very best of intentions, but she obviously didn’t love his father the way a wife loves a husband. Maybe by stepping between them Marcus had done them both a favor. Vanessa was so sweet and kind, he could imagine her compromising her own happiness to make his father happy. Eventually though, they would have both been miserable. In essence, he had saved them from an inevitable failed marriage.

Or was he just trying to rationalize a situation that was completely irrational?

She reached down and laced her fingers through his. “It’s not your fault that this happened, so please don’t ever blame yourself.”

He squeezed her hand. “It’s no one’s fault. Sometimes things just…happen. It doesn’t have to make sense.”

She looked over at him. “You know that no matter how we feel, you and I, we can’t ever…”

“I know.” And the thought caused an actual pain in his chest. A longing so deep he felt hollowed out and raw. He had little doubt that Vanessa was the one for him. She was his destiny, she *and* Mia, but he could never have them. Not if he ever hoped to have a civilized relationship with his father. It was as if the universe was playing a cruel trick on them. But in his world honor reigned supreme, and family always came first. His feelings, his happiness, were inconsequential.

It wasn’t fair, but when was life ever?

“I need to call him and tell him,” Vanessa said. “That it’s over, I mean. I won’t tell him about us.”

The minute she ended her relationship with his father, she would have to leave. There would be no justifiable reason to stay. And the idea that this was it, that Marcus would never be with Vanessa again, that he had to give her up so soon, made his heart pound and adrenaline rush. He wasn't ready to let her go. Not yet.

"That's not the sort of thing that you should do over the phone, or through Skype," he told her. "Shouldn't you wait until he returns?"

Her brow furrowed into a frown. "It just doesn't seem fair to let him think that everything is okay, then dump him the second he gets back. That just seems… cruel."

And this was the woman he'd been convinced was a devious gold digger. How could he have been so wrong? Because he was an idiot, or at least, he had been. And he would be again if he let her go now.

"Do you really think now is the right time?" he said, grasping for a reason, any reason, to get her to stay. "He's so upset over my aunt."

She blinked. "I guess I hadn't really thought about it that way. That would be pretty thoughtless. But I don't think I can wait until he comes back. That could be weeks still."

"Then at least wait until she's out of intensive care."

"I don't know…"

Oh, to hell with this. Here she was being honest and he was trying to manipulate her.

"The truth is, I don't care about my father's feelings. This is pure selfishness. Because the minute you tell him, it's over, and I just can't let you go yet." He pulled her close, cupped her face in his hands. "Stay with me, Vanessa. Just a few days more."

She looked conflicted, and sad. "You know we'll just be torturing ourselves."

"I don't care. I just want a little more time with you." Not wanted. *Needed.* And he had never needed anyone in his life.

"We would have to be discreet. No one can know. If Gabriel found out—"

"He won't. I promise."

She hesitated a moment, then smiled and touched his cheek. "Okay. A few more days."

He breathed a quiet sigh of relief. Was this wrong in more ways than he could count, and were they just delaying the inevitable? Of course. And did he care? Not really. He'd spent his entire life making sacrifices, catering to the whims of others. This one time he was going to be selfish, take something for himself.

"But then I have to go," she said. "I have to get on with my life."

"I understand." Because he did too, as difficult as that was to imagine. But for now she was his, and he planned to make the most of what little time they had left together.

"You did what?" Jessy shrieked into the phone, so loud that Vanessa had to hold it away from her ear. "I don't talk to you for a couple of days and this happens?"

Vanessa cringed. Maybe telling Jessy that she'd slept with Marcus, several times now, hadn't been such a hot idea after all. But if she didn't tell *someone,* she felt as if she would burst.

"You realize I was kidding when I suggested he could be a viable second choice," Jessy said.

"I know. And it's not something I planned on happening."

"He didn't, you know...*force* you."

"God no! Of course not. What is your hang-up about the men in this country being brutes?"

"I'm just worried about you."

"Well, don't be. Marcus would never do that. He's one of the sweetest and kindest men I've ever met. It was one hundred percent mutual."

"But you've barely known him a week. You don't sleep with guys you've known a week. Hell, sometimes you make them wait *months*."

"I know. And it's a wonder we held out as long as we did."

Jessy laughed. "Oh my God. Who are you and what have you done with my best friend?"

"I know, this isn't like me at all. And the weird thing is, if I could go back and do it differently, I wouldn't. I'm glad for what happened. And I'm glad I met him. It's changed me."

"In five days?"

"It sounds impossible, I know. I have a hard time believing it myself, but I just feel *different*. I feel...gosh, I don't know, like a better person, I guess."

Jessy laughed again. "You're sleeping with the son of the man you're supposed to marry, and you feel like a better person?"

It did sound weird when she said it like that. "It's hard to explain. And though I hate to admit it, I think what you said about Gabriel being a father figure was true. Nothing I do is good enough for my dad, and I guess in a way I transferred my feelings onto Gabriel. Deep down I knew that I didn't love him the way a wife should love a husband, that I never would. But he seemed to love me so much, and I didn't want to let him down. But then I met Marcus and something just... clicked. If it hadn't been for him, I may have made another terrible mistake."

"So you must really like him."

If only it were that simple. "That would be a major understatement."

Jessy was quiet for a second, then she said, "Are you saying that you *love* him? After *five* days?"

"Weird, huh?"

"How does he feel?"

She shrugged. "What does it matter?"

"It seems to me like it would matter an awful lot."

If only. "We can't be together. How do you think Gabriel would feel if I told him I was dumping him for his son? He might never forgive Marcus."

"You don't think Marcus would choose you over his father?"

"It doesn't matter because I would never ask him to. Nor would I want him to. Family and honor mean everything to Marcus. It's one of the things I love most about him."

"So, the thing you love most is what's keeping you apart."

"I guess so, yeah." And the thought of leaving, of giving him up, filled her belly with painful knots, and she knew that the longer she stayed the worse it would be when she left, yet here she still was. "This is making me sad. Let's talk about something else. How was your trip?"

"It was good," Jessy said, sounding surprised. "It was actually...fun."

"His family is nice?"

"Yeah. They're very small-town, if you know what I mean, and very traditional. Wayne and I had to sleep in separate rooms. They have this big old farmhouse with lots of land and though I've always been more of a city girl, it was really beautiful. Hot as hell though."

Vanessa smiled. "I'm really glad that it went well."

At least one of them was in a relationship that might actually work.

"I know you don't want to talk about it," Jessy said, "but can I just say one more thing about your affair with the prince?"

Vanessa sighed. "Okay."

"This is going to sound strange. But I'm proud of you."

It was Vanessa who laughed this time. "I slept with the son of the man I was planning to marry and you're *proud* of me?"

"You're always so hell-bent on making other people happy, but you did something selfish, something for yourself. That's a huge step for you."

"I guess I never thought of being selfish as a good thing."

"Sometimes it is."

"You know what the hardest part about leaving will be? Mia has become so attached to him, and he really seems to love her. I think he would be an awesome dad."

"You'll meet someone else, Vanessa. You'll fall in love again, I promise."

Vanessa wasn't so sure about that. In her entire life she'd never felt this way about anyone, she hadn't even known it was possible to love someone the way she loved Marcus. To need someone as much as she needed him, yet feel more free than she had in her life. And she just couldn't imagine it ever happening again. What if Marcus was it? What if he was her destiny? Was it also her destiny to let him go?

Fourteen

Vanessa woke to another message from her father, the third one that he had left in as many days, this one sounding more gruff and irritated than the last two.

"Nessy, why haven't you called me back? I called the hotel and they said you took a leave of absence. I want to know what's going on. Have you gotten yourself into trouble again?"

Of course that would be his first assumption, that she had done something wrong. What else would he think? She sighed, not so disappointed as she was resigned to the way things were. And a little sad that he always seemed to see the worst in her.

"Call me as soon as you get this," he demanded, and that's where the message ended. She dropped her phone on the bedside table and fell back against the pillows.

Beside her, Marcus stirred, waking slowly, the way he always did. Or at least, the last three mornings when they woke up together, he had. First he stretched, lengthening every inch of that long, lean body, then he yawned deeply, and finally he opened his eyes, saw her lying there next to him, and gave her a sleepy smile, his hair all rumpled and sexy. Creases from his pillow lined his cheek.

Watching this ritual had become her new favorite way to spend her morning. Even though what they were doing still filled her with guilt. She just couldn't seem to stay away.

"What time is it?" he asked in a voice still gravelly from sleep.

"Almost eight."

He rolled onto his back and laughed, the covers sliding down to expose his beautiful bare chest. "That makes last night the third night in a row that I slept over seven hours straight. Do you have any idea how long it's been since I got a decent night's sleep?"

"I'm that boring, huh?"

He grinned and pulled her on top of him, so she was straddling his thighs, his beard stubble rough against her chin as he kissed her. "More like you're wearing me out."

It had rained the past two days and Marcus had decided it would be best to spend them in the palace, in her suite. Wearing as little clothing as possible. They mostly just talked, and played with Mia, and when Mia took her naps, they spent the entire time making love. A few times Vanessa had even let Karin watch Mia for an extra hour or so, so they had a little more time together. And though it had been a week now, neither Vanessa nor Marcus had brought up the subject of her leaving, but it loomed between them, unspoken. A dark shadow and a constant element of shame that hung over what had been—other than Mia's birth—the best time of her life. She kept telling herself that when the time was right to leave, they would just know it. So far that time hadn't come, and deep down she wished it never would.

Marcus was it for her. He was the one, her *soul mate,*

and of that she was one hundred and ten percent sure. For the first time in her life she had no doubts. She wasn't second-guessing herself, or worrying that she was making a mistake.

She wasn't exactly sure if he felt the same way. He seemed to, and he clearly didn't want her to leave, but did he love her? He hadn't actually said so. But to be fair, neither had she. At this point, what difference did it make? They were just words. Even if he did love her, his relationship with his father *had* to come first.

After that first time making love, she'd dreaded having to face Gabriel on Skype, sure that he would know the second he saw her face, but while she waited on her computer for over an hour, he'd been a no-show. She'd been more relieved than anything. He'd phoned the next day, apologizing, complaining of security issues, and said it might be better if they limited their calls to voice only. Which actually worked out pretty well for her. Already she could feel herself pulling away.

Their conversations were shorter now, and more superficial. And one day, when Marcus had taken them for a drive to see the royal family's mountain cabin—although to call the lavish vacation home a cabin was akin to calling the Louvre a cute little art gallery—she'd been out of cell range and had missed his call completely. She hadn't even remembered to check for a message. And though it was clearly her fault that they hadn't spoken, he had been the one to apologize the next day. He said he was swamped with work and tending to Trina, and he hadn't had a chance to call back.

She kept waiting for him to ask her if there was a problem, but if he had noticed any change in their relationship, he hadn't mentioned it yet. But Trina had been improving, and though she was still very weak, and Gabriel hadn't felt comfortable leaving her yet, it was only a matter of time.

And then of course she had her father to deal with.

"You look troubled," Marcus said, brushing her hair back and tucking it behind her ear.

He had an uncanny way of always knowing what she was thinking. "My dad called again."

He sighed. "That would explain it."

"He called the hotel and found out that I took a leave, so of course he's assuming that I'm in some sort of trouble. He demanded that I call him immediately."

"You should. You should have called him days ago."

"I know." She let out a sigh and draped herself across his warm, solid chest, pressing her ear to the center, to hear the thump of his heart beating.

"So do it now."

"I don't want to."

"Stop acting like a coward and just call him."

She sat up and looked down at him. "I'm acting like a coward because I *am* one."

"No, you aren't."

Yes, she was. When it came to dealing with her father anyway. "I'll call him tomorrow. I promise."

"You'll call him now," he said, dumping her off his lap and onto the mattress. Then he got up and walked to the bathroom, all naked and gorgeous, his tight behind looking so squeezable.

He stopped in the doorway, turned to her and grinned. "Now, I'm going to take a shower, and if you want to join me, you had better start dialing."

The door closed behind him, then she heard the shower switch on. Damn him. He knew how much she loved taking their morning shower together. He brought a change of clothes to her room every night so no one would see him the next morning wearing the same clothes from the night before. He also rolled around in his bed and mussed up the covers so it would look as if he'd slept there. It had to be obvious to pretty much everyone how much time they had been spending together, but if anyone suspected inappropriate behavior, they'd kept it to themselves.

Vanessa sighed and looked over at the bathroom door, then her phone. Well, here goes nothing.

She sat up, grabbed it and dialed her father's number before she chickened out. He answered on the first ring. "Nessy, where the hell have you been? I've been worried sick. Where's Mia? Is she okay?"

He'd been worried sick about both of them, or just Mia, she wondered. "Sorry, Dad, I would have called you sooner but I've actually been out of the country."

"Out of the country?" he barked, as if that were some unforgivable crime. "Why didn't you tell me? And where is my granddaughter?"

"She's with me."

"Where are you?" he said, sounding no less irate. She knew he was only acting this way because he was worried, and he hated not being in control of every situation every minute. If she gave him hourly reports of her activities he would be ecstatic. And usually when he spoke to her this way it made her feel about two inches tall. Right now, she just felt annoyed.

"I'm in Varieo, you know that little country near—"

"I *know* where it is. What in God's name are you doing there?"

"It's sort of…a work thing." Because she had met Gabriel at work, right?

"I thought you took a leave from the hotel. Or was that just a fancy way of saying they fired you?"

Of course he would think that.

Her annoyance multiplied by fifty. "No, I was not *fired,*" she snapped.

"Do not take that tone with me, young lady," he barked back at her.

Young lady? Was she *five?*

In that instant something inside of her snapped and she'd had enough of being treated like an irresponsible child. And if standing up for herself meant disappointing him, so be it. "I'm twenty-four, Dad. I'll take whatever tone I damned well please. And for the record, I deserve the same respect that you demand from me. I am sick to death of you talking down to me, and always thinking the worst of me. And I'm finished with you making me feel as if anything I do is never good enough for you. I'm smart, and successful, and brave, and I have lots of friends and people who love me. So unless you can think of something positive to say to me, don't bother calling anymore."

She disconnected the call, and even though her heart was thumping, and her hands were trembling, she felt… good. In fact, she felt pretty freaking fantastic. Maybe Marcus was right. Maybe she really was brave. And though she didn't honestly believe this would change anything, at least now he knew how she felt.

Her phone began to ring and she jerked with surprise. It was her dad. She was tempted to let it go to voice mail, but she'd started this, and she needed to finish it.

Bracing herself for the inevitable shouting, she answered. "Hello."

"I'm sorry."

Her jaw actually dropped. "W-what?"

"I said I'm sorry," he repeated, and she'd never heard him sound so humbled. She couldn't recall a single time he'd ever apologized for anything.

"And I'm sorry I raised my voice," she said, then realized that she had done nothing wrong. "Actually, no, I'm not sorry. You deserved it."

"You're right. I had no right to snap at you like that. But when I didn't hear from you, I was just afraid that something bad had happened to you."

"I'm fine. Mia is fine. And I'm sorry that I frightened you. We're here visiting a…friend."

"I didn't know you had any friends there."

"I met him at the hotel. He was a guest."

"He?"

"Yes, he. He's…" Oh what the hell, why not just tell him the truth? Since she didn't really care what he thought at this point anyway. "He's the king."

"The *king?*"

"Yes, and believe it or not, he wants to marry me."

"You're getting married? To a king?" He actually sounded excited. He was finally happy about something she had done, and now she had to burst his bubble. Figures.

"He wants me to marry him, but I'm not going to."

"Why not?"

"Because I'm in love with someone else."

"Another king," he joked.

"Um, no."

"Then who?"

If he was going to blow his top, this would be the time. "I'm in love with the prince. His son."

"Vanessa!"

She braced herself for the fireworks. For the shouting and the berating, but it never happened. She could practically feel the tension through the phone line, but he didn't make a sound. He must have been biting a hole right through his tongue. And could she blame him? Sometimes even she couldn't believe what they were doing.

"You okay, Dad?"

"Just…confused. When did all this happen? *How* did it happen?"

"Like I said, he was visiting the hotel and we became friends."

"The king or the prince?"

"The king, Gabriel, and he fell in love with me, but I only ever loved him as a friend. But he was convinced I would grow to love him if I got to know him better, so he invited me to stay at the palace, but then he was called away when I got here. He asked Marcus—he's the prince—to be my companion and we…well, we fell for each other. Hard."

"How old is this prince?"

"Um, twenty-eight, I think."

"And the king?"

"Fifty-six," she said, and she could practically hear him chomping down on his tongue again. "Which was part of the reason I wasn't sure about marrying him."

"I see," was all he said, but she knew he wanted to say more. He was going to need stitches by the end of this conversation. But she gave him credit for making the effort, and she wished she had confronted him years ago. Though he probably hadn't been ready to hear it before now. Or maybe she was the one who hadn't been ready for this. Maybe she needed to make changes first.

"So, I assume you'll be marrying the prince instead?" he said.

If only. "I won't be marrying anybody."

"But I thought you love him."

"I do love him, but I could never do that to Gabriel. He's a really good man, Dad, and he's been through so much heartache. He loves me, and I could never betray him that way. I feel horrible that it worked out this way, as if I've let him down. Not to mention that it would most likely ruin his relationship with his son. I couldn't do that to either of them. They need each other more than they need me."

He was quiet for several seconds, then he said, "Well, you've had a busy couple of weeks, haven't you?"

Though normally a comment like that would come off as bitter or condescending, now he just sounded surprised. She smiled, feeling both happy and sad, which seemed to be a regular thing for her lately. "You have no idea."

"So I guess I won't be seeing you Thursday."

"No, but we should be flying home soon. Maybe we can make a quick stop in Florida on our way."

"I'd like that." He paused and said, "So you really love this guy?"

"I really love him. Mia does too. She's grown so attached to him, and she loves being here in the palace."

"Are you sure you're doing the right thing? By leaving, I mean."

"There isn't anything else that I can do."

"Well, I'll keep my fingers crossed that you work it

out somehow. And Nessy, I know I've been pretty hard on you, and maybe I don't say it often enough, but I am proud of you."

She'd waited an awfully long time to hear that, and as good as it felt, her entire self-worth no longer depended on it. "Thanks, Dad."

"It's admirable what you're doing. Sacrificing your own happiness for the king's feelings."

"I'm not doing it to be admirable."

"I know. That's why it is. Give me a call when you're coming home and I'll get the guest room ready."

"I will. I love you, Dad."

"I love you too, Nessy."

She hung up and set her phone on the table, thinking that was probably one of the nicest things her dad had ever said to her, and one of the most civilized conversations they had ever had.

"Now aren't you glad you called?"

She looked up to find Marcus standing naked in the bathroom doorway, towel-drying his hair. She wondered how much of that he'd heard. Had he heard her tell her father that she loved Marcus?

"I confronted him about the way he makes me feel, and instead of freaking out, he actually apologized."

"That took guts."

"Maybe I am brave after all. I'm not naive enough to think it will be smooth sailing from here. I'm sure he'll have relapses, because that's just who he is, and I'll have to stand firm. But at least it's a start."

He dropped the towel and walked toward the bed. And my goodness he looked hot. The man just oozed sex appeal. It boggled the mind that a woman would be unfaithful to him. His ex must have been out of her mind.

He yanked the covers away and climbed into bed, tugging her down onto her back, spreading her thighs with his knee and making himself comfortable between them.

"Thank you," she said, running her hand across his smooth, just shaved cheek. "Thank you for making me believe in myself."

"That wasn't me," he said, kissing her gently. His lips were soft and tasted like mint. "I just pointed out what was already there. You chose to see it."

And without him she might never have. She was a different person now. A better person. In part because of him.

"There's one more thing," he said, kissing her chin, her throat, the shell of her ear.

She closed her eyes and sighed. "Hmm?"

"For the record," he whispered, "I love you, too."

Fifteen

After a week of torrential rain the weather finally broke and though Marcus would have been more than happy to spend the day in Vanessa's suite again, sunny skies and mild temperatures lured them back out into the world. A calm sea made it the perfect day for water sports, and since Vanessa had never been on a personal watercraft, he figured it was time she learned.

They left Mia with Karin, who he thought looked relieved to have something to do. Many of the young parents he knew took full advantage of their nannies—especially the fathers, to the point that they'd never even changed a diaper—but Vanessa was very much a hands-on parent. He had the feeling Karin was bored more often than not. And because Mia was usually with them, they always took the limo on their outings, so today he decided they would take *his* baby for a spin.

"This looks really old," Vanessa said, as he opened the passenger door, which for her was on the wrong side of the car.

"It's a 1965. It was my grandfather's. He was a huge Ian Fleming fan."

"Oh my God! Is this—"

"An Aston Martin DB5 Saloon," he said. "An exact replica of the car 007 drove."

She slipped inside, running her hand along the dash, as gently as a lover's caress. "It's amazing!"

He walked around and climbed in. He started the engine, which still purred as sweetly as the day they drove it off the line, put it in gear and steered the car through the open gates, and in the direction of the marina. "I've always loved this car. My grandfather and I used to sneak off on Sundays and drive out into the country for hours. He would tell me stories about his childhood. He was only nineteen when his father died, and he would tell me what it was like to be a king at such a young age. At the time, I just thought it sounded exciting to be so important and have everyone look up to you. Only as I got older and began to learn how much hard work was involved did I begin to realize what a huge responsibility it would be. I used to worry that my father would die and I would be king before I was ready."

"How old was your father when he became king?"

"Forty-three."

She was quiet for a minute, then she turned to him and said, "Let's not go to the marina. Let's take a drive in the country instead. Like you and your grandfather used to do."

"Really?"

"Yeah. I would love to see the places he took you."

"You wouldn't be bored?"

She reached over, took his hand, and smiled, "With you, never."

"Okay, let's go."

He couldn't recall ever getting in a car with a woman and just driving. In his experience they preferred constant stimulation and entertainment, and required lavish gifts and attention. In contrast, Vanessa seemed to relish the times they simply sat around and talked, or played with her daughter. And as far as gifts go, besides the earrings—which she wore every day—he'd bought nothing but the occasional meal or snack. She required little, demanded nothing, yet gave more of herself than he could ever ask. Before now, he hadn't even known women like her existed. That he once thought she had ulterior motives was ridiculous to him now.

"Can I ask you a question?" she said, and he nodded. "When did you stop thinking that I was after your dad's money?"

And she was apparently a mind reader. "It was when we went to the village and you didn't once use the credit card my father left for you."

Her mouth dropped open in surprise. "You knew about that?"

"His assistant told me. She was concerned."

"Gabriel insisted that I use it, but the truth is I haven't even taken it out of the drawer. It didn't seem right. He gave me lots of gifts, and I insisted he take them back."

"Well, if the credit card hadn't convinced me, your reaction to the earrings really drove the message home."

She reached up to finger the silver swirls dangling from her ears. "Why?"

"Because I've never seen a woman so thrilled over such an inexpensive gift."

"Value has nothing to do with it. It's the thought that counts. You bought them because you wanted to, because you knew that I liked them. You weren't trying to buy my affections or win me over. You bought the earrings because you're a sweet guy."

He glared at her. “I am not sweet.”

She grinned. “Yes, you are. You’re one of the sweetest, kindest men I’ve ever met.” She paused, gave his hand a squeeze. “You know I have to go soon. I’ve probably stayed too long already. I feel like we’re tempting fate, like someone is going to figure out what we’re doing and it will get back to Gabriel. I don’t want to hurt him.”

Though it was irrational, he almost wished it would. He didn’t want to hurt his father either, but it was getting more and more difficult to imagine letting her go. He wasn’t even sure if he could. “What if he did find out? Maybe you wouldn’t have to leave. Maybe we could explain to him. Make him understand.”

She closed her eyes and sighed. “I can’t, Marcus. I can’t do that to him. Or to you. If our relationship came between the two of you I would never forgive myself.”

“We don’t know for certain that he would be upset.”

She shot him a look.

“Okay, he probably would, but he could get over it. In fact, when he sees how much it means to me, I’m sure he will.”

“But what if he doesn’t? That isn’t a chance I’m willing to take.”

If she were anything like the women he’d dated in the past, this wouldn’t be an issue. She wouldn’t care who she hurt as long as she got what she wanted. Of course, then he wouldn’t love her. And he knew that once she’d made up her mind, nothing would change it.

Her stubborn streak was one of her most frustrating yet endearing qualities. He liked that she continually challenged him. She kept him honest. And he loved her too much to risk losing her respect.

* * *

After a three-hour drive that they spent talking about their childhoods and families, then a stop in a small village for lunch, Marcus drove them back to the palace. He walked with her up to the nursery, only to discover that Mia had just gone down for a nap.

"Just call me when she wakes up," Vanessa told Karin, then she turned to Marcus and gave him the *look,* the one that said she had naughtiness on her mind. He followed her across the hall, but stopped her just outside her suite door.

"How about a change of pace?"

"What did you have in mind?" she asked, looking intrigued.

"Let's go to my room."

The smile slipped from her face. "Marcus…"

"But you've never even seen it."

"If someone sees us go in there—"

"The family wing is very private. And if you want, we won't do anything but talk. We can even leave the door open. We can pretend like I'm giving you a tour of the family wing."

She looked hesitant. "I don't know."

Despite the risk of being discovered by a passing employee, he took her hand. "We haven't got much time left. Give me the chance to share at least a small part of my life with you."

He could see her melting before his eyes. Finally she smiled and said, "Okay."

What he hadn't told was that just the other day Cleo had confronted him about all the time they had been spending together.

"Talk to my father," he'd told Cleo. "He's the one who wanted me to keep her entertained."

Her brows rose. "Entertained?"

"You *know* what I mean."

She flashed him a told-you-so smile. "I take it you're finding that she's not as terrible as you thought?"

"Not terrible at all," he'd told her, diffusing the situation entirely. Because if she believed the relationship was platonic, no one on the staff, except maybe George, would question it. But he still didn't dare tell Vanessa about the exchange. Especially now.

Under the ruse of tour guide, Marcus led Vanessa through the palace to the family wing, and the employees they did encounter only bowed politely, and showed not even a hint of suspicion. When they got to his suite, the hall was deserted. He opened the door and gestured her inside.

"Wow," she said, walking to the center of the living room and gazing around. He stood by the open door watching her take it all in. "It's huge. As big as an apartment. You even have a kitchen."

"I insisted. I figured, if I have to live here in the palace, I need a space of my own."

"I like it. It's very tasteful, and masculine without being too overpowering." She turned to him. "Comfortable."

"Thank you. And my designer thanks you."

"How many rooms?"

"Master suite, office, kitchen and living room."

She nodded slowly. "It's nice."

"I'm glad you like it."

She dropped her purse on the leather sofa and turned to him. "Maybe you should close the door."

"But I thought we agreed—"

"Close the door, Marcus." She was wearing that look again, so he closed it. "Lock it too."

He locked it, and crossed the room to where she was standing. "Changed your mind, did you?"

She slid her hands up his chest, started unfastening the buttons on his shirt. "Maybe it's the element of danger, but the closer we got to your room, the more turned on I got." She rose up on her toes and kissed him, yanking his shirt from the waist of his slacks. "Or maybe, when we're alone, I just can't keep my hands off you."

The feeling was mutual.

"I know it's wrong, but I just can't stop myself. Doesn't that make me a terrible person?"

"If it does, I'm a terrible person, too. Which could very well mean we deserve each other."

She tugged his shirt off, but before she could get to work on his belt, he picked her up and hoisted her over his shoulder. She let out a screech of surprise, then laughed.

"Marcus, what are you doing!"

"Manhandling you," he said, carrying her to the bedroom and kicking the door open.

"Not that I mind, but why?"

He tossed her down onto the bed, on top of the duvet, then he reached under her dress, hooked his fingers in the waist of her panties and yanked them down. "Because I am not *sweet*."

She grinned up at him. "Well, I stand corrected."

Then she grabbed him by the shoulders, pulled him down on top of her and kissed him.

Every time he made love to her he thought it couldn't possibly get better, but she always managed to top herself. She was sexy and adventurous, and completely confident in her abilities as a lover, and *modest* was a word not even in her vocabulary. She seemed to instinctively know exactly what to do to drive him out of his mind, and she was so damned easy to please—she had a sensitive spot behind her knees that if stroked just right would set her off like a rocket.

She liked it slow and sensual, hard and fast, and she even went a little kinky on him at times. If there were an ideal sexual mate for everyone, there was no doubt in his mind that she was his. And each time they made love that became more clear.

Maybe, he thought, as she unfastened his pants, it was less about skill, and more about the intense feelings of love and affection they shared. But then she slid her hand inside his boxers, wrapped it around his erection and slowly stroked him, and his thoughts became all hazy and muddled. She made it so easy to forget the world around him, to focus on her and her alone. And he wondered what it would be like this time, slow and tender or maybe hot and sweaty. Or would she get that mischievous twinkle in her eyes and do something that would make most women blush?

Vanessa pushed him over onto his back and climbed on top of him, then she yanked her dress up over her head and tossed it onto the floor. Hot and sweaty, he thought with a grin—his particular favorite—and as she thrust against him, impaling herself on his erection, she was so hot and tight and wet, he stopped thinking altogether. And as they reached their climax together, then collapsed in each other's arms, he told himself that there had to be some way to talk her into staying.

And at the same time, his conscience asked the question: To what end?

Sixteen

Somewhere in the back of Marcus's mind he heard pounding.

What the hell was that? he wondered, and what could he do to make it stop? Then he realized, it was his door. Someone was knocking on his bedroom door.

His eyes flew open, and he tried to sit up, but there was a warm body draped across his chest. He and Vanessa must have fallen asleep. He looked over at the clock, and realized that it was past suppertime. Oh hell. No doubt Mia was awake by now.

He shook Vanessa. "Wake up!"

Her eyes fluttered open and she gave him a sleepy smile. "Hey."

"We fell asleep. It's late."

She shot up in bed and squinted at the clock, then she uttered a very unladylike curse. "Where's my phone? Mia must be awake by now. Why didn't Karin call me?"

The pounding started again as they both jumped out of bed.

"Who is that?" Vanessa asked, frantically looking around, he assumed, for her purse.

He tugged his pants on. "Stay here. I'll go see."

He rushed out to the living room, unlocked the door

and yanked it open. Cleo's hand was in the air, poised to knock again.

"There you are!" she said.

"I was…taking a nap," he said, raking a hand through his tousled hair. "I haven't been sleeping well."

"Well, we have a problem. Poor Karin is frantic. Mia woke from her nap an hour ago but she can't find Vanessa. She's not answering her phone and I can't find her anywhere in the palace. I thought perhaps you knew where I might find her."

Was that suspicion in her eyes? "She probably went for a walk," Marcus said. "Maybe she forgot her phone."

"If she left the palace, security would know about it."

He opened his mouth to reply and she added, "But just in case, I had them check the gardens and she isn't out there. It's as if she disappeared."

"Give me a minute to get dressed and I'll find her."

Behind him Marcus heard an "oof!" then a loud crash. He swung around to find Vanessa on the floor by the couch, wrapped in a bed sheet, wincing and cradling her left foot. Beside her lay the floor lamp that had been standing there. Then he heard a noise from the hall and whipped back around to find that in his haste he'd pushed the door open, and Cleo could see the entire sordid scenario.

"Miss Reynolds," Cleo said, her jaw rigid. "Would you please call Karin and let her know that you are in fact fine, and haven't been abducted by terrorists?"

"Yes, ma'am," Vanessa said, her voice trembling, her cheeks crimson with shame.

Cleo turned to Marcus and said tightly, "A word in private, your highness?"

"Are you okay?" he asked Vanessa, who looked utterly miserable, and she nodded. "I'll be right back."

He stepped out into the hall, pulling the door closed behind him, and the look Cleo gave him curdled his blood.

"You lied to me?"

"What was I supposed to do? Tell you the truth? I can see how well that's going over."

"Marcus, what were you thinking?"

Had it been anyone but her berating him this way, he would have dismissed them on the spot. But Cleo had earned this right through years of loyal service. She was more an extension of family than an employee.

"Cleo, believe me when I say, we didn't plan for this to happen. And if it's any consolation, she's not going to marry my father."

"I should hope not! Your father deserves better than a woman who would—"

"This was not her fault," he said sharply, because he absolutely drew the line at any disparaging remarks against Vanessa. She didn't deserve it. "I pursued her."

"Look, Marcus," she said, touching his arm. "I know you're upset over Carmela, and maybe this is your way of getting revenge, but would you risk your relationship with your father for a—a cheap *fling?*"

"No, but I would for the woman who I've fallen hopelessly in love with."

She pulled her hand back in surprise. "You love her?"

"She's everything I have ever imagined I could want in a woman, and a few things I didn't even know I wanted until I met her. And she loves me too, which, considering my track record with women, is pretty damned astonishing. And the irony of it all is that those things I admire most about her are the reason we can never be together."

"You can't?"

"She thinks our relationship will come between me and my father, and she absolutely refuses to let that happen."

"You know that she's right."

"Sometimes I think that I don't even care. But she does, and as much as I'd like to, I would never go against her wishes."

Cleo shook her head. "I don't know what to say. I'm just…I'm so sorry things have to be this way."

"I can count on you to keep this conversation private," he said.

"Of course, Marcus."

He leaned down and kissed her papery cheek. "Thanks."

He stepped back into his suite, leaving her in the hall looking unbelievably sad.

Vanessa was dressed and sitting on the couch, putting her sandals on, when Marcus stepped back into the room. And from his expression she couldn't tell what had happened. "Marcus, I am so sorry."

"It's okay."

"I left my phone in my purse on the couch, that's why I didn't hear Karin calling me. Then I tripped on that stupid lamp. And I didn't mean to fall asleep."

"I fell asleep too. I take it Mia is okay."

"Fine. I figured we would need to talk, so I asked Karin to feed Mia her dinner and get her into bed for me."

He sat down on the couch beside her. "There's nothing to talk about. It's no one's fault."

No, they had plenty to talk about. "Cleo looked so… disappointed."

He sighed. "Yeah, she's good at that. But I explained the entire situation and she understands."

"That's not good enough."

"Vanessa—"

"I can't do this anymore, Marcus."

"I'm not ready for you to go."

"We knew this was inevitable. We kept saying that eventually the day would come that I'd have to leave. And I honestly think that it's here."

He squeezed her hand, gave her a sad smile. "I can't lose you. Not yet."

She shook her head. "My mind is made up. But I want you to know that this has been the happiest couple of weeks in my life, and I will never, as long as I live, forget you."

"Say you'll leave tomorrow. That you'll give me one more night."

She touched his cheek. It was rough from afternoon stubble. "I'm sorry. I just can't."

He leaned in to kiss her, and someone knocked on his door again. Marcus muttered a curse.

"Marcus, it's Cleo!"

"Come in!" he called, sounding exasperated, and he didn't even let go of her hand.

She opened the door and poked her head in. "I'm sorry to bother you again, but I thought you might like to know that your father's limo just pulled up out front. He's home."

sire she may have had to marry him was gone. In this case absence did not make the heart grow fonder. She was too busy falling in love with someone else. And she couldn't put this off any longer. She had to end it now.

"Gabriel," she said, forcing a smile. "Can we talk? Privately, I mean."

"Yes, yes, of course. Why don't we go up to your suite." He turned to Marcus, whose jaw was so tight it could have snapped like a twig. "Please excuse us, son. We'll catch up later. I have news."

Marcus nodded. He was jealous, Vanessa could see it in his eyes, but he stayed silent. What choice did he have?

As they walked up the stairs together, Gabriel didn't even hold her hand, and he made idle chitchat, much the way he had during their recent phone conversations. When they got to her suite, she held her breath, scared to death that he might suddenly take her in his arms and kiss her, because the idea of pushing him away, of having to be so cruel, broke her heart. But he made no attempt to touch her, and when he gestured toward the sofa and asked her to sit down, he didn't even sit beside her. He sat across from her in the wing back chair. And he was definitely nervous. Had someone told him that they suspected her and Marcus of something inappropriate? And if he asked her for the truth, what should she say? Could she lie to him?

Or what if…*oh God*, was he going to *propose?*

"Gabriel, before you say anything, there's something I really need to tell you."

He rubbed his palms together. "And there's something I need to tell you."

"I'll go first," she said.

"No, it would be better if I did."

Vanessa leaned forward slightly. "Actually, it would probably be better if I did."

"No, mine is pretty important," he said, looking slightly annoyed.

"Well, so is mine," she said, feeling a little annoyed herself.

"Vanessa—"

"Gabriel—"

Then they said in perfect unison, "I can't marry you."

Seventeen

Marcus watched Vanessa and his father walk up the stairs together thinking, *what is wrong with this picture.*

If his father was happy to see her, why hadn't he kissed her? Why wasn't he holding her hand? And why had he looked so…nervous? He never got nervous.

"Something is up," Cleo said behind him, and he turned to her.

"So it's not just me who noticed."

"As giddy in love as he was when he came back from America, I thought he would sweep her into his arms the instant he walked in the door, then promptly drop to one knee to propose."

"Are you thinking what I'm thinking?" Marcus asked.

"He doesn't want to marry her."

Marcus was already moving toward the stairs when Cleo grabbed his sleeve.

"This doesn't mean he won't be angry, Marcus, or feel betrayed."

No, it didn't, but every time Marcus imagined Vanessa leaving he got a pain in his chest so sharp, it was as if someone had reached into his chest, grabbed his heart and was squeezing the life from him. The thought of watching her and Mia get on a plane, of seeing it take them away from Varieo forever, filled him with a feeling of panic so intense it was difficult to draw a breath.

He shrugged. "I don't care, Cleo. I can't do it. I can't let her go."

Cleo let go of his sleeve, and smiled up at him. "So what are you waiting for?"

He charged up the stairs to the second floor and raced down the hall to her room. Not even bothering to knock, he flung the door open. Vanessa was seated on the sofa, his father in the chair across from her, and the sudden intrusion surprised them both.

"Marcus," Vanessa said. "What are you doing here?"

"I need to have a word with my father," he told her.

His father frowned. "Is something wrong, son?"

"Yes and no. I guess it just depends on how you look at it."

Vanessa rose to her feet, shaking her head. "Marcus, don't—"

"I *have* to, Vanessa."

"But—"

"I know." He shrugged helplessly. "But I have to."

She sat back down, as if she'd gotten tired of fighting it too, and whatever happened, she was willing to live with the consequences.

"Marcus, can this wait? I really need to talk to Vanessa."

"No, it can't. What I need to tell you must be said right now."

His father looked to Vanessa, who sat there silently. "All right," he said, sounding annoyed. "Talk."

Marcus took a deep breath and blew it out, hoping his father would at least try to understand. "Remember when you thanked me for agreeing to spend time with Vanessa, and said in return, if I ever needed anything, to just ask?"

He nodded. "I remember."

"Did you really mean it?"

"Of course I did. I'm a man of my word. You know that."

"Then I need you to do something for me."

"Anything, Marcus."

"Let Vanessa go."

He drew back slightly, blinking in confusion. "Let her go? But…I just did. I just now told her that I couldn't marry her."

"That's not good enough. I need you to *really* let her go, forget you ever wanted to marry her."

He frowned. "Marcus, what on earth are you talking about? Why would I do that?"

"So I can marry her."

His father's mouth actually dropped open.

"You told me that Vanessa is a remarkable woman, and said that once I got to know her, I would love her. Well, you were right. I do love her." He turned to Vanessa. "More than she could possibly imagine. Too much to ever let her leave."

She smiled, tears filling her eyes. "I love you, too, Marcus."

He turned back to his father, who sat there looking stunned. "You have to understand that we didn't mean for this to happen, and we did fight it. But we just…" He shrugged. "We just couldn't help it."

"You had an affair," his father said, as if to clarify.

"This was no affair," Marcus said. "We fell in love."

"So," his father said, turning to Vanessa, "this is why you couldn't marry me?"

"Yes. I'm so sorry. But like Marcus said, we didn't mean for this to happen. At first, he didn't even like me."

His father slowly nodded, as though he were letting it sink in, but oddly enough, he didn't look angry. Maybe the depth of their betrayal had left him temporarily numb.

"We had agreed not to say anything, to end it," Marcus told him. "She was going to do the honorable thing and leave. Neither of us could bear the thought of hurting you. But I need her. Her and Mia."

His father just sat there, eyes lowered, slowly shaking his head, rubbing his palms together. Marcus glanced over at Vanessa who looked both sad and relieved, and a little worried. He could relate. Telling his father the truth had been hard as hell, but he knew that living a lie would have been so much worse. It would have weighed on him the rest of his life.

"Would you please say something?" Marcus said. "Tell me what you're thinking."

His father finally looked over to him. "I find it ironic, I guess."

"Ironic how?"

"Because I have a secret, too."

"The reason you couldn't marry me?" Vanessa asked.

He nodded. "Because I'm engaged to someone else."

For a second Vanessa just sat there, looking dumbfounded, then she laughed.

"You think that's funny?" Marcus asked.

"Not funny ha-ha, but funny ironic. I guess because

I was so focused on Marcus, I didn't really see it. Suddenly everything makes sense."

Marcus was completely confused. "See *what?*"

"Why he stopped Skyping, why his calls were less frequent and increasingly impersonal. You were falling in love with her."

"It was difficult to look you in the eye," his father said, "to just hear your voice. I felt so guilty. I knew I had to end it but I didn't want to hurt you."

"I know exactly what you mean!" she said. "You have no idea how relieved I felt when you said we couldn't Skype anymore. I was so scared that the second you saw my face you would know what I was thinking."

Gabriel smiled. "Me, too."

"Excuse me," Marcus said, raising his hand. "Would someone like to tell me who is it that you were falling in love with?"

Vanessa looked at him like he was a moron, and right now, he sort of felt like one. "It's your Aunt Trina."

Marcus turned to his father, and could see by the look on his face that it was true. "You're engaged to *Trina?*"

He nodded. "Almost losing her opened my eyes to my feelings for her."

He and Aunt Trina had always been close, but Marcus honestly believed their relationship had been platonic.

"We didn't mean for it to happen," his father said. "But after spending so much time together, we just knew. I guess you can understand how that goes."

"When mother was still alive, did you and Trina…?

"Marcus, *no!* Of course not. I loved your mother. I *still* love her. And until recently I never thought of

Trina as anything but a friend. I'm still not sure what happened, what changed, I just know that it's right." He turned to Vanessa. "I was going to tell you this, and apologize profusely for dragging you and your daughter halfway around the world, and for making promises I couldn't keep. It's not that I don't care for you deeply. It's because of you that I was able to open up my heart again. I was so lonely, and unhappy, and then I met you and for the first time in months I felt alive again. And hopeful. I wanted to hold on to that feeling, but deep down I think I knew that it wasn't going to last. I knew that we would never love each other the way a wife and husband should."

"I wanted to love you that way," she said. "I wanted to be that woman."

"You are that woman, Vanessa." He looked to Marcus and smiled. "Just not for me."

"So, you're not angry?" Marcus asked.

"When I'm guilty of the same thing? You two love each other. And you were going to forsake your feelings to protect mine."

"Well, that was the plan," Vanessa said, shooting Marcus a look, but she was smiling.

"Then how could I possibly be angry. Besides, I can't imagine anyone else I would rather have as my daughter-in-law. And at my age, I think I'd much prefer being a grandfather to Mia than a father. I know men my age do it all the time, but I'm just too old and set in my ways to start over."

And Marcus felt as if his life was just beginning. As if everything up until now had just been a rehearsal in preparation for the real thing. It was so perfect that for an instant he couldn't help wondering if they might still be asleep in his bed and this whole thing was just a dream.

Marcus reached his hand out to Vanessa, and she reached for him, and the instant their fingers touched he knew this was very real. And very right.

"Father, could you give us a moment alone?" he asked.

He rose from the sofa, a smile on his face. "Take all the time you need."

The door had barely closed behind him and Vanessa was in his arms.

Vanessa buried her face against Marcus's chest, holding on tight, almost afraid to believe this was really happening. That it had worked out. That somehow, by breaking the rules and doing the *wrong* thing, she got exactly what she wanted.

"Is it real?" she asked him. "Could we be that lucky?"

He tightened his hold on her and she heard him sigh. "It sure feels real to me. But I don't think luck had anything to do with it."

She pulled back to look at him. "Why did you do it, Marcus? You risked so much."

"When I thought of you and Mia leaving…I just couldn't stand it. And when I saw the way he greeted you, I just had a feeling that something was wrong."

"He still could have been angry."

"I know. But that was a chance I had to take."

"For me?"

"Of course." He touched her cheek. "I love you, Vanessa."

He'd said it before, but until now, she hadn't allowed herself to really believe it. It would have been too painful when he let her down. But now, all that love, all those feelings she had been holding back, welled up inside her and she couldn't have held them back if her life depended on it. "I love you, Marcus. So much. I honestly didn't know it was possible to feel this happy."

"Well, get used to it," he said, kissing her gently. "Because if you'll have me, I'm going to spend the rest of my life making sure you stay that way."

"That's a long time."

"Vanessa, to truly express how much I love you, how much I *need* you, it would take an eternity."

She smiled. "Then I guess I'll just have to take your word for it."

"Does that mean you'll stay here with me, that you'll be my wife and make me the happiest man alive?"

In all the different places she had lived, Vanessa had never felt as if she truly belonged, but here, in Varieo with Marcus, she knew without a doubt that she was finally home.

"Yes," she told him, never feeling more sure about anything in her life. "I definitely will."

* * * * *

SPECIAL EXCERPT FROM

HARLEQUIN Desire

Will Rafe Montoro have to choose between the throne and newfound fatherhood?

Read on for a sneak preview of CARRYING A KING'S CHILD, a ***DYNASTIES: THE MONTOROS*** *novel by* USA TODAY *bestselling author Katherine Garbera.*

Pregnant!

He knew Emily wouldn't be standing in his penthouse apartment telling him this if he wasn't the father. His first reaction was joy.

A child.

It wasn't something he'd ever thought he wanted, but the idea that Emily was carrying his baby seemed right to him.

Maybe that was just because it gave him something other than his royal duties to think about. He'd been dreading his trip to Alma. He was flattered that the country that had once driven his family out had come back to them, asked them—him, as it turned out—to be the next king. But he had grown up here in Miami. He didn't want to be a stuffy royal.

He didn't want European paparazzi following him around and trying to catch him doing anything that would bring shame to his family. Including having a child out of wedlock.

HDEXP0515

"Rafe, did you hear what I said?"

"Yeah, I did. Are you sure?" he asked at last.

She gave him a fiery look from those aqua-blue eyes of hers. He'd seen the passionate side of her nature, and he guessed he was about to witness her temper. Hurricane Em was about to unleash all of her fury on him, and he didn't blame her one bit.

He held his hand up. "Slow down, Red. I didn't mean are you sure it's mine. I meant…are you sure you're pregnant?"

"Damned straight. And I wouldn't be here if I wasn't sure it was yours. Listen, I don't want anything from you. I know you can't turn your back on your family and marry me, and frankly, we only had one weekend together, so I'd have to say no to a proposal anyway. But…I don't want this kid to grow up without knowing you."

"Me neither."

She glanced up, surprised.

He'd sort of surprised himself. But it didn't seem right for a kid of his to grow up without him. He wanted that. He wanted a chance to impart the Montoro legacy…not the one newly sprung on him involving a throne, but the one he'd carved for himself in business. "Don't look shocked."

"You've kind of got a lot going on right now. And having a kid with me isn't going to go over well."

"Tough," he said. "I still make my own decisions."

Love the Harlequin book you just read?

Your opinion matters.

Review this book on your favorite book site, review site, blog or your own social media properties and share your opinion with other readers!

HARLEQUIN®
A Romance FOR EVERY MOOD™